CRUEL TIDE

CRUEL TIDE

RUTH SUTTON

HOAD
PRESS

First published in United Kingdom
by **Hoad Press** in 2015
2 Lowther Street, Waberthwaite, Millom, Cumbria LA19 5YN
www.ruthsutton.co.uk ruth@ruthsutton.co.uk

ISBN–13: 978-0-9929314-0-7

A CIP catalogue record for this book is available from the British Library.

Prepared for publication by Aldridge Press
enquiries@aldridgepress.co.uk

Editorial: Charlotte Rolfe
Design: John Aldridge
Cover design: Kevin Ancient
Cover photos: Jeff Dalt iStock; Ron Jeffreys rgbstock (Morecambe Bay)
Typeset in Bembo 11.5/14.5pt

Printed and bound in UK by TJ International, Padstow

Acknowledgements

This first foray into crime fiction has been greatly assisted by expert support provided by Matthew Hall and William Ryan. Thanks are also due, as ever, to John Aldridge and Charlotte Rolfe of Aldridge Press, and to Kevin Ancient for his creative translation of a vague idea into a striking cover image. Special gratitude goes to Mick Shaw for his unfailing encouragement and practical advice throughout.

Author's note
Some of the locations of this book are real and recognisable, but many place names have been changed. The story and the characters are all entirely fictional, and bear no connection to any events or people, living or dead. In particular, no such institution as Montgomery House ever existed on the north shore of Morecambe Bay, and the culture and procedures of journalism and policing in 1969 were very different than they are today.

RS, Waberthwaite, October 2015

Chapter 1

Judith Pharaoh pushed open the heavy door of the police station. She pulled strands of wayward hair back into place and tasted brick dust blown from the demolition site across the street. Now that the ironworks had finally closed, Barrow was slowly coming to terms with a different future. It was not a pretty town.

The overnight incident book was disappointing: another stolen bicycle, another midnight scuffle outside the Hope and Anchor. Nothing meaty to keep her editor at the *Furness News* happy. 'Better luck tomorrow maybe,' said Sergeant Clark. She had already turned to leave when the phone jangled. She watched the sergeant's face as he listened.

'You're in luck,' he told her, putting the black phone back on its cradle. 'Call from Attercliff. Looks like a body in the mud at the shore. No details, uniform on the scene with a witness. We'll get someone from plain-clothes down there, probably the new lad with the funny name. Could be your story, Judith, if you can persuade your boss.'

'What's the new bloke's funny name, then?' Judith asked. She knew most of the Barrow police after six months of following them around.

1

'Detective Constable Tognarelli. Would you credit it? A bloody I-tie – 'is dad was from Glasgow apparently. Lots of them there, all making ice cream.'

'Poor lad, with a name like that,' said Judith. 'What do you lot call him?'

'Nelly mostly, or Dago.'

She winced.

'He plays it by the book, so watch yourself. They're all pissed off with him already and 'e's only been 'ere a few weeks. Came from Lancashire when they joined up with us.'

'Sounds like a fascinating day ahead,' said Judith, 'and it's my birthday.'

'Birthday, is it? Many happy returns. Celebrating tonight, are we?'

She shook her head, and more recalcitrant hair fell out of its restraining elastic band.

'Brings back some not so good memories,' she said.

'That's a bugger,' said Sergeant Clark.

Judith shrugged. 'What do they call you, by the way?' she asked. 'Everybody has a nickname round here. I know they call me Red. So what's yours?'

'Never you mind,' he said.

She was crossing the street when the birthday memory hit her again. She reached the kerb and leaned on a wall to breathe, slowly, until the wave of humiliation passed. That was ten years ago, she told herself. She had to let it go. She was stronger now, less foolish, more wary, in charge of her own life. No one could ever hurt her like that, not again.

'You all right, love?' someone asked.

'I'm fine,' she said. 'Thanks.'

When Judith opened the door of the newsroom at the paper something was going on. Hattie, the secretary, motioned to her to be quiet, pointing towards the closed door of the editor's office. 'They're in there,' she whispered.

'Who?' Judith asked.

Ed Cunningham was leaning on the doorframe of his sub-editor's cubbyhole, cigarette in hand. 'George Falcon and his missus,' he said, smiling.

'Shouting,' said Hattie. 'Marjorie's been shouting.' She giggled into her hand.

'What about?' asked Judith. Cunningham shrugged. 'My guess,' he said, 'George wants to stay off and the boss said no.'

'But he's ill,' said Judith.

'And we've got a paper to run,' said Cunningham.

The door to the editor's office opened. Bill Skelly, *Furness News*' chief reporter for the past twenty-something years, stood for a moment in the open doorway, his face red, before he stomped across the room, jammed his hat onto his head, and pushed past Judith, followed by George Falcon looking pale and Marjorie close to tears. All three left the newsroom without a word as Judith watched, intrigued.

She was still wondering what was going on when Alan Thornhill, the paper's editor, appeared at his office door 'Ah, Judith,' he said. 'Good. Can you come in a moment please?'

Hattie watched intently as Judith, still wearing her coat, followed him into the office.

'Close the door,' he said, easing himself into his big chair on the far side of the desk. He sat back, his fingers steepled together in front of his mouth. Judith gazed round the room to avoid looking at him. One wall was hung with dozens of photographs of Thornhill at various functions. She recognised some of the faces that beamed out at her, the mayor, someone from the TV, all looking pleased with themselves.

'Bit of a problem,' Thornhill said, still looking at his hands. 'George Falcon isn't well, poor chap. Marjorie insists he can't come back to work. He's not willing to resign, and I can't sack him, not yet, so we'll have to make a few changes. How long have you been with us now?'

'Six months,' said Judith. Her heart was beating loudly in her chest. She wanted to sit down.

'Bill says he's quite pleased, but you just don't have the experience, do you? We took a chance, taking you on, never employed a young woman as a news reporter before, but now, well, we may have to think again.'

'What do you mean?' said Judith, aware of the croak in her voice.

'We need an experienced journalist. Bill can't do everything.'

'But I am experienced,' she said. 'Three years...'

'Not enough,' he cut her off. 'George wants to stay on the books for now, and we're duty bound to that for a while at least, but in a few weeks, well...' He spread his arms wide. 'If George stays off sick, we're a man down. If he goes, well, either way we'll have to reconsider. Budget, you know. We're on a knife-edge here, every penny counts. You know how it is.'

Judith stared at him. 'That doesn't make sense —' she began.

Thornhill held up his hand. 'I'm the best judge of that, young lady,' he said, still not looking at her. 'I'm being straight with you, but you can't count on being here past Christmas. You could start looking elsewhere right now, or stick around and convince me that you're too valuable to lose. That's your choice. Understood?'

'But...'

'Good. Now is there anything else?'

She swallowed, making up her mind.

'There is a story I'm working on. It could be big. Just got it from Sergeant Clark. A body, in the bay, buried in the mud.'

'Are you saying you want the story?'

'Who else is there? Bill's run off his feet as it is. And young Andrew, well.'

Thornhill looked at her over the top of his glasses. 'Where is this body?'

'Attercliff. It's our patch. I've got the scooter.'

He stared out of the window. Gulls shrieked on the neighbouring roofs.

'OK,' he said finally. 'My decision, I'll tell Bill. He won't like it, and you know what he's like.'

'He's gone,' said Judith.

'He'll be back. I'll tell him I've given you this story to see what you can do with it. So you report to me on this one, OK?'

'Yes,' she said. 'Thank you, Mr Thornhill.'

'Alan,' he said. 'We're all on the same team here, Judith. My job is to get the best possible stories out of you, squeeze them past Führer Cunningham out there and into the paper for people to buy and make us all rich.' He smiled. 'OK?'

'OK,' she said. 'Thanks. I'll get on with it, then.'

'Go,' he said, waving his hand towards the door.

'Well?' Hattie whispered as Judith reappeared.

'He's given me a big story.'

Cunningham's voice said, 'And what did you give him, I wonder?'

Andrew giggled. He was the office trainee and observed the goings-on around him as if he were watching Coronation Street.

'Shut up, Andrew,' said Judith. She picked up her helmet off the desk where she'd abandoned it and left the room with as much dignity as she could muster. It was only when she got outside that she realised her hands were still clenched tight.

The red Vespa scooter parked invitingly round the back of the *Furness News* office brought a smile to Judith's face. It was her parents' Christmas present and felt like belated recognition of her adult independence. For her stepfather, John Pharaoh, Judith's independence wouldn't have been a problem. But Judith's relationship with her mother, Maggie, was more complicated, constantly soured by unrealised expectations. And then there was Vince's accident, and things had gone from bad to worse: Maggie blamed Judith for not looking after her little brother carefully enough, even though Vince was twelve when he fell off the back garden wall. Buying the scooter, from both of them, was a step back towards trust. It was a new start. And it had transformed Judith's life. She didn't have to wait around for buses any more, or feel beholden to people for lifts. When she needed to be somewhere, she could just go.

The day had brightened into breezy blue and within a few minutes of leaving town she was out at Rampside and the start of the coast road. She purred up and down its quiet slopes and curves, smelling the sea. For the first time in months, she felt she was being given a chance to prove what she could do. Whatever it took, she would do it. She had to. She couldn't bear the look on her mother's face if she lost this job. 'Unsuitable', Maggie had called it. 'A waste of a good education.' Judith remembered the conversation. 'Plenty of proper steady jobs going at Sellafield. Your father would help, of course.

Good clean work, and prospects for a bright young woman like you. Jessie did well there, before she threw it all away.'

'Granny didn't throw it away,' Judith had protested. 'She made a choice.'

'Too many choices, if you ask me,' Maggie had said, with a twist of her chin that signified the conversation was over.

Judith wasn't sure exactly how far down the coast road she was aiming for but any unusual activity at the shore would probably be obvious, and it was. As she approached Attercliff two cars were already parked on the side of the road by an open gate, and fresh muddy tracks pointed the way to the shore where a tractor and an ambulance were standing, and a van that was probably the coastguard.

She stopped, put her feet down to hold the scooter steady and looked out towards the bay. The morning light was still casting long shadows, and flat acres of sand and mud beyond the shore gleamed like pewter. Only minutes earlier the tide had left the shingle bank, sliding noiselessly back to where a flock of oystercatchers stalked and probed. Every day the shallow waters of Morecambe Bay flooded across a hundred square miles of mud flats and then retreated, flooded again and retreated, faster than a man could run: relentless moon-driven motion that transformed the landscape and the light.

Judith parked the scooter by the hedge, took off her helmet and raised a hand to her eyes against the glare. Across the road behind an old limestone wall was a stand of oak trees, the last few withered leaves snatched by the breeze. Further east, out of her sight, the bay narrowed towards river estuaries where fresh water clashed with the incoming sea, churning mud into froth. Several miles away on the southern shore of the bay was the grey blur of land, the streets and promenades of More-cambe that blazed with light when the night air was clear.

Wishing she'd brought some Wellington boots Judith set off gingerly across the field, picking her way round cowpats and the worst of the mud churned up by the passing wheels. A cluster of figures stood on the edge of the sands, holding large boards on end, like ancient soldiers carrying massive shields. Of course, she thought, they need to rest the boards on the quicksand to avoid being sucked down. She imagined the body hidden below the surface, and the final minutes as cloying mud extinguished light and air.

The back door of the ambulance was open and a man appeared, watching her progress down the field. She knew Doc Hayward from another accident she'd reported, and liked him, a rare exception to her aversion for professional men of a certain age. He raised his hand and as she waved back another figure emerged from behind the ambulance. This was a younger man, who walked briskly towards her looking official but not in uniform; Judith guessed he was the detective constable with the Italian name. He was quite short, wearing a tweed jacket that sat square over his shoulders but was too long at the hips. Cropped hair, a young man trying to look older, thought Judith, as he came closer and she could see his boyish face and the faintest trace of a moustache above his lip.

'Who are you?' he asked, as if he had the right to know.

'Press,' she said, holding out her ID card. He looked carefully at the card, took a small notebook and a very small pencil out of his inside pocket and wrote some miniscule notes before looking back at her.

'This is a crime scene,' he said. His voice had a petulant expression, as if responding to a social gaffe.

Judith wondered about the unfamiliar tone, a Lancashire accent mixed with something else. 'What crime?' she asked.

'Well, it could be a crime scene,' he said, 'and you're in the way. You're contaminating the area.'

Judith looked around. 'Me and a few others, by the look of it. I've every right to be here.'

'How did you find out about it?'

'I was at the station when someone phoned it in,' she said. 'You're DC Tognarelli aren't you?'

He blushed.

'It's my job to find things out,' she said, taking full advantage of his surprise. 'Sergeant Clark knows what we do,' she continued. 'I check the incident book every morning, to see what stories we need to follow up.'

'Isn't there someone more senior?' he asked. 'Shouldn't you be doing the WI meeting reports or something?'

Judith restrained an impulse to hit him. 'I've got your name already,' she said. 'So watch what you say.'

'That's all you're going to get from me,' he said, turning away. 'I've got a job to do.'

Prat, she said to herself, and she walked off, towards the ambulance. The rear doors were open.

'Morning, doc,' she said, looking into the gloom of the interior. 'How long do you reckon it'll take them to get it out?'

'Morning, Judith. Come in and have a seat. Won't take long, now they've got the boards down. That stuff's like wet concrete. If you struggle, it drags you down. Lost a dog in the quicksand once. He cried and wriggled until the end, but there was nothing I could do.' Dr Hayward shook his head, and began to cough, deep and prolonged. He held up his hand, as if to tell Judith that he was all right, but the fit left him breathless. She looked away towards the shore to give the old man time to recover.

'Are they sure it's a person down there?' she asked.

'More like a child actually. There was a hand sticking out.

9

Very small fingers. That young detective asked me to have a look, even before they'd starting digging.'

'Do you know that bloke? Sergeant Clark at the cop shop told me he's new and nobody likes him. Have you seen him before?

'Don't know him. He looks about twelve, or is that me getting old?'

'I must be getting old too, then,' said Judith. 'Young and arrogant, that's a great combination. He asked me why I wasn't doing WI reports.'

Dr Hayward winced. 'Oh dear, not a great start for police-press relations.'

'I get so tired of it,' said Judith. 'I'm twenty-eight years old, properly qualified and I've been in this business for nearly four years, but they still treat me like some kid straight from school. Is it because I'm female?'

'Probably,' he said. 'No women in the police, at least not detectives, and the ones there are get all the menial things to do. My wife tells me things have to change, but I don't see it, not here.'

'Nor me, more's the pity. Bet it's different in London.'

'That doesn't help you much does it? We live here, in the outer darkness, and we just have to get on with it. At least we're well away from rioting students and the Kray twins.'

'True,' said Judith. She got out her notebook. 'OK, back to business. When will you do the post-mortem?'

'Not today. Two on the slab already. Tell Bill Skelly the report'll be available early next week. Not retired yet, has he?'

'They'll have to carry him out,' said Judith, 'especially now that George Falcon is off for a while.'

'Oh yes, poor George. Well, if Bill stays a bit longer, that'll improve your chances when he goes.'

'Of taking over his job? Chief reporter Judith Pharaoh? That would make our young friend over there choke on his pencil.'

They heard the sound of raised voices and peered round the side of the ambulance towards the shore. Two men were walking back across the boards, holding something between them.

'Is that the body?' said Judith. 'It's so small. Oh God, what a way to go. Poor little mite.' She thought for a moment. 'No report of a missing child locally, as far as I know. How could that happen?'

'Some parents don't seem to know or care,' said Dr Hayward. 'Things have gone to pot since the war: no discipline, no respect.' He shook his head, watching the men carrying the stretcher between them.

'He could be from Montgomery House,' he said. 'Do you know it? Used to be the sanatorium. Big house in its own grounds, a bit further down the coast road. It's a children's home now, has been since after the war. The boss, what's his name now? I should know that, dammit. Simplest things to remember and they just disappear. Edwards, that's it, Captain Edwards.'

Judith looked down at the shore for a moment, watching the young detective.

'I bet he doesn't have a clue where to start,' she said. 'But I do. Thanks, doc. I could be identifying that body while he's still writing in his little book.'

He smiled at her, and she remembered why she'd always liked him. 'Big day for me, doc,' she said. 'And it's my birthday.'

'Your birthday! Many happy returns. May I?' He leaned across and kissed her on the cheek. 'Pretty grim work for your birthday, but you'll be celebrating later won't you?'

'I don't make much of it,' she said. 'It's not been a good day in the past. Put me off a bit.'

'What happened?'

Just for a moment, she thought about telling him, but the idea froze in her mind. She'd told no one, not even her parents, just announced that university was a mistake and she was leaving. Maggie assumed that this was Judith getting back at her, and John was sad. Not telling them was hard, but doing so would have been worse. The longer she left it, the more impossible it seemed. But Judith longed to tell someone, and Doc Hayward wouldn't judge or blame, she was sure of that. She looked at his watery blue eyes, and began to form the words she needed, but then she noticed the young man striding up the hill. She locked the words away, turned and walked back up the hill, to start the fight for her job.

Chapter 2

It was only when she was standing on the doorstep of Montgomery House that Judith realised that she'd jumped the gun. There was no reason to think that this was the place to start trying to piece the story together. She'd seen that arrogant policeman coming towards them and been so keen to avoid him that she'd forgotten to ask about the witness who called the police. That would have made a good story in itself. Too late now. She'd have to go back and hope the policeman was still there.

She was cursing herself for rushing at things yet again when the door opened. A large woman in a blue uniform with a white cap on her head looked down at her.

'Yes?' she said.

Judith fumbled for her ID card. 'Sorry to bother you,' she said, holding out the card. 'We have reason to believe that a child may have gone missing in the area and I wondered –'

'What makes you think a child could have gone missing from here? We take excellent care of our boys.'

'Just boys, is it?' Judith asked, grasping at straws.

'I don't think that's any of your business, young lady,' said the woman. 'Now, I have work to do, and don't have time to answer impertinent questions. Good day to you.'

'And your name is?' asked Judith, but the woman stepped back into the dark hallway and had half closed the heavy door when it swung open again. This time a tall man was standing there, looking down on Judith from an even greater height. A handsome man, with full grey hair, wearing a dark suit and a shirt so white that it glowed in the gloom.

'I'm Captain Edwards, the director here. Did I hear something about a missing child?'

Judith smiled her most placatory smile. 'Judith Pharaoh, *Furness News*. I'm so sorry to disturb you, but we believe a local child has gone missing and I wondered…?'

'Mrs Robinson is our matron here. I'm sure she would know if the child were one of ours, would she not?' The man spoke with quiet authority and precision, making Judith feel even more gauche.

'Well, yes, but…'

'Thank you for your concern, Miss Pharaoh,' he went on, inclining his head, 'but I think your enquiries may be premature, don't you? Good day.'

The door closed with a determined click and Judith was left standing, staring at its polished surface. She turned away and down the steps, cursing herself yet again. 'Idiot, idiot. Get your facts straight. One thing at a time, you know that.'

The Vespa's wheels crunched the gravel on the spacious driveway as she pushed the scooter away from the front door, not daring to start the engine until she was out of sight. At the end of the drive she stopped, uncertain where to go. There was no choice: she would have to go back and ask more questions, and he would think she was a complete fool.

Ten minutes after she had left the field where the vehicles

were parked she was back, working out a story that would explain her early return without too much embarrassment. The ambulance was still there, and the men were down by the shore, looking for clues, she surmised. With any luck they wouldn't see her yet and she could make a better excuse for her return. She didn't have to worry about Doc Hayward, who had caught sight of her and stood, his head on one side, wondering.

'Back so soon?' he called.

'That's me all over, I'm afraid. I rushed off to avoid our tiresome friend before I'd asked him everything I needed to know. Names, dates and details, they drum it in to you at journalists' college and then I get out here and forget the basics. I need to know who first saw the body and called it in. Do you know?'

'I think they said it was a woman walking her dog, early on, but I don't have a name.'

'Damn,' said Judith. 'That means I'll have to ask his lordship and give him a chance to sneer at me again. Is he still down there?'

Dr Hayward squinted into the glare of light from the sands. 'They're all there. They brought the body up here, and went back down to look for anything else they could find before the tide comes back in.'

'It's in the ambulance?' said Judith, peering into the gloom. A small bundle covered in sheets lay on a stretcher inside. 'How old?'

'A boy, about ten I would guess, but I haven't had a proper look. I need to get him back to the mortuary and wash all the mud off before I can tell you much more than that.'

'Ten. That's dreadful,' said Judith, remembering her brothers at that age, their innocence and naivety.

'Did you go to Montgomery House? You came back pretty quickly.'

'Wasted journey, I'm afraid. They weren't about to tell me that one of theirs was missing. I met a woman who looked like the matron and the man in charge, the one you mentioned. She was pretty frosty but he was polite. Very well spoken, isn't he? Not from round here.'

'He's a gentleman, is Captain Edwards. A war hero. Did you notice the limp?'

'No. What happened to him?'

'He was in Malaya, during the war there, in the fifties. Damaged his knee somehow. Invalided out and ended up running a kids' home. People think he's just the type they need.'

Judith caught his tone. 'Do you think that?'

He shrugged. 'Kids like that need to learn respect. What did Edwards say to you?'

'Just that they didn't know if a child was missing. Basically told me to push off, and I don't blame him really. It was far too soon to start asking questions. I'm under the gun at work, did I tell you? The editor called me in and said unless I could prove myself I would be out of a job. They're upset about George not being around, but I don't see why that would involve sacking me.'

'They think people work harder if they're threatened. Rubbish of course. People under pressure make mistakes.'

'Like me,' she said. 'And now I have to crawl back to young Sherlock and start again. Wish me luck.'

She was almost within touching distance of Tognarelli before he realised she was there. He blushed as he turned towards her.

'Miss Pharaoh,' he said. 'I thought you'd taken your enquiries elsewhere.'

'I did, but I have a few more questions.'

'What now?'

'It's about the witness who alerted the police. And are there any reports of a missing child?'

'No one has reported a missing child, as far as I'm aware,' he said. 'But you will need to check with the station in Barrow about that. Men can land on the moon but our radios don't work out here, so I've no way of knowing. And the other matter…'

He took off one of his muddy gloves and looked in an inside pocket for his notebook, turning the pages awkwardly with his fingers to find the right page.

'Can I help?' she asked.

He ignored the offer. Eventually he found the page he wanted, and craned his head to see what was written there. 'Mrs Bracegirdle, 8 Church Road, Barfield. She called 999 at 7.19 this morning. I'm not sure she'll want to talk to you, but does that answer your question?'

'It does, thanks,' said Judith, surprised at the cooperative response when she'd expected a lecture.

'Always pleased to assist the press,' he said, with the faintest smile, or was it that sneer again? No matter, she had what she wanted, and the morning was still young. She wanted to give Mr Editor Thornhill lots of factual stuff today, to show how capable she was. He wouldn't know how careless she'd been along the way, and she certainly wouldn't tell him.

Less than twenty minutes later Judith was knocking on a door again, a smaller one this time, at the end of a short, neatly paved path. The door remained closed but a voice came from within. 'Who is it?'

'It's Judith Pharaoh, Mrs Bracegirdle,' Judith replied, and the door was opened immediately. Mrs Bracegirdle smiled. 'Thank goodness,' she said. 'I thought it might be some dreadful newspaperman. Are you from the Council? Come in, do. That's pretty quick, I must say, I only wrote in last week about the bins and thought it would be weeks before anyone got back to me.'

'The bins?' said Judith.

'The dustbins and the foxes, or seagulls or whatever it is making all the mess. Did you get my letter?' She had led the way into the small front room and gestured for Judith to sit down.

'No, but, I think you may have… I'm not from the Council.'

'Well who are you then, dear?' asked her hostess, still smiling. Judith fished in her bag for the ID card and proffered it.

'I'm one of those dreadful newspaper people,' she said. 'I'm sorry I didn't say so earlier.'

'You don't look like one of them.'

'No, well, that's fortunate, isn't it? The ones I know look pretty awful.' Judith smiled hopefully, and to her surprise Mrs Bracegirdle smiled too.

'Well, Miss Pharaoh,' she said. 'Now you're here, I suppose it's about what happened this morning.'

'Can you tell me anything about it? It was very clever of you to realise that something wasn't right.' The flattery was blatant, but Mrs Bracegirdle seemed to appreciate it and settled back in her chair. 'Well, it was Meg who spotted it actually. My dog. I had her on a long lead, she's only a puppy and I worry about her running into one of those quicksands. She bolted right to the end of the lead and started barking and carrying on. It was all I could do to pull her back. I looked to see what she was barking at and then I saw what looked like twigs sticking out of the mud. Oh dear...' She took a handkerchief from her sleeve and dabbed her eyes. 'When I think now, it's very upsetting.'

'I'm sure,' said Judith.

'I tied Meg to a tree to stop her pulling and then I walked a bit further out, on the bank where the samphire grows. The sun was in my eyes but I looked as hard as I could and I realised they were fingers. Little fingers. Oh dear.' She wiped her eyes again. 'I couldn't believe it. So close to the shore. It must be deep enough to swallow a child, and leave just the hand sticking up.' She blew her nose. Her eyes were full of tears.

Judith felt her own eyes pricking as her mind worked on what could have happened. 'What could a child have been doing out there?' she wondered aloud. 'All on his own.'

Mrs Bracegirdle looked up. 'A boy?'

Judith nodded. 'They dug him out. Very young. The doctor isn't sure how old.'

'The poor mite. I have a grandson, he's just eight, such a bright little thing.'

'I have two brothers,' said Judith. 'I remember them at that age.'

'That plain-clothes policeman was a real gent,' said Mrs Bracegirdle. 'He had a funny name, Italian.'

'Tognarelli,' said Judith.

'That's it. I was very upset, and he was patient, you know, very polite. Not from round here.'

'Further south?' said Judith.

'Aye, that it was. You know him, do you?'

'I met him,' said Judith.

Mrs Bracegirdle was quiet for a moment before she asked, 'Has anyone reported a missing boy?'

'I asked the policeman but he didn't know.'

'Maybe the tide caught him. It sweeps in so fast here. You could be out on the sands and get cut off, and if there's a quicksand…'

'My friend lost his dog in a quicksand,' said Judith. 'He's still upset about it.' She looked at the woman, weeping for a nameless child. 'Can I get you anything? A cup of tea?'

'You stay there, love,' said Mrs Bracegirdle, rising from her chair. 'I'll do it.'

'You look a bit better, lass' said Sergeant Clark, when Judith got back to the police station to check about a missing child. 'Just had Montgomery House on the phone, the kids' place near where that body was found. Looks like it's one of theirs.'

Judith was indignant. 'But I went there myself and they knew nothing about it.'

'Well, they do now. Apparently they did their own search before they called it in. It's a big place, and all the grounds, too. Anyway, that were about twenty minutes ago.'

'Has DC Tognarelli been told?'

'Not called in yet, so probably not. Sergeant Morrison's gone down there and Doc Hayward's taking the body to the mortuary.'

Judith didn't mention to Sergeant Clark that she was going to head straight back to Montgomery House. She'd already decided that 'ask questions first, apologise later', was the best motto for the time being if she wanted to get her story without one of the other papers getting there first.

This time she had the words prepared for her conversation with Captain Edwards, who answered the door himself.

'Miss Pharaoh?'

Behind him in the hall Judith could see a man standing, tall and heavy, like a rugby player gone to seed. She couldn't see his face clearly but the shape looked familiar. One button of his coat was fastened, pulling across his stomach. He didn't speak to Judith, and pushed the door to obscure her view. She heard the two men talking in whispers before the door opened again. Captain Edwards cleared his throat. 'You can come in, but whatever it is will have to be quick,' he said. He was still outwardly calm but his eyes were nervous, and his fingers fidgeting.

'Of course,' said Judith. 'I understand how distressing this must be for you all, and I'd like to help by getting something into the news tonight. No names, you understand, just appealing for information. I've talked to the lady who called the police first thing this morning and there could have been other people out there around the same time who might have information.'

The man in the tight coat had been standing off to one side, but now he stepped into the light and Judith recognised him. Captain Edwards turned towards the man, 'You know Sergeant Morrison, I expect,' he said. 'It might be useful for the police to find witnesses, so you'd better come in. I'll call your editor to check, of course. I trust he'll handle the details.'

He pointed to a door and they went through a dark empty hallway into an office. Judith went in, and the sergeant followed her and stood with his back to the wall. Captain Edwards pulled out a chair for Judith but remained standing himself, in front of the fireplace.

'We need to do everything we can to discover what happened to this poor lad,' he said. 'His name is Steven Stringer by the way, but of course that must remain between us. We're doing our best to contact his family, but there's no phone and it sometimes takes quite a while to track people down. Some families don't want to be found, for various reasons. So the boy's name cannot be released, as I'm sure you understand.'

'Of course,' said Judith.

'Naturally we are all terribly distressed,' he went on. 'Our boys' safety is so important to us, and nothing like this has ever happened here before. It's a tragedy. Our matron, Mrs Robinson, is too distressed to see anyone. Dr Graham, one of our trustees, has come from Broughton, and he's with her now. Sergeant Morrison is already here and I'm sure his constable…' He hesitated and looked at Morrison.

'DC Tognarelli,' said Morrison.

'Yes, the constable will be here soon. Perhaps you should come back later?'

Judith was already thinking about catching the final edition of the paper, but she would have to work fast. She smiled at the captain. 'I'm sure my editor would be pleased to get an appeal for witnesses into the afternoon edition, if we can gather just a few facts now, captain,' she said. Captain Edwards looked over her head to Sergeant Morrison standing behind her.

'While the sergeant is here,' she said quickly, 'perhaps we could talk to one or two of the boys, just to pin down a time when Steven might have gone missing? Of course, whatever we say at this stage would make no mention of any names, not until you've told the boy's family. I understand that completely.'

Judith was surprised when no further objection was raised.

'I was just about to talk to them myself,' said Captain Edwards. 'Perhaps it would be useful to have you here. Some of the boys feel more comfortable with a woman, and poor Mrs Robinson is in no fit state. If you'll excuse me for a moment.'

Judith stood up as the captain left the room, and turned towards the sergeant who was still standing behind her.

Morrison looked down at her. 'I'm letting this happen because it might be useful,' he said. 'Don't get any ideas. One step out of line and that editor of yours will confiscate your pencil. Got it?'

Judith got it. She felt uncomfortable, as if the two men were using her, but she didn't respond. The office door was pushed open by a thin-faced man with sparse hair, wearing grey trousers and a grey jumper. He held out his hand: it was cold. 'Desmond Harries,' he said. 'I'm the padre here. This is a terrible day for us.' He noticed Morrison and stopped.

'This is Sergeant Morrison, from Barrow CID,' said Judith. 'I think he's going to ask the boys a few questions, about what happened.'

Desmond Harries looked at Morrison, and back to Judith, and then stepped back towards the door. 'It'll be too crowded in here,' he said. 'I'm sure you don't need me.' And he was gone.

Captain Edwards came back into the room, pushing ahead of him a lad of about twelve, who seemed very reluctant to come in.

'Come on, Leonard,' Edwards said. 'This is Miss Pharaoh. She's trying to find out what Steven was doing out on his own last night.'

The boy saw Morrison. 'Who's 'e?'

'Never mind who I am, sonny,' said Morrison quietly. 'I'm just here to make sure you tell the truth.'

Captain Edwards pointed to Judith. 'This young lady is from the newspaper.' Leonard stared at Judith, and she smiled reassuringly, but got no response. The captain stood back where he'd been before, and Leonard turned to look at him. 'When did you last see Steven, Leonard? Was it last night or this morning?'

'Last night, sir –'e said he was going to see 'is mam. She wanted 'im back and 'e said someone would come for 'im and take 'im 'ome.'

Morrison's voice spoke from behind Judith's chair. 'Who was going to come for him?'

Leonard didn't look round. 'Didn't say, did 'e?'

Captain Edwards looked carefully at Leonard. 'When did Steven first say that someone was coming to fetch him?'

'Monday, sir. That's when we 'ave a bath.'

'That was three days ago, Leonard,' said the captain. 'Why didn't you mention this to me, or to Mrs Robinson?'

'E said we 'adn't got to tell, sir, so we didn't.'

'Steven told other boys as well?'

'There were a group of us – me, Spud, Mikey, couple of others.'

'And do you know when Steven actually went away?'

'His roomie said 'e was there when 'e went to sleep and gone when 'e woke up.'

'When did he wake up?' said Morrison.

'Sir,' said Leonard, without turning to face him, 'dunno sir. It was light, 'e said.'

Captain Edwards looked over Judith's head again before he went on. 'Is there anything else you need to tell us, Leonard?'

The boy looked at him. 'What 'appened to 'im, sir?'

'We don't know yet,' said the captain. 'And we don't want any gossip or rumours, Leonard, do you understand? You and the other older boys have to set an example for the younger ones.' He looked down at the boy and raised his chin with his fingers. 'Understand, Leonard? How old are you now?'

'Thirteen, sir,' Leonard mumbled, his eyes averted.

'Old enough to set an example,' said the captain, releasing the boy's chin. 'Off you go, now.'

Leonard scratched his head. 'Sir,' he said. 'Thank you, miss.' He shuffled out of the door and they heard his shoes heavy on the staircase.

'Where does Steven's mother live?' Judith asked, seeing the story in all its pathos stretching into next week. Morrison came round her to stand by the door. 'No more information about the lad until we've found the family. If the boy is Stringer, then we have tragic news that must come from us, not from you. If the boy isn't Stringer, then that's a different matter.'

'Are you not sure?' she asked.

'No formal identification has been made yet, although I'm sure that won't be long. I'll take Captain Edwards to the morgue when we hear the body has arrived. Until then, watch your step, Miss Pharaoh.'

Judith nodded, realising there was nothing more she would get from him or the captain, who was steering her towards the door. 'That's all we can do for now, Miss Pharaoh,' he said.

Judith was halfway down the drive, guiding the scooter round a patch of mud, when the glossy leaves of a rhododendron bush close by moved suddenly and a face appeared. She put her foot down to steady the scooter. There was no one around, except the owner of the pale adolescent face, cheeks sprinkled with small red spots, eyes wide and checking nervously around.

'Are you the woman from the paper?'

Judith nodded.

'Len saw you in the office. We want to tell you summat. Stevie's mam lives in Morecambe — 'e said something'd 'appened and 'e 'ad to go 'ome.'

'Is that where he was going?' Judith asked. 'And what's your name?'

'Mikey, miss. One of 'is mates. Stevie said someone would take him back 'ome to 'is mam.'

'Did he say who was going to come for him?'

Mikey shook his head. 'No, miss.'

'And what about school? Do you know what school he went to?'

'School? He said summat about Holy Joe's but 'e hated school. We all did, miss.'

They heard voices from the direction of the house. Mikey's eyes widened. Judith knew she was running out of time.

'We can't talk here, Mikey,' she whispered, 'but I'd like to talk some more. Where could I meet you?'

'They don't want us talking, miss.'

'I know that, but you're a big lad, sensible, aren't you?'

'Aye.'

'So you're not going to tell me anything that isn't true, are you?'

'Me, miss? No, miss.'

'So is there anywhere we could talk, just you and me. I'd love to know more about Stevie.'

'Next Wednesday, miss, we 'ave digging. Just next door,' he jerked his head, 'that way, there's lots of spuds and stuff in t'field and a shed. We do all the work and Harries just sits in there reading the paper.'

'So if I come back then, we might talk?'

'Other lads'll keep lookout, miss. Come about ten. Hide the scooter and stand by the bushes. I'll find you. Gotta go.'

And he was gone. Like the Cheshire Cat, thought Judith, as she rode her Vespa back along the coast road for the second time that morning.

CHAPTER 3

The newsroom was quiet, and the air not as heavy with cigarette smoke as it usually was. Judith could hear Thornhill on the phone in his office, and Hattie's typewriter was rattling away. No sign of Cunningham in his cubbyhole, which was always a relief. Ever since she'd started work there she felt his eyes on her, infecting the small space like a virus.

She was hungry. It was well past her normal lunchtime and the pasty she'd bought on the way home was one of yesterday's by the look of it, the last one that no one else wanted. She took a bite but the pastry was greasy and tough and she threw it away. I need some decent food, she thought, and remembered where she might get some. Time to visit Elspeth, something to look forward to at the end of the day.

The most urgent task for now was to sort out all the notes she'd been making, and write something to go in the final edition. She checked the time; a couple of hours at most to get something written, subbed, and away. There were some loose ends to check first. The phone to the mortuary rang for a long time, but she knew how long it took for someone to get to it with clean hands, if they could be bothered at all, and persistence was rewarded when a familiar voice said, 'Mortuary, Hayward.'

'Identification?' he responded to her question. 'Aye, they've been and gone. Steven Clifford Stringer. Aged eleven apparently. Underweight for his age.'

'Who came from the home?' Judith asked.

'Captain Edwards himself,' he paused, 'and a Mrs Robinson. She couldn't speak, she was so upset. Just nodded.'

'She's the matron,' said Judith. 'Too distressed to see me when I was there.'

'Are you putting anything in the paper today?' he asked.

'Working on that now. Can't mention the kid's name of course, but just saying that a body was found *et cetera* and asking for anyone with information to contact the police.'

'Have they found the family yet?'

'Doubt it. Sounds like they may not want to be found, although the lad told his mates he had to go home for some reason.'

'How do you know that?'

'Sorry, doc, can't reveal my sources.'

'Spoken like a real hack, Judith.'

'Date for the PM yet?' she asked.

'Where are we now? Friday today, two bodies in the queue. Could be Wednesday.'

'Can you not jump the queue for this, doc? If we find the family, they need to know what happened. He was just a kid.'

There was silence for a moment. 'Monday. Tell Bill Skelly the police will have my report by the end of Monday if he wants to check.'

Judith looked up to see Hattie go into the editor's office and close the door. 'I'm reporting direct to Thornhill on this one,' she whispered into the phone. 'Skelly's not happy and he's probably said so.'

'My report goes to the police anyway, not to the press,' said

Dr Hayward. 'Monday. 'Bye now.'

Judith thought for a while, made a few notes and then wrote a short piece with the barest details and an appeal for anyone with information to contact the police at Barrow. When Hattie emerged from the inner office, Judith took her chance. Alan Thornhill read what she'd written, took off his glasses, pinched the bridge of his nose and looked up at her. 'Is this all you've got?'

'It's all we can say for the time being. We know the kid's name but have to hold it until they've found the family. And I have some feelers out.'

'About what?'

'The family, what the kid was up to, that kind of stuff. Apparently he was trying to get home to Morecambe. Could have thought the sands was the quickest way.'

Thornhill groaned. 'How many people have been lost out there over the years? Must be hundreds. What with the tide and the quicksands it's like setting off through a minefield.'

'He was just a kid,' she said. 'Awful way to go. PM on Monday. If it's accidental death the funeral might be next week.'

'Is Cunningham back yet?' He looked at his watch. 'Two o'clock. Lunch seems to be getting longer and longer. If he's not back by half-past I'll sub it myself.'

Judith had just got back to her desk when Ed Cunningham returned, smelling strongly of tobacco and alcohol. Judith tried to avoid him on boozy afternoons but today she had no choice. He was slumped in his chair, surrounded by the clutter of what he called his office, which was actually no more than a cupboard without a door, deep enough for the chair to be out of sight. She took a deep breath before she knocked on the wall.

He turned the chair round and smiled when he saw her.

'Well, well,' he said. 'The editor's pet of the week. Come into my lair, dear, and tell me everything.' He stretched out his hand towards her and she stepped back, as she had done many times before when he reached for her.

'I have to get something in the final edition, about the body on the sands this morning. We're appealing for information, so it has to go out tonight. Just two-fifty words, not much to say at this stage.'

'Give me your deathless prose,' he slurred his words a little, taking the paper that she held out for him. 'If it's as bad as that piece you did on the stolen boat, it'll go on the spike.'

'The editor wants it to go out tonight. He's seen it already.'

He looked at her. 'You little crawler,' he sneered, turning back to his desk. 'It'll do, once I've tidied it up.' A moment later he turned towards her and leaned back in the chair, his hands behind his head, adding the smell of stale sweat to the mix. 'I could be helpful to you, sweetheart,' he said, 'with just a wee bit of encouragement. Nothing much, just a smile, maybe a little hug and a squeeze every now and then, just like you'd give your dear old dad.'

'You're nothing like my dear old dad,' said Judith. She wanted to get away but knew he could keep her story out of the paper for as long as he chose.

'Tell you what,' he said, 'just let me touch your hair, feel it in my fingers. Like this.' He pushed himself up out of the creaking chair and stretched out his hand. Judith stepped back out of his reach. 'Get off,' she said. 'Don't touch me.'

Cunningham fell back into the battered chair in mock horror, holding up both hands. 'Just a bit of fun, dear. You a lessie or something? Can't fool me. I know what you want. And don't think about telling anyone. I'll just say it was your idea. Don't forget who decides what happens to your copy, no matter what the boss says. That's a big spike on my desk. If all your stuff ends up there, it'll be back to the weddings and parish councils for you, girlie.'

He laughed and coughed, taking another cigarette from the packet on his desk. 'Don't touch me,' he mimicked in a whining voice.

Hattie looked up as Judith went back to her desk, pointed mutely towards Cunningham's cubbyhole and mimed a vomit, which made Judith smile. It also made her yearn for someone to confide in.

The move from Lancaster to Barrow six months before had left Judith without a friend she could talk to, not just on the phone or in scribbled notes, but a real talk, face to face. Her little flat in Cannon Street was actually the upstairs of a small terraced house just off Abbey Road. Abbey Road was impressive but Cannon Street was not, and Judith's three rooms were cramped and shabby. The downstairs flat was empty. Even before the tenant had moved out to a job further north at Sellafield, he'd been so quiet that it was like having the house to herself. The owner of the house lived miles away. 'Tenants are just a nuisance,' he'd said when he showed Judith round. 'But I'm too busy to sell the place.'

Charming, Judith had thought. Hello and welcome to you, too.

It had been a shock to realise that there was no one in her life closer to her than her stepfather. It was her own fault, she knew that. John was the only man she really trusted; her mother was either easily shocked or pretended to be so, and the girls she'd known at school and university had drifted away, embroiled in family and children. She felt the girls were judging her, 'Poor Judith, left on the shelf.' And then she'd met Elspeth.

One unusually hot day in August when there'd been nothing happening in the newsroom, Judith had gone out to Bruciani's for a cold drink and noticed a young woman there with a child of seven or so with a shock of golden hair. The child was pestering her for something and the woman caught Judith's eye, not impatient or embarrassed by the child's behaviour but with a laugh in her eyes if not in her mouth.

'I promised him an ice cream,' she said, 'but we seem to have forgotten about his side of the deal.'

'Did you promise Mummy something?' said Judith to the boy who turned round to look at her. He shook his head. 'Are you sure?' she said.

'What about sitting quietly at the table?' said his mother. 'This is a place for grown-ups, like this lady, and they don't want to listen to whiny children.'

'Certainly not,' said Judith. 'And if I sit at your table, you can sit nicely with us, can't you?'

'Yes, please join us,' said the mother. The boy climbed up on the chair without another word and picked up the long spoon to finish the ice cream that was turning to liquid in the bottom of a tall fluted glass.

'Thank you, Tommy,' said his mother, winking at Judith over his head. 'Say hello to the lady.'

'What's your name?' Tommy said to Judith, licking the pink foam from round his mouth.

'Judith.'

'Do you live here?'

'In Bruciani's?' She laughed. 'No, but my boss thinks I do.'

'I'm Elspeth, by the way,' said the young woman. 'Thanks for this. I was just about to give up and take him home.'

And so the conversation had flowed, covering Judith's work, and the boy's school, and the weather, the usual things. Elspeth invited Judith back to their little house in Roose for a cup of tea, and an hour or two later Judith's ingrained habit of fact-finding had established that they'd lived in Roose since January, and before that they'd lived with Elspeth's parents for two years. She had a part-time job in the same primary school as Tommy, which was really handy, and they'd come into town to buy Tommy some new trousers for school because he was growing so fast. 'He's tall, like his father,' said Elspeth. Judith waited for more. 'But it's just the two of us here, isn't it Tommy? And Gran and Grandad in Chorley.'

Judith had to wait until the Sunday afternoon when they all went for a walk together on the beach at Walney to hear the rest of the story about Tommy's tall father. The first surprise was that Elspeth, like Judith, had been a student at Liverpool University, but they hadn't overlapped; Judith had gone by the time Elspeth arrived fresh from school in 1962. Judith did not mention her reason for leaving, saying only that she'd been pushed into going to university by her mother and had never felt comfortable there, which wasn't far from the truth.

They walked along side by side, and stopped to watch Tommy playing tag with the incoming tide.

'Are you wondering about Tommy's father like everyone else does?' said Elspeth.

Judith smiled. 'Is it that obvious? Sorry. It's my job, you know. Nosey.'

Elspeth took a deep breath. 'OK, here's the potted version. I met Ralph during freshers' week, a few days after I'd left home. I was straight out of school, and he was on one of the stands, very confident, a real charmer. He was only there to get poor saps like me to sign up, but he made me feel good, and I fell for him, right there. Never met anyone like him before. He asked me to go for a drink, and then said he would show me round the hall of residence where he lived. It was full of boys, of course, all joking around and having a good time. I thought it was wonderful.'

'Something happened, didn't it?' said Judith. 'I know where this story's going.'

'It's as old as the hills, I know,' said Elspeth. 'He took me to his room, locked the door, – for privacy, he said – and that was that. Just that once, and again at the weekend, and then he decided I was too quiet and it wouldn't work, and he dumped me. I'd only been at university a week and my life changed, just like that. Found out I was pregnant a couple of months later. I went to the doctor on campus to ask about contraception and she told me I was eight weeks gone. I couldn't believe it.'

Tommy ran up to them. 'I fell over, Mam,' he said pointing to his scuffed knee.

'Mummy,' said Elspeth. 'I fell over, Mummy. Let's see.' She peered at the knee, and rubbed it gently. 'You'll live,' she said. 'Off you go.' He scampered away again, down the pebble bank towards the waves.

'You're very good with him,' said Judith.

'It just comes I suppose. You remember what your parents said to you. Sometimes you sound like your own mother. It's frightening.'

'What did your parents say, about you being pregnant?'

'I didn't tell them for a while. First thing was to tell Ralph, and he freaked out. I was shocked actually. He was almost hysterical about what his parents would say. Said his father would never allow it.'

'Allow what?'

'Us getting married. Ralph thought we would have to get married and live in a hovel and his life would be over. "I have to be a lawyer," he kept saying. I knew then I could never marry him, not because of his dad but because he was so horrid. I just told him not to bother about his precious life and his precious father and walked away. Then it hit me what I'd done, but I couldn't go back. So I had to tell Mum and Dad. That was pretty gruesome but they were OK in the end, after a lot of crying and upset. I think it helped that Tommy was so gorgeous when he was a baby, but we're all dark and that hair is a bit of a giveaway. Loads of people ask about it. I just pretend I'm divorced and that shuts them up.' Elspeth giggled suddenly. 'I remember one thing Ralph told me. I must have been an idiot to believe this. He said he had to have sex once a week or he got spots.'

They both laughed.

'Dad said Ralph's people had to take some responsibility to help out with the baby. He did his best, but they were all lawyers, the whole clan, and they played it really hard. Dad didn't dare take them to court over it, so in the end we just got some cash for somewhere to live and some money for the baby, nothing for me. It's not much, but it helps, until Tommy's sixteen and then it all stops. But he should be on his way by then, or I'll have married someone with pots of money and it won't matter.'

Judith was still curious. 'So you lived at home for a while, and then moved here. Why Barrow?'

'Good question! My aunty Molly lives in Ireleth, and her neighbour works in the school in Roose, and they needed a part-time teacher, which was easier for me than trying to work full time. And the houses were cheap, to buy, not just to rent. Things just added up, so we put the money from Ralph's family and some from my dad down for a deposit and here we are. It's better here. I needed to get away. We both did. And it's an OK place to live. The sea's so close, Morecambe Bay on one side and Walney just across the bridge. We can get on the train and be back in Chorley in no time, and Windermere in an hour or two, or up the coast to Ravenglass. Have you been up there?'

'I was born in Whitehaven,' said Judith, 'and then we moved to St Bees.'

'There you are then. You know how beautiful it is up the coast,' said Elspeth. 'People here complain all the time, but I'm glad we came. I'm making a life for myself, for us.'

For a moment Judith envied her new friend with shocking intensity. What did she have in her own life? Work, a small flat that wasn't even hers, a family she saw infrequently and when she did it was full of tension.

'You're very lucky,' she said to Elspeth.

'Lucky?' Elspeth laughed. 'That's rich.'

Over the two months since then Judith had gone to see Elspeth a few times on her way home from work. They were both busy once the school year began and the weekends filled up with chores. But Elspeth's little house felt more of a home than Judith's flat. It was clean and tidy, and there was always cake in the tin and real food in the pantry. Tommy was a lively boy, noisy sometimes but curious and funny and he reminded Judith of her brothers. And she hoped that some of Elspeth's contentment would rub off on her.

It was nearly six when Judith parked the scooter outside Elspeth's. Tommy opened the door and shouted over his shoulder, 'It's that lady!' Elspeth emerged, wiping her hands on a towel.

'It's Judith, Tommy. You know her name.' She looked up at Judith, smiling. 'Come in, love. I'm just serving up. Want some?'

Judith was impressed at how Elspeth was able to provide for three without warning when she struggled to provide just for herself. She was a few years older than Elspeth but seemed much younger in some ways.

'Not had rabbit in years,' she said when their plates were empty and Tommy had been released to watch the tiny TV in the front room.

'I get it in the market,' said Elspeth. 'No questions asked about where it came from. It's cheap protein.'

'And delicious. Thanks.'

Judith brewed tea and they sat together in the relative peace of the back room.

'You were at Liverpool for a year, weren't you?' Elspeth asked.

Judith nodded.

'So why did you leave? Did you fail exams or something?'

It was time. Judith badly needed to tell someone. She started right at the beginning, with the wartime death of her real father, Isaac Lowery, and how her mother Maggie and John had got together. 'It's all a bit rags to riches, isn't it?' she said. 'But John changed our lives, and he is a lovely man. His mam was special, too. I called her Jessie when it was just the two of us, not Granny like they wanted me to. She stuck up for me when I was a teenager and having rows with Mum all the time. But she got cancer and she died, about three years ago. I miss her. It was Mum's idea to send me to a posh school and then university, but Mum wanted it more than I did. I'd had enough of exams, just wanted to get a job and earn enough money to get away from home.'

'I'm the same,' said Elspeth, 'even though my parents seem a bit easier than yours.'

'I've never told my parents why I left university.'

'Tell me,' said Elspeth. 'Get it off your chest.'

The tears came easily and Elspeth produced a large hand-kerchief from somewhere. 'He was my tutor, and I never thought he could do something like that. It wasn't just that he hurt me,' said Judith. 'He humiliated me, throwing me out of his office in such a mess. People stared at me in the corridor. I couldn't go back there again.'

'Why didn't you just change course, or tell someone about what he'd done? He could be still there, doing the same thing again.'

'I know, I know. I should have reported it, but what if they didn't believe me? And Mum would have found out. I couldn't bear it, so I just left. Told Mum I never really wanted to be there, couldn't face another year of boredom, all that. It was tough for a while, but I found a job in a bookshop in Liverpool and enjoyed it. Interesting people, plenty to read, enough money to get myself a room. It was great for a few years and then I got bored. Dad said he would pay for jour-nalism school in Preston and after that I got a job on the evening paper. Peanuts for wages and crappy stuff to do, but it was a start. I did three years and was getting some decent assignments when this posh kid turned up whose dad knew the editor and all of a sudden I was "surplus to requirements". It was probably time to move on anyway, but sometimes it feels like I've had to start all over again in Barrow. To get a decent story I have to get past Skelly who thinks I should be at home in the kitchen, and then everything I write has to go to Cunningham.'

'Is he the creepy one?'

'Hattie calls him the groper. He's harmless enough I suppose, but every time he starts on me I get the memory of what happened before. Makes me feel physically sick. Just wish it would wear off. I might have to move again, and that's just not fair.'

Judith blew her nose noisily. 'Sorry about the hankie,' she said. 'I'll wash it properly, promise.'

Elspeth laughed. 'Keep it,' she said. 'What's a hankie between friends? Or drop it in the basket in the bathroom and it'll go in my new washing machine! Sam's buying one for me as a moving in present and I'm so excited. Pathetic isn't it?'

Judith looked at her. 'Sam? Who's Sam?'

'My half-brother. Didn't I tell you about him? I thought I had.'

'Give me the short version, or we'll be here for hours.'

'My mum was married before to a man from Glasgow, and had Sam, but her husband died suddenly and Mum was left on her own. My dad, the one in Chorley, was an old friend of the family and they, you know, got together and married and had me. Sam's three years older than me. He lived with us while I was growing up but I don't think he and my dad got on that well. Sam joined the army when he was sixteen but that didn't work out, so he left the first chance he could and joined the police instead.'

'He must like uniforms,' said Judith.

'You'd think so wouldn't you, but now he doesn't wear one. He's plain-clothes, a detective. Done very well. Transferred to Barrow, lived in digs for a while and hated it, and then Mum suggested he could have my spare room. I get the money and Tommy gets a man around. Seemed like a good plan, so he's moving in and we'll see if it works. I haven't seen much of him for ten years. It could be awful.'

'Has he always lived on his own before?'

'Ah, well that's another story,' said Elspeth. 'He's a pretty straight man, you'd know that if you met him. Nothing swinging sixties about him. He went out with one girl from school, the beautiful Christine, the childhood sweetheart, and then of course they got married, far too young. He was only twenty-one, just a young copper. We all told him it was a mistake, but he wouldn't have it.'

'What happened? Sounds like it didn't work out.'

Elspeth laughed. 'That's the polite version. I'd say he was happy for a year or two, maybe less, then you could tell it was going wrong. He wanted to be at home when he was off duty, she always wanted to go out. He was on late shifts, she only worked mornings. One day he came home and found her in their bed with some bloke, both naked. Sam went nuts, there was a big fight and Sam threw him out and chucked his clothes out of the window. The bloke ran off in his pants and socks! Christine had the gall to blame Sam for leaving her alone too much, but he wouldn't leave the police and they seemed to patch it up. God knows why he didn't throw her out as well. He obviously thought it was a one-off, never happen again, all that stuff. Then a couple of weeks later he got home from work and found the house empty.'

'She'd gone?'

'Empty! No Christine, and nothing else either. Everything gone. She'd taken the lot, furniture, carpets, even the light bulbs. No note. The neighbours said two blokes came with a van and just loaded everything up and drove away. Poor Sam.

He called me and when I got there he was sitting on the floor in the empty sitting room, arms round his knees, rocking back and forth like a crazy person. That was ages ago now, just after I had Tommy. He's lived like a saint ever since, as far as I can see. No girlfriend, just work and an occasional drink with his mates.'

Something dawned on Judith.

'What's his name?'

'He went back to his real dad's name when he left home. Detective Constable Samuel Tognarelli! Pretty impressive isn't it?'

Chapter 4

Judith looked around her tiny flat and was ashamed. Living alone, treating the place as somewhere to sleep and eat the occasional meal, she'd lost track of what her mother would have called normal housework, the chores that any self-respecting person would have done without thinking. Judith certainly didn't think about it, despite the daily irritations of losing things, not having clean clothes to wear and a permanent lack of teaspoons. She knew she should reciprocate Elspeth's regular hospitality, but dreaded the idea of anyone else seeing how she lived. On Saturday morning she decided to take herself in hand.

She discovered that housework was good for thinking. There was something about the mindlessness of the activity that let her thoughts wander more freely. As the weekend stretched ahead of her, Judith scrubbed away with Ajax on the stained kitchen sink and wondered why she hadn't told Elspeth about her first meeting with Sam. Maybe it was the same reason that had stopped her inviting Elspeth to the flat. Despite all her apparent confidence, Judith worried about how people would perceive her, especially if she cared about them. She didn't know Sam; he probably thought she was a jumped-up, pushy newshound, but who cared? The thought that Sam was close to Elspeth, whom she did know and whose respect she wanted, came as a shock to Judith. She'd had the chance to admit that she and Sam had met, and had avoided saying anything and created another unnecessary secret. It was foolish, she was foolish. Sometimes she didn't like herself much at all.

She rinsed the sink, took off the Marigold gloves, made herself a cup of tea and looked around. The sink was clean, but the rest of the flat was a mess. For an hour she tackled the accumulated piles of discarded stuff that lay in every room, putting things away or in big bags for the dustbin. She found things she thought she'd lost, uncovered surfaces that had been hidden for months, dusted, wiped and even polished. In the cupboards she found food she'd forgotten buying, some of which was still edible, and a late lunch consisted of cold baked beans followed by tinned fruit salad floating in evaporated milk.

Bedsheets were changed for the first time in weeks, and the dirty ones and grubby towels festered in a bag by the door waiting for a trip to the launderette. The clean bed looked crisp and inviting and she couldn't resist, falling immediately into a deep sleep. But it lasted only a couple of hours and she woke with a start, feeling mud closing over her head, thrashing out against a pillow that had covered her face. It took a few minutes to find her bearings, realise it was mid-afternoon not early morning, and pull herself together.

Domestic redemption and the launderette were forgotten as she let her mind wander back to Steven Stringer and his short life. She wanted to make the most of his story, to make sure he was not forgotten. Could this be a 'poor unwanted child's death goes unnoticed by the world' story, or a 'grieving family speaks of their loss at a packed funeral service' story?

She'd have to wait and see, but she thought the editor would be pleased with either. 'Thank you, George, for being ill,' she said to herself, 'and giving me this chance.' There was still the meeting with Mikey at Montgomery House. Wednesday, she hadn't forgotten. If and when she saw Tognarelli again she would avoid any mention of Elspeth, and leave any awkwardness till later.

By the end of the afternoon it was almost dark, but Judith had no desire to go out. She had a comfortable clean room, some interesting food, and a Saturday night play to listen to on the radio. Early to bed, an early start, the Sunday papers and a walk at Earnse Bay completed the weekend, one of the happiest she'd spent since moving to Barrow, and she was proud of herself for making it so.

The new sense of satisfaction propelled Judith to work early on Monday morning, to do a similar clean-up at her desk and she was astonished to hear herself having a conversation with Hattie about the merits of different types of paperclips. Yet again, undemanding activity made the hours slip away. When Bill Skelly approached her newly cleared desk late in the afternoon, Judith hoped he would bring news of Steven Stringer's post-mortem, but instead he muttered something about nest-building before he crammed his hat onto his head and went home. It wouldn't be the first time that Skelly had kept something to himself just to prove who was boss. She would have to ask him directly about it, and probably more than once. Before she left the newsrooom she called Montgomery House. This time the secretary, Mrs Clough, answered and obviously knew who Judith was.

'All I can tell you, Miss Pharaoh,' said Mrs Clough in her

best telephone voice, 'is that the poor boy's family have now been informed about his death. That's all, goodbye.'

It wasn't much, but enough for her to catch Alan Thornhill at his desk the following morning and persuade him to let her track down the mother for herself and add some flesh to the story before it went cold. Using the details supplied unwittingly by Mikey it didn't take long to find a school called St Joseph's in Morecambe, and that was definitely a place to start. They might not tell her anything, but that didn't mean she couldn't find an address if she stretched the rules a bit. And with an address would come the mother and her story. It was worth the trip, especially as Thornhill had given her expenses money for the train. Things were beginning to look up: a day out on a proper job and no more stolen bicycle stories for a while at least.

The school was a walk from Morecambe station, in miserable fine rain that blew off the sea and blotted out the view across the bay to the north. The view of Morecambe from the other side of the bay was very familiar to her but she'd never actually seen it close up, and wouldn't see much of it today either, unless the visibility improved. When she found the main entrance of St Joseph's School there was no one in the little office and Judith stood for a minute, listening to the sounds of children running in the hall and wondering whether to walk straight in and brazen it out. Before she could decide, a small child peered round a door to the right.

'Who are you?' said the child.

'I want to talk to the Head,' said Judith, bending her knees. 'Do you know where he is?'

The child disappeared without a word, and again Judith

waited, wondering who else was watching her.

The door was pulled open and a small white-haired woman said, 'Can I help you?' She was wearing a startling red blouse with a little scarf, a long dark skirt and sensible shoes.

'I'm looking for the headmaster,' said Judith.

'Headmistress. I am she,' replied the woman. 'Mildred Bennett,' she extended a dry hand, which Judith shook. 'And you are?'

'Ah,' said Judith. Why did she have to fumble for her ID every time when she could have it ready in her hand? Made her look foolish. 'Judith Pharaoh. I'm from the *Furness News* in Barrow.'

Mildred Bennett held the card at arm's length and squinted at it. 'You're a long way off your patch, Miss Pharaoh. What brings you to St Joseph's?'

'Can we talk somewhere else perhaps?' said Judith. 'It could be a bit tricky.'

Miss Bennett exhaled in irritation. 'Well, it'll have to be quick. I promised Form 1 I'd hear them read. You could have rung ahead, couldn't you?' She led the way into the office and shut the door, but didn't sit down. 'Well?'

'I believe you have, or had, a pupil here called Steven Clifford Stringer.'

'And if we did?'

'A child by that name was found on the sands, on the other side of the bay, last week.'

'What do you mean, found? Is he coming back to us?'

'No, Miss Bennett, I'm afraid he's dead. He was identified by the director of the children's home where he's been living.'

'Oh dear, goodness me,' said Marjorie Bennett, sitting down suddenly. 'What a dreadful thing. How did it happen?'

'We don't know. The family have been informed, but I'm

anxious to talk to his mother myself, and wonder if you could let me have an address.'

Miss Bennett took a paper handkerchief from the box on the desk and blew her nose. 'I don't think we would be able to do that. We have a duty of confidentiality you understand.' She looked up at Judith who was still standing.

'Does anyone know what happened to him?'

Judith shook her head. 'The police are investigating.'

Mildred Bennett dabbed at her eyes with the edge of the handkerchief. 'His poor mother. Will you excuse me a moment? I need to check…' She stood up, squeezed past Judith and left the room, closing the door behind her.

Judith looked around the small office. Two large filing cabinets loomed against the far wall. On the front of a top drawer, written in a neat dark script, was the label, *Pupil contact details, 1969-70*. She hesitated. Would that include Steven Stringer if he had left the school earlier? Maybe not, but if there were siblings… She waited again, listening for the sound of returning footsteps but there was nothing. 'Do it,' she told herself. The filing cabinet drawer was unlocked and slid noiselessly open. Thank God for alphabetical filing. She looked at the S section and there it was, *Gloria Stringer*, probably a sibling or even a cousin, it didn't matter. She read the address and memorised it – no time to write it down. She had just closed the drawer and stepped back when the quick footsteps made her cough to cover the sound, reach into her bag and throw something from it into the floor. When the door opened Judith was bending down, picking up paperclips that had scattered everywhere.

'So sorry,' she said. 'I was looking for my card to leave with you and the box broke.'

By the time they had found all the clips on the floor they

both stood up rather pink in the face, which served to mask Judith's embarrassment.

'Well, Miss Pharaoh,' Miss Bennett said, adjusting the paisley scarf at her neck, 'I have confirmed that we cannot offer you any information about the family. If you were the police, perhaps, but you're not, are you?'

'Have they been here?'

'The police? No, thank heaven. That would have caused far too much excitement if the children had spotted them. But I can't help you, I'm afraid. And now I need to get back to the class. May I escort you to the door?'

Judith was as gracious as someone who'd just got what she wanted despite being told it was impossible. She wrote down the address from memory quickly, before she forgot. It took a few minutes and questions to passers-by before she found the street where the Stringer family lived. The number she wanted was at the far end of a long row of red brick terraced houses, which began with quite attractive bow windows and tiny yards at the front but ended with neither, where the houses looked in need of repair and some were boarded up. She checked the number, and her spirits sank when one of the boarded-up houses was the one she was looking for. The hardboard nailed over the small front window looked fresh, unstained by time and rain. They may have gone after the police were here, she thought. But where?

A window curtain in the next house twitched and seconds later an elderly woman appeared on the doorstep. 'You from the Social?' she asked. 'Cos they've gone.'

'Ah,' said Judith. 'Do you know where?'

The woman shrugged. 'Her boyfriend bought a van round, last night early on and they loaded up some stuff and buggered off. Coro was on, I 'ad to turn the sound up. I was going to say summat but then I saw who it was, so I just let them go. Why bother? They were a noisy lot. Good riddance to 'em.'

'That's Mrs Stringer and her family, you mean?' Judith said, involuntarily smartening up her voice to sound more like someone from the Social.

'Yes, 'er, though she calls herself Bell these days. Yvonne Bell.'

'Are there any other family members around I could speak to?' asked Judith, in precise tones, trying to act the part.

'There was an older lad, but he went off years ago. Don't know where. Anyway, he disappeared. And that Donna, she left home too. She's at the station.'

'Catching a train?'

The woman laughed. 'No, she works there, in the café. Been there since she left school. She must be twenty-something now.'

The rain had blown through and Judith could see the grey outline of the north shore of the bay as she walked back to the station she'd left less than an hour before. The building spoke of better days and the café was dreary and unsurprisingly empty. A young woman with black hair hidden under a white hat was wiping tables with a grey cloth. Judith walked across.

'Are you Donna?' she said quietly.

The young woman looked up sharply and then across at the counter. 'What do you want?' she said. 'I'm working.'

'I'd like a word with you, if possible. It's personal, perhaps we could go somewhere else?'

'Who are you?'

'I'm from the *Furness News*, it's about Stevie.'

49

'Stevie? What's 'e done now?'

Judith hesitated. This woman was Stevie's elder sister and she didn't know he was dead. 'When you get off for lunch, maybe,' said Judith. 'I would like to talk to you.'

Donna nodded towards the bar next door. 'Wait in there,' she said. 'I'll tell them I want a break. Not like we're busy or anything.'

And so it was that Donna Stringer learned of the death of her youngest brother, and cried. 'Poor little bugger,' she said, wiping her nose on a napkin from one of the tables in the empty bar. 'He never really had a life, did 'e? People coming and going all the time, pushed from one place to another. That's no good for a kid. She's been a useless mam to him, and the rest of us. Used to be think I 'ad to be loyal to 'er, stick together, us against the world and all that – but not no more. She knew 'e was dead and she didn't even tell me. You can put that in the paper if you want, I don't care.' She sniffed. 'What about the funeral?'

'Steven's body – he's still being examined by the police surgeon.'

'Not cutting him up, are they?'

Judith shrugged. 'I don't know about that, Donna, but you can't have a funeral until they release the – until he can be taken to the undertaker. Procedure, you know.'

A man with slicked down hair, a red face and an apron stood in the doorway.

'You all right, Donna?' he said. 'Is this woman bothering you?'

'It's OK, Fred,' said Donna. She walked unsteadily to the door and spoke quietly into the man's ear. He put an arm round her shoulders and she cried again. He looked across at Judith. 'Can you take her home? She's in no fit state and I can deal with things here.' He bent down and spoke to Donna. 'Go home, have a cuppa and get your feet up,' he said. 'Come back tomorrow and we'll talk about getting to the funeral when it happens, OK?'

Donna sniffed and smiled.

'I'll walk home with you,' said Judith.

The two women, not far apart in age, walked together through the bleak streets to another terraced house where Donna opened the front door and they stepped inside. In the tiny cluttered kitchen, Donna made tea. Judith loathed the unmistakable flavour of sterilised milk but she drank the tea anyway.

''E's out at work,' Donna said, without explanation. 'If 'e comes back, don't say anything to 'im. You'll have to go pretty sharp, 'e doesn't like me 'aving anyone in.'

Judith wondered what went on in the house, behind the closed front door.

'Where do you think your mother may have gone?' Judith asked.

Donna shrugged. 'Could be anywhere. If the police've been to the 'ouse, they'd get as far away as possible, I reckon. Don't like people knowing where they are. That's why it were a shock when our Anthony turned up.'

'Who's Anthony?' asked Judith.

'My big brother,' said Donna. ''E went away years ago, when 'e was not much older than Stevie, and then 'e turned up again, out of the blue.'

'When was this?' Judith said. She needed her notebook but knew that could stop Donna talking, so she listened intently to hold the details in her mind.

'Two weeks ago, mebbe,' said Donna. 'Hardly recognised 'im. Much bigger, you know, and quite tanned, like 'e'd been to Majorca or summat, and a funny voice. Looked like a stranger, but it was 'im all right. God knows how he found me, or Mam, but 'e did. And then the police.' She smiled. 'Bet they were shitting themselves.'

'What about your mother's friend?'

'Friend! Him? Not really, not like any friend I'd want. E's been around a while. They're not married or anything. She just calls 'erself whatever suits 'er at the time. He 'its her, but then they all do, don't they?'

'Do you want me to tell you about the funeral, when it's arranged? That nice man at the café, I'm sure he'd let you have the time.'

'Oh 'e would, like, but I might not get paid, and then there's getting over there. I know someone who wouldn't be 'appy about that. Every penny counts, 'e says, tight git.'

They heard a key turn in the front door, and Donna looked up. Judith saw the panic in her eyes. 'Don't say anything. Let me –'

The kitchen door opened. 'Donna?' said the man. He looked quite young, an overgrown boy trying to prove his manhood. 'Who's this? No one in the house, I told you.'

'She's going, Ian. From the Social, looking for our Stevie. Told 'er to mind 'er own business and she's going.'

'Get out,' said the man, putting down his bag and pushing up the sleeves of his jacket. 'Private property. Bugger off.'

Judith looked at Donna, saw the expression in her eyes, and left without a word, hurrying away down the street before the man decided to come after her.

On the train back to Barrow she wrote up her notes, pulling the details from her memory. Both addresses, Donna's place of work and the address of the house. Mother calls herself Yvonne Bell, so that's probably the latest boyfriend's name.

Older brother Anthony, but she had no confirmed second name for him either. Could be Anthony Stringer. Age? Must be in his late twenties if he disappeared some years ago, and older than Donna who must be in her early twenties. Maybe Anthony's arrival was what made Stevie want to go home. She made a list of questions to ask Mikey when they met, or the captain or Mrs Robinson at Montgomery House. Then she went over her notes again, making sense of the information she'd accumulated. Steven Clifford Stringer had left the home, probably at night on the previous Thursday or early in the morning of Friday. With or without someone else, he'd ventured onto the sands and got stuck almost immediately, or had been caught by the incoming tide and forced back to shore, where he disappeared into a quicksand and drowned. Or else he died from some other cause before ending up in the mud. The thought of those final few minutes of the boy's life haunted her. She stared out of the window and tried not to care as the train rattled over the Furness viaducts. She had to keep this story, and make something of it. No good getting sentimental about it.

By the time she got back to Barrow it was too late to go back to the newsroom. Instead she bought herself a coffee in Bruciani's and wrote the start of a piece about Stevie and his brief life, not knowing whether she would ever have the chance to publish it. She wondered whether the policeman who was now revealed as Elspeth's half-brother would have gathered the same information she had. Surely Donna or Miss Bennett would have mentioned a visit from a detective? So was she obliged to share what she knew?

Judith stopped writing and sat back to sort out what she'd been told. Elspeth had said that her brother Sam was three years older, which would make him about the same age as

Judith, despite his boyish looks. So he must have been in the police force for seven or eight years, long enough to make it through to CID and keep that status when he changed jobs. Joining a new force must be hard, she thought. Maybe that's why he seemed so officious. She would have to talk to him. If there was someone with Stevie when he left Attercliff, the police needed to know. Judith remembered the mud and mess by the shore after the men had finished digging him out. Impossible to tell how many people would have been down there originally, and if the boy had left the shore with someone else and been driven back by the tide, there wouldn't be anything to find anyway.

She remembered the post-mortem report, which had to be ready by now. Would Skelly share it with her? He would have to eventually if Thornhill insisted, but he might deliberately slow everything down, just to spite her. Maybe she could go direct to the source. She checked the time. Just after six. She knew where Doc Hayward might be found after work, so she stuffed her notebook into her bag and set off to find him.

He was where she expected him to be, in the usual pub, at the usual table, with the usual drink in front of him. It looked as if he'd been there for some time. He glanced up and smiled when he saw her.

'Judith! Thank God for a cheerful young face before the end of the day,' he said. 'Looking at dead bodies all day long drags you down after a while. And the smell. Everyone said I'd get used to it but I never have. And how are you, my dear? Let me get you a drink.' He began to get unsteadily to his feet and the small table wobbled, empty glasses tinkling against each other.

'No, doc, you stay there,' she said. 'I can get my own. They do serve women in pubs these days, as long as there's nothing more important to be doing.'

From the bar she watched him lifting another glass of whisky carefully towards his mouth. He took a sip, put down the glass and began to cough, covering his mouth with a large handkerchief.

'Were you looking for me?' he asked when she sat down with her half of cider.

'I knew where you'd be and that you might save me some time,' she said. 'Things in the newsroom are a bit tricky. Skelly thinks his territory is being invaded by his boss, so he's out to show me who's in charge, and that means hiding things from me, slowing everything down, the usual games.'

'Happy days,' said Dr Hayward. He was quiet for a moment. 'I suppose you want to know how that poor lad died?'

'Have you done the post-mortem?' she asked.

He waited, staring into his drink. She wondered how much he'd already had.

'Yes, I've done it,' he said finally.

'I knew it,' said Judith. 'Not a word about it from Bill, but I have been out all day, so maybe I'm doing him a disservice. Anything you can tell me?'

He looked up at her. His eyes were wet and he wiped them with the handkerchief. He beckoned with his fingers and Judith leaned close to hear what he said.

'He didn't drown. No water or mud in the lungs. If he'd got sucked into that quicksand there would have been.' He hesitated. 'I'll put it all in the report. Tomorrow, I'll do it tomorrow. You'll have to read the rest for yourself.'

Judith stared at him. 'If he didn't drown –' she began. He held up his hand. 'It'll be in the report,' he repeated. 'And that's where it should be, not under discussion in a public house.' He picked up the glass and finished it. 'You're a fine woman, Judith,' he said, getting up from the table. 'Don't let them change that. Find something to believe in and stick to it.'

He patted her head and left her wondering about the boy, and death, and loneliness.

Chapter 5

On Wednesday, Judith was at her desk early, impatient for something to happen. How long would it take before Stevie's post-mortem report filtered through the porous network of policemen and then the press, she wondered? Doc Hayward said the boy didn't drown, but could he have made a mistake? He wasn't well, Judith could see that, and probably drinking too much. She had to see the full report herself. Or maybe she would have to get Doc Hayward on his own again and pester him until he told her all the details. Couldn't print it of course, but it would help to fill in the picture she needed.

And what about Brother Sam, the zealous detective? He would know what the PM had uncovered. She could ask him, use him as a source of information and by-pass the newsroom gang all together. He might refuse of course, but she could trade some stuff that she knew and he didn't. Mikey might tell her something he wouldn't tell the police. Edwards had said the lads liked talking to women more than men. That could work in her favour.

In the meantime, she'd made up her mind about something else. Maybe it was telling Elspeth about what had happened to her that brought it to a head, but suddenly Judith couldn't stand being around Cunningham any longer. The smell of him, his eyes on her, she couldn't bear it. She needed to make a call, but couldn't use the phone in the newsroom. There was a public phone box in the street outside and she gathered up her change to call the only person she could think of who might advise her what to do. Eight-thirty. He always went to work early and would be at his desk by now, hopefully.

'Mr Pharaoh's office,' said a crisp voice. Judith explained who she was. 'Hold on a moment, Judith,' said the secretary.

'Judith,' said her father, 'Is anything wrong?'

'No, Dad, nothing. I'm OK. Sorry to call at such a funny time. Didn't want to call you at home. Mum, well you know how she is.'

'What is it, pet, that can't be discussed with your mother?'

Judith hesitated. 'It's something at work, and you're a man, so I thought…'

'Good heavens, Judith. I'm imagining all sorts of things now.'

'It's nothing bad, really. I just don't know what to do about a man in the office who…' She stalled again. It all sounded so feeble. 'He stares at me all the time, and tries to touch me, and he says I should be nice to him if I want him to help me, that kind of thing.'

John Pharaoh was silent.

'Are you there, Dad?'

'How long's this been going on?'

'Since I started on the paper. He's been there for years. He must be your age, maybe older. He says I should give him a hug and kiss him like I would do with my father. It's really disgusting.'

'Is he your boss?'

'Sort of. He's the sub-editor, the one that has to approve all my work.'

'And you think he'll block your work if you don't go along with this?'

'Yes.'

'You poor thing,' said John. 'Of course you meet men like that, but I haven't really thought about the girls and what a spot it puts them in. Girls like you –'

'I'm not a girl, Dad, I'm a grown woman.'

'But he's not treating you like one, is he? I could come down and knock his block off but that wouldn't help much, would it?'

'Probably not,' said Judith 'but I'd love to see you do it.'

'Is there someone you could tell, someone more senior? What about the editor?'

'Mr Thornhill?' Judith couldn't imagine it. 'I could try I suppose. Don't know what he could do. I think Cunningham bullies him too.'

John sighed. 'Let's not tell your mother, Judith. She'd want me to call the police or she'd come down and deal with it herself, heaven help us.'

Judith could hear him smiling at the thought, and she laughed too at the vision of Maggie beating Cunningham over the head with her handbag.

'I'll try telling the editor, Dad. Could make it worse but I have to do something. I have to work with a sub-editor, can't get round that, but if he touches my hair again I'll hit him myself and lose my job.'

'No, don't do that. Talking to his boss is the only thing I can think of,' said her father. He was quiet for a moment. 'None of this would happen if you just came to work with me, Judith. Not in finance like me, in the press office. They'd jump at someone with your experience, someone local who knows about Sellafield and how important it is to us up here. The

59

Irish are kicking up again about pollution in the sea. We need all the help we can get.'

'Maybe sometime, Dad, but not yet. Have to get some more experience on a proper paper, and I'm not sure I want to deal with Sellafield stuff the whole time. How's Vince?' she asked, anxious to change the subject.

'Doing remarkably well, considering. His sight's no better, just light and shapes but no detail. He would love to see you, Judith. Why don't you come up this weekend? It's been ages since we saw you last.'

Judith remembered all too clearly the blame in her mother's voice, but John heard the silence and understood. 'She doesn't blame you, you know. She knows it was an accident. Vince was old enough to know that he shouldn't climb that wall, and you weren't close enough to stop him.'

'But she still blames me. You know she does.'

'Maybe at the time, but that's all forgotten now.'

It was no good talking any more; Maggie would blame her daughter for her younger son's blindness till her dying day. For Judith the thought of living in St Bees was out of the question.

'I'll have to go, Dad. Running out of money. I'll let you know what happens but don't say anything to Mum.'

She put the rest of the unused change back in her purse, and pushed open the door of the phone box, relieved to escape the lingering smell of urine She'd be early for her meeting with Mikey but she would need plenty of time to ask the growing list of questions in the bag that she slung over her shoulder on her way out.

❖ ❖ ❖

Judith parked the Vespa well away from Montgomery House and walked round to reach the digging field without going near the building. From the top end of the field she looked down to find the best place for their conversation. The hut Mikey had mentioned, where the teacher would be engrossed in his newspaper, was down at the bottom of the field near the path that led through the rhododendron bushes surrounding Montgomery House. Dividing the field from the house was a fence that ran up the slope and then bent round to the west. If Judith could find a spot among the bushes and Mikey arranged to work close by, they could talk without her being seen and their conversation being overheard. The top gate into the field led directly off the little road up to the village. There was no one around. Judith closed the gate behind her and walked across to the corner of the fence, climbed over it with ease and found a place in the thickest part of the bushes where she couldn't see the hut but found herself within a few feet of the edge of the field. The boys had obviously been working here. There were rows of sprouts waiting to be picked, and other areas where the reddish soil had been tilled ready for some winter planting.

From her hiding place she heard a bell ring in the main house and some minutes later a group of boys in rubber boots appeared near the hut followed by a man that Judith realised she had seen before. Harries – the name came back to her at once. Desmond Harries. He'd been in Edwards' office the day they found Steven's body, but had said nothing that she could remember. And Mikey had mentioned him, as the digging teacher who left the boys to their own devices.

She ducked back into the bushes while the boys collected their various implements and set off to their tasks around the field. Mikey hadn't forgotten. He was looking around as he walked slowly across the field and spotted her almost at once, altering his path to bring him up the field towards her. He spoke to another smaller boy, who glanced up at Judith and then began his work closer to the hut. Harries stood at the door for a while checking on the activity before he disappeared inside.

'That's good, miss,' said Mikey as he bent to fiddle with the sprouts a few feet away from Judith's hiding place. 'Harries wouldn't see you unless 'e knows where to look. Can you 'ear me or should I come a bit nearer?'

'That's OK, Mikey. Glad you remembered.'

'We miss Stevie,' he said. 'We want to know what 'appened to 'im, just like you do.'

'Have the police been?' she asked.

'Oh, aye. Copper looked about the same age as me. Not from round 'ere though and 'e had a funny name. He asked what time Stevie left that night, what 'e'd said to us, usual sort of stuff.'

'Did you tell him about someone coming to fetch Stevie?'

''E never asked about no one else. We told 'im Stevie'd talked about going home to 'is mam, and that was all. Never tell the cops nothing you don't 'ave to, that's what me dad told me. So I don't.'

'What time did Stevie leave that night, do you know?'

'Late, miss. Darren was in his room and said he was gone when he woke to go to the lav about midnight.' He stood up.

'Are we still OK?' asked Judith. 'Any sign of the teacher?'

'Old 'Arries won't stir till we have to go in, 'e never does. Reads that big paper from cover to cover. We could be off over the fence and away but 'e don't care.'

'Well, keep checking,' said Judith. 'Mikey, do you lads ever get hold of any drink, you know, alcohol?'

'Booze, miss? Would if we could. One of the lads brought some back from home once, but 'e put it in 'is hot water bottle and it tasted 'orrible. Stevie drank some, I remember that. Not much, but 'e threw up in the lav. Stank the place out.'

'Is there any alcohol on the premises, in Captain Edwards' office maybe, for visitors?'

'I saw Matron with a glass of sherry or summat once, on 'er birthday. And there's a posh bottle with whisky in it that they get out at Christmas. That might be in the office, but it'll be locked up.'

'So you hadn't been drinking the night Stevie disappeared?'

'We 'adn't, but there were some visitors making a bit of a racket. Wouldn't be surprised if they'd 'ad a few. Captain has 'is mates over sometimes and they get a bit noisy.'

'You said that Stevie told you someone was coming to get him.'

'Yes, 'e said that. We thought 'e were making it up, showing off. No one ever came to see 'im.'

Mikey looked up suddenly, away from Judith. The boy he'd spoken to earlier was standing up, whistling a tune. Beyond him, Judith could see Mr Harries standing outside the hut, looking away from them out to the shore and the flat expanse of the bay beyond. Judith ducked back into the darkness of the trees while Mikey bent to his task of picking sprouts with convincing commitment. A few minutes later the whistling started again and Mikey whispered. 'E's gone, back in the hut. Is that it, miss? Me back's killing me.'

'Nearly done. I've got some pocket money for you if we can just finish this off.'

'Fire away, miss,' said Mikey.

'You say no one ever came to see him, but did you see anyone hanging around the home at all, or out here even, over the past few weeks?'

Mikey was thinking and Judith wished she hadn't mentioned

the money. Maybe he would make something up just to keep her interested.

'There was someone,' he said. 'Couple of weeks back. A man. He looked cold but it weren't a cold day. He were standing by the road, near where the hut is, looking down the path towards the house. We were in the van coming back from town. Must've been the Saturday, not the one just gone, or the previous, the one before that.'

'About two weeks ago,' said Judith.

'That's it. When 'e saw the van slow down to come in the drive, 'e just turned and walked away, but 'e'd a good look at us when we passed.'

'Was Stevie with you?'

'Nah, 'e were in trouble again and couldn't come out. That's what they do. You 'ave treats like trips out and comics and that, and if you mess around they take them off you.'

'And Stevie was in trouble a lot was he?'

''E were an idiot, miss. Never knew when to shut up, except when it suited 'im. One day 'e spat out the window over the back door, and someone was coming in. Gob hit him right on the 'ead. The bloke went mental and stormed up the stairs to where we all were and said he wanted the kid who'd gobbed on him and we all knew it was Stevie and 'e never said a word the little runt, so we all copped it. No trips, no comics, for two weeks. We gave 'im hell over that.'

'Could Stevie have run away to get away from you lads, then?'

Mikey stood up to stretch his back. Judith could see that he was smiling. 'Run away from us? Nah,' he said. 'We're 'is family, poor little bugger. Sorry miss.'

He looked down towards the hut. 'Eyup,' he said. ''Ere 'e comes, 'Arries.' Mikey coughed and put a hand to his mouth.

'Leave the money right there, miss, and I'll pick it up later. Gotta go, before he comes up 'ere. Stay there until you 'ear the bell in the house and then get out quick before the next lot of kids come.'

He picked up the bucket of sprouts and set off down the field. Judith stepped back and waited, putting two half crown coins under a stone near her feet. The voices diminished and when she heard the bell she looked around once more, climbed the fence and hurried back to where the scooter was parked near the post office.

She'd learned a few things but nothing that would stand up, or even make much sense. The only person she could think of who might have been hanging around Montgomery House recently was the man that Donna had mentioned, Stevie's elder brother who'd suddenly turned up in Morecambe. But why didn't he visit properly, if he was part of the family? Judith made a mental note to check the tide times for the night of Stevie's death. If he left before midnight, could the incoming tide have been the problem? But he wasn't drowned. None of it made any sense. For the time being, the only facts she could pull together would be about the funeral, and she needed the date of that, too.

Back at the office she made a phone call.

'Stevie's funeral?' said Mrs Clough. 'One moment please.' She was back almost immediately. 'It'll be at the crematorium in Barrow, this Friday at eleven in the morning. Some of the boys will be going, and some of the staff of course.'

'What about the family?'

'The family were expected to arrange the funeral, obviously, but the mother declined apparently. You didn't hear that from me, Miss Pharaoh. They left it to us, and the Captain will probably have to find the funds from his own pocket, a very noble gesture if you ask me. But what can you do with parents like that? They should be prevented from having children, in my view. Don't print that.'

'I won't, Mrs Clough,' said Judith. She pictured the small coffin, going through those final curtains into the flames. Then there would be nothing left of him but a plaque on a wall somewhere. She remembered Vince at eleven, bursting with energy and questions and jokes and life. She would go to the funeral and then she would go and see her own brother who was still alive.

She looked up suddenly as Bill Skelly began roaring at Andrew, the young trainee who had claimed he had nothing to do. Judith listened to the tirade, smiled sympathetically at Andrew and was reading her various messages when Bill sat himself down on the spare chair beside her. 'Even you weren't as pathetic as that, were you, Judith?'

It was an impossible question to answer and she didn't try. 'How's that story going,' Bill went on, 'about the kiddie who drowned?'

He hadn't seen the PM report, she decided, and her question about it dried in her mouth. 'We're still waiting for the PM report,' she said. 'Will you get the details from the cops or shall I?'

'They usually call me first, but I'll just pass it on. The kid drowned, right? Not much of a story in that but we could do something with it. Another death in Morecambe Bay, when will people learn, the old refrain. Funeral?'

'Friday morning,' said Judith. 'I rang the home.'

'Must have released the body then,' said Bill. 'You go, don't forget to get all the names. Won't be many, but people want to see their names in the paper. What about the family?'

'Only story there is: "Can parents like this be rewarded for having children, child allowance, irresponsible families *et cetera*." They might turn up to the funeral but I doubt it. Seem to have dumped the whole thing back on social services.'

For a moment Judith thought of saying something about the man who she thought might be the long-lost brother, but that might jeopardise her deal with Mikey and it wasn't worth it. If the brother turned up at the funeral she would have something more solid to go on.

'Make something of it, if you can,' said Bill. 'Stories about kids always sell papers. If you put something out before Friday it might make a better funeral. Talk to Cunningham about it, if you can find him.'

'Is he in?' asked Judith.

Bill shook his head. 'Meeting at the Town Hall about something. And then the usual long lunch I expect.'

'While he's out, can I have a word?'

'About Cunningham? I know he's drinking, and so does Thornhill.'

'No, it's not the drinking, although…' She knew it was probably hopeless.

'Come on girl, spit it out. Don't bother about cloth ears over there, and Hattie's off powdering her nose somewhere. What about Cunningham?'

'He's pestering me,' said Judith. 'Has done ever since I started here.'

'What do you mean, pestering? Hand up your skirt, is that it? If you ever wore a skirt. Why don't you wear a skirt? Something wrong with your legs?'

Judith was shocked. 'No, not a hand up my skirt. But, you know, trying to touch me, says he wants to feel my hair.'

'Your hair, for God's sake, what's wrong with that? It's not even close to your tits.'

'But,' said Judith, 'I don't like it. I want him not to do it.'

Bill got up. 'For fuck's sake, girl,' he said. 'You're a big girl now. Men do that kind of stuff. Always have, always will, makes the world go round. Where have you been all these years? If that's the worst you can say about him, then just grow up and shut up. Honestly,' he continued, 'don't waste my time.' He turned back towards her. 'And don't waste his time either,' he jerked his head towards Thornhill's closed door. 'We've got a paper to run here. I know all about what he said to you last week. The last thing you need right now is some nonsense about being pestered. Understood? Just get on with the bloody job.' He put on his hat and left, banging the news-room door behind him.

Andrew put his head up. 'Shut up, Andrew,' said Judith.

She was writing up her notes from the conversation with Mikey a while later when the newsroom door opened and a waft of expensive perfume caught Judith's nostrils by surprise. She knew it was Irene Thornhill even before she raised her head to check, and the sight of several bags from the more expensive shops in Barrow confirmed it.

'It's Judith, isn't it?' said Irene, looking down at Judith over the shoulder-high partition.

'Yes, Mrs Thornhill, Judith Pharaoh.'

'Such a quaint name,' said Irene. She'd said that before, and Judith wasn't sure what 'quaint' actually signified. 'Is that a local name, Pharaoh?' she continued.

'Up the coast, Whitehaven way I think,' said Judith, 'but there seem to be Pharaohs all over the place.'

'Just like Ancient Egypt.' Irene's laugh had a curious tinkle, refined, like the rest of her.

Irene took the few steps that it took to glimpse into Cunningham's cubbyhole. 'Not in, I see,' she said. 'Alan tells me his lunchtimes are getting longer. I wonder what he's up to.'

'We wonder too,' said Judith. Irene looked at her sharply. 'What do you think, dear? Any ideas?'

'Just the usual, picking up stories in the pub, seeing contacts, that sort of thing. Mr Skelly says that's the way to catch the stories.'

'I'm sure that's true, and he should know after all these years, shouldn't he? I don't suppose my husband's in either is he?'

'He's out,' Andrew's voice, surprisingly forceful, spoke from the darkness on the far side of the room.

'A phantom speaks,' said Irene. 'My own fault, to find a deserted office when I come in unannounced. I was just doing a bit of shopping and thought I'd pop in and catch you all unawares. I'm dying for a nice cup of tea.'

'I can make you one,' said Judith. She'd always admired Irene Thornhill's style and it certainly made a change for the better today.

'Here? I said a *nice* cup of tea,' said Irene with emphasis. 'Heaven knows what ghastly bugs there are around here. No, I was heading for the Blue Teapot, on the corner. Can't abide the ghastly noise of that machine in Bruciani's and if I hear that dreadful "Boom, Bang-a-bang" song once more I shall scream. Care to join me, Judith? You and I have never really talked, have we, and you look like such an interesting young woman.'

Judith looked at the papers on her desk.

'Don't tell me you can't afford half an hour away from your desk, when the two men are hardly ever here. Hattie can hold the fort, and whoever that voice belongs to over there. The *Furness News* will be in good hands for a little while.'

Why should I argue, thought Judith. The notes are almost complete, and I deserve a break. She picked up her jacket and followed Irene out of the newsroom and down the stairs to the street. Once on the pavement, Irene asked her to carry some of the bags and slipped her arm through Judith's as they walked to the café, where she appeared to be a welcome and frequent guest.

'There now,' said Irene, as they settled into the best table by the window. 'We can watch the world go by, such as it is, and have a good chat. I'm just so short of female company. Too many men in this world, dear, don't you agree?'

Judith said nothing; what was there to say?

The waitress came over, pad in hand. 'Tea for two,' said Irene. 'Half Earl Grey, you know how I like it. And maybe a scone? What do you think, Judith?'

Judith was very hungry and could have cheerfully demolished one of the café's sandwiches but she restrained herself. 'A scone would be lovely, thanks.'

'Two scones, with cream and jam, strawberry jam mind, none of that other stuff.'

The waitress didn't wait for any further pleasantries and departed.

'Now then, Judith,' said Irene, easing her coat from her shoulders. 'Tell me all about yourself. I don't think there's ever been a young woman like you in the newsroom and I'd love to know how you ended up here. Barrow-in-Furness isn't everybody's cup of tea, after all. I'd much prefer to live somewhere more civilized, like Ulverston, such a pleasant town, but Alan insists we have to live here, closer to the office. Can't shift him on that one. Did you say your people come from Whitehaven?'

'Originally, yes,' said Judith. She was already calculating how to avoid the fact that both her mother and grandmother had been screen lasses at Haig Pit, at the lowest end of the social ladder. 'But then we moved to St Bees.'

'That's another lovely spot, but too far away again. Whereabouts in St Bees?'

'Beach Road, quite close to the sea.'

'Lovely,' said Irene. 'Quite large houses down there I recall, south facing. Does your father work in the village?'

'No, he's at Sellafield,' said Judith. 'He's one of the finance managers there.'

'And what does he think of your choice of career, I wonder?' Irene asked, smiling.

The tea and scones were being placed with conspicuous care on the small table and Irene stopped the interrogation for a while, much to Judith's relief. She took her chance.

'It's quite difficult actually, as the only woman in the newsroom,' she said, 'apart from Hattie, that is. I've got all the qualifications, and experience too, but they still seem to think of me as a novice who knows nothing. I do get fed up with it sometimes.'

'I'm sure you do,' said Irene. 'I remember that feeling from my days at work, but that was ten years or so ago. I thought it might be different by now. Nearly 1970 and still women aren't respected in the workplace. Of course I gave up work when I married.' She sipped her tea. 'Sometimes I think getting married was a mistake. Alan seemed so glamorous when we met – a young journalist in Manchester, at the heart of the city. I honestly thought we'd be going to London next, but then he suddenly turned into the dutiful son and came rushing up here to look after his parents and took a job in this godawful place. Of course he's in line to be editor of a bigger paper, maybe in Kendal or Newcastle even, somewhere with a bit of class, but now we're stuck here in this dump. I'm so bored I could scream.'

Judith drank her tea, wondering how to respond to these confidences. She'd always thought Irene Thornhill was an ambitious woman and admired her for it, and didn't want to hear that she was actually frustrated and unhappy. Irene seemed bent on telling her more than she wanted to know, and continued as if Judith wasn't even there.

'Even before we moved up here, things weren't good. I know Alan had a hard time with his National Service, before I met him. They all had to go, you know, no matter what. The timing was rotten and he got sent to Malaya. Now he says that whole experience knocked the stuffing out of him. He thought it would be so exciting. Won't tell me much of course, they never do, do they? But he has nightmares about it still. Wakes up shouting.' Irene was gazing into the distance as she spoke, stirring her tea.

This is my boss she's talking about, thought Judith, completely nonplussed by the revelations, and desperate to change the subject. She turned the conversation back towards herself.

'I'm my own worst enemy in some ways. I should give up worrying about how I look, but my hair drives me crazy. It's as frizzy as a hedge. My mother's hair is curly too, but it's a lovely rich red colour while mine's just a dirty orange. I don't know what to do with it.'

Irene seemed to have come back to the present and looked closely at the young woman opposite. 'That's easily sorted out, dear. A good hairdresser is all you need. And you have so much to offer. Lovely bone structure, you can probably thank your mother for that, too. I'm sure there are plenty of young men who find you very attractive. They're all so gauche these days. No idea how to make a woman feel good about herself.'

I wonder, Judith thought. Irene would never put up with the treatment I get from Cunningham, or Bill, or even her husband. Could I risk telling her about what's happening and ask for help, woman to woman?

'There is something I'd like your advice about,' she began.

'About your hair?' asked Irene, cutting her scone into delicate portions.

'No,' said Judith, 'about the things a man I know has been saying to me. Things that I don't think he should be saying, or doing, but I don't know how to deal with him.'

Irene put down the piece of scone that was halfway to her mouth. 'What kind of things?'

'He says he wants to touch me, and I ought to be affectionate towards him, a squeeze, a hug, that kind of thing. He's much older than me. It just doesn't feel right. He says I should treat him like my father, but that doesn't feel right either.'

'Is he a friend of your family?'

'No. They don't know him. It's at work.'

'Not Mr Skelly?' said Irene. 'Surely not.'

'No, said Judith. 'It's Ed Cunningham. I don't know what to do.'

For the first time Irene seemed too stunned to speak. She reached into her bag for her compact, opened the lid and looked carefully at her reflection.

'Oh dear,' she said finally. 'I'm sorry to hear that. Now let's finish our tea and get you back to work. Just leave it with me.'

'That's the last time I mention Mr Groper,' Judith said to

herself as she sat down again at her desk. 'No one's taking it seriously except my father, and his standards must be higher. Nothing to be done, so I might as well take the only advice on offer, shut up and just keep out of his way as much as I can.'

Later she woke in the night with the same old dream running through her brain. Only it was a memory rather than a dream. The shock, the hurt and humiliation. Cunningham was making her feel bad all over again. It was time to put it behind her.

Chapter 6

Judith woke early on Friday morning wishing she'd paid a bit more for curtains that would actually keep out the light. During the winter months the sun's first light caught the edge of her bedroom window and pierced her sleep more effectively than any alarm clock. Once awake, her head was too full to let her sleep again. She'd realised two things clearly in the past few days. One was that she dreaded going to work: not an acute fear but a low rumbling anxiety that was partly about her competence and partly about the people she had to work with. The second realisation was that nobody would help her deal with the work problem and her choices were stark. Either she drove herself through this despondency or she had to quit. There were no alternatives.

She could leave the job tomorrow and go to Sellafield, where her father's reputation and influence would swing her a job and probably a good one, too. She wouldn't have to live at home, and there were places on the Irish Sea coast that were more attractive than where she lived, in a back street in Barrow. But it felt like going backwards, and she knew enough about Sellafield to realise that the atmosphere there wouldn't suit her.

If she needed to stay with the *Furness News* for the time

being she would just have to deal with the men herself, as best she could, and not let it get tangled up with memories of losing her virginity to a middle-aged man whom she should have been able to trust. They weren't all like that. Bill was just blinkered about work and dismissive of anything else. And Alan Thornhill? What about him? Irene's description of him in his younger days had made Judith think of him differently. National Service had probably changed his life. One good thing about being female is that you didn't have your life interrupted by the requirement to go and kill people.

She'd had a few boyfriends – what a stupid title that was for a grown man – since she left university. There was Adrian from the bookshop, but he turned out to be too solemn and slow. Then there was Paul, who was fun, he liked her much more than she liked him, and he was much younger, just a boy. That was all in the past, she told herself, staring at the rain-stained ceiling of her room. Grandmother Jessie had been alone for years, making her way in the world, unwilling to risk her independence. So far, having a man around had been fraught with compromise for Judith too, and she was better off without, for a little longer at least. Sometimes she wished she preferred women, but she knew by now that there were no sexual sparks in that direction. Pity really. Life might have been a bit easier if there were. She wondered whether Detective Sam might have given up on women after the Christine debacle and turned his attention towards men instead, but he was probably just off sex all together. She could understand that.

She'd been lying watching the light on the wall and encouraging herself to get up and face the day, when the alarm jangled into life. It was hours yet until Stevie's funeral but already it was weighing on her. Children's funerals were almost unbearable. Would the family come? Would anybody come apart from some from the home and herself? Detective Sam would probably be there. Damn. He was Elspeth's relative, and that meant Judith would have to be polite to him, if nothing more. Was she obliged to tell him what she knew? Was any of her information solid enough for the police to act upon? She doubted it. So maybe she could wait until it was. He was paid to check things out. If he wasn't as energetic about it as she was, that was his problem, not hers. So far the story had potential, and she wanted to keep it that way.

By the time she'd found something suitable and relatively presentable to wear, and eaten something to fortify herself against the misery of the hours to come, it was gone nine. Was there really time to go to work, or could she sneak a walk by the shore while the sun was still shining?

The newsroom prevailed, but she compromised by taking the scooter down to the shore on her way in. It was one of those days when the light and colour of the sky was reflected in the wet surface of the sand, white and silver and blue and grey, changing patterns as the clouds moved across. Sometimes the reflections were sharp, sometimes blurred. She rested both feet on the ground on either side of the scooter and watched for a few minutes before turning round and heading into town.

Andrew looked up when she came in. 'There was a call for you,' he said. He had such a quiet voice normally that everyone strained to hear him and Bill Skelly had been shouting at him again, which made him even more nervous. 'She wanted to speak to you, no one else, about ten minutes ago.' He handed her a slip of paper. *Donna*, it said, *Please call back on this number*

before ten o'clock. Judith glanced at the clock. It was just gone ten but worth a try and she dialled the number. 'Café' said a man's voice. 'Donna? She's here, love, hang on.'

'Is that you, miss?' said Donna, a moment later. 'Look, I've only got a minute. Fred's let me use the phone. I wanted to come to the funeral, saw it in the paper, but 'e won't let me.'

'Who won't? Fred?'

'No, he's been great, but Ian won't hear of it. I told you, 'e hates me going anywhere, seeing anyone. Just work and 'ome.'

'But he wouldn't have to know, would he? You could get the train and be here and back before he gets home.'

''E'd know,' said Donna. ''E says 'e 'as to protect me, and 'e does love me, I know that. But I wish…' her voice tailed away.

Judith cursed Ian with all her heart, but said nothing.

'Are you going?' Donna asked.

'Yes, of course.'

'Say a prayer for 'im, please miss. Can you buy a few flowers and I'll owe you for them?'

'I'll do that, Donna, and don't worry about owing me anything. It's the least I can do. Stevie would understand, wouldn't he?'

Donna sobbed. ''E never 'ad a chance, poor little sod. Tell me where 'e ends up and I'll get there when I can.'

'Of course you will.'

'Got to go, miss. Thanks.'

As she put the phone down, Bill Skelly emerged from Thornhill's office.

'You going to the boy's funeral?' he called to her. 'Morrison got the PM report yesterday apparently. They were cutting it fine. Must've released the body in a hurry.'

'Anything interesting?' she asked. He shrugged.

Judith was puzzled. If it was clear the boy hadn't drowned

the report would have said something about that, surely, and Skelly's nose for a story would have picked it up. But she didn't want to break Doc Hayward's confidence. Maybe no one cared enough to bother about what actually happened. It was an accident, one way or another, and Stevie's relatives weren't going to ask any questions.

Judith bought a bunch of flowers and waited for the bus up to the crematorium. She didn't want to take the scooter and it was a long way to walk up the hill. She was early and stood under the porch at the crematorium for a while, waiting. She'd put the time and place of the funeral in the paper on Wednesday, but feared that nobody would care enough to turn up who didn't know Stevie already, and there were precious few of those. There was no one around. A robin was foraging among the leaves before it flew to a branch just a few feet from where Judith was standing and sang its song, more beautiful than she remembered. Maybe she should stop and listen more often.

At the far end of the long drive a car appeared, came slowly closer and turned around to park beside the square brick building. Captain Edwards emerged awkwardly from the driver's side, and Mrs Robinson's head and black hat also appeared. She noticed Judith and raised a gloved hand, just slightly.

'Good morning, Miss Pharaoh,' said the captain doffing his hat in a vague salute. 'A lovely day for a sad occasion, is it not.'

'It is indeed,' said Judith as they approached the porch.

'Thank you for coming, Miss Pharaoh,' said Iris Robinson, squeezing Judith's arm.

'Are any of the boys coming?' Judith asked. She remembered Mikey's confidence that he and others would be there. Iris looked down, saying nothing.

'We had hoped,' said the captain, 'but as it turned out, we've not been able to do so. Sometimes hard choices have to be made. We had a short service at the home, but that was all we could provide. Mr Harries is our padre, as you know, and he led us in the prayers, but he was too unwell this morning to take the service here. We've had to ask someone else. A pity, but there we are,' he paused, then added briskly. 'Cold out here, shall we go inside, Iris?'

Judith wanted to wait until the hearse arrived with the coffin. She couldn't let the lad go to his funeral on his own.

Another figure was walking smartly along the drive. Judith squinted into the glare and realised it was the detective whose nickname she couldn't get out of her head.

'Miss Pharaoh, is it?' he said, pulling off his gloves and extending his hand. 'I wondered whether the press would turn up.' He looked around. 'Nobody else here?'

'Captain Edwards and Mrs Robinson are inside.'

'None of the lads?'

Judith shook her head. 'Captain Edwards said something about hard choices. They use things like this, anything the boys want to do, as bargaining counters, to be promised and cancelled, like carrots and sticks. I suppose that's better than beating them.'

'I expect they do that too. Kids in school get strapped still, so I'll bet the Montgomery House lads do, more than most probably.'

Judith remembered her school days in St Bees where children were caned regularly, before she was sent to the more refined school at Casterton where young ladies could be punished in ways much more subtle than a beating.

The soft throb of the hearse's engine made them both turn. The plain coffin in the back of the hearse was pathetically small and Judith could hardly bear to see two men raise it between them as if it weighed almost nothing. She went ahead to put the bunch of flowers onto the coffin and then went to sit with Sam behind Captain Edwards and the matron. Rows of empty seats served to remind them that Steven Stringer's untimely death was like a leaf that falls in the forest, unnoticed.

'No family?' he whispered. She wanted to tell him about Donna's phone call, but that would have opened up a can of worms about her visit to Morecambe. Instead she shrugged slightly.

Someone in clerical clothes said the familiar words, and Judith was surprised when Captain Edwards rose from his seat, stepped towards the coffin and then turned towards the empty space. He stood up very straight and began to speak, his voice reverberating off the walls.

'Steven was not with us long,' he said. 'His short life was difficult in ways that are hard for us to imagine. For a brief spell we were his family, and enjoyed his energy and his jokes. All that is gone, and we grieve for him.'

Mrs Robinson wept quietly and Judith felt her eyes fill with tears. To her right Sam handed her a large white handkerchief without looking round, which she took gratefully. 'Thanks,' she whispered. He nodded.

In the last final act of the short ceremony, the coffin slid forward and dark red curtains closed noiselessly, hiding it from view. Soon the boy's remains would stream as smoke from the crematorium's high chimney and out into the wind. Judith wiped her eyes and blew her nose. Mrs Robinson was still sitting with her head bowed, and Judith followed Sam out into the sunshine.

Suddenly and without explanation Sam ran towards the bushes at the edge of the car park. Judith turned to watch as he pushed forward into the dense foliage. She heard him shout, then the disturbance in the bushes moved to the left towards the drive and Sam emerged, looking around him. He walked back to her, brushing leaves and twigs from his dark grey coat.

'What happened there?' asked Judith.

'Didn't you see him?' Sam asked, pointing towards the bushes.

'All I saw was you dashing off into the trees,' she said.

Sam looked around again and stood still listening. 'There was someone standing there, at the edge of the car park, when we came out. He ducked back into the bushes pretty quick and I just went after him. That's what happens sometimes at dodgy funerals, people of interest turn up. That's why Morrison sent me, to see who would be here.'

'Dodgy funerals?'

'You know what I mean, when the death is unexplained. It's like people who go back to the scene of a crime. They get a kick out of seeing the results of what they did.'

Mrs Robinson appeared in the porch and walked towards them, wiping her eyes, with the captain just behind her.

'Always hard when the padre doesn't know the person who's in the coffin,' he said. 'Sorry to keep you waiting.'

'DC Tognarelli's been busy,' said Judith.

'Ah,' said Edwards, looking at her and then at Sam, who reached to shake the older man's hand.

'It was good of you to say a few words,' Sam said gravely. 'I know you'll feel his loss.'

'Seen a few good men die,' said the captain, adjusting his hat against the glare. 'Some of them no more than boys. But we've never had something like this happen at Montgomery House, and it's hit us all very hard. I hope you'll have some answers for us soon, constable. I know you and your sergeant are doing everything you can. And the post-mortem will be completed by now?'

'We understand so,' said Sam. 'Not seen the report yet myself, but I'll be in touch again when there's any information that would help you protect your lads in the future.'

'I'm obliged to you,' said Captain Edwards. Mrs Robinson, her eyes still red, clasped Sam's hand warmly, and then Judith's.

Sam said 'Just one more thing, captain, before we go. You said that the boys were not allowed to come to the funeral today. May I ask you why?'

Captain Edwards looked down at his highly polished shoes. 'It was a difficult decision, but the right one I believe. They have to realise that actions have consequences.'

'So there's been some trouble?'

'I don't feel I have to explain the circumstances to you, young man,' said the captain, but Sam persisted. 'Does that mean that other staff members had to stay and supervise?'

'Of course, someone must be left in charge if Mrs Robinson and I are both away.'

'And that would be Mr Harries?'

'Yes, as it happens. Mr Harries is looking after things for us. He has led our prayers for Steven, with his experience, you know, but I can't see what that has to do with the police.'

'No, no, of course,' said Sam apologetically. 'Sorry about all the questions, I'm just trying, you know, to get things straight. It's just that, a few minutes ago I saw someone just over there,' he pointed towards the bushes, 'who seemed to be watching or waiting for someone, or something. He moved away quite quickly, and I didn't have a chance to ask who he was. It just crossed my mind, you know, that it might be someone from the home who wanted to be here, to say goodbye to the lad.'

'Did you see this person clearly?' Edwards asked. 'It could have been someone waiting for the next funeral, nothing to do with us.'

'Of course,' said Sam.

'Or it could have been one of Stevie's relatives,' said Mrs Robinson. 'They didn't respond, but who knows what's been going on with them?'

The words were out of Judith's mouth before she could stop them.

'His sister rang this morning,' she said. 'I mean…' Too late.

'His sister?' said Mrs Robinson. 'He never said anything about a sister to me.'

'How did she know where to find you?' asked Sam.

They were all silent, waiting for her answer, but she couldn't think of anything to say that wouldn't make matters worse.

'No doubt we'll be informed in due course,' said Captain Edwards. 'In the meantime, we'll drop you both by the police station, shall we? We all have work to do, I'm sure.'

There was silence in the car as they drove down the hill and into the confusion of building work in the centre of Barrow. Judith remembered Ed Cunningham's remark when someone had mentioned the swinging sixties. 'Only thing swinging in Barrow is the demolition crew's wrecking ball,' he'd said, at which Bill Skelly had actually applauded. Sitting in the back of the car, Judith could feel Captain Edwards' annoyance with Sam and all the unasked questions hanging in the air. It was only when she and Sam were standing together outside the police station that his irritation spilled out.

'Right,' he said, turning to her. 'Shall we go in? I've a few things I need to ask you, Miss Pharaoh. And don't try the usual

84

journalists' whine about protecting sources. This is an active investigation into an unexplained death, and you have some explaining to do.'

'And so do you,' she countered. 'How could you call that a dodgy funeral? I was there because he was just a kid that no one seems to care about. You were there because your sergeant told you to go and spy on it. It was just work for you, wasn't it? No wonder people don't like policemen. Captain Edwards doesn't like you much, that's fairly obvious.'

Sam stared at her. 'I'm just doing my job. People don't have to like me. Of course I feel for the lad and what happened to him, but sympathy's no good, not without trying to find out what happened. If you must know, I would have been at the funeral, whether or not Morrison sent me. Now do you want to give me some more information or not? Holding it back isn't going to help the boy, is it?'

'He's not *the boy*,' said Judith. 'His name was Steven.'

'Steven, OK,' Sam repeated. 'So where shall we have this conversation about Steven?'

'Not in there,' said Judith, gesturing towards the police station. 'And not at the paper either. Too many ears flapping.'

'So unless you want to talk to me right here on the windy street, I suggest we find somewhere warmer where we won't be overheard.'

It was the noise in Bruciani's that made it the best place. The hiss of the coffee machine and the steady thump of the Rolling Stones from the jukebox made talking difficult, and listening worse, unless the talkers were quite close together. Judith watched as Sam went to the counter to order their coffees. She didn't like his attitude. Job first, everything else second and now she needed to decide pretty quickly how much to tell him.

Sam stirred two sugars into his cup and got out his notebook and the tiny pencil.

'Where do you want to start?' he asked.

Judith frowned. 'You make it sound as if I know everything and I'm keeping it from you deliberately. It's not like that. I've been told a few things, but all very vague. Nothing I've got would stand up in court. That's why I've kept most of it to myself, and I still have to consider protecting my sources, so don't sneer.'

Sam rolled his eyes. 'This is the *Furness News* we're talking about, not the *Manchester Guardian*.'

'But this could be a criminal case, you said so yourself. I don't want to incriminate anyone.'

'Do you know how Steven Stringer died?' he asked. 'Let's start there and work backwards and you tell me as much as you can. All I've had so far is dead ends. Who's this sister, for a start?'

Judith told Sam what she knew, which wasn't much. She had no idea how Stevie had died. His sister was called Donna and she was obviously afraid of the man she lived with. 'Names?' asked Sam. 'I forgot to ask,' Judith admitted. 'No really, I forgot,' she insisted as Sam's eyebrows went up. 'I think Steve's mother calls herself Mrs Bell now, Yvonne Bell, and I think that Donna's surname is Stringer, like her brother. She lives with someone called Ian. I've got their address but please don't just turn up there. He nearly threw me out of the house and he'd take it out on Donna if the police showed up, I know he would.'

Sam was scribbling assiduously in his notebook.

'How did you find them?' he asked.

Judith explained about the school, saying that the address was on the desk, not in a filing cabinet, and that she had followed the trail until she found Donna, but not the mother. As she recounted all this, a thought occurred to her.

'That man you saw outside the crem. Donna told me about another brother, older, who'd disappeared years ago and then turned up.'

'What do you mean, turned up? When, where?'

'In Morecambe, at Donna's I think, but it could have been at the mother's. About three weeks or so ago, and out of the blue apparently.' Judith dredged her memory for any more details but couldn't find anything. 'I might have more in my notes. I worked out he must be in his twenties, a year or two older than Donna. Maybe twenty-five. Donna spoke to him, said he had a funny accent. And she said he looked quite tanned, as if he'd been in the sun, or working out of doors.'

'What did he say? What did he want?'

Judith shook her head, realising that she was pretty hopeless at finding things out. 'I didn't get the chance to ask her any more. The man she called Ian came back early and threw me out. Sounds like he doesn't let her go anywhere except work, or see anybody. A real shit.'

Sam raised his eyebrows.

'Well, he is,' said Judith, 'and I know worse words than that to describe him.'

'No thanks,' said Sam, 'You've made yourself quite clear. Now, while we're in confessional mode, is there anything else you haven't told me that might help?'

Judith hesitated. 'I learned a few things from the lads at Montgomery House but I'm not prepared to give you any names.'

'What did you do, smile at them?' said Sam.

'Are you inferring I'm dishonest with people?'

'I'm not inferring anything.'

'I just listened,' said Judith. 'They don't like the police, no surprise they wouldn't talk to you.'

'Anything useful?

'They said that Stevie had told them he had to go home, and that someone was going to come and fetch him.'

'Who?'

'No idea.' She paused. 'But it crossed my mind that Stevie's big brother might have wanted to see him for some reason.'

'So it could have been the brother at the crematorium today? But how could he have talked to Steven at Monty House without them knowing?'

'Not difficult. They don't know I've talked to any of the lads this week. At least, I don't think they do.'

Sam looked at her. 'You're as keen on your job as I am on mine,' he said. 'Is there anything else?'

'Have you seen the PM report?' Judith asked.

He put his pencil down on the table, annoyed. 'You're not telling me you've seen it, have you?'

Judith shook her head. 'But Doc Hayward said something about how Stevie died. I've been trying to get back to him, but the mortuary won't pick up the phone.'

'What did he tell you?'

'He said that Stevie didn't drown. He must have been dead before he went into that quicksand.'

Sam sat back in his chair. 'Bloody Nora!'

CHAPTER 7

Back at the station, Sam sat at his desk, irritated and completely out of his depth. He was supposed to be the detective and there was this pushy woman, hair all over the place, banging down doors that looked locked tight, getting people to tell her things. The school in Morecambe had dithered around with the address and finally said they had no address for Steven Stringer, so how did Judith find it? It had taken him a while to get the go-ahead to visit Attercliff and the delay had given the Montgomery House lads plenty of time to decide to play dumb. The older boys had been brought down to the office by Captain Edwards and instructed to tell Sam everything they knew, but they'd just hung their heads and told him nothing. He always thought being out of uniform would make people more willing to talk, but it wasn't the uniform, it was the mere fact of being a policeman of any description that put these lads off. Or was it the captain standing there watching their every move and word? He should have asked him to leave.

Detective Sergeant Morrison came into the CID room. 'How was the funeral? Anyone break down and confess all?'

'Hardly anyone there,' said Sam. 'Not even the lads from the home. Edwards didn't say much but there must have been something going on.'

'Lazy bastards most of 'em,' said the sergeant, standing in the doorway now, his head so close to the top of the frame that he ducked involuntarily every time he came and went. 'Probably couldn't be bothered getting up.'

'It's not like that, though, is it?' said Sam. 'Looks like a well-run place to me. The matron was there today, weeping into her hankie.'

'She's a good soul,' agreed the sergeant. 'Been there since it opened. Edwards too, come to that. One or two of the others are more recent. Have you checked them all out?'

'On to it, sarge,' said Sam. 'Things are going too slowly.'

'Kids like them, there's no sanity in their lives,' Morrison went on. 'Families all over the place, flitting around. You found the mother to tell her about the kid and then they were off again, right?'

'House was boarded up when I got there. Neighbours probably knew what was going on but as soon as the warrant card appears they go blind and deaf.'

'Any other family?' Morrison asked.

Sam hesitated. 'Some hints about an older sister and possibly a brother too. I'm looking into it.'

'Carry on, constable,' said Sergeant Morrison, pushing away from the doorframe and out of the room.

'Sir,' Sam called after him. 'Any sign of that PM report? Doc Hayward is too sick to talk, and I haven't seen it. PM must be done or the body couldn't be released.'

'Might be on my desk,' Sergeant Morrison called back down the long corridor. 'Have a rummage.'

Sam crossed the corridor and looked through the open door at the sergeant's desk, piled high with papers, yellow message slips, files, cigarette packets. What a mess. He'd told himself not to say anything but the whole place was unbearably sloppy. He'd given up counting the number of times he'd heard someone else say, 'That's the way it works round 'ere.' It didn't work, but no one was ever prepared to admit that. Scene-of-crime stuff was a nightmare, people trampling about, evidence in paper bags that could have been in someone's pocket for days, scrawled notes on them that nobody could read. Sam had done the training and read the books, twice over probably, and knew how things ought to be done. What could he say when procedures weren't followed? He'd tried suggesting changes at the beginning but the rest of the blokes just laughed and called him Nelly and told him to calm down. And now this missing PM report. If the doc had confided in him like he seemed to have done in Judith bloody Pharaoh, Ace Reporter, he might have something to go on, but it was too vague. Maybe he could persuade her to tell him more. He was sure she was holding something back. But why? What if he promised her first sight of any firm information? He'd met reporters like her, usually young men, always on the make. All they wanted was to get something out before their rivals on another paper beat them to it. Have to get a scoop! What a ridiculous word.

His expectations weren't high, but Sam started sifting methodically through the chaos on the sergeant's desk, putting all the yellow telephone messages in one pile, all handwritten notes in another, all typed up stuff in a third. While he was at it he filed assorted documents back into the folders they had come from and stood them up neatly on the shelf. Someone whistled. 'Great job, Nelly. Want to do mine as well?' Bloody Harry Grayson. They'd been at training college together, but since then Harry seemed to have abandoned most of what they were supposed to have learned. Line of least resistance, that was Harry all over. If everyone else called Sam 'Nelly' then Harry would do the same, just to fit in. He'd gone again by the time Sam turned round.

When he'd sorted almost everything, there were a few items left that didn't seem to fit anywhere. One was a scrap of lined paper, not the neat yellow slip off the message pad. *Call me – AT*, was all it said, handwritten, as if someone had written it at the desk, not a phone message written up like so many of the other messages that had littered the desk. Another was the unused part of a train ticket to Manchester, from months before. Sam looked for the bin, but then thought better of it and put these two back on the cleared desk under a mug with mould in the bottom of it.

He leafed through the telephone messages, looking for something about the report. The post-mortem had probably been on Monday, after the body was found on the Friday. October 27th – here was something. Hayward, it said, in the box labelled: From. *Call about Stringer PM*. There were two messages in fact, one at 10.42 a.m. and another at 5.23 p.m. Sam wondered if they'd been followed up. Maybe Hayward was saying the report would be delayed. He walked through to the front desk for a word with the omniscient Sergeant Clark.

'Heard anything about Doc Hayward?' Sam asked. 'I need to talk to him.'

'Went into hospital late Wednesday, I heard. Blue lights, sirens, the lot, apparently. Took him to North Lonsdale. Something to do with his breathing. You might be able to talk to him if you go there and ask.' Sam stared, his mind racing.

'Thanks, sarge,' was all he could think of to say.

Back in Morrison's office, Sam took a deep breath and looked again at the piles of papers on the desk. First things first, he reminded himself. Finish one job before you start another. Systematic, patient. The rest of those so-called coppers could take the piss as much as they wanted but he would do this job right or not at all. He looked at every document in the various piles but found no further sign of or reference to a PM report on Steven Clifford Stringer. Next job, call the hospital. The sister on the men's medical ward told him that Dr Hayward was as well as could be expected, and yes it might be possible to talk to him if the patient's doctor allowed it at the time.

Sam's second call was more of a long shot. He asked Records to check on anyone called Stringer, male, born between 1940 and 1950, last known address in Morecambe. 'Not much to go on,' he said, 'but see what you can find.' Sam paused for a while, then made another call, to Directory Enquiries and thence to Morecambe Social Services, but the phone rang for a while with no reponse and he finally left a message with the switchboard. What else could he try? Judith had said that this elder brother had disappeared and then reappeared. Given the family history the first disappearance could have been into care. But that would have been years before. If the man was hanging around in Barrow now, where had he been? If he'd been in jail, Records would probably find it.

Sam sat back in his chair, hands behind his head, and tried to think it through. If the boy didn't drown, how did he die? Could have been hypothermia, but it hadn't been that cold. But then the kid was tiny, underweight according to Mrs Robinson, although he was doing better with proper nourishment at the home. 'He was a changed boy,' she'd told him proudly. 'That's all it takes for so many of them. Decent food, enough sleep, regular wash or bath, clean clothes, regular checks by Dr Graham, and we have a dentist too.' Sam couldn't believe that Iris Robinson would have let anything preventable happen to the boy.

One of the boys – which one, Sam wondered? – had said

that Steven thought someone would come and fetch him, but if it was true that must have been unofficial. Maybe he ran off that night to meet someone, who killed him, or let him die. And if the lad was heading off across the sands to Morecambe, did he start from that spot? Or had he been somewhere else and the tide had caught up with him? Too many questions. Sam went back to thinking about the older brother. Could he have been hanging around at the funeral to say goodbye, or to soften his guilt? And when Sam pushed his way into those trees, where had the man gone? People don't just disappear. Sam turned back to the piles of papers and checked them through again, just in case. No point in wasting time at the hospital if there was no need.

The phone rang. 'DC Tog…Tog.'

'Tognarelli, yes,' Sam snapped at the phone. It was a perfectly straightforward name, why did people make such a meal of it?

'Morecambe Social Services, Mrs Craven here. You rang earlier about someone from here who might have been in care with us ten or fifteen years ago. Nothing on an Anthony Stringer, but we have a record here that an Anthony James Lennon from Morecambe was placed in a Barnardo's home near Lancaster in 1953. The notes mention a younger sister named Donna, who stayed with the mother. Does that sound about right? It says here the boy was eight years old at the time.'

Sam scribbled in his notebook. 'Does it say where he went after that?'

'Nothing more than that, I'm afraid. The home doesn't actually exist anymore. Barnardo's like to keep children closer to home these days and support them there. Not sure it works, but there we are. Is that all?'

Sam made sure he had the woman's name and phone

number before she rang off. At last, something clear-cut. Could be someone else of course, but the chances were high that this was the man Steven's sister, Donna, had mentioned. The man had been somewhere else in the meantime, and he came back for some reason, but at least Sam had something specific to do and he worked faster than most of the other blokes in the squad. He couldn't bear the idea of stretching out the work to fill the maximum possible time, like some of them did.

It was gone four already, and he'd promised Elspeth he'd be back in time to have supper with them and play with Tommy before bedtime, but it was far too early to stop yet. He picked up the phone and dialled the familiar number. Paying for the phone at Elspeth's had been one of his better ideas.

Elspeth and Tommy had just got home. 'I won't be late, promise,' said Sam. 'Someone I've got to see.'

The hospital was the same Victorian building that had been there for years. There were rumours of a new hospital being built out towards Furness Abbey, but there were rumours about everything and most of them came to nothing. The bridge over to Millom for example: they'd been talking about that for fifty years and still nothing. It took Sam less time to walk from the police station to the hospital than to find the ward he wanted in the maze of wings and extensions. The men's medical ward was large, and he wasn't sure he would recognise the elderly doctor in these very different surroundings. It was quiet and he took a few minutes to find someone in a nurse's uniform.

'Nurse,' he began, pulling out his warrant card.

'Staff nurse,' she interrupted, and he felt the blush starting on his neck.

'DC Tognarelli, Barrow CID. I believe Dr Hayward is on the ward here?'

'And if he is?'

'If possible, I would like a quick word with him. Won't take long.'

The nurse checked the small-face watch hanging on her apron. 'Could it not wait till tomorrow? We've just got everyone nicely settled.'

'I'm afraid it can't wait, Staff Nurse Fleming,' he said reading the name on her badge. 'Part of an enquiry into a child's death.'

'Go on then. He's not well, mind, so don't tire him. Take it slow, and give him time to speak. Seventh bed down, on the right.'

Dr Hayward was lying quite still, propped up on several pillows, his eyes closed. Sam was shocked by how frail he looked. The old man stirred and opened his eyes just a little and then wider as he focused on the young face so close to his. Sam leaned back quickly.

'Dr Hayward?' he said. 'You awake?'

'Who the hell are you?'

'DC Sam Tognarelli, from Barrow. We have met before. I work with Sergeant Morrison.'

'Lucky you,' said the doctor.

'It's about a post-mortem report you did earlier this week on a eleven-year-old boy, Steven Stringer.'

Dr Hayward tried to sit up higher, and started to cough. 'Yes,' he said, after a few deep breaths that rattled in his chest. 'What about it?'

'Couple of things, sir,' said Sam. 'I believe you told someone that the boy didn't drown as we first thought, so he must have died from some other cause.'

'I did? Who did I say that to?'

'Judith Pharaoh, from the *Furness News*.'

Hayward took a breath deep enough for Sam to hear the rattle in his chest.

'Ah, Judith,' he said. 'She found me in the pub and I probably talked when I shouldn't. What did I say to her?'

'That the boy didn't drown. There was no water in his lungs, you said.'

'Did I? Well that was stupid of me. I must have been confused. I get confused you know and that was a bad week.' He paused, thinking. 'I should have walked across here and admitted myself there and then, silly old fool.' He said nothing for a few minutes, lying on his back. Then he turned towards Sam and looked at him.

'Judith told you about this, did she? About what she thought I'd said? Why you, I wonder?'

Sam was wondering too, about what she'd told him, and why. Surely she would have asked more questions, or realised that the old man was confused. Or was she just trying to wind him up?

Hayward looked hard at Sam. 'How long have you been in Barrow?' he asked.

'Only a few months, after the reorganisation, when Barrow joined up with Lancashire.'

'Oh, that. Waste of money. And how old are you? Look about sixteen to me, but that's because I'm old.'

'I'm twenty-eight actually,' said Sam, wondering what this had to do with anything.

'Good God. Just a child. And what do you think of our noble police force here in Barrow?'

'To be honest, I think we're a bit of a shower. I like to do things by the book, but I don't think most people do.'

'Bet they love you,' said Hayward. In the next bed, another

old man was coughing and heaving, his fingers gripping the sheets. Sam wanted to get away, from the ward and from Doc Hayward who was beginning to irritate him.

'So,' he said, 'about the PM report.'

'Did I send it in?'

'That's what I came to ask you. It's Friday now and I haven't seen it.'

'Friday?' There was another long pause. Sam looked down at his notes.

'I'll be honest with you, young man,' said Dr Hayward, lowering his voice. 'I wasn't at all well earlier in the week, and well, some bits of it I just can't remember. Might have to dig up the wee lad and start again, eh?'

'Too late for that now,' said Sam. 'He was cremated this morning.'

Dr Hayward looked at Sam but said nothing. Staff Nurse Fleming walked past, pointing at her watch. It was probably time to go.

'What about the report?' Sam persisted.

'I sent it to Morrison, I must have done.' After a moment he continued. 'It could have been an accident. What do the boy's mates say?'

'Nothing to me, but I believe some of them talked to Judith.'

'Bet that pissed you off, eh? And what did they tell the fair Judith?'

'Not a lot. I think we'll need to interview them properly.'

'And if they decide to clam up there'll be nothing you can do. They're all too young to be bullied, even by your sergeant who has a good line in bullying, so I hear.' He breathed heavily again. 'So, is that all you want?'

Sam looked down at his notes. 'Yes, I think so. Thanks, you've been very helpful. I'm sorry to have disturbed you.'

Hayward pulled himself up a little and leaned towards Sam. 'Listen to me, lad. Keep all this to yourself.'

'What d'you mean?'

'I mean, just be careful. Don't trust people, lad. And stick to your guns. It's too late for me, but you're young. That's all, now push off and leave me alone.'

Sam walked out of the hospital and took the road towards Roose and Elspeth's house. He was worried. Was Hayward just tired and ill, or so confused that anything he said was suspect? Why did he lie to Judith about the boy not drowning? And what was all that about sticking to your guns?

Supper was on the table by the time he opened the front door and he could smell it. Living with Elspeth and Tommy may have meant a loss of privacy, but it had its compensations. Elspeth could make a good meal out of anything, and Tommy was a tonic after a long day with crims and perverts and people whose lives were collapsing around them. Tommy ran to him and Sam caught him just in time to whisk him into the air.

'My, you're heavy,' he said. 'How much does he weigh, Elspeth?'

'Too much for me to do that. Wash your hands both of you, it's all ready.'

Later Sam and Tommy read a book together while Elspeth washed up. Even with her back to them she could hear them and smiled at Tommy's questions. 'Yes, but why?' seemed to be the continual response, and Sam was surprisingly patient. This was going to work out, Elspeth thought to herself. Drying her hands she said, 'Have you met my friend Judith yet?'

Sam looked up at her. 'Not Judith Pharaoh?'

'Yes, Judith Pharaoh. She works for the *Furness News*. I mentioned you to her last time she was here but she didn't say anything so I assumed you hadn't come across each other.'

'Oh, we have,' said Sam.

'What does that mean?' asked Elspeth.

'It means we're getting in each other's way. That's the politest way to describe her meddling in my case.' Sam warmed to the theme. 'I suspect like many others of her ilk she's just after the story, whatever it takes, and I don't like it.'

'Oh,' said Elspeth. 'Well she's still a friend of mine, and I still intend to invite her for supper one day soon, so you might have to arrange to be elsewhere.'

'I might have to do that,' he said. '"No fear, no favours", that's the way it should be. Police, press, criminals, we need to keep a good distance from each other. It's all too chummy round here.'

'Has anyone ever said you sound a bit sanctimonious?'

'They have indeed, and that wasn't the word they used. But if it means I should go out while Miss Pharaoh comes to supper, that's maybe how we have to play it. Straight. If I need to talk to her, I'll do it somewhere else.'

'She's all right, you know. I think she's pretty straight too, as newspaper people go.'

'That's not saying much,' he said.

Elspeth stretched out her hand to touch his arm. 'And not all women are Christine.'

He pulled away. 'No,' he said. 'Just forget it.'

CHAPTER 8

Whatever difficulties might lie ahead, the Sunday morning train ride to St Bees was as enjoyable as ever, once they'd pulled away from Barrow itself. Judith had a book to read and her notebook, but she didn't look at either of them, preferring to watch as the familiar beauty rolled past the window, marred only by the state of the window itself and its veneer of smuts and salt. For a while the best view was across the threaded channels of Duddon Sands. After Millom the line rounded the most northerly headland of Morecambe Bay and from then on the sea to the west was grey and wild, stretching from the railway to the horizon. For a short while the line skirted the nuclear plant at Sellafield, where steel and brick and barbed wire replaced the natural colours of sea and sand and stone. It felt like another planet, but a few minutes brought a return to the sea and the beach houses down on the shore. The tide was coming in. A curlew pushed its long curved beak into wet sand.

On the station platform at St Bees, Judith swung her bag over her shoulder and waited until the train had pulled away, and the traffic held up by the level crossing had dispersed. She breathed in deeply, savouring the smell of the sea, and set off to walk the few hundred yards to her parents' house. The front door was open and she walked in as quietly as she could, dropping her bag at the bottom of the stairs.

'That you Jude?' came a young man's voice from the front room. 'I'm in here.'

She looked round the door of the front room. Vince was sitting on an easy chair by the window. 'I sat here to see if I could make out any change in the light when someone came up the path,' he said, turning towards her. 'And I could. I could see there was someone there, but I wouldn't have known it was you. I heard the door of course, and your bag hitting the floor. That's the giveaway. Who else puts a bag just there when they come in?'

'OK, smart arse,' said Judith. 'This is me giving you a hug.' She leaned down and put her arms round her brother, and planted a kiss on his cheek.

'Steady on,' said Vince. 'People will talk.'

'Nothing new there,' said Judith. 'Not much else to do in St Bees on a Sunday morning.'

'Not true. Mam's gone to the Abbey, Dad's out with the dog. The place is buzzing.'

'The Abbey? What happened to Mum's obsession with Our Lady and the Holy Father and all that?'

'I think she's been seduced by all the history and mystery of the place, but she'd never admit it of course. Keeps going to the Catholic church as well, and confession, all the same old things.'

'So how have you been?' Judith asked. The question had to be asked, even if the answer was always the same.

'I'm fine,' said Vince. 'Bit bored today but college is good. The bus picks me up and brings me home. Door to door service.'

'When will the others be back?' she asked.

'Dad any minute I should think. He just went down to the beach with Sandy. What time is it?'

'Just gone eleven.'

'So Mum will be back in about an hour, unless she stays for coffee. I think that makes her feel more guilty than actually going to the service. Fraternising with the opposition. What would Father Price say?'

'Father Price, is he still around?'

'Still there, ministering to the faithful of Kells in that massive new church,' said Vince smiling. 'And Granny Violet still thinks he walks on water. Nothing changes. What about you, Jude, keeping busy in your unladylike job?'

'Mum still calls it that?'

'Most of the time she pulls a face when it's mentioned, or sniffs, like she does.'

'Vince,' Judith asked, 'have you heard anything about a boy found in quicksand between Barrow and Ulverston?'

'No, was he dead?'

'Yep. Poor kid. Just eleven. That's the story I'm working on at the moment. For as long as they let me.'

'Quicksand. What a way to die.' He hesitated, turning his head to the window. 'I could have been killed that day, you know, but at least it would have been quick.'

'Don't,' she said. 'Don't make me think about that.'

John Pharaoh appeared beyond the seaward side of the bay window and turned up the path. 'Footsteps,' said Vince. 'It must be Dad. I'll get the towel for sandy Sandy.'

John came into the room as Vince left it. 'I saw the bag,' John said, giving his daughter a kiss on the cheek. 'Good to see you, sweetheart. How long?'

'Got here just now and I'll stay for lunch, if that's OK. Walk on the beach this afternoon if the rain holds off and then train back about five. Will that be all right with you?'

'Of course it will. We're always so pleased when you come home, even for just a few hours. Your mother too, no matter what you may think. Now, important business. I've left Sandy in the porch. Can you hold him while I towel him down?'

For a short while Judith had her father and brother to herself, talking, catching up with news, helping with tasks that Maggie had left for them. Judith made no further mention of the Stringer case. It wasn't far as the crow flew between here and Attercliff but it felt like a long way and she needed the distance. The family here didn't know much about how she lived, only what she chose to tell them. At one point Vince asked Judith if she had another unfortunate man in tow, which was his way of enquiring about a boyfriend, but Judith didn't respond and John told Vince to mind his own business.

When Maggie returned, the emotional climate changed, as always. Maggie's first comment was about Judith's appearance, her clothes and her hair. Vince followed the voices as mother and daughter exchanged the usual remarks. It was a well-worn script and he smiled at its familiarity. John patted his daughter's shoulder, knowing it was best to keep quiet. Sunday lunch provided a merciful interruption; it was as delicious as ever and Judith ate as much as she could within the bounds of politeness. Suddenly Maggie said, 'It's been a while since you finished with that nice young man. He was called Paul, wasn't he? Have you found someone more your own age?'

Vince choked on a roast potato, giving Judith time to think.

'Paul was very young, that's why it didn't last,' she said carefully. 'And there's no one else around just now. We're very busy at work.'

'Oh, that job of yours,' said Maggie. 'I can never understand why you ended up working there. Why did you pay for the training, John? Might have known it would lead to something unsuitable.'

'It was what she wanted,' said John. 'She's always been good at writing, but you can't make a living out of it, can you? Have to have some more qualifications, like with any job. And you are making a living, aren't you, Judith?'

Maggie would not be deflected. 'Well, there are other ways to do that. Look at our Frank. He pays Granny Violet a bit for room and board, but not nearly as much as he would living on his own. He's got his job at Marchon just down the road, and we know that Granny has someone to help her when she needs it. Work, home, family, all linked up. Judith could work with you at the plant. Always room for her here, and she'd save a lot of money too.'

'I'm right here, Mum,' said Judith. 'Don't talk about me as if I wasn't. And the job's fine, just a bit busy.'

Maggie sniffed, and got up from the table, lifting empty plates towards the sink.

'I'll do that,' said John. 'Judith, why don't you and Vince go for a walk while it's still fine, and we can have the apple pie when you get back, before you go for the train.'

Maggie sniffed again and turned towards the sink. John gestured to Judith to go, and Vince didn't take long to follow Judith into the hall and put on his coat. 'Quick,' he said, taking his sister's arm. 'Let's get out before you two start again.'

Once out of the house, Judith calmed down a little. 'Honestly Vince, it's no wonder I don't come home much. In about two minutes she's managed to insult my choice of clothes and friends and my job, and talk about me as if I'm a half-wit. I'm sure Violet never treated her that way when she was my age.'

'They lived together and worked together, didn't they?' said Vince. 'And Grandad Frank had this thing about families always supporting each other.'

'So what happened to Mum?' Judith asked. 'How did she turn into such a snob?'

'Maybe it was because she was a screen lass and had to hide it from everyone. Dad told me once it was ages before she admitted it to him. And then he got that big job and we moved here. Much posher than Kells, or Sandwith where Dad lived. She may feel she has to keep up with everyone else.'

'She could be proud of me,' said Judith. 'If she saw me at work, she'd be amazed.'

'So would I,' said Vince. 'Tell me more about the story you're working on, and that poor boy who died.'

'It's not a proper story yet but I'm sure there's something in it,' said Judith. 'We know he came from a boys' home down the Barrow coast road. But no one knows what he was doing out on the sands. I think he may have been running away from something, or maybe he just wanted to get home to Morecambe and that seemed like the easiest way to get there.'

'Oh God,' said Vince. 'What an idiot.'

'He was just a kid,' said Judith. 'We don't know what was going through his head, or what happens in those homes, although the boys there seem OK to me.'

They were approaching the beach and the wind was picking up.

'Wait a minute,' said Vince. 'Do you remember when Granny Jessie lived in Seascale she had a friend who lived in Maryport who worked with kids in care?'

'Hold on, too many things at once,' said Judith laughing. 'Jessie had a friend in Maryport, I remember that, and do you know who he was?'

'Who?' asked Vince.

'He was the priest who married Mum and Dad, when Father Price wouldn't do it. Granny Violet thought he was the devil incarnate.'

'I didn't know that part,' said Vince.

'Well now you do. His name was Father O'Toole,' said Judith. 'So, what about him?'

'I remember Granny Jessie telling us how he helped kids in trouble. She used to say how lucky we were to have two parents who cared for us.'

Judith squeezed her brother's arm. 'I know we are,' she said. 'It's just … well, I can't do right for her now, can I? Everything I do seems to be wrong.' She paused, looking across to the sandstone cliffs and the open sea beyond. The tide had turned.

'Tide's coming in now,' said Judith. Vince turned his face into the wind. 'I can see a difference in the light,' he said. 'And I can smell it, and feel the wind pick up. I'm sure it makes a different sound when it's coming in, but that may be just the wind.'

They stood side by side, Vince's head raised, sniffing the air. 'I like the tide here,' said Judith. 'You know where you stand. It goes out in a straight line from the beach for six hours or so, and then it turns and comes in again, in a straight line, back towards the beach. It's predictable and straightforward, not like in Morecambe Bay.'

'I've never seen it there,' said Vince. 'What's the difference?'

'Well, the bay's massive and flat and full of river channels that wind around, and the tide follows those channels when it comes in. So it sneaks all over the place, pushing up the channels until it spills over and comes at you from all angles, not from the front like it does here. Not many big waves in the bay either. The water just pushes and surges, and then it picks up speed. Sometimes there's a wave at the front that doesn't break but just keeps coming, faster than you can run.'

Judith thought of a small boy, out on the sands alone. 'The tide's unstoppable,' she said. 'And cruel. It chases people and drowns them.'

They turned their backs to the wind and set off towards the house.

'Are you coming back to stay?' asked Vince. 'It'd be more fun at home with you here.'

'Not sure about that,' she said. 'Me and Mum, well you know how that is. I got on with Granny Jessie better, but she's gone. I could talk to her and she never judged me.'

'She couldn't judge anyone really, could she?' said Vince. 'First she had our dad and gave him away, and then she lived with Lawrence without getting married. You should hear what our Frank and Granny Violet say about Jessie when they get started. Frank goes on as if he's the guardian of the family's morals. Don't know where that comes from.'

'Probably picked it up from Mum. She and Jessie got on all right at the end, when Jessie was weak, but it was always tricky before that.' said Judith. 'Anyway, let's hope she's finished having a go at me. If we go back now there'll be just time to scoff the apple pie and then I'll go for the train.' Judith laughed as she remembered something. 'Do you remember that time at Gosforth Show, when you showed us all up and Mum went mad?'

Vince laughed too. 'No one's ever forgotten that.'

'You were about six and you stood in the middle of the showground and said "Our dad's a bastard," in a very loud voice and Mum said, "What did you say?" and you said it again, even louder.'

'I got a slap,' said Vince, and Judith laughed again.

Later, on the train, with the sky turning pink over the incoming tide, Judith got out her notebook and scribbled a list of things to do. There were a few things she could trade with Sherlock Sam if necessary. Is this the way it works, she wondered, trading information, sniffing out a story like a pig looking for truffles?

It was dark when the train got back to Barrow. The wind had subsided and there was fog in the air. It wasn't far from the station up Abbey Road and through the narrow streets to her flat and she pulled her coat closer to her as she walked. After the usual noise of Saturday night around the station it was quiet with not many people about apart from footsteps behind her. She turned and looked back but saw no one. As she turned the last corner, a movement caught her eye and she saw someone standing at the far end of the street. It was a man in a long coat and big hat, his head bent over a cigarette, but when she looked again he must have walked on and was gone. 'Get a grip, Judith,' she said. 'People are allowed to walk about and light cigarettes in the street.' She unlocked her front door, climbed the stairs to her newly tidy rooms and forgot about it.

Bill Skelly was in full cry when she got to the newsroom on Monday morning, yelling at young Andrew again. 'Don't tell me there aren't any stories. I could sit in Bruciani's for half an hour and come back with a dozen ideas, just by keeping my eyes and ears open. You have to get out there, lad, and ferret around. Things won't just land in your lap.' He noticed Judith as she slipped into her chair. 'Ah, Miss Pharaoh. A word with you, please.'

Here it comes, thought Judith. George is back, I'm off the story and out on my ear.

She followed him into his little office, which was a bit bigger than Cunningham's cubbyhole but no more than a space confined by shelves and screens rather than proper walls.

'Thornhill says we have to keep an eye on you for some reason. Make sure you get what you need on this story. God knows why, but he had a word on Friday and that's what he said.'

'He did?'

'Strange but true. You're not, you know, with him, are you?' He made a rude gesture.

'Please,' said Judith. 'Not every woman has to sleep her way to success. I can do this job, and I'm just getting on with it now that I've got something to work on other than stolen bicycles and parish council meetings. And it's going well, thanks for asking. I'm keeping one step ahead of the CID bloke, which pleases me no end. What I need now is sight of the post-mortem report on the kid.'

Skelly held up his hands. 'No sign. Morrison's always losing things, but he's pretty helpful, most of the time. It cuts both ways of course. We scratch their backs, and all that.'

'Hayward did the PM before he got hauled off to hospital.'

'Are you sure?'

'That's what he told me, in the pub.'

'That's my girl,' said Skelly. 'You're catching on.'

'But since then, nothing.'

'What about that new bloke, the shortarse, who works for Morrison? Wheedle it out of him, use the feminine wiles we hired you for, the ones poor George and I don't have.'

Apart from the innuendo about Thornhill, Skelly's tone was almost respectful and Judith wondered what was going on.

'What's making you and Thornhill take an interest in me all of a sudden?' she asked.

He shrugged again, then looked around. '*Cherchez la femme*,' he said. 'That's French for some woman sticking her oar in. Now get on with it.'

She left. Curious, she peeped into Cunningham's cubbyhole in the newsroom. He was there, and she knocked on the wall outside as she normally did. He turned, saw her and looked away.

'Yes?' he said.

'I'm doing a piece about the kid's funeral, a bit more than the normal, just to follow up the previous stuff.'

'And?'

'Is that OK? I'll get it to you in good time.'

'Good,' said Cunningham without turning round. 'Fine.'

Back at her desk, Judith sat down for a while to digest these encounters. Something must have been said to him, too. Then she remembered the conversation with Irene that had seemed to fall on deaf ears. She'd told Irene what was going on and she must have told her husband to sort it out. Shouldn't have to be that way, but what the hell, Judith said to herself. Sisterhood – was that what they called it? She felt as if someone had taken a weight off her back.

Finding the list she'd written on the train she pinned it to the board propped up at her desk and began to see a way ahead, for the first time in days. The necessary conversation with Mikey would wait till the next digging day on Wednesday, but she would need to decide exactly what she wanted to know and why, in case there was little time or opportunity to talk. Then she tried the mortuary one more time and was so surprised when someone picked up the phone that she stumbled over the question.

'Hayward's not here,' said a man's voice, 'and we found his PM report on Steven Stringer on his desk earlier this morning, when that detective, the new one, called in. He took it with him.'

'You mean the doc didn't actually send it in himself last week. He told me he had.'

'Between you and me, love,' said the man, 'most of last week the doc didn't know what day it was. He should have got help but you know what they're like, doctors. Don't trust each other, most of them. You didn't hear any of that from me.' The phone went dead. Judith thought about what to do next. Item one on her list was ticked off, even though she was no further forward with knowing what the PM actually revealed. If she had to get that from the police, she needed something to trade. She picked up the phone to speak to someone at the Morecambe Social Services.

'Are you from the police?' said the woman she spoke to.

'No, press. *Furness News.*'

'I'm afraid I can't divulge any information about children in our care, now or in the past, Miss Pharaoh. When the police ask, that's different.'

Judith couldn't believe he'd got there ahead of her again.

'Has someone from the police here asked you about this?'

'Yes, a few days ago a detective called. Funny name.'

'I know who it is, thanks,' said Judith. Damn the man.

Her next call was to the station café in Morecambe. A man answered the phone. 'Is that Fred?' she asked, checking his name from her notes. 'It's Judith Pharaoh, from the *Furness News.*'

'You're the woman who came to see Donna.'

'That's right. Is she there?'

'She hasn't come in this morning. Sometimes late on a Monday, and when she gets here she looks rough. That feller of hers…'

Judith hesitated. She wanted to know more, but she couldn't get involved. It was none of her business. 'When she does come in, could you tell her I called, and ask her to ring me back and reverse the charges?' She gave Fred the number and rang off. Another blank. One more try, to make some progress. The phone at Montgomery House rang for quite a while and the voice that responded finally sounded familiar.

'Mrs Clough?' Judith asked.

'She's not in today, it's Mrs Robinson here.'

'And this is Judith Pharaoh. Maybe you can help me. I'd like to speak to Mr Harries if possible.'

'Mr Harries? No. I'm afraid that's not possible. Not at all. I'm sorry.'

Judith waited a moment. 'That's a pity,' she said. 'When should I call again to speak to him?'

'You'd be wasting your time. Captain Edwards has told all of us, and the boys too, not to speak to the press. Goodbye, Miss Pharaoh.'

Judith sat for a while looking glumly at the blank page in her notebook. She didn't see Alan Thornhill until he was standing next to her. When he spoke her heart sank.

'Can you brief me on the story about the boy?' he said, 'Seems to have gone cold. What's going on? We need to keep it running or move on. Come and tell me what's happening.'

Judith did her best to make it look as if the story was shaping up, but Thornhill was too experienced to be fooled. 'So there's nothing more,' he said, 'except bits of stuff that don't add up to much.'

'I'm working on it,' she said. 'Things are pretty slow.'

'You know Skelly's motto,' he said. 'Get out there and ferret about. Don't wait for things to come to you.' He straightened the items on his very tidy desk. 'You need to give us the goods on this one. George is fretting at home, no matter what his wife says. If he comes back, and with sales the way they are, I'll have to reconsider. I did warn you.'

'Give me a few more days.' Judith was trying not to plead with him, but she could hear it in her voice. 'I've a few more leads. I'll have something in a day or two.'

'You'd better,' said Thornhill. 'We're trying hard to give you a chance on this one, all of us. Don't let us down.'

If Irene had told her husband to give Judith a chance, this was it. The only lead left was the talk with Mikey on Wednesday, and even that looked shaky after what Mrs Robinson had said. There was only one other door open to her, for the time being at least. On the way home, after a ghastly day with parish council reports, Judith went to Roose to track down the policeman who definitely knew more than she did.

CHAPTER 9

Sam Tognarelli sat in the empty CID room and leafed through his notes, before going back to the folder which had Steven Clifford Stringer's name written on the front. He'd read the PM report twice and it seemed straightforward. So why was Hayward so odd about it? Was there something he'd had doubts about? Sam wanted to talk to him again, just in case. The ward sister on men's medical at North Lonsdale was polite but no use at all. 'Dr Hayward is responding to treatment, but he's not well enough to see anyone but immediate family. I told that to Sergeant Morrison this morning. The doctor's waiting, DC Patelli, so I have to go.'

Sam slammed down the phone. It felt like ploughing through wet concrete. The only outcome from an hour on the phone was a name for the dead boy's elder brother that he'd got finally from Morecambe Social Services. Anthony Gerald Lennon, born 13th April,1948. Taken into care in Lancaster aged eight. No further information. Records had nothing on that name, although the man who must have been his father, George Albert Lennon, had a record as long as your arm for violent offending. He'd ended up in Strangeways in Manchester for attempted murder and was probably still there. Steven had been better off in care, Sam was sure of that, but then the family genes got the better of him. He didn't stand a chance. Sam looked back at his notes. Anthony Lennon was his only lead. It was a pretty thin connection, but it might be worth a trip to Lancaster. The car pool gave him the first good news of the day.

'You're in luck. Just had a car come back from the repair shop. Booked out tomorrow but you can have it today.'

At the main police station in Lancaster Sam introduced himself, explained what he needed and found the CID room. Then and only then did he call Barrow and tell his boss where he was, and why.

'What the hell are you doing there?' shouted Morrison. 'The kid ran away and drowned on the sands because he was an idiot and didn't know how dangerous it is.'

'But the brother tried to see him,' Sam said. 'He might know what happened.'

'So what?' roared Morrison. 'You work for me or not? They may have given you a long lead in Garstang or wherever you were, to roam about like bloody Sherlock Holmes, but we keep things simple here, lad. Plenty else here for you to be getting on with, not swanning around wasting time and petrol on open and shut stuff like this. So get your arse back here sharpish, and report to me, like you should have done this morning.'

Someone in the Lancaster CID room looked across at Sam. 'Get your ear chewed off?'

Sam shrugged. 'That's what happens when you're new in. Barrow force was on its own till this year, and now it's part of Lancashire and that seems to be all my fault.' The man laughed. 'One more call?' asked Sam.

When he called the local social services number, having a name and date of birth helped, but the home where young

Anthony Lennon had been placed no longer existed. Sam checked his watch. He could spend another hour here and blame the traffic if he was late back. 'Can I come and see you myself,' he asked, 'now I've come all this way?'

'It was a Barnardo's home,' said Mrs Anderson, checking the dusty file on her desk. Her nails were painted an incongruous pink, which spoke to Sam of a life away from the drab surroundings of Lancaster Social Services. She spoke without looking at him. 'And they changed things a few years ago. Sold off most of the homes and put the money into finding the children placements with families.' She paused as if remembering something. 'Actually, some of the children went to families overseas, for a "fresh start", they called it. Just what they needed, some of them. Getting away from their families was the only way out. It was all voluntary, of course. The boys were asked if they would like to go, and the family were consulted, naturally.'

'Where overseas?'

'Canada mainly, some to Australia. New Zealand even, I'm not sure. The old Empire, you know.'

'Where would I find information about where Anthony was placed?'

'That would be with Barnardo's, not us. Sorry. Now if there's nothing else? We are very busy,' she added.

'As if we're not,' Sam said to himself. He was tired of being fobbed off.

Before setting off back to Barrow he spent a few minutes updating his notes. Was it possible that the man he'd seen at the funeral was Anthony Lennon? A photo would have helped but no one seemed to have one. Maybe Anthony Lennon had contacted his brother Steven at the home and encouraged the lad to leave. But there was no evidence that Steven had actually met someone that night. Sam scribbled a few more questions in his tiny neat writing. It sounded as if Morrison would be checking on him, and he needed everything straight.

He needn't have bothered about checking in. Sergeant Morrison wasn't there when he got back.

'Monday, isn't it,' said the secretary. 'Usually goes to see Thornhill at the *News* on a Monday, doesn't he?'

'What for?'

'God knows. Making sure they're sharing what they know, I suppose. That's the way it works here.'

Sam remembered the note on Morrison's desk from 'AT'. He hadn't realised the two men were so close, and made a mental note to remember that in future. Then he turned his attention to the mound of messages, and to the almost illegible list of tedious jobs Morrison had left, to re-assert control over his constable's time.

It was half-past six when Sam finally got back to Roose, grateful yet again that he would find a warm house, food and a sympathetic ear when he got inside. But the first person he saw behind Tommy in the hall when the child opened the door was not Elspeth. The smile froze on his face.

'Elspeth's in the kitchen,' said Judith. 'She put supper back a bit hoping you'd be home.'

'I'm starving,' said Tommy, running back to his mother and the smell of bacon.

'What are you doing here?' said Sam. He'd told Elspeth he didn't want informal contact with reporters, and here she was again.

'I just dropped in on my way home,' she said. 'Elspeth invited me for supper.'

'Tell her I'll be down in a minute,' he said, going up to the bathroom.

Judith could see he was annoyed. Maybe this wouldn't be a good time for a chat about Stevie's fate, but she had to get some more information for Thornhill, and soon.

'He'll be down in a minute,' she said to Elspeth in the kitchen. 'Didn't look very pleased to see me.'

'Tired, I expect,' said Elspeth. 'And he's a bit prissy about contact with the press. Thinks the police need to keep their distance.'

'Great,' said Judith. 'Should I go?'

'You will not,' said Elspeth. 'I've invited you for supper and here you'll stay. He'll have to get over it. You're my friend, and this is my house.' She got cutlery out of a drawer and gave it to Judith. 'And anyway, from what he tells me, you two need to pool your information, not fight over it.'

'I'm getting nowhere,' Judith admitted, 'and the editor's breathing down my neck. I could be going back to St Bees with my tail between my legs unless I can come up with something.'

Elspeth smiled. 'Let's see,' she said.

They sat around the small table in the kitchen to eat supper. Thank heaven for Tommy, Judith thought as the boy distracted them with tales from school and a joke he'd learned that day.

'What's yellow and dangerous?' he asked them. They shook their heads. 'Shark-infested custard,' he cried, and Sam laughed.

'OK,' said Sam. 'I've got another of those. What's purple and conquered the world?' Tommy tried and failed to find an answer. 'Alexander the Grape,' said Sam. Tommy was puzzled and looked at his mother. 'Honestly Sam, he's only six. Come on Tommy, time for bed. 'What's Alexander the Grape?' they heard Tommy ask as he climbed the stairs.

Judith took her chance. 'You forget what they don't know yet,' she said. Sam sat quietly, picking at the remains of the food on his plate. She tried again. 'Elspeth says you're not happy about me being here.'

He looked up. 'Of course you can be here,' he said. 'It's Elspeth's house. It's just that, with your job and everything…'

'You think police and the press should keep away from each other?'

'Not officially, of course, but there's all sorts going on here, you know as well as I do. Drinking together, back scratching. They're probably all in the Masons as well.'

'You think so?' said Judith. 'You hear about it, but how do you know?'

'I just assume unless I know otherwise. It's part of life round here.'

'Thornhill? Skelly?'

'Probably,' he said.

'But not me?'

'Hardly. You're the wrong sex and not their type at all. Can't see you at the Lodge dinners or what ever they invite the wives to.' He smiled at the thought of Judith in a dress and gloves, maybe a little hat?

Elspeth had come back to the kitchen to pour some milk for Tommy. She glanced at her brother and winked at Judith as she passed. 'I told Tommy you're too tired to read to him tonight, Sam,' she said. 'There's a beer in the fridge if you want it.'

As he got up to find the beer, Judith began quite nonchalantly, 'Well I don't know about you, but I'm not getting very far. Thornhill wanted a report today and it was pitiful. Not sure how long I can convince him to keep me on.'

'They're going to sack you?' said Elspeth. 'What for?'

'Surplus to requirements again, I guess. Seems to be the story of my life. The only possible link to a proper story is an old friend of the family who used to work with children in trouble. I want to find out a bit more about how these kids get into care and what happens to them.' She hesitated. 'I'm supposed to be talking to one of the lads again tomorrow at Monty House, but he might not be able to risk it.'

Elspeth took Tommy's milk upstairs.

Sam had been listening. 'What do you mean?' he said.

'Mrs Robinson told me today that Edwards had told them all not to talk to the press, and the boys too. It's that carrot and stick thing again. If Mikey thinks he might lose something by talking to me, he won't do it.'

'Well he won't talk to me, that's for sure. Don't suppose any of them will.' Sam's annoyance about the frustrations of the day and now this intrusion into his evening spilled over. 'What did Doc Hayward really say to you about Steven Stringer's post-mortem?' he asked suddenly.

Judith was taken aback, by the question and the tone.

'He said the boy didn't drown,' she said.

'Are you sure? He told me he was confused and ill that week.'

'You've seen him?'

'I went to the hospital. They let me talk to him, I said it was police business.'

'You've got a nerve,' she said. 'And what did he say?'

'What I said, that he was probably drunk when he spoke to you and must have got it wrong.'

Judith stared at him. 'That's ridiculous,' she said. 'Why would he do that?'

Sam shrugged. 'That's what he told me. He could hardly talk, coughing really badly and he looked awful.'

'I'll bet having to talk to you didn't make him feel any better,' she said.

'Can't be helped,' he said. 'What with that and Morrison pushing me around, I won't be able to do much more about Steven's death now. I want to follow up about the older brother, but Morrison says I'm wasting my time.'

'Do you still think that was the bloke we saw at the funeral?'

'It could have been. Apparently he went to a Barnardo's home, and they sent boys overseas to find a fresh start, after the war. That might be where he's been all this time.'

At the mention of Barnardo's, Judith sat up straight. She wanted to keep Sam talking and this was a chance. 'The family friend I mentioned, he worked for Barnardo's. He might know about all that. Is it worth finding out?'

'Anthony's our only lead right now,' said Sam. 'If he did visit Steven, he might know why the boy ran away.'

'Do you want to talk to this friend of mine?' asked Judith. 'I think he lives up Maryport way, or he used to. My gran used to go up there to see him, in the fifties, when she lived in Seascale. He was a Catholic priest before that.'

Sam looked puzzled. 'I thought Catholic priests were there for life, like the Pope. Did they throw him out?'

Judith shrugged. 'Don't know. If I can find him, maybe we could see him together. He's getting on a bit, you going on your own might put him off.' It was a long shot, she knew, but he didn't say no. Keep going, she told herself. Aloud, she added, 'Don't just let this drop, please, Sam, I need the story.'

She knew immediately that she'd pushed too far. Sam looked up and she could see the anger in his face.

'It's not a story, Judith, it's a case, and it's mine not "ours".

A boy died and I'm trying to find out how that happened, not for some stupid byline but because we need to know, his family needs to know. I told Elspeth that I'd go out if she invited you for supper. You and I have different jobs to do. I should have gone out tonight, but I was too tired and it's been another shitty day.' He got up from the table and pushed back his chair. 'So I'm going to bed. You get on with your job and don't expect me to do it for you. Good night.'

Sam pushed past Elspeth who had come downstairs at the sound of Sam's raised voice. She stood for a moment looking at Judith, her eyebrows raised, her hands up, questioning, before she called up the stairs. 'Sam?' There was no reply.

'What happened?' she said. 'You seemed to be getting on OK.'

Judith groaned. 'We were,' she said. 'I must have asked the wrong question and he just went on about not doing my job for me. He's so, I don't know, so tight. Sorry Elspeth, but he is.'

'He is, I know. He means well, but I called him sanctimonious the other day. That's what he was, banging on about the principle of keeping his distance from the press. I had to tell him you're my friend and if he doesn't want to see you he'll have to go out.'

'I should have asked if I could come tonight.'

'Well you didn't, and I was pleased to see you and he'd said he would be late. Anyway, I'm not going to tread eggs around his sensitivities. Not in my own home.'

'Well the damage is done now,' said Judith. 'He's stormed off and I'm no further forward, and now you two are cross with each other.'

'We'll survive,' said Elspeth. 'He'll probably be sorry in the morning about raising his voice. Sometimes I wish he wouldn't apologise so much.'

Later that evening, Judith sat on her bed and wondered what to do. Her chances of getting any more information from DC Tognarelli were slim to none. Maybe Skelly could use his links with Morrison, but she'd get no credit for that. So much for Skelly's instruction to use her wiles on Sam. She obviously hadn't got any wiles, whatever they were. The only things she had left to follow up were the date with Mikey and a conversation with Father O'Toole in Maryport, if he was still alive. She didn't sleep much that night.

On Wednesday morning Judith followed the same instructions that Mikey had given her for their meeting the previous week. It was raining and although she was sheltered from the wind off the sea as she stood in the bushes at the digging field by Montgomery House she could feel water dripping off the trees, past her upturned collar and down her neck. She looked at her watch. It was after ten. When the boys arrived down the path from the home they didn't spread out round the field like they had before but stayed clustered by the hut. Mr Harries was with them but he seemed to be talking to them and showing them something, and before long they traipsed back towards the path and out of sight. If Mikey had been in the group, and she wasn't even sure he was there, he'd made no effort to contact her. She was annoyed and frustrated and very wet, but she wasn't surprised. She knew the boys were under pressure, and what did any of them have to gain from talking to her?

By the time she got into town on the Vespa she was so wet that she stopped off at the flat to dry out and change her clothes. Back in the newsroom, she put on her most confident expression to avoid any unwanted attention and sat at her desk writing with studied concentration, as if her story was taking shape instead of falling apart. The task of tracking down Father O'Toole took only two phone calls, one to Directory Enquiries and the other to a house on Camp Road in Maryport. The voice that answered the phone was hard to follow. 'Father?' said the old lady. 'No, he died in the war, you know, fighting for his country.'

'Father O'Toole?' Judith repeated, wondering who this old person thought she was talking about.

'Father O'Toole?' said the high-pitched voice. 'Oh, he's not a father any more. He's just Mr O'Toole…'

Judith heard a whispering voice and then knockings on the line, as the receiver was handed over.

'Who is this please?' said a man's voice.

'My name is Judith Pharaoh,' said Judith.

'Judith Pharaoh? Oh, my goodness,' said the man. 'Jessie's granddaughter?'

'Yes,' said Judith. 'Is that Mr O'Toole?'

'It is indeed,' he said. She could hear the smile in his voice. 'Many years ago I married your parents, but that was in another life. Well, well. And where are you now, Judith?'

'At work, in Barrow,' she said. 'I work for the *Furness News*.'

'That's splendid,' he said. 'Jessie would be so proud. And what can I do for you, my dear?'

Judith gave away as little as she could about her reasons for wanting to talk to Pat O'Toole. She told him only that it was a story about a local boys' home and she recalled that he'd worked with boys in care and might give him some background information. Going up to Maryport would get her out of the office and away from her colleagues' scrutiny for a while, a bonus that she did not share with Pat. Getting instructions about how to find his house was a long process during which her questions were greeted by questions rather than answers.

'Now you know the road up from the harbour?' he said.

No, Judith didn't know it. 'Where do I go when I come out of the station?' she asked.

'Ah, well you know where the fort is, up on the hill there?'

And so it went. Pat seemed to find it hard to understand that Judith had never actually been to Maryport before.

When Judith arrived in the newsroom the following morning to deal with some bits and pieces before heading off to Maryport, Irene Thornhill was emerging from her husband's office, looking as well groomed as ever. Yet again, Judith was immediately conscious of her own unkempt appearance, even after she'd put on a decent pair of trousers for her trip north. Her embarrassment seemed to attract Irene's attention like a hawk to a mouse in the grass. Judith began to understand what 'feminine wiles' really meant.

'There you are, dear,' said Irene in a low conspiratorial tone. 'I've been dying to ask you whether things have improved at all, you know, after our little chat.' She took a quick look into Cunningham's cubbyhole but it was far too early for him to make an appearance. Judith too had a look round the newsroom, wondering whose ears might be alert to some gossip. She gestured to Irene and they stepped out into the stairwell.

'Did you say something about the problem I was having?' Judith asked. She didn't want to assume that Irene had intervened on her behalf.

Irene beamed. Even in the gloom of the stairwell her carefully made up face seemed to shine. 'I told you I could deal with it, and I did. And it worked?'

'It looks like it,' said Judith. 'Ed's hardly said a word to me, and not bothered me at all. Alan's still after me about the story I'm working on, but I don't feel he and Bill are trying to find fault all the time. They both seem genuinely interested in how it's going.'

'Splendid,' Irene responded, pulling on her gloves.

'What did you say, if you don't mind me asking?'

Irene tapped the side of her nose. 'Never you mind, dear. Just a few home truths, that's all. It was the least I could do. We women have struggled with men at work for far too long. I thought I might be able to help.'

'And it worked,' said Judith. 'Thanks. I was going to write you a note about it, but I was leaving it a bit longer, to see whether it was really going to be better.'

'If you have any more trouble with any of them, come back to me.' Irene smiled at Judith, squeezed her arm and tapped off down the stairs on her high heels. Judith carried a faint aroma of face powder and Chanel perfume back into the newsroom, to clash incongruously with the usual smells of sweat and tobacco.

CHAPTER 10

The house on Camp Road in Maryport was bigger than Judith expected, but it looked neglected. The front hedge was wild, the garden uncared for and she noticed as she rang the bell that the front door needed painting, Chimes echoed inside before the door opened and a man stood in front of her who was nearly as wide as the doorframe. He had a thick mop of grey hair and round glasses perched on a small nose. Like Friar Tuck, Judith thought.

'Judith Pharaoh,' cried the man, stretching out his hand to shake hers. 'I'm Pat O'Toole. Come in, come in.'

She stepped into the dark hallway and saw another smaller figure emerge from a room at the end of the passage. Pat O'Toole saw her too. 'Come and meet Judith, Winnie. This is Jessie's granddaughter. You remember Jessie?' He was speaking very loudly; Judith guessed that the old lady must be deaf.

Pat turned to Judith, who had clasped the dry hand that was extended to her. 'Mrs Foster has been looking after me for many years now, ever since I moved up here, when was it, Winnie?

'After Bill died,' she said, 'and that was in 1950.'

'Nearly twenty years then,' he said. 'Would you believe it?'

'Not a day too long,' said the old lady, squeezing Pat's arm.

'He's such a gentleman,' she said to Judith. 'I look after him and he looks after me.'

'We do indeed,' said Pat. 'And now Judith and I need to talk about some business, Winnie, so could you bring us some tea in the front room, and maybe some of your cherry cake?' He said this bending over to speak to the old lady who was tiny next to him. 'She makes a wonderful cherry cake, so she does,' he said to Judith, straightening up again. 'Come away into the sitting room, Judith. Let me take your coat.'

'Well, well, let me look at you,' he continued, as Judith settled into a chair by the bay window. 'Jessie told me all about you. You were going off to boarding school, as I remember.'

'Did she tell you about that?' said Judith. 'Jessie wasn't sure it was the best plan for me.'

'And was it?' he asked, leaning forward. Jessie had always said that Pat O'Toole was a good listener, and Judith didn't doubt it. They talked about those days for a while, about Vince's accident and Maggie's reaction, and Judith's job on the paper. The door opened slowly and Mrs Foster carried in a tray that looked more than she could manage. A curious dance ensued as Pat tried to relieve her of the tray and she tried to keep hold of it. Once the tray was safe and the tea poured, Mrs Foster sat and looked hard at Judith. 'I remember Jessie,' she said. 'She was a fine-looking woman, I must say. She and Pat here, well I thought they were heading for the altar, I can tell you.' She sat back with an air of finality, while Pat looked on, nodding.

'It didn't work out, did it, Winnie, and here I am still. Just a sad old bachelor.'

Not very sad, thought Judith, looking at his beaming face. She'd never heard anything about Jessie and Pat being so close, but then her grandmother had always been very circumspect about her private affairs.

Mrs Foster showed no sign of leaving, but when the tea was drunk and the cherry cake consumed, Pat helped her up and kindly steered her towards the door, carrying the tray. A minute later he was back, and Judith felt those grey eyes focus closely on her again.

'Why didn't you and Jessie get together?' she asked. He smiled and clasped his big hands together. 'Well, you know, we both had our own views of the world and they didn't always coincide. I was very fond of her, always had been since we first met just after the war, but I don't think she felt the same about me.' He paused, thinking. 'Anyway, you haven't come all this way to talk about me and your grandmother. You said something on the phone about a story you're doing, about a boys' home?'

Judith decided to come clean before he got too much of the real story out of her.

'Well, actually,' she said, 'the story is about a boy from a local home who was found dead by the shore at Morecambe Bay a couple of weeks ago. I'm trying to piece his life together. I've talked to some of the other boys there and they seem bright and lively. I wonder how children end up in care like that, what their lives are like now and will be like when they go out into the world. If this lad was trying to get back to a family that doesn't seem to care about him, why was that?'

Pat put his fingertips together. 'How sad,' he said. 'Do the police know how he died?' For a moment Judith wanted to tell him much more, but the thought was interrupted. 'You say the family doesn't care,' Pat went on, 'but they do, you know, in their own way. It's often mum who has to hold things together and sometimes the mothers just get overwhelmed. They can't provide for the kids and they actually think that someone else would do a better job. Yes, it's an abdication of responsibility, but we must be careful not to judge. We've no idea what problems they might be facing. Could be debt, or eviction, or violence. The children may not have the right food, or any food. Some of the boys I worked with used to beg for food from neighbours, and have to share beds or sleep on the floor. Being in care was a better place for them, safer.'

'The boy had an older brother I've been trying to track down,' said Judith. 'He went into care, too, into a Barnardo's home in Lancaster, around 1957, maybe earlier. It's not there any more.'

'Well things change, as I said. Maybe it was the cost of running the homes, I don't know. We began to think that the children, some of them at least, would be better off in families rather than in big institutions. Some of those Barnardo's homes were huge, you know. How big is the home this boy of yours lived in?'

'There are only about twenty boys at most, I think. Some of them are apprentices or working, and still living there. For the younger boys it must be like living in a very large family. Just three full-time staff as far as I know, although there may be others I haven't met.'

'You see, that could work well,' said Pat. 'As you said, like a large family, but all boys?' Judith nodded. 'And up to all sorts of things I've no doubt,' he went on. 'There will have to be rules and structures, of course, and some children will always find those difficult after what they've been used to. The very big homes were the ones I had my doubts about.'

'In what way?' said Judith.

'Too many rules, perhaps, and not enough real care. Boys in large numbers can be a real handful.' He got up and looked across a bookshelf beside the fireplace, picking out one and handing it to Judith. She looked at the title, *Lord of the Flies*.

'We read this at school,' said Judith, recognising it. 'But those boys were on an island, with no adults.'

'You'd be surprised how much like that island a big place full of boys can be, even if there are adults around. They're not around for every minute of every day. Unsupervised lads can do pretty harmful things to each other.'

Judith thought about this for a moment. Had Steven been bullied by the others, and tried to get away from them? Had they got him drunk that time against his will? Had Mikey told her the truth about anything?

She glanced at the notebook on her lap, open at the page of questions she'd written on the train. 'There was some mention of boys from Barnardo's going to live with families overseas. Can you tell me anything about that?'

'Ah,' said Pat. 'Well that wasn't just Barnardo's of course. After the war, things were very difficult in Britain and looked much better in the old Empire. There was quite a push to offer children the chance to go to Canada or Australia. A healthier life, don't you know, often on farms where they would get decent food and exercise. It all sounded very attractive if the boy wanted to make a fresh start, or the family thought it would be best.'

'A bit final, wasn't it?' said Judith. 'What if it didn't work out?'

Pat hesitated. 'I'm sure there were procedures to deal with that. You can't just send children away and forget all about them.'

'So if a boy went overseas, he could come back again once he was old enough, and able to find the money for a ticket?'

'I'm sure that could happen,' said Pat. But he didn't sound sure, thought Judith.

'Do you still work for Barnardo's?' she asked.

Pat shook his head. 'No. I wasn't with them long actually. In the 1960s I got involved in the anti-nuclear movement, writing, campaigning, that sort of thing. Had to do all sorts of jobs to make ends meet, but I've never worried much about the money. God will provide, I say, and He has done so for me. I've been very fortunate.' He paused. 'You've probably worked out that I'm not a priest any more, not even one of those modern ones who don't wear the uniform.'

'I'm sure you had your reasons for leaving,' said Judith. Suddenly, from nowhere, she remembered something that Captain Edwards had said, although not where or when.

'When you were a priest in Millom, or when you moved up here, did you ever come across a man called Desmond Harries?'

Pat O'Toole looked up sharply. 'Harries? How old is this man?

Judith thought about it. 'Hard to tell actually. I only met him briefly, and since then I've only seen him at a distance. About forty I should say, maybe less, or more. I'm not sure.' She watched Pat thinking, remembering, and prodded his memory. 'The Desmond Harries I've met works at Mont-gomery House in Attercliff. He led the prayers there for the boy who died. I wondered if he had a religious background.'

'Who's the man in charge there?'

'Captain Edwards. He was a war hero I believe. Walks with a limp.'

'Don't know him,' said Pat. He was quiet for a while longer before he asked, 'You're sure this man's name is Desmond? What does he look like?'

Judith described the man as well as she could. 'He seems a sad man,' she said, 'as if the energy's gone out of him. Looks as if he's not very well.'

'I think I may have come across him,' said Pat slowly, 'although he was Jerome then, Father Jerome.'

'A priest?'

Pat nodded. 'Just a young priest, here on the west coast. When he left, he went into the navy I think, or was it the army? That must have been ten years or so ago. I've not heard of him since. And he's working at a boys' home, you said?'

Judith nodded.

Pat leaned forward in his chair. 'I'm going to tell you something Judith, and I want you to be very careful with it. Priests are often the subject of gossip, and some of it is malicious. I've had that trouble myself. There was gossip about Father Jerome, enough to reach me, and I worked at the other end of the county at the time. But it's a small world, you know.'

'What was the gossip about?'

'There was some talk about Father Jerome being too friendly with some of the boys in his parish. One of the boys' fathers complained, and it went to the bishop apparently. Nothing came of it as far as I know, but Jerome did leave the parish. He went off to be a padre in the forces, as I said, and I've heard nothing about him until today. That's why I want you to be careful, my dear. Is he a good man?'

Judith had no idea how to answer Pat's question. 'Montgomery House is highly thought of, I know that. Captain Edwards and the matron, Mrs Robinson, seem like fine people to me. Why would they appoint someone to work with them if they weren't sure about him?'

'Why indeed?' said Pat.

Judith wrote nothing in her notebook, but her mind was buzzing. It might be nothing, but this was information that she had to treat with care. She'd heard all the jokes about scoutmasters and such like, but this was a Catholic priest. Was it something she could keep to herself? Why share it with the police when Sam Tognarelli was being so self-righteous about liaising with the press?

'Is there any more you can tell me about this?' she asked.

Pat looked up at her. His eyes were sad. 'You're a real journalist, aren't you now?' he said. 'No, there's nothing more. I wish I hadn't remembered. It was a long time ago.' He seemed uncomfortable, shifting in his chair, looking out of the window at the overgrown hedge that blocked their view out to Solway Firth and the Scottish coast. She looked at her watch.

'I'll have to be going,' she said. 'It's a fair way back to Barrow.'

Pat held up his hand. 'Before you go, let me say a prayer for the poor boy who died. What was his name?'

'Steven Stringer,' she said. She didn't want to pray, but he took her hand and she bowed her head.

'Dear Lord,' he said. 'We pray for the soul of Steve Stringer, who left this life too young. And we pray for his grieving family and friends, who will miss him always. May he rest in peace. Amen.'

'Amen,' echoed Judith, in spite of herself.

Pat helped Judith on with her coat. 'Winnie,' he called towards the back of the house. The tiny figure appeared in the doorway. 'I'm walking Judith down to the station. Is there anything you want from the shops?'

Mrs Foster walked slowly towards them. 'You see, my dear,' she said, looking up at Pat, 'how he looks after me?'

'I do indeed,' said Judith.

'So I'm glad your grandmother didn't take him away,' the old lady went on, looking up at the corpulent figure beside her. 'I thought she would, you know. He brought her here to tea, didn't you, Pat? And he went to her house in Seascale, too.'

'Yes, yes,' said Pat, embarrassed. 'But that was a long time ago, and then Jessie married the man from Windscale. I told you about it. And after that she was so ill and was taken from us. I was in London and I didn't hear she'd gone until I came home. I wrote to your father, with my condolences. It was very sad, so young, and such a fine woman too.'

'She was, wasn't she?' said Judith. 'Brave and independent.'

'Like you, my dear,' said Pat. Judith blushed. She wanted to say that she felt like a manipulative cheat.

Together they walked down the hill to the station. At the harbour the gulls were screaming and wheeling on the wind and white tops broke on the open sea.

As she turned to go to the train, Pat reached for her hand and held it. 'You'll remember what I said about Father Jerome?'

'I remember,' she said.

'Gossip is a wicked business. Be kind, Judith.'

'I will, Pat,' she said. 'Thanks for giving me your time, and thank Mrs Foster, too.'

'Come and see us again,' he said. 'We need young company.'

'I will,' she said. But sitting on the train as it headed south Judith wondered if she ever would see them again.

She wasn't sure what to do. Sam must have checked out Desmond Harries as a matter of routine, but maybe he hadn't gone far enough back. And where would he find what she had learned today? Gossip, maybe, but smoke and fire were closely connected. The possibilities swirled around in her head. And there was another question in Judith's mind, about Anthony Lennon. Donna had mentioned his funny voice and that fact that he looked as if he'd been in the sun. Maybe he was one of the boys who went off to a new life somewhere. She'd never heard of such a thing before, but someone had to know about it. She scribbled in her notebook as the train bumped along, before the view distracted her again.

❖ ❖ ❖

It was early afternoon by the time she got back to Barrow. The newsroom was quiet, apart from the thud of Hattie's typewriter. She looked up as Judith pushed back her chair.

'Where is everybody?' Judith asked.

'Ed's at lunch, Alan's at a meeting somewhere and Skelly's at the cop shop. There's a flap on. Not seen him so excited in ages.'

'What about?'

'More trouble at Attercliff, that boys' home. Another body, in the woods this time. Sounds like someone topped himself.'

Judith put her coat back on and ran all the way to her flat to get the Vespa.

Chapter 11

By the time Judith reached Montgomery House it was almost completely dark, and any remaining light was blocked by large trees that surrounded the front of the building. The gravel drive crunched as she parked her scooter out of sight against the side wall. She felt like a trespasser; secreting the scooter seemed like a necessary act, and there was no time to reflect on why that should be so.

This time she didn't approach the main door but found her way round the outside of the house to where she guessed the path would lead down into the woods towards the shore. Reaching the end of the path she could see lights on the other side of the road, where more old tall trees spread down to the sea. Lights in the wood shone like early stars that had fallen to earth. A car was parked by the side of the road and she climbed the fence to get to the scene as directly as she could. Beams of torches flashed intermittently among the trees and she heard the men's voices before she saw where they came from. Suddenly she stopped. Something long and dark swung gently from a low branch a few yards ahead of her. On the ground beside it, next to an overturned wooden box, stood a policeman in uniform and two others in plain clothes. One of them was Sam Tognarelli. She stood quite still, watching, listening.

A torch beam found her face and she blinked into it, aware only of a figure moving towards her. The uniformed policeman's hand reached to grip her arm, and pulled her forward.

'What the hell's *she* doing here?' said one of the men, and another of them groaned. It was Sam. 'Bloody press!' he said. 'The jungle drums have been busy, and here she is again.' He turned to the man standing next to him. 'Harry, you've probably met Judith Pharaoh from the *Furness News*. Don't tell her anything, and keep her away from here, constable. There's enough people tramping around as it is.'

'Park her by the tree where she was, well out of the way,' said Harry Grayson. 'And where the hell are the scene of crime gang? Can't get the body down till they've checked everything out.'

'Who is it, do you know?' asked Judith, looking at the gently swinging corpse.

Harry turned back to Sam, who shrugged. 'She'll recognise him anyway. It's Harries from the home.'

'Desmond Harries?'

'Yes, Desmond Harries,' Sam repeated scornfully. 'How many men called Harries did you meet there? I only met one.'

Judith smarted. You pompous prick, she thought, tempted to tell them what she had discovered that they had no clue about, but she said nothing, pulled herself away from the constable's grip and reached for her notebook.

'What can you tell me?' she said.

Harry Grayson walked over to her and led her back into the trees, away from the scene towards the road. 'Look,' he said, 'a couple walking a dog through the woods about an hour ago spotted him and ran up to the road to flag down a ride to Barfield and the phone. Your friend DC Tognarelli and I got here ten minutes ago and now we're waiting for people to check the scene and you are waiting for what we choose to tell you, when we know something ourselves. All clear so far, Miss Pharaoh? We've had old man Skelly here already, and his mate from the *Ulverston Record*, and we sent them packing, too. They're probably propping up the bar at the Bay Horse as we speak, reminiscing about old times, so why don't you push off and join them? I'm sure they'll love your fresh young company.'

Judith ignored the snub. 'Has anyone been up to Montgomery House?' she asked.

'No they haven't and if you dare interfere with our investigation by going up there yourself, I'll have your editor in for obstructing the police. Got that?'

There was nothing Judith could say, but she wondered if someone at the house had already seen her. Thank goodness she'd hidden the scooter.

She checked her watch. It was coming up to seven o'clock. Best thing was say nothing, leave quietly, pick up the scooter without being seen and check in with Skelly at the Bay Horse. With Sam around there was no chance of rules being bent at the scene, so the only plan was to latch on to Skelly's coat-tails and hope he would let her keep the story.

Left alone, and with only the faintest gleam from the lights, Judith climbed the fence, crossed the empty road and walked back towards Montgomery House, not on the path but to the side of it in the trees, to end up on the side of the building where she'd left the scooter. At the edge of the trees she stopped. The house was full of lights, upstairs and down. She could hear children's voices and saw their shadows pass one of the windows on the first floor. An adult voice sounded dangerously close and she shrank back into the protective darkness of the trees. Two young women, arm in arm, walked quickly round from the back of the house and down the path that led to the road into the village. They were talking together but too softly for her to hear.

'Nobody knows,' Judith said to herself. 'Harries is hanging from a tree a few hundred yards away and nobody knows he's there.' The urge to tell them, to ring the front door bell and stand there and tell them what she knew, all of it, was very strong. Captain Edwards, Sam, Grayson, even the dumbo in the uniform, she wanted all of them to notice her and listen to her and take her seriously. But instead, keeping in the shelter of the trees, she crept round the back of the house, waited until she was sure she would not be spotted, and pushed the scooter beside her into the woods and down the back path to the road. She could see the lights and torches in the wood to her right as she started the engine, turned the scooter to the left, and headed towards the Bay Horse.

'Well, well,' said Harry as they heard her scooter purring down the road. 'She was pretty quick off the mark.' His face and its raised eyebrows were in shadow, but Sam could hear the inference in the voice. 'Not what you're thinking,' he said. 'I didn't tip her off. OK, she's better-looking than Bill Skelly but she thinks the same way, anything for a story. Trouble is she's a friend of Elspeth's and keeps hanging around. God knows what Elspeth's up to, but if she keeps on trying to make us all get on with each other I might have to leave.'

Harry said, 'She won't say anything, up at Monty House, will she? We'll have to go up there as soon as the scene of crime blokes get here. We've had a positive ID from you, but I want to see how they react up there.'

'She wouldn't dare,' said Sam. 'She told me herself that her job's on the line and she has to keep in with the boss.'

'I laid it on pretty thick about obstructing the police, and threw in that I'd report to her editor if she got in our way.'

'Thornhill's OK. Skelly's like a dog with a bone. Not sure why they gave Judith the story, but someone's off sick. They must be short of people.'

'Judith, eh?' Harry tried again.

'Give it up, Harry. I'm not interested, and even if I was, she'd have to go through proper channels to get any information, right?'

'Right,' Harry agreed, and Sam knew what he was thinking.

'They're 'ere,' said the constable, as lights approached through the trees.

The two detectives greeted the new arrivals and briefed them. More lights were set up and photographs taken, the flash lighting the scene with gruesome brilliance. The wooden box was photographed from various angles and examined carefully before being lifted with gloved hands and tagged. A ladder was placed carefully against the trunk of the oak tree that the dead man had chosen as the last place on earth that he would see, and after a few more minutes of examining knots, the body was lowered to the ground and onto a stretcher. Harry looked carefully through the pockets of the dead man's jacket.

'Eyup,' he said, and his gloved fingers pulled something into the light. The paper shone white in the torchlight as Harry unfolded it and the two men read the few words together. *Tell Mam I'm sorry.* That was all.

'Maybe he was in a hurry,' said Sam.

'Or maybe someone else wrote it,' Harry added. 'But it would have to be someone who knew his mam was still around. We'll get some of his writing from up at the house. Must be plenty of it around, him being a teacher.'

Sam took an evidence bag from the case he'd brought with him, refolded the note and dropped it in.

'OK, lads,' he said. 'He's all yours, and we need a fingertip search all round this patch. Looks pretty straightforward but you never know.'

The scene of crime team divided up the small clearing in which they were standing and dropped to their knees, keen to discover as much as they could before possible rain overnight made the facts, however obvious they might appear, even harder to ascertain. The two detectives watched for a while, deciding how to break the news to Edwards and the others at Montgomery House.

The Bay Horse was deserted apart from two men leaning on the bar, and the barman who was standing to one side reading the paper. They all looked up when Judith walked in.

'Judith Pharaoh, Ace Reporter,' said Bill Skelly. The cigarette hanging from the side of his mouth waggled as he spoke. 'What'll you have, my dear?'

'Introduction, please Bill,' said the other man. 'Not met this young lady before. I would have remembered.'

Judith stood her ground, wondering what Skelly would say next and remembering Irene's assurance that she would be treated properly from now on. And it was all right. Bill introduced Judith to his counterpart from the *Ulverston Record* without a trace of innuendo or disrespect. 'John Shaw,' said the other man, shaking Judith's hand. 'Pleased to meet you.'

'Hattie told me where you were,' said Judith, perching beside Bill on a stool at the bar. 'I'll have a lime and lemonade please.'

'Steady on,' said Bill, but he ordered what she asked for

without further comment.

'We got a call, probably from the same people that called the police,' said John Shaw. 'They must have been from our patch and they called our newsroom. I knew about that kid in the quicksand that the Barrow force are handling, put two and two together, and called Bill.'

'That new CID bloke's down there,' said Judith. 'Have you met him, Bill?'

'Pain in the arse, by all accounts,' said Bill. 'And that's the polite version. Do they know who it is?'

'They do, and I do too. It's a bloke called Harries, from Montgomery House. Met him last week when they found the kid's body. He didn't say much, but he looked pretty upset.' She paused. 'And today I found out a bit more about him.'

'Wondered where you were today,' said Bill.

Judith's explanation about why she went to Maryport to see Pat O'Toole took a little while, as she made up her mind about how much to share. She knew that as soon as Bill learned what she knew, she'd lose control of it. She remembered what Pat O'Toole had said about being kind, but Bill was her boss and the lure of a story trumped 'kind' every time with him. She decided she had to tell them. 'There were complaints from parents about Harries and then he left the parish,' she said.

John Shaw slapped his spare hand on his thigh. 'I knew it,' he said. 'A pervy priest. Oldest story in the book, but it always goes down well with everyone, bar the Catholics.'

'And there are plenty of those around,' said Bill. 'My missus for a start.'

Judith was surprised. She wondered whether Bill ever confessed anything in the dark box to invisible clerical ears.

'What else did this priest friend of yours tell you?' Bill asked.

'Ex-priest,' Judith corrected him. 'And he was a friend of

144

my grandmother, not me. He only agreed to talk to me out of respect for her.'

'I hear more plots thickening,' said Shaw.

'Very old plots in that case,' said Judith, 'and irrelevant.'

'Leave Judith's granny out of it, John,' said Bill Skelly. 'Next question is whether Edwards and company at Montgomery House know that their dear departed colleague has been found.'

'And why he did it,' said Shaw. 'Looks pretty clear to me. Dodgy priest has his hand down the kid's trousers, Catholic guilt, kid runs away and turns up dead, more guilt, dodgy priest tops himself before they catch up with him. Open and shut.'

'Sad,' said Judith, sipping on her fizzy drink.

'Who for?' said Bill. 'Come on, Judith. Don't feel sorry for some perv who molests kids. If he touched a kid of mine, I'd cut his balls off.'

'But we can't just jump to that conclusion, can we? What my friend told me was gossip he heard a long time ago, and it was a long way from where anything might have happened.'

'So why would he top himself?' said John Shaw.

'Why do people kill themselves?' Judith went on, watching the last of the bubbles rise in her drink. 'All sorts of reasons. He could have been ill, some woman might have jilted him, we've no idea. It's just guesswork, and we can't print that.'

'She's right,' said Bill, looking into his pint. 'Need more to go on.'

'Good story in the making, though,' said John Shaw, calling the barman over.

Harries's body was moved to one side to wait for transport to the mortuary, and the policemen adjusted the lights to see as much as they could. Grayson pulled Sam by the arm out of the lighted area into the darkness of the surrounding trees, and lowered his voice. 'I know everyone thinks you're a pain, Sam, but to be honest, I'd rather work with you than with Morrison. You and I trained together and I know how things should be done, even if you don't think I do.'

Sam was surprised. He'd written Grayson off as just another time-server who cut corners and beat up suspects to get a 'confession' and save them the time on proper police work. More than once, Sam had left an interview room when things got really rough and he wasn't sure how much longer he could keep quiet about what went on. Slapping a suspect around was routine and he was used to it, but he drew the line at kicking.

'Does Morrison know we're both here?' Sam asked. 'I'd already started asking questions about all the staff at Montgomery House and about the kid who died in the quicksand down the road.'

'Something I wondered,' said Grayson. 'If the kid was from here, how come he ended up on the shore where he did?'

'I thought about that too,' said Sam. 'Still haven't figured out exactly how he died.'

'So what are we going to do about the press guys?'

'Tell them something to keep them off our backs. Ask for help finding witnesses, all the usual stuff.'

'Do you think that Pharaoh girl knows things she's not telling us?'

Sam thought for a minute. 'She's no fool, I know that. And she told me herself that she needs this story to keep her job.'

'Could you find out what's she's been up to, on the quiet like?'

Sam shrugged. 'Last week I gave her a lecture about the evils of police and press getting into bed together.' He realised too late that the words were poorly chosen.

Harry patted Sam on the back. 'Now there's a thought,' he said. 'Is that called killing two birds with one stone?'

They turned back to help the scene of crime team tie yellow 'Do Not Cross' tape from tree to tree around the scene. 'Need someone here overnight,' said the scene-of-crime sergeant to Harry. 'Done as much as we can tonight. We'll get the body back to the mortuary and see what the doc says in the morning. We can guess it was suicide but you never know.'

'Found anything?'

'Not much. Two cigarette ends,' the sergeant held up a brown evidence bag with writing on it. 'Look like the same brand but we'll get forensics to check that out. Untipped, don't see so many of them around these days. As soon as we have enough light we'll go over it again, and further up towards the road. What about Montgomery House?'

'We're on our way up there now,' said Harry. 'I'll take Sam with me as he knows them. We'll see you back here tomorrow, first thing, right?' The sergeant nodded.

A few minutes later DCs Tognarelli and Grayson stood side by side in the porch as the front door of Montgomery House opened, flooding the steps with light. Both men produced their warrant cards and introduced themselves. Captain Edwards looked from one to the other, and nodded to Sam.

'Not more bad news?' said the captain.

In Edwards' office Grayson told him what they'd found in the woods across the road, while Sam stood quietly by the door, watching, gauging the reaction. The captain was hard to read: shock, yes, and confusion. Alarm? Definitely, but that was understandable as the reputation of Montgomery House was about to be badly tarnished. Captain Edwards sat down heavily in his chair. The two police officers remained standing.

'Did he…?' Edwards' voice tailed away.

'It's possible he killed himself, sir, too early be sure as yet, although there is a brief note that seems to support this. We've made a preliminary search of the scene and will carry on at first light. In the meantime, we're sure that the body is that of Desmond Harries, as my colleague had already spoken to him about the other matter.'

'Do you think there's a connection…' he paused, 'with the other matter?' Edwards' voice was barely more than a whisper.

'Again, too early to tell. Sometimes one event just triggers another without there being any other link. Did you notice anything unusual about Mr Harries's behaviour in the past few days, or longer?'

Edwards produced a large white handkerchief from an inside pocket and blew his nose. 'Well of course he was very upset by what happened to Steven, but then we all were. Such a tragic business.'

'And bad for the reputation of this place?' Sam asked.

'Of course, how could it not be? But in that case it would be me feeling that responsibility, not poor Mr Harries.' He blew his nose again. 'And how am I going to tell Matron? She needed to see Dr Graham after what happened to Steven. I'd better alert him.'

'We'll have to talk to both of them, sir, so perhaps the initial news might come from you? She's bound to know that something's up when we search Mr Harries's room.'

'Do you have to do that now? The boys are still around. It's been hard enough with them the past few days, and now this.'

'You could tell them that we're worried about Mr Harries and need to look in his room. That's as much as they need to know for the time being.' Harry looked down at his notebook, while behind him Sam opened his to a fresh page and began to write with his very small pencil.

'That's what I'll tell them, and Iris too, just for now,' said Edwards. 'Something vague, just until the morning. Can you wait here please, to give me time to gather them up and say what needs saying.'

'We'd like to be there, too,' said Sam. He wanted to see any reactions from the boys.

Ten minutes later the two policemen stood at the back of the dining room while Captain Edwards, with Iris Robinson by his side, spoke to the twenty or so boys who sat straight and quiet along the long benches by the old wooden tables.

'These two gentlemen are police officers,' said the captain, and heads turned to stare at Sam and Harry. 'They have some concerns about the whereabouts of Mr Harries and they need to have a look in his room and perhaps ask us about when we last saw him, and so on.'

The boys looked at each other. Sam saw nothing much register on their faces, but most of them had dealings with the police many times before and knew how to keep their reactions to themselves.

'You may go to your rooms, boys, but don't get ready for bed just yet. We'll call you down to my office if we need to talk to you. Before you go – Mr Harries had a day off today. Did any of you see him leave this morning?'

'I saw him talking to someone, sir,' said a voice. 'This morning, sir.'

'Thank you, Leonard,' said the captain. 'Anyone else?' There was silence. 'So if you could come with us please, Leonard,' said the captain, 'and Mrs Robinson will see the rest of you up to your rooms.'

The matron helped and herded as the boys scraped back their benches and shuffled out of the dining room towards the stairs. None of them spoke until they had left the room, but then their raised voices and Mrs Robinson's calm adult tone reached the policemen's ears as they walked ahead of Leonard and the captain back to the office.

'If I go with the captain up to Mr Harries's room, could you have a word with Leonard here?' said Harry Grayson to Sam as they stood in the doorway. Leonard was obviously not happy about being interviewed again and had to be steered into the office. As he hovered uncomfortably by the door Sam pulled out a chair for him to sit on, and another one next to it for himself, positioned so that he was beside the boy rather than facing him. They sat in silence side by side for a moment before Sam spoke.

'Do you remember me, Leonard?' he asked. 'I came a few days ago, after we found Steven.'

Leonard nodded, looking down at his knees.

'So tell me as much as you can remember about seeing Mr Harries.'

''E were with this man, sir,' Leonard began.

'Slowly, please,' said Sam. 'I'll have to write things down, or I forget.' It was a lie; Sam rarely forgot anything but he wanted the boy to think slowly and carefully about what he said. 'Now let's start at the beginning, shall we? What time did you see Mr Harries?'

'After breakfast. Must've been about half eight. Me and the other school lads were going across the yard to t' schoolroom but I forgot summat and I went back in. When I came out again, Mr Harries were standing by the bins, with a man.'

'Did they seem to know each other?'

Leonard screwed up his face in thought. 'Nah,' he said after a pause. 'Mr Harries had a look, you know, as if 'e didn't know the man. And 'e looked upset like.'

'What can you remember about this man?'

'Taller than you, more like that other copper. And a thin face.'

'A thin face?'

'Yeh, he 'ad a long chin. That makes your face look thin, dunnit?'

'What was he wearing?'

'A big 'at,' said the boy, without hesitation. 'It were pulled right down.'

'But you said you could see his thin face and his chin.'

'Aye, well, 'e'd pulled it down at the front and to one side, like them gangsters do in old films, but I could still see some of 'is face.'

'Would you recognise him again?'

Leonard shook his head.

Sam looked at the boy carefully for a moment before he went on. 'Were he and Mr Harries talking?'

'The man were talking, but Harries weren't saying much.'

'Could you hear what he was saying?'

'Couldn't 'ear 'owt, but he were pointing at Mr Harries, jabbing 'im in the shoulder,' said Leonard. 'Couldn't just stand there listening. Didn't want Harries to see me. So I went back in and waited till they went away.'

'Where did they go?'

Leonard shrugged his shoulders. 'Dunno,' he said. 'When I come out again, they'd both gone.' He thought for a minute. 'Could still see the smoke, though.'

'What smoke?'

'From a cig. Smoke were 'anging in the air, like.'

'Did Mr Harries smoke?' Sam asked.

''Im? Nay,' said Leonard. 'E allus knew when we'd been. Said he could smell it 'cos 'e didn't smoke 'imself.'

Sam wrote in his book. 'Could you show me where you saw Mr Harries and the man?'

Leonard got up from his chair and walked out of the office with Sam following behind. There didn't appear to be anyone around or on the stairs but Sam could feel eyes watching as they went down the hall to the back door. Leonard opened it and stood just outside, at the top of the steps that led down into the back yard. 'I were standing 'ere, sir,' he said to Sam. 'And they were over there.' He pointed to his left, towards a low fence behind which were the large refuse bins. Piled up against the fence were some old orange boxes and an axe that someone was using to chop them up for kindling.

'Right,' said Sam. 'And that's where you saw the smoke.'

'Yes, sir,' said Leonard.

'One last thing before you go, Leonard. You're sure you never saw this man before.' The boy shook his head. 'And you don't think Mr Harries knew him?' Leonard shrugged. 'Did you see Mr Harries speak to the man, even if you couldn't hear what he said?'

'He said summat. Well, 'is mouth moved, like. I told you, 'e looked scared. Maybe 'e thought the man were going to 'it 'im.'

'You think that?'

'That's how I look when someone's going to 'it me,' said Leonard. 'Somebody big, like. Not one of the lads.'

'So he looked a strong man, big.'

'Aye, 'ard,' said Leonard. He dropped his head. 'Can I go now, sir?'

'Yes, Leonard. If I need to talk to you again, I know where you are.'

Sam had asked Leonard not to talk to the rest of the lads about their conversation but he knew that it was a waste of breath. Alone on the step, he looked across again at the area where the encounter had apparently taken place. He took a torch from his pocket and walked slowly and carefully across the flagstones, shining the light on his feet as he did so. Close to the low fence he stopped and crouched down. He took a pair of tweezers and a brown bag out of his inside pocket, picked up a cigarette stub from the ground, put it in the brown bag and went back up the steps and into the house.

There was no sign of Grayson, but the door of the captain's office was open and he could hear Mrs Robinson's voice, and her tears. Sam walked to the stairs and up. There was no one around and the doors were closed. As he passed down one of the long corridors he heard a door open behind him, but by the time he looked around it had closed again. Harry's voice caught his ear.

'That you, Sam? I'm up here. You need to see this.'

Chapter 12

Harry Grayson stood silhouetted in the doorway of a room at the far end of a long corridor.

'Look at this,' he said.

Sam looked inside and saw a large brightly lit room, windows black against the night sky beyond. On one side a narrow bed was made with hospital precision and sharp corners. A desk, a chair, a rail with a few clothes hanging, a chest of drawers. Sam looked at Harry.

'Too tidy,' said Harry. 'No one lives as neatly as this. Harries was a tidy man, obviously. Didn't someone say he'd been in the forces? He may have cleared up when he decided to top himself, clear out anything too personal.'

Sam pulled on his gloves. 'Or someone else did it, someone who knew that we might be looking. Whoever did it, they might have missed something. We need to go through it all.'

'Leave it, Sam. It'll keep till the morning. We need to talk to whoever cleans the rooms, check when they came in here, see if they found anything. And we need an example of Harries's writing to check that note.'

'There'll be plenty of those around.'

'All that can wait till the morning as well,' said Harry. 'I'll tell the boss we'll be back, and that this room must be locked, off limits to everyone. I could do with the overtime but I could do with the sleep more.'

On the way from Roose to Attercliff the following morning Sam had been wondering about the fog, or was it mist, lying in swathes, patchy and shallow across the flat expanse of the bay. Bonfire Night tonight, he remembered, November 5th. There'd be smoke as well as fog around later, and the usual rash of kids in casualty with burns of various degrees. From the brow of the hill near Attercliff he looked down onto the top of the mist before descending into the murk as the road curved away down the hill towards the shore. There was no wind and when the rain started it fell softly and verti- cally, straight down the upturned collar of Sam's coat. Harry Grayson was already at the scene, talking to Sergeant Brewster from the crime scene team. He gestured to Sam to join them.

'Brewster's been filling me in on what they've found so far.'

Sergeant Brewster drew on his cigarette, and tapped the ash into his cupped hand. 'That box we found. Looks like an orange box, with a divider in the middle. Could be strong enough to take his weight, before he kicked it away.

'I saw a stack of orange boxes last night,' said Sam, 'behind Monty House, by the bins. He could have carried one of them down here.'

'If he wanted to do a proper job, he would have needed something to stand on,' said Harry. 'If this bloke was serious about doing himself in he'd put it up on one end, stand on it, tie the rope round his neck and the branch and then kick the box away.'

'Without the box, he might have just choked slowly, not the snap that does the job quickly,' said Brewster.

'Forensics will have a good look at the box, and the others up at the house, but it looks pretty straightforward to me. Could be some prints too, on the labels orange boxes usually have '

'Talking of forensics,' said Sam, taking a brown evidence bag from his inside pocket, 'I found another cig butt last night up at the house, in the back yard. That's where I saw the orange boxes. You lot were gone when I got back down here.' He handed it over to Brewster. 'Drop that in for us will you? Could be the same brand as the ones we found here but that doesn't tell us much. If they were all smoked by the same person that would be very interesting, even if it wouldn't hold up in court.'

'Did the dead bloke smoke?'

'Not according to the kid I spoke to last night. Kid's no reason to lie and we can always check further.'

'So if someone was smoking down here last night, and we should be able to find that out, then someone else was right here either before, during, or after Harries topped himself.'

'We don't even know he did it to himself,' said Sam. 'He could have been drugged, or hit over the head and strung up to make it look like suicide.'

'That should all show up in the PM,' said Brewster.

'Footprints?' Sam asked, knowing the answer.

Sergeant Brewster shrugged. 'Look at this mess,' he said. 'People who found the body, you two and that PC from last night. Now the rain. All we can say for sure was that several pairs of boots have been plodding around. Not much chance of finding out how many, or whose bootprints fit where.'

The three men stood in silence, looking around them.

'Not sure who'll do the PM,' said Sam. 'Our police doc's in hospital and I reckon he's gone a bit doolally. Made a right cockup of the kid's PM.'

'What do we know about Harries?'

Sam looked at his notes. 'Looks like he was a priest up on the west coast somewhere, and then joined up as a padre. Not sure if he served here or overseas. Then he turned up here for a job last year, 1968. Desmond Jerome Harries, born March,1925, in Rochdale. Edwards said Harries wasn't married, and he thought both parents were dead, but obviously not if the note's genuine. I need to check that with Mrs Robinson. She looks like the type who someone might talk to. I have a nasty feeling that reporter might know more but she's keeping it to herself.' He shut his notebook and put it away.

Harry said, 'If we're going to claim suicide and save ourselves a shitload of effort we need something to back it up. We'll have proper look at Harries's room for a start. I'll dig out the medical records, and you have a word with Pharaoh's editor if you have to about withholding information. And tell Brewster what the kid told you, about Harries having a visitor.'

Sam re-told the details of Leonard's story. 'The kid said he looked "hard" and threatening. Could have been enough to tip Harries over the edge.'

'Or the bloke might have marched Harries down into the wood with the orange box and strung him up,' Harry added.

'Or,' said Brewster, 'the hard man just bumped him off somehow down here and strung him up to put us off. The note and the orange box were just to cover his tracks.'

The three men looked at each other. 'We need that post-mortem, fast,' said Sam. 'And a proper look in Harries's room. Come on.'

In the full light of day, the clinically tidy room on the top floor of Montgomery House looked as implausible as it had the previous night. Harry and Sam pulled on their gloves and started with the desk drawers, looking for anything in the dead man's handwriting. Nothing. No letters, no notes, no photos. Nothing in the pockets of any of the clothes hanging on the rail. Nothing in the empty rubbish bin under the desk. The cleaners had been in the previous day, after the time when Harries had last been seen at the house; they would have tidied up, but not removed all signs that the dead man had ever inhabited this soulless space.

'Waste of time,' said Harry eventually.

Sam agreed. 'Why don't you go back to check what they've found on Harries's body?' he suggested as they returned downstairs. 'I know the people here, so I'll take statements from Edwards and the matron, and get what I can about the handwriting and the next of kin.'

Captain Edwards was clearly still shaken about the tragedies that had overtaken them. He sat straight in the chair behind his desk but Sam could see the anxiety in his face. 'I need to know whatever you can tell me about this awful business, as soon as you can,' he said to Sam as soon as their conversation began. 'The trustees have called an emergency meeting for next week. They're as appalled by all this as I am, of course.'

'What about Mr Harries's next of kin?' asked Sam. 'We have a duty to inform them, and there's been mention of his mother, but we don't know where she is. We'll need to find her.'

'Did you find anything at all in his room?' asked Edwards. 'Mr Harries was always a very tidy person, and the cleaners did their usual work before we … before we knew.'

Sam persisted. 'You need to check your files, sir, to help us find the mother.'

Edwards got up and opened the middle drawer of a large filing cabinet that stood in the corner of the office. He took out a thin folder, brought it back to his desk, opened it and leafed through the various papers.

'His application form said that he wasn't married. Nothing about parents in the file, but I seem to remember some mention of the north-east. Maybe Newcastle?'

'Would Mrs Robinson know?' asked Sam.

'I haven't seen Iris this morning,' said Edwards. 'She was so upset last night, the doctor gave her something to help her sleep.'

'Is that the local doctor?' Sam asked, taking his notebook from his pocket.

'Dr Graham comes from Broughton,' said Edwards. 'He's one of our trustees. A wonderful supporter of our work here since I began here.'

'And that was?' asked Sam.

'Ten years ago,' said the captain. 'Montgomery House was opened after the war, and I took over as director when I came out of the army.' He tapped his leg. 'Invalided out, you see,' he said. 'Being in Malaya made me want to do something worthwhile when I came out. Things were pretty dreadful out there for children, displaced, separated from families and so on. Some of them were forced to fight for the guerillas, the Communists.'

'And Mrs Robinson?' said Sam.

'Iris has been here from the start,' said Edwards. 'She's been immensely loyal to Montgomery House, and to me. Do you need to speak to her?'

'Poor woman,' thought Sam when Iris Robinson came into the office a short while later. Her eyes were swollen and red, the usually immaculate hair tousled. Abandoning any pretence of being in control of herself, she slumped in the chair that the captain pulled out for her. He patted her hand. 'Have you had tea, Iris?' he asked gently. 'Shall I get you some?' Sam nodded, and Edwards left the two of them alone.

'I'm very sorry about what's happened,' said Sam. 'There are just a couple of things I need to ask you, Mrs Robinson, if you can manage that?' She nodded. 'We've looked in Mr Harries's room upstairs, but we haven't found any information about his next of kin. Can you help us with that?'

Iris raised her eyes, which filled with tears. 'He was a very private man,' she said. 'And lonely too, I think.' She wiped her eyes and blew her nose. 'He told me once that his father had died, and he was concerned about his mother left alone, but that was last year when he joined us, and I don't recall anything recently.'

'Was he married?' Sam asked.

She shook her head. 'Not as far as I know. He'd been a Catholic priest, I believe, then a padre. He wouldn't have been married, would he?'

'No,' said Sam, 'unless he'd left the church for some reason.'

'But why would he?' she said. 'He still had his faith, that was obvious to me. Such a gentle, quiet man. I can't believe…' Her voice tailed away, and she wiped her eyes again.

'Did he ever write to you,' asked Sam, 'a letter perhaps, or a note? In his own writing?'

She looked at him, questioning, but saying nothing. 'The captain would have that kind of thing, wouldn't he?'

'Of course,' said Sam. 'Captain Edwards mentioned something about family in Newcastle. Does that ring any bells?'

Iris thought for a moment and remembered. 'Last New Year,' she said, 'he said something about "first footing", you know, on New Year's Eve, and how he was often asked to do it when he was young man in Gateshead. But that would have been a long time ago.'

Sam scribbled in his notebook. 'That's very helpful, thank you. We'll see what we can do.'

'His funeral,' said Iris. 'He was Catholic, and if he…' she left the sentence unfinished.

'We'll do our best to find his family,' said Sam. 'They'll look after all that, I'm sure.'

'The poor man,' she said. 'To die like that all alone. He was very upset about poor Steven, you know, but I never thought – none of us did. The captain is terribly upset, you know. We're like a family here. And the trustees, they'll want to know what happened.' She sniffed. 'The captain is a wonderful man, constable,' she said. 'So dedicated to these boys. He was away fighting you know, and I think that's what drives him, to make up for what he saw over there.'

Sam smiled and nodded, wondering. They both looked up as the door opened and Betty from the kitchen brought in a tray of tea and toast. Sam wanted to get away, but he stayed a while in the vain hope that more information would be forthcoming. It was hard to accept that Desmond Harries had disappeared leaving no trace of his existence behind him.

In the newsroom of the *Furness News* Bill Skelly outlined to his editor his theory of the case with unassailable confidence. 'Looks like this Harries guy was a Catholic priest who was shifted out of the parish for fiddling with little boys, buggered off to the army or somewhere out of reach for a while and then turned up wanting to work in a boys' home. Surprise, surprise. Harries fools with a kid who runs away and dies, Harries feels guilty, can't live with himself any more, finds a tree and a rope and Bob's your uncle.'

Judith winced; so much for Pat's advice to be kind and not

jump to conclusions. Thornhill sucked his bottom lip. 'How much of this is speculation?' he asked.

'Too much of it,' said Judith quickly. 'I heard about it from another ex-priest who said the stuff about the little boys was just gossip.'

'No smoke,' retorted Bill triumphantly. 'He's just a pervy priest. God knows there's enough of 'em around.'

'It's not enough, Bill,' said Thornhill. 'You know that. We'll have the bishop and all his angels on us in a flash if we print something like that.'

'I could find out more,' said Judith. 'The diocese would have information about where he went, even if they're keeping quiet about why. And wouldn't the army or whatever it is have records about when someone left? Why did he turn up at Monty House last year, looking for a job?'

'Edwards would never employ someone really dodgy,' said Thornhill. 'We never hear a bad word about the man. He must be mortified.' He was staring at the papers on his desk; Judith wondered why he wasn't more enthusiastic about the story.

'Couldn't get near him last night, with the police warning me off,' said Judith, 'but I could go back now, see what he says, if he'll see me at all.'

'Probably rather see you than me,' said Bill, 'but who wouldn't, eh?'

Judith stared at him and he looked away.

An hour later, she was getting ready to go back to Montgomery House when the phone rang. It was Tognarelli.

'Just in case you were thinking of snooping around after last night, Miss Pharaoh, I've been asked by Sergeant Morrison to make sure you get the message to leave this alone. Montgomery House could be part of a crime scene and you and your colleagues should not be there until we say so.'

'My editor's just asked me to keep on with my enquiries, and that's my job.'

'That's why I'm about to call your editor and meet with him as soon as maybe,' said Sam. 'That will include you, and I expect to be down there forthwith. Goodbye, Miss Pharaoh.' The phone went dead.

'Forthwith?' Judith repeated into the silence. 'Straight out of the pompous policeman's almanac.'

She heard the phone ring in Thornhill's office and a few moments later Thornhill appeared at the door.

'I know,' called Judith from her desk. 'He called me, too.'

'Who did?'

'That new DC, Tognarelli.'

'Well it was his boss who called me. Detective Sergeant Morrison and DC whatever his name is will be here in ten minutes, so you'd better bring a couple of chairs in here in case we have to let them sit down.'

It was not a comfortable meeting. Judith remembered that Thornhill and Morrison knew each other, and it was obvious, despite their efforts to maintain some professional distance. Morrison let Sam do most of the talking about the case, and all three men looked at Judith when he said quite clearly that he believed that Judith had information that would be useful to the investigation. Secretly Judith was pleased that Thornhill would see how hard she'd been working, but she looked gravely down at her shoes and gave nothing away.

'What do you need to know?' said Thornhill.

'We think that the deaths of Steven Stringer and Desmond Harries are probably connected.'

'One's an accident and the other a suicide,' said Thornhill.

'Maybe and maybe,' said Sam. 'Not enough evidence yet to confirm or deny that.'

'But there will be soon,' said Morrison.

'That's reassuring,' said Thornhill.

Morrison glared at him. 'We expect all your people to cooperate with us in sharing information,' he said.

'As we always do,' countered Thornhill. 'Now is that all? We have a paper to put to bed.' He moved just a short distance across the crowded space to make his point. 'Miss Pharaoh here will do whatever's necessary to bring our DC up to speed, and you and I will make sure they join all the dots.'

Ten minutes later, Judith and Sam sat in the corner of the newsroom with their respective notebooks in their hands. There didn't seem to be many dots to join.

'My contact in Maryport who told me the gossip about Harries is Pat O'Toole,' said Judith, giving Sam the address and phone number. 'He was Father O'Toole, but he left the priesthood some years ago.'

Sam looked up and raised his eyebrows. 'No,' said Judith firmly. 'This has nothing to do with him. Not a chance, so forget it. What about the PM report?' she added, determined to get some information before she offered any more.

Sam shook his head. 'The report confirms that the boy drowned, and would lead to an assumption of accidental death.'

'But–' said Judith.

'But nothing,' he interrupted. 'Whatever Doc Hayward said to you, off the record, there's no doubt about the report.'

'Have you asked him about it?'

'Not since I saw him in the hospital, and you know what he said then.'

Judith knew he was right, and changed tack. 'There's the Barnardo's connection and the older brother,' she said. 'Anthony Lennon could have been sent overseas by Barnardo's, probably Canada or Australia. Somehow the brother gets back to England and finds out the younger brother is in care as well. Wants to protect him, tracks him down, says he'll come and fetch him, kid sets off, gets lost, ends up in the mudhole,' she said.

Sam listened. He'd already worked out that possibility but Judith didn't know what he'd discovered from social services. 'OK,' he said. 'And what about Harries?'

Judith thought for a moment. 'Anthony might guess that someone had been messing with Steven, takes it out on Harries who is terrified of more accusations like last time and kills himself to avoid it.'

Sam nodded again. 'We may, repeat may, have Anthony meeting with Harries outside Monty House just hours before Harries died,' he said.

'Well, then,' said Judith. 'Looks pretty cut and dried to me.'

Sam sat back and shook his head. 'But I'm a trained police detective and you're not are you, Miss Pharaoh? You can help though. We need more information from Steven's sister about the elder brother, and there's no chance of her talking to me. And I need to talk to your friend in Maryport and pick up Harries's history from there. If it was a suicide we need to convince the coroner and at present it's all guesswork. You'd better call O'Toole and let him know about Harries and that I will want to see him. Can you do that?'

Judith nodded. It wasn't something she wanted to do, but she had little room for manoeuvre.

'And the sister,' Sam went on. 'You have to get her to tell us more about the elder brother. That man's in this picture somewhere, and currently he's just a ghost.'

Judith said suddenly, 'The man you saw at the crematorium. What did he look like?'

'Hardly saw him at all, just a glance before he disappeared

into the bushes,' said Sam. 'One of the boys may have seen him too, at Monty House last night.'

'And?' asked Judith.

'It could be the same person. Taller than me, wearing a long coat and hat, big enough to pull down over his face. The lad at Monty House said he looked hard.'

'And he probably smokes,' said Judith.

'Why?' asked Sam.

'It was a few days ago now,' said Judith. 'I was walking from the station to my flat just off Abbey Road and I wondered if someone was watching me. He was wearing a long coat and a big hat, too, and smoking. He was standing at the end of the street but when I stopped to look, he walked round the corner. I'd actually forgotten about it.'

Sam got to his feet. 'If it happens again, tell us,' he said. 'Probably nothing, but until we pin this man down he could be anywhere. Keep good notes when you talk to the sister and get in touch as soon as you've seen her. PM results for Harries shouldn't be long and those will help. Probably just confirm the most likely course of events, the one we've all guessed at already.'

'Is it OK for me to visit Elspeth again without you going off in a huff?' asked Judith.

Sam didn't smile. 'We're co-operating on a case not because we want to but it's the most efficient way to proceed,' he said. 'I still feel that press and police should keep their distance from each other. You and Elspeth are friends, but don't include me in that. I'm not being nasty, that's just the way it needs to be.'

And that was all he said as he made his way across the newsroom and out. Andrew's head went up.

'Shut up, Andrew,' said Judith.

❖ ❖ ❖

When she rang Fred at the station café in Morecambe, Donna had still not appeared and her boss seemed genuinely anxious about what had happened to her. 'She phoned in sick last week, Thursday,' he said, 'but it's nearly a week now and not another word. It's that man of hers, he hurts her you know. "Walked into a door", my arse. Are you going to check at home? Go during the day. If he's there he can be real trouble, that bloke.'

Judith reassured him on that point and thought about how long it would take her to get to Morecambe and find Donna's house. She might have to wait for her to come home.

She was working on the logistics of a trip to Morecambe when Bill Skelly came back into the newsroom, hung up his hat and started opening letters and messages that had accumulated on his desk during the morning. While Judith was checking train times, Bill began to rummage around in a cupboard by Ed Cunningham's office, which brought him out to see what was going on.

'Looking for a tape recorder,' said Bill. Judith was watching them now. 'Sure there's one here somewhere. Here it is.' He stood up with a large machine in his hands.

'Haven't used one of those for a while. Too bloody heavy to lug around,' said Ed Cunningham.

Bill put the tape machine on top of the messy desk and picked up an envelope. 'This arrived some time this morning,' he said. 'Anyone know where it came from? Hattie?'

'She came back from lunch a while back,' said Andrew.

'Reel of tape,' said Bill. 'Nothing else. No note. *Head Reporter* written on the envelope, in capitals. Looks like someone can't write to save his life.'

Judith, Ed and Andrew stood round Bill Skelly's desk as he struggled to set up the tape to playback. Andrew found an extension lead and the machine sprang to life. Bill pressed the 'Play' button and they waited. For a few moments there was nothing to be heard but clicks and scratching noises. Then the sound of someone breathing and a voice began to speak, distorted but quite audible:

'The kid was murdered. Police are bloody useless. You'll have to get it done, get them done, you and that girl with the red hair. I've done my part, now you do something. I'm watching. I'll know.'

CHAPTER 13

'Play it again,' said Thornhill from behind his desk. Bill rewound the tape, pressed 'Play' again and they watched as the reel jerked into action, then crowded closer, straining to hear the words.

'It's a crank. Somebody winding us up,' said Thornhill. 'Must be.'

'Someone who knows the lass has a lot of hair,' said Cunningham.

Judith stepped away from the group towards the window. Suddenly she felt very trapped.

'Those kids at the home,' said Cunningham, 'they know Judith. They're stirring things up, just from devilment, little bastards. Nothing better to do likely. Life of Riley down there. I'd put them all out to work, or get them making something, earning their keep.'

'Sewing mailbags?' asked Judith.

'Well, that's what they'll end up doing, isn't it, at Her Majesty's Pleasure in one of those holiday camps called prisons.'

'Shut up Ed, for God's sake,' said Bill, pointing to the envelope. 'Look, this was addressed to me. Who brought it? There's no stamps or postmark.'

'Hattie!' yelled Thornhill. 'Get in here.'

Hattie didn't have far to go as she and Andrew were already standing in the doorway, trying to see and hear what was going on.

'Where did this package for Bill come from?' asked Thornhill. 'It didn't come in the post, so who brought it?'

Hattie straightened her hair. She wasn't used to being spoken to so brusquely. 'It was just there, when I got back from lunch,' she began.

'Where, woman?' roared Thornhill. Judith noticed his red face, and looked across at Hattie whose eyes were beginning to fill with tears

'It's all right, Hattie,' said Judith. 'No one's blaming you for anything. We just need to know if you saw whoever brought this in.'

Hattie shook her head. 'It was propped up against the door,' she whispered.

'Outside or inside?' Judith asked. The men had taken their cue from her and kept quiet.

'Outside,' said Hattie, 'just leaning on the door, at the side of the pavement. I picked it up, saw what it said and brought it upstairs for Bill. I thought he must be expecting something and whoever left it couldn't be bothered to bring it up themselves.'

Ed lowered his voice. 'Did you see anyone, in the street?'

'No, no one,' Hattie whispered again and fumbled for a handkerchief in her sleeve.

'OK,' said Thornhill. He was calmer now and his face had resumed its normal colour, although the usual expression of mild boredom had been replaced by anxiety. He picked up the envelope. 'So this came from someone out there who just left it on our doorstep, literally, and walked away.'

'Fingerprints,' said Judith. Thornhill dropped the envelope

immediately and it slid onto Thornhill's desk and down again onto the floor. There was a scramble as everyone tried not to tread on it. Judith pulled down her sleeve and picked up the envelope without touching it with her fingers.

'We need the police,' said Cunningham.

Bill groaned. 'Damn the police,' he said. 'Apart from possibly finding some fingerprints, what could they tell us that we don't know already?'

'It's evidence,' said Judith. 'It may have something to do with what happened to Stevie.'

'Who the hell's Stevie?' said Cunningham. The others looked at him.

'What do you actually do in that filthy cubbyhole of yours all day?' said Thornhill, leaning across towards Cunningham's face. 'Stevie is the kid from Montgomery House who was found dead in the mud last week. Judith's been working on the story, we've put stuff out about the funeral, appeals for help and all that, and you've supposedly read them all. I wonder what we're paying you for?' Cunningham blinked but didn't respond.

'Whoa,' said Bill. 'Not now, right?'

Thornhill sat down heavily in his chair and looked out of the window. Hattie looked at each man in turn, eyes wide. Judith stretched out a hand towards her. 'You can go back to your desk now, Hattie. We need someone on the phones while we sort out what to do. Take Andrew with you.'

Hattie and Andrew did as they were bid and the rest of them were able to shuffle apart from each other a little. Judith noticed her heart was beating quite quickly.

'We'd better not touch the tape or the envelope again,' she said. 'I can call DC Tognarelli, or Sergeant Morrison, or Sergeant Clark if we can't find anyone else.'

Cunningham turned away towards the door of the crowded office. 'I'm not waiting for the entire Barrow police force, who our friend Miss Pharaoh seems to know so well, to descend on us. Despite your assumption that I'm a waste of space, Alan, I for one have some proper work to do. There's a big spike out there waiting for some more rubbish to go on it.' He left, and Thornhill's office felt less claustrophobic without him. Bill sat down and Judith leaned against the windowsill.

Judith said, 'Ed's right. We need the police. We all need to know who dropped this thing off and what they're really getting at. 'What does "I've done my part" mean? And who's he going to be watching?'

Thornhill shook his head. Bill said nothing. 'Right then,' said Judith. 'If you're not going to do it, I'll call Tognarelli.'

'No you won't,' said Thornhill suddenly. 'My paper, my office, my call, and it'll be Sergeant Morrison, not some pipsqueak of a constable.' He looked at them. 'I think I can manage this, unaided, thank you.'

Judith took the hint and went back to her desk, with Bill more reluctantly behind her.

'He wouldn't know a real story if it got up and bit him,' Bill muttered to Judith as he went back to his desk. 'If there's no response from the police in a few minutes, Judith, you call that I-tie copper.'

'Tognarelli,' said Judith. She could see why Sam got so irritated by this refusal to use his proper name.

'Yes, him,' said Bill. 'He sounds all right, better than that useless Morrison.'

'Thornhill won't like it,' said Judith.

'Sod him,' Bill hissed through the side of his mouth. 'This story needs to move before it's stone cold. Nothing like a good voiceover to perk things up. The radio will love it.'

'No one on the radio knows much about Barrow,' said Judith.

'Well, they will soon,' said Bill, 'if we play this right.'

It didn't take long for Sergeant Morrison to push open the door of the newsroom, with Sam Tognarelli just a few steps behind him. Morrison nodded to Bill and Sam to Judith before the two men went into Thornhill's office and closed the door. Hattie sniffed and blew her nose before the regular thud of her typewriter started again. Bill watched the door. Judith knew that he expected to be invited into the office at any moment, but they could hear the tape playing again, once, twice, before the editor's office door opened a fraction and Thornhill's voice shouted, 'Bill, Judith, get in here!' In his cubbyhole Ed Cunningham sneered and lit another cigarette.

'We'll need a statement from Hattie,' Morrison was saying. 'And we'll take the tape and the envelope straight over to Forensics. If we're lucky, there'll be something to lift and we might even have the prints on file already, whoever it is. Any ideas, anybody?'

Judith was surprised that she was the only one to respond. 'The only person I can think of is Steven Stringer's brother Anthony Lennon. He's been away for years but the sister Donna said he reappeared a few weeks ago. It might have been him who told Stevie that he was needed at home. Can you play it one more time? Donna said he had a funny voice.'

'He probably disguised it anyway,' said Morrison.

'Please?' said Judith. Morrison's gloved hand rewound and played the tape yet again. 'We'll need a copy,' he said. 'We're going to wear it out if this carries on.'

Judith listened, trying to picture the man Donna had

described to her. There was a faint twang of something in the voice, but nothing she could recognise. She shrugged and shook her head. Morrison took a couple of evidence bags out of his coat pocket, took the tape off the machine and placed it carefully into one bag. Then he picked up the envelope, held it up to the light and turned it round, looking at it carefully before he placed this, too, in an evidence bag, and turned to go. 'DC Tognarelli here will take a statement from Hattie, and from you Bill, and we'll let you know if and when we get any results. In the meantime, if you think of anything else, anything at all, get hold of the lad here.' He pointed at Sam. Morrison left the newsroom and Sam walked across to speak to Hattie, taking his little notebook and pencil out of his pocket as he went. From her desk Judith was able to see and hear most of their conversation.

Sam introduced himself quietly and it sounded as if he was explaining about himself and his name. Hattie smiled, and began to repeat what she'd told them a while before, but this time more carefully, as she anticipated what might be important. 'I'd been to the Co-op,' she said, 'to get some bits for supper you know, and walked back down here.'

'Time?' asked Sam, without looking up.

'About quarter past one,' said Hattie. 'That's when I usually get back after lunch.'

'So you were walking down the street, coming from the Co-op?'

Patiently, Sam got more and more detail out of Hattie as she recalled what had happened just before she found and picked up the envelope.

'It was just propped up against the door, outside, by the street?'

'They must have known it would be found by someone

coming in, or it could have been taken by someone just passing by,' said Hattie.

'That's right,' said Sam, and she beamed at him.

'When you said "they", Hattie,' said Sam, 'do you think there was more than one person?' Judith heard a faint Scottish accent in his voice, with 'person' sounding like 'pairson'. She'd not noticed it much before. Hattie shook her head. 'I didn't see anyone in the street,' she repeated. 'Nobody.'

Sam thanked her, chatted to Bill for a few minutes taking notes all the while, nodded again to Judith and left. The newsroom felt suddenly very quiet.

'What a nice young man,' said Hattie. 'And such a charming voice, not like that awful man on the tape.'

Sam had been back in the CID room only a few minutes when he got a call. 'Morrison?' said the voice. 'Hobbs, Forensics. About the PM report on Steven Stringer?'

'Yes,' said Sam, 'it's my case.'

'Nothing untoward,' said Hobbs. 'Hardly anything at all actually. Just a few lines. Hayward's usually pretty thorough but he must have been in a hurry. Even the signature's more of a scrawl than usual.'

'Is that it?' Sam persisted. He still didn't understand why Hayward had said something different to Judith, or why she would lie about it.

'Makes life easier all round,' said Hobbs. 'You lot should be happy about that.' He rang off.

The phone rang again. 'Morrison here. That call from Hobbs in Forensics, that was for me. It's my case. I'm the sergeant, you're the constable. That means it's my case that you might work on for me, got that?'

'Yes, sarge, said Sam. 'Sorry, sarge.'

The phone went dead and Sam looked at it before putting the receiver down again. His face was hot. For a while he flicked idly through his notes before he realised what he still needed to know. Where was Grayson? Sam asked around and finally tracked him down in the cafeteria. Harry's mouth was too full of bacon sandwich to allow for conversation, but he fished his notebook out of his inside pocket and handed it to Sam, who peered at the scribbled notes and asked, 'This is what Forensics told you?' Harry nodded, swallowed and took another slurp of tea before he took back his notebook and read the notes himself. 'Yes,' he said finally, 'the three cigarettes butts, two from the scene and one picked up behind Montgomery House were all the same brand, but it's not certain that they were smoked by the same person. The time of death was estimated between nine and midday.'

'Funny time of day to top yourself, isn't it?' Sam asked.

'Don't know whether people in that state worry about what time it is,' said Harry. 'What did Forensics say about the rope?'

'Nothing much. Ordinary rope, could have come from any garden shed. Wasn't new, so not bought for the purpose. Again, no real sign of premeditation.'

'And harder to track down?'

'Impossible, I'd say.'

'It's probably the most obvious,' said Harry. 'The guy killed himself for some reason, and we need to know more about him.'

'Morrison's said he's going up there to see Edwards and the matron about Harries's next of kin, and get the handwriting sample we need to check the note.'

'Morrison's going there? Too many cooks. We could go round in circles unless someone sorts out who's doing what.'

'What are you doing tonight?' Sam asked.

'Not a lot,' said Harry. 'I'll be off around six, all being well, down the Feathers for a pint or two. Why?'

'We need to get our act together if Morrison's going to start poking his nose in,' said Sam, 'and that means meeting outside the office. I'll see you in the Feathers, around half six. OK?'

Sam fell asleep for a while when he got home and Harry was on his second pint by the time Sam found him, sitting by a smouldering fire in the corner of the snug at the Feathers, reading the *Furness News*.

'What's up then?' he said. 'What's Morrison moaning about now?'

Sam grimaced. 'It's typical really. He gives me all the work to do but he wants it to look as if he's doing it all. Gets very snotty if anyone twigs that's he's not doing much. Like today, when the Forensics bloke rang. He asked to speak to Morrison about the lad's PM report that we've been waiting for. Morrison was actually on his way over there and I said something about it being my case. So the bloke tells me a few things, and next thing I know Morrison's on the phone shouting about it being his case. I can't trust him to do his job properly or let me do it.'

'Hold on, too much at once,' said Harry, putting down his pint and wiping his mouth on his sleeve. 'What did Forensics tell you?

'That the PM report confirmed the kid had drowned so that was that. Said that the report was pretty sketchy.'

'Could Hayward have missed something? He's off sick now, isn't he?'

Sam hesitated. 'Apparently he told someone that the kid didn't drown, that was no water in his lungs.'

'What?' said Harry, putting down his drink. 'When?'

'A few days before we got the report. That Pharaoh girl talked to Hayward in the pub and he told her.'

'So why did he change his mind?'

'God knows. When I saw him he insisted he'd been wrong and got mixed up. He was in a bad way, gave me a line about not trusting people, but I don't know what it was all about.'

'Where is he now?'

'Still in hospital apparently. Sounds as if Morrison has been asking to talk to him, from what they told me this morning. Must have left unfinished business all over the place, and Morrison hates that. Sometimes I think his only aim in life is to make it as easy as possible for himself, regardless of what really needs doing.'

'So Morrison gave you a hard time,' said Harry. 'What did you say?'

'Yes, sarge, sorry, sarge. What else could I say?'

'Very wise,' said Harry.

The two men drank in silence for a while.

'Let's say Hayward was telling the truth and the lad didn't drown,' said Harry. 'We know Harries had a history of fiddling with little boys.'

'Rumours,' said Sam.

'No smoke and all that,' Harry went on. 'With Harries dead we'll never know whether the kid died by accident, or Harries might have killed him deliberately to shut him up. Harries takes the kid, however he died, and dumps him somewhere out on the sands. He probably knew the kid was threatening to run away. The body could be washed up miles away, but instead it's sucked into that mudhole nearby.'

'Didn't take much to pick the lad up,' said Sam, remembering the small coffin being lifted from the hearse.

'Exactly,' said Harry. 'Harries was pretty puny by all accounts, but even he could manage that. Then afterwards he's so overcome with remorse, or guilt, or fear, whatever these pervy bastards feel, that he writes a note, sticks it in his pocket, takes a rope and something to stand on down to the wood and tops himself. Case closed. Monty House rebuilds its reputation and takes more care about who it employs. End of story.'

Sam put his glass down. 'But that's all speculation isn't it, and there's no medical evidence to back it up. All we've got is a PM report which is contradicted by something Hayward may or may not have said, and now denies.'

'And no body,' added Harry.

'And no body,' Sam repeated, remembering the curtains closing over the little coffin and the smoke that drifted over the crematorium.

'No wonder someone thinks we're useless,' said Sam. He told Harry the details of the appearance of the tape.

'So who sent it?' Harry asked.

'I reckon it must be the dead kid's older brother. He could have guessed what Harries was up to, threatened him, and wants to tell us that he got the result.'

'Why?' asked Harry.

'God knows. Ego, wants the credit for dealing with Harries. Wants to make us look useless. But why the tape, not a note or something? Where would he get a tape recorder from?'

'For God's sake, Nelly,' said Harry. 'Give over trying to prove how clever you are. You're as bad as he is. Leave it alone. And it's your round.'

When Sergeant Morrison appeared in the CID room the following morning, Sam wished he hadn't had that extra pint.

'This is getting out of hand,' Morrison began. 'We started off with a dead kid, and now we've got a suicide and a nutter sending anonymous messages to the press. Making us look like fools, Nelly, and I want it sorted. High-ups want it sorted, too. They lean on me and I lean on you, that's the way it works round here. So tell me what's going on, so at least I know who to blame. Come on, haven't got all day.'

Sam recounted the state of play as concisely as he could and for once Morrison seemed to be listening and asking reasonable questions, although Sam didn't have many of the answers. He ended up with a list of things to do: check for next of kin in Gateshead, find the older brother and get him to admit sending the tape, stop making life so complicated, and keep any information as far away from Bill Skelly and that bloody Pharaoh woman as possible.

'Grayson reckons it's pretty obvious what happened,' said Sam.

'Of course it's bloody obvious,' said Morrison. 'Open and shut. We wait till all the reports are finished off, then we can close the kid's case and get on with something else. Is this elder brother a problem?'

'Sounds as if he had something to do with Harries's death,' said Sam.

'Of course he did,' said Morrison. 'He threatened Harries and Harries topped himself. And Harries wrote a note. I checked the writing I got from Edwards, and it matches, so no mystery there. You're not saying this Lennon bloke actually strung him up, are you?'

'Well –' Sam began.

'Well, nothing. Harries topped himself. That's it. Finished. Just tie up the loose ends, constable,' said Morrison finally. He slapped both hands on his knees, and pulled himself out of the chair. He hovered briefly by his desk, skimmed through a pile of messages, dumped most of them in the bin, shoved others in his jacket pocket and slammed his office door on his way out.

Sam sighed. First Harry, now Morrison, and he could guess what the *Furness News* mob would be hinting at, even if they couldn't say it outright. Maybe they were all right. He picked up the phone to find the CID in Gateshead.

Chapter 14

'Judith?' said Pat O'Toole..

'Yes, I wondered if you would call me.'

'I saw the piece in last's night's *Star*, up here,' he said. 'No name, just that a body had been found in the woods, near Attercliff. Is it Harries?'

'Yes,' she said. 'It's him.'

'What I told you about him was just gossip. You understood that, didn't you?'

Judith heard the reproach in his voice. 'I told no one about it, until afterwards, when it looked as if someone had been threatening Harries, about the boy who died on the sands.'

'What have you said?' he asked.

She didn't want to lie to him. 'I told my boss that there'd been rumours before, that's all. They wanted to print stuff about Harries's history but I told them there were no real facts, just speculation. They agreed with me in the end.'

Pat was silent for a while. 'What happened to you, Judith?' he said. 'Jessie always told me what a lovely girl you were, and she was very fond of you. Is it the job? They are vultures, these people you work with, finding bodies and picking over them.'

'Only if the bodies smell,' said Judith, regretting it as soon as she'd said it.

'I asked you to be kind,' he said. 'Is that so hard?'

'In this job, yes it is.'

'Well, get out then, before it's too late. Leave it to the vultures. Don't become one of them yourself.'

'It's not as easy as that, Pat,' she replied. 'And I'm not like them. I made them re-consider, I did, truly. You might have been proud of me. It's not easy standing up to your boss.'

Pat sighed. 'So poor Harries took his own life?'

'That's what it looks like. Maybe he was afraid of rumours catching up with him again.'

'His poor mother,' said Pat. 'She must be heartbroken.'

'Where is his mother?' said Judith. 'The police are trying to find the next of kin. Do you know where she is?'

'I don't know much about him at all, but everyone has a mother, don't they? Alive or dead, I can feel sorry for the poor woman.'

Judith hesitated. 'Do you ever see people from when you were a priest, Pat, when you knew about Harries?'

'Occasionally,' he said. 'At funerals mainly, these days.'

'Could you do something for me? Could you ask around, see who knew him, ask about his family? He can't just disappear as if he never existed. The police will be looking I know, but you don't want to be bothered with them. Most of the police round here are either lazy or pompous, or both.'

She remembered something else she wanted to tell him. 'I'm going to check about what happened to the boys who were sent away,' she said.

'What boys?'

'The Barnardo's boys,' she said, 'who were sent overseas. I think the older brother of the boy who died may have been one of them.'

'And he came back?'

'Yes, I think so. Not sure, I'm still trying to find out more.'

'Haven't you got enough on your plate already? There can't be much of a story in that, can there?'

Judith didn't want to mention the tape, or her suspicions about who had sent it.

'I have to prove myself somehow,' she told him. 'I want a story with my name on it. Something that no one else has written about. This could be it.'

'Find another job, my dear,' he said. 'You're beginning to talk like they do. Don't let them suck you into their world.'

Judith thought about the old man on the other end of the line, and suddenly she was angry with him.

'I'm a grown woman now, Pat,' she said, 'not the little girl my grandmother talked about. Jessie made her own decisions about how to make her way in the world, and that's what I'm doing. You might not be proud of me but I think she would be. I'll try to keep it like that, so don't worry about me. 'Bye, Pat.'

She put the phone down and sat back, wondering what to do next. She had to do something.

The woman who looked after the *Furness News* archives worked on the next floor down from the newsroom, at a tiny desk surrounded by piles of shelves and cupboards.

'Do you have a filing system?' Judith asked, daunted by the amount of paper that confronted her.

Miss Hobson looked at her witheringly. 'It's an archive, dear,' she said, 'not just a random collection of papers. Of course I have a system. What do you want to find? Or are you the errand girl for one of the grumpy old chaps up there?'

Judith smiled. 'They're not all grumpy and old,' she said. 'Mr

Thornhill's quite young and he's been very helpful to me just recently. Or at least his wife has.'

'Irene Thornhill,' said Miss Hobson. 'Quite a case, isn't she? Still wearing those high shoes and Chanel?'

'Oh yes,' said Judith. 'And she's trying to get me to do the same. Bit of an uphill battle there.'

'Well, I'm glad they're looking after you,' said Miss Hobson. 'I was very pleased to get out into my little dusty heaven down here where no one bothers me. That's why I've got a good system, because no one wants me to use it!'

Judith explained that that she was looking for was anything about Barnardo's boys being sent overseas, after the war. 'Most likely to Canada,' she added, 'but possibly Australia, or New Zealand.'

'Can I ask why?' said Miss Hobson.

'Just a story,' Judith replied. 'A feature, not news.' It was a lie, but Miss Hobson didn't need to know any more.

'Fine,' said Miss Hobson. 'I'll look into it and get back to you, as soon as I find anything.'

Judith had only just got back from lunch at Bruciani's with something by the Hollies running in her head when the internal phone rang.

'Found a few pictures,' said Miss Hobson. 'Do you want to come down or shall I send them up?'

Within a few minutes Judith was looking through images of the bright young faces and bare knees of boys, who stood stiffly or waved at the camera. Underneath, the captions told of excited young migrants heading for a new life working on farms in far-flung corners of the old Empire. The language was corny and contrived, like old newsreel commentary. How things have changed, thought Judith. She borrowed a magnifying glass and squinted at the blurred faces of the boys, but nothing seemed familiar about any of them. She was hoping that the older brother, Anthony, might have looked like Steven when he was the same age, but the image of Steven Stringer that Judith carried in her head was that of a corpse, with eyes closed and face streaked with mud, lying on a stretcher in the back of an ambulance.

She closed her own eyes to block out the boy's face. Maybe Pat was right. It was the death of that abandoned child that had started this whole business off and he seemed to have been forgotten, swept aside. Desmond Harries had been caught up in it and he was dead, too. Two victims, and the mood in the newsroom was almost gleeful. And she was part of it, no matter how she tried to excuse herself. Doing this job was a choice, and staying in it until it corrupted her was a choice, too. Maybe writing about boys in care and what happens to them was just about making the job seem worthwhile, about redeeming herself.

In one of the photographs she noticed a woman standing at the end of a row, wearing a smart coat with a belt and a cap on her head, like a uniform of some kind. The caption said that this was a Mrs Nora Amblethorpe from Barrow Children's Department who would accompany the boys on the trip to Montreal in 1954. Fifteen years before. Worth a shot. Judith finished her notes, thanked Miss Hobson and headed back to use the phone.

When she got back to the newsroom Hattie called across to her. 'There was a phone call for you a minute ago, a young woman. She was trying to reverse the charges. I told her not to be so cheeky and she rang off. Said her name was Donna. What a nerve.'

Judith flicked back through her notebook to find the number she wanted and dialled it, fumbling the numbers in haste and having to start again. A man's voice answered. Judith introduced herself. 'Was Donna trying to reach me a minute ago?' she asked. 'Is she still there?' A moment later, a quiet voice said, 'Is that you, miss?'

'Donna,' said Judith, 'thanks for calling me. I forgot to tell my office about reversing the charges. Are you all right?'

'He'd kill me if he knew I were talking to you, miss,' said Donna. 'But I don't want to lose Anthony like I lost Stevie. They're family.'

'Do you know where Anthony is now, Donna? The police think he may be over this side of the bay, in Barrow, trying to find out what happened to Stevie.'

'What will 'appen to 'im, miss?'

'Nothing, I'm sure,' Judith lied. 'They just need to ask him some questions.'

'He won't want that, miss. Never 'ad a good word for the police, got that from 'is dad.'

'Do you know where he was for all those years when you didn't see him?'

Silence. 'Honest, miss, I thought he were inside, prison. He'd be all right in care, like, but then 'e'd 'ave to come out, and then, well, I thought 'e'd end up in the nick.'

'I think he may have been overseas somewhere, in Canada or Australia. He might have done OK for himself and come back to see you all. Then he found out about Stevie and he wanted to know what happened, like any family would.'

'Really? Our Anthony, overseas?'

'On a farm or something, yes,' said Judith. 'And if that's true, it would make a wonderful story for my paper. I'd love to talk to him about it.'

'In the paper! None of our lot's ever been in the paper, except for being in trouble, court stuff.'

'This wouldn't be like that, Donna, I swear. Your Anthony could tell his story, show what he's made of his life. But I need to talk to him. Do you know where he is?'

Donna hesitated. 'He did try and find me, like you did, to see I was all right. I was off ill. He told them he'd try again, but he 'asn't done, not yet.'

'When he does,' said Judith, 'could you tell him about the story I want to write? See what he says. There'd be something in it for him, too. Might even make the big papers, the nationals. Pictures, everything.'

'I'll tell 'im, miss,' said Donna. 'Gotta go.'

'Wait,' said Judith, but it was too late. The phone buzzed. 'Hattie,' Judith called across the room. 'If that young woman ever rings again and reverses the charge, take the call and her number, will you?'

'You mean we pay?' said Hattie. 'Mr Thornhill won't like that.'

'He doesn't haven't to know, does he?'

There was no response.

One more phone call, before Judith would feel perfectly justified in leaving early and doing some shopping on the way home. She'd been warned off going to Montgomery House, and anyway the boys there had been told not to talk to her. Sam Sherlock had cut her out of anything interesting. If she could keep the Barnardo's project going it could get her all the points she needed with Thornhill.

Barrow Children's Department had no one called Mrs Nora Amblethorpe, but after being passed from one person to the next Judith eventually found someone who knew where she was living in her retirement. It didn't take Judith more than twenty minutes on the scooter to cross the bridge onto Walney and follow the road across to Biggar Bank on the far side, looking out over the Irish Sea. Mrs Amblethorpe and her husband, both retired, seemed delighted to have some interruption to their afternoon. Nora remembered the story in the paper and found her own cutting of it in the bureau with only a few minutes' search.

'That was a wonderful trip for me,' she said. 'First time on a big ship like that. No one from Barnardo's could go, so they asked for one of us. Bill went to his mother's, didn't you, dear?'

Bill Amblethorpe rolled his eyes. 'She did that deliberately so I'd appreciate her cooking more after a week or two with my mam,' he said.

'And it worked,' said his wife. 'And the boys were so excited. So young, some of them. One of them told me his mam had said she didn't want him back so he said he would go. "What's to lose?" he said to me. Just a child really, but it was a fresh start for him and the others.'

'Who picked them up?'

'Someone like me, a social worker,' she said. 'Nice enough man, said he had homes for all of them, mostly on farms out west. He was going to take them on the train.'

'What if it didn't work out, Nora?' asked Judith.

Nora shrugged. 'No idea,' she said. 'It was up to the lads to make it work, wasn't it? It was their last chance.'

Judith rode back the long way round, watching the wading birds dabbling in the shallows on the shoreward side of Walney Island. The shipyard workers were coming out, so she parked her scooter and did some shopping while the busy roads quietened down a little. Since she'd been trying to keep the flat tidy and take more care of it, she'd been happy to get home of an evening instead of heading to the pub or Bruciani's. She hadn't seen Elspeth for a while, but Sam's presence there made it more difficult for all of them. Maybe if she and Elspeth planned a visit ahead of time, Sam could make sure he was out and spare them both all the embarrassment of bumping into him there.

By the time she parked the scooter in the back yard of her digs and walked back down the alley to the front door it was getting dark. She glanced down the road while she was looking for her key and saw a light flicker as someone standing further down lit a cigarette. She put down her bag and stepped slowly out onto the street to get a better view. The smoking man turned towards her. She couldn't see his face but the long coat and the hat made her step back to the pavement and then run towards him. But it was too far. By the time she'd reached the end of the street and turned the corner there was no sign of him.

Back in the house she leaned against the wall inside the front door to get her breath back before picking up the pay phone and dialling Elspeth's number.

'Is Sam there?' she asked.

'You all right Judith? Have you been running?'

'I'm fine, is he there?'

'No he's not back yet.'

'When he comes in, could you tell him something from me. Tell him that I've seen Anthony again, in the street by my house. I ran but I lost him. Can you tell him that?'

'Who's Anthony?' asked Elspeth.

'He'll know. He asked me to tell him if I saw him, so I have. That's all, thanks.'

She lay on her bed and looked at the damp spot on the ceiling above her head. She'd had to reassure Elspeth more than once that she was OK, but she didn't want to tell her any more. This wasn't a cry for help or an admission that she was afraid. It was just a fact. If the man was Anthony, he knew where she lived and he was watching her comings and goings, and she didn't know why. And if the same man had made that tape, he expected her to do something, not just weave some sob story about kids being sent overseas.

She thought again about the voice on the tape. It was probably distorted, either by the tape machine or deliberately, but she knew it could tell them more. There was an accent, but she couldn't pin it down. Suddenly she thought of Vince. Since his accident he seemed able to hear things that no one else even noticed. If he could hear that tape, he could tell them something about the voice and the person behind it, the same person who'd been looking for his little brother, the same person who could have threatened Harries, and might even have helped him die. Judith got up and went back to the phone in the hallway.

CHAPTER 15

'Is she out?' Judith asked Vince when he opened the front door.

'Regular as clockwork,' said Vince. 'She and Granny Violet go to the Catholic ladies' knitting circle or whatever it is, up at Kells every Friday afternoon. For two blessed hours I have the house to myself. I can play the music loud, that kind of stuff. Love it.'

He led the way into the sitting room where afternoon light flooded in.

'Any change?' she asked.

He shrugged. 'Don't think so. Hard to tell really. Docs still don't really know what's going on. One of them said that if I could crack my head again like I did the first time it might come back again. Not sure whether that was good news or bad news. Mum was really cross.' He sat down and turned towards her. 'Anyway, what was all the mystery on the phone? I had to tell her it was something about Dad's birthday to stop her asking questions.'

Judith leaned forward and put her hand on his arm to hold his attention. 'I want you to listen to a tape someone sent us at work. Did you manage to find our old tape recorder? The one from work was so heavy I didn't want to bring it unless

I had to.'

'It was under my bed,' said Vince. 'Haven't used it for a bit, but it seems to be working OK. Don't tell me, we're going to play *Name That Tune* just like the good old days.'

'No,' she said. 'Nothing like that. Stay here, it's going to take me a while to set it up.'

'I can do it,' he said.

Judith gave him the tape and watched in amazement as he turned it round in his long fingers, threaded the tape into the various slots and round the various wheels and felt along the row of knobs for the one he wanted. 'They all feel a bit different,' he said. 'Does it look right?'

Judith leaned over to check. 'Looks OK.'

'And is this the "play" button?'

'Right.'

'Now before we listen to whatever it is, tell me what this is for. You've come all the way up here for the second time in a couple of weeks, and you didn't want to have to tell Mum. What's going on?'

Judith told Vince an edited version of the events. She said that a relative of the boy who'd been found dead claimed the culprits weren't being tracked down fast enough and had sent this tape to the newsroom to tell them to do what the police weren't doing.

'Why didn't he just go to the police?' asked Vince.

'Must be some reason. Probably afraid of being picked up for something he's done, so he's going the long way round, through us.'

'Come on then,' said Vince, his finger leaning on the 'play' button. He pressed it down and the two of them listened, then rewound and listened again.

'What do you want me to say?' asked Vince.

'Tell me anything you can hear in that man's voice. It is a man, isn't it.'

'Oh yes,' said Vince. 'He's angry. Frustrated. Sort of spitting out the words, as if he was really wanting to shout, or get hold of someone.'

'Violent?'

'Could be, if he's angry enough. Who's "the girl with the hair"? Is that you? I hope he doesn't know where you live.'

Judith said nothing to that, glad that Vince couldn't see her face clearly. 'What about the accent?' she said.

'It's a funny one, isn't it. Not from round here, although, bits of it sound like Lancashire. Play it one more time.'

'Is it North American?' said Judith. 'There's a chance this person spent some time there.' Vince shook his head. 'Not like any American accent I know, and you hear them on the TV enough these days... Wait a minute. One more time.'

Vince listened attentively. 'I think it's Australian,' he said, 'with bits of Lancashire, or the other way round. Maybe someone born here who went there. It's not just the individual words, it's the way they go up and down. You've heard Rod Laver talking at Wimbledon. Somewhere between him and Al Read.'

Judith listened again. 'You're right,' she said. 'So he's an angry man who was brought up in Lancashire and then went to Australia, and now he's come back.'

Vince leaned forward. 'And he's looking for someone to blame. If I were you I'd keep out of his way.'

'That's the problem,' said Judith. 'We're actually trying to find him.'

'You and whose army? You're not doing some super heroine act are you? Judith Pharaoh, Ace Reporter, tracks down Ozzie madman. Leave it alone, I say. Let some big brawny policeman handle it.'

Judith thought of Sam and laughed. She checked her watch. 'What time's Mum due back?'

'Never before four,' he said.

'Can I use the phone?'

'Carry on,' he said. 'I don't pay the bill.'

Judith called the familiar number in Roose, where Elspeth had just got in from school. 'I gave him your message,' she said. 'He said he'd try to call you at work today. He seemed cross about it, for some reason. What's going on?'

'Do you have his number? I haven't got it on me.'

Judith wrote down the number, checked the time again and rang it, while Vince sat on the bottom stair, listening and intrigued.

'Sam? It's Judith Pharaoh. Yes I know. I've been out since lunchtime. I think I've pinned down the accent of the man on the tape, it's Australian.' She listened for a few moments. 'No, he's not an expert, he's my brother, but he has a knack for voices, and…' Vince couldn't see his sister roll her eyes. 'I know it wouldn't stand up in court but it doesn't have to, does it? It might make it easier to track down where Anthony's been the past so many years. His sister assumed he'd been in jail… No, not in Australia, over here. Look, are you interested or not? … I've seen him twice near my flat, but when I try to get closer he disappears. I don't know how he knows where I live… Why, do you think he's dangerous?'

She listened for longer this time. 'Why haven't you told me all this before? Yes I could come to Elspeth's but I thought you wanted me to leave you alone… When? Tonight? … Yes, I suppose so. Any chance of having supper?'

Vince mimed the hands of the clock going round. Judith rang off, kissed her brother, let herself out of the house and went the long way round back to the station to avoid bumping into her mother.

She walked from the station at Roose and it was after six by the time she got to Elspeth's. Sam opened the door, pulled her into the house and then stepped out to the gate to look up and down the road.

'Were you followed?' he said.

Judith laughed. 'I don't think so. You can't be serious about Anthony having a go at me, surely. I just think he knows I'm working on the story and wants to know what I'm finding out.'

Elspeth turned from the cooker. 'What are you two on about now? Don't spoil supper, and not in front of Tommy.'

So it was after supper, with Tommy in bed and Elspeth reading him a story, before Sam and Judith could continue their conversation.

'We think Anthony Lennon may have murdered Harries,' said Sam, keeping his voice low. 'That's why you need to be careful. If he thinks you, or me come to that, might be on to him, we could be next.'

'But Harries hanged himself,' said Judith, 'didn't he?'

'That's what it looked like, and there was a note in his pocket that we think he wrote himself, but that could have been under duress, you know, someone made him write it. The autopsy report came back but it was inconclusive. He could have been choked by someone and then strung up to make it look like a suicide. We still don't know enough to satisfy a coroner. Don't make me explain everything. Just trust me will you? It's possible someone murdered Harries, and that could have been Anthony Lennon, and now he's hanging around outside your house. Of course I'm worried about it. And Morrison is, too.'

'You told Morrison?'

'Of course I did. He's my boss. The last thing any of us want is being accused of putting you in danger, or not doing enough to protect you.'

Judith sat back, deflated, thinking. 'What are you going to do?'

'Not sure yet. We're trying to track him down, obviously. Looks like he stole the tape recorder from a secondhand shop in town. Place was such a tip to start with it took the owner a while to realise that anything had been taken.'

'But why go to all that trouble?' asked Judith. 'He could have written a note, or come to see you.'

'Not if he's already in trouble with the police, here or wherever he comes from. What if he hasn't got the right papers? False passport or something. If he came in, we'd probably check. What if he can't write?'

'Not write? Who can't write these days?'

'Lots of people,' said Sam. 'I meet them all the time. They cover it up, but they never learned as children and then it's too late. If you're right about Anthony, what chance did he have? If he was shipped off to Australia or wherever it was to work, that was the end of his schooling.'

'So the tape was the only way he had?'

'Looks like it.'

'It still doesn't make sense,' said Judith. 'If he killed Harries, or even if he goaded him into hanging himself, why would he draw attention to himself like this?'

'Arrogance,' said Sam. 'See why I'm worried about him following you around? God knows what he's capable of with a woman.'

'I still don't think he wants to harm me,' Judith said after she'd thought about it for a few minutes. She cleared plates from the table and took them over to the sink. 'Maybe he's just looking for information about how Stevie died. That's what he wants, not me.'

'What's the matter with you?' Sam cried out, and then lowered his voice when Judith turned and put a finger to her lips to quieten him. 'Think about it. He wants something you have, and hasn't any scruples abut how to get it. If he didn't get what he wanted from Harries, then he'll be after you next.'

'Why not come after you?' said Judith.

'Because we're the police and you're not. And he must know by now that you're a pushy, nosey reporter who's poking around in matters that you should have left us to get on with.'

As his voice rose again, Elspeth came down the stairs and into the kitchen. She was not happy. 'Look you two, I don't mind cooking for you both, but this is our home, me and Tommy, and I don't want it messed around by you two shouting at each other. If you want to talk, fine, but if you want to argue, go and do it somewhere else.'

Sam picked up his jacket from the back of the chair. 'I'm taking Judith home,' he said. Judith was about to protest but the look on Elspeth's face told her it was time to leave.

It was foggy outside and the two of them walked in silence through streets that seemed ethereal as the fog turned the orange street light into swirling strands and made their footsteps echo. 'I feel as if I've wasted the whole day,' she said, 'and now I'm being frogmarched back to my own place. You couldn't care less about Lennon being Australian, could you?'

'Frankly, Judith, I wouldn't care if he came from Mars. It makes no difference to anything about this case, and you probably have wasted the whole day, and made more work for us, too.'

She stopped. 'How come?'

'You've made yourself vulnerable, and now we'll have to protect you. If you'd just left things alone, I wouldn't have to frogmarch you home, as you put it.'

'It's my job, just like you have yours. I was given a story, and told to get on with it, so I did.'

'Why did they give you the story, instead of Skelly?'

'To give me a chance, maybe?' said Judith, thinking of the encouragement she'd had from Irene Thornhill.

'Or because there was no one else,' said Sam.

They walked the rest of the way in silence. Before they turned into Cannon Street Sam held Judith back and peered down the street into the gloom. 'Just checking,' he said. 'No one here, but I can only see halfway down.'

When they reached Judith's door, she pulled her keys from her bag and turned to face him. 'Thank you for walking me home, constable,' she said, with as much irony as she could muster. 'I'm sure I can manage to climb the staircase to my own front door without assistance.'

Sam said nothing, still looking around, up and down the street. 'No lights on downstairs,' he said. 'The other tenant must be out.'

'The downstairs flat's empty,' said Judith. 'I'm all on my own in the house. Poor me. Do you want to come in and look under my bed, just in case?'

Sam said nothing, but he stayed where he was. 'You go in,' he said. 'I'll wait till you turn the upstairs lights on.'

Judith turned away without another word, unlocked the front door and closed it, pushed the light switch and climbed the stairs with an extra hard thump so that Sam could hear. At the top of the stairs, she hesitated. The door to her flat was slightly ajar. She pushed it and the door swung open. She waited. The light switch timer clicked off and there was darkness. Her heart thumped. She listened for the slightest noise, but there was none. Judith turned and ran down the stairs. Sam was still standing in the street when she opened the front door.

'Sam,' she said. 'There's something...'

He pushed past her and up the stairs. In the darkness she fumbled for the light and heard his voice above.

'Police!' he shouted. 'Come out!'

There was no sound. Light flooded the tiny hall and stairs as she found the switch and followed him, breathing hard, seeing light from above now as Sam found the next switch. At the open door of her flat she caught her breath. To her left was the tiny kitchen, where broken crockery spilled across the floor. Smashed eggs. Something orange oozed over them. 'My orange juice,' she whispered. Cupboard doors were open, one of them pulled off its hinges. Sam appeared at the door of her bedroom. His face was pale.

'Don't come in here,' he said. She pushed past him. The bed was upturned, the mattress slashed. A mess of clothes on the floor, ripped and soiled. The smell of urine. Sam was trying to turn her away, to push her out of the room but she caught sight of the wall. A stick figure with breasts and hair sticking out from the head on either side.

Judith felt Sam's arm round her shoulders as he pushed her out of the room. Her eyes were wet and smarting and her head thumped.

'Come on,' he said. 'Downstairs.'

Judith sat down on the bottom step. Sam pulled his radio from his pocket and stood outside to get a better signal. She heard him give the address and talk for a while before he came back and sat on the step beside her as she sobbed.

'More police are coming,' he said. 'We'll find him, whoever did this.'

'All my things,' Judith whispered. 'It was so tidy.'

'Don't worry,' he said, putting his arm back round her shoulders. 'We'll find you somewhere to stay. It's only stuff, after all. You're all right, that's the main thing.'

They sat for a while, the light from the street and the fog seeping through the open door. When the first car arrived, Judith was led to sit in the back while two men in uniforms went with Sam back up the stairs. She saw the lights go on behind curtains that she had drawn back that morning.

'My scooter,' she cried, suddenly, remembering. She tried to open the car door but it was locked. She squeezed herself over the back seat into the front, catching her knee on the handbrake before she pushed the passenger door open and fell out onto the pavement. Her knee throbbed but she limped to the alley that ran between the houses, through a wooden door halfway down into the back yard and there it was, shining dark red in the shadow of the back wall. Judith leaned over the machine, felt its smooth hardness under her fingers, and cried.

'Judith!' a man's voice shouted. She heard the sound of running footsteps and the squawk of the radio. 'I'm here,' she said, but her voice croaked. She got to her feet and pushed herself back along the narrow passage. A man in uniform stood at the end of the alley and shone his torch into her eyes. The light went away and she heard him shout, 'She's here.' He pulled her arm and she stumbled onto the pavement. Sam picked her up. 'My scooter,' she whispered. 'It's still there.'

Over her head, the three policemen looked at each other.

Twenty minutes later, Judith sipped her tea at Elspeth's kitchen table. She could hear Sam and Elspeth talking in the other room but not much of what they were saying. Their voices were low and urgent. Sam came back into the kitchen and sat beside her at the table, his head close to hers. 'We've secured the flat, Judith, and the team will go in tomorrow and see what we can find about who did this.'

'What about my things?' she said, sniffing. He handed her a handkerchief.

'Some of them will be fine, I'm sure,' he said. 'Have you got insurance?'

She nodded. 'Dad paid it for me.'

'So when we've finished in there we can make a list of all the stuff that will need replacing, and that'll be all looked after.'

'But where can I sleep?'

'You can have my room here tonight, I'll sleep on the sofa in the other room.'

'No,' she said.

'Yes,' said Elspeth. 'It'll feel different in the morning and we'll work out what to do. It'll be fine Judith, don't worry.'

'Don't tell my mum,' she said. 'She'll make me go home.'

'That might be for the best,' said Sam. 'Just until we get things back to normal.'

'No,' said Judith, again. She tried to get up.

Elspeth pushed Sam away and put both arms around her friend. 'Tomorrow,' she said. 'We'll work it out. You've had a shock, Judith, and you need to sleep. Finish your tea. Sam's going back to the station now, to organise what they'll do tomorrow. We have to let him do his job.'

In the unfamiliar bed, her mind full of images of broken, precious things, Judith Pharaoh cried herself to sleep for the second time in her adult life.

CHAPTER 16

Sam left the two women in the house and went back to the CID room at the police station. He was angry, with Judith for getting herself into this mess, with himself for not seeing it coming, and with the bloody man who'd wrecked the flat. He must have been looking for something, but why trash the place like that? Why piss all over her things? Judith was a nuisance, but not a threat to anyone. She was interested in the bloke and his miserable life in Australia or wherever he'd been sent. She was going to write a story about him and others like him, and now this.

He wrote up his notes into a report of the incident and left it on Morrison's desk. There would be questions about what he was doing walking Judith home at that time of night but he didn't care. At least he'd tried to keep out of her way, not going off drinking with the press guys like so many of his colleagues did. Before they left the ruined flat he'd had a good look, without disturbing anything so that the scene-of-crime team could get the photos they needed in the morning. The bedroom was the worst. The kitchen was a mess but at least no one had pissed in there. In the tiny living room all the drawers of the old desk had been pulled out and their contents dumped on the floor. It looked as if someone had picked their way through them, looking for something, but there was no way of telling if anything had been taken. The cushion of the old red armchair was ripped by something sharp, the foam spilling out like white fat from an open wound. There were human faeces on the carpet, ground in and smeared across whatever was on the floor. He must have been there for a while, to do so much damage. No one downstairs to hear anything, but next door? Sam made a list of the enquiries that would begin as soon as it was light and the neighbours were stirring. He left a message for the scene-of-crime team and a copy of his report with the duty sergeant and walked back to Elspeth's house, letting himself in as quietly as he could. Elspeth had made up a bed for him on the sofa. It was past midnight and the house was mercifully quiet.

The next morning he was woken by Tommy carrying a cup of tea with exaggerated care while Elspeth held open the door for him. Sam smiled at the boy and thanked him before Elspeth ushered him back to the kitchen table to finish his breakfast. It was after eight. Sam pulled on his trousers and took his tea into the kitchen.

'Is she up?' he asked. Elspeth shook her head. 'I'm going to leave her as long as I can,' she said. 'We'll need to think about where she can stay.'

'I could move out for a while,' said Sam.

'You'll do no such thing,' said his sister. 'This is your home, supported by your money and you'll stay where you are. God knows your job is hard enough without sleeping on sofas. If it comes to it, Judith has a home to go to and it sounds as if her mam would be happy to have her back.'

Sam smiled. 'Don't think that's going to happen,' he said. 'Judith's stubborn. And she wants that job.'

'Well the people at the *Furness News* will have to deal with it,' said Elspeth. 'If they want her to carry on working, they'll have to help her find a place so she can. That's what a good employer should do.'

'We'll see,' said Sam.

Tommy came back into the kitchen in his football kit holding his boots in his hand and Sam helped him tie the laces. 'I'll take him to the field,' he said. 'Ten minutes while I get washed and shaved. It's on my way. OK?'

Elspeth smiled. 'Yes,' she said.

The front door had just closed behind Sam and Tommy when Judith came slowly down the stairs.

'I need to phone in,' she said. 'I'm on till noon today and I'll be late.'

'I'll do it,' said Elspeth. 'I'll tell them what happened and you're taking time off to sort things out.'

Judith shook her head. 'No, don't say that. Just tell them I'm not well. I need to think about what to do. If they know about the flat they'll be all over me, asking questions, telling me I should go home to my dad, treating me like a kid.'

'You'll have to tell them in the end.'

'But not yet.'

Elspeth shrugged. 'Up to you,' she said. 'Do you want some breakfast?'

Judith felt ravenous. As she ate her toast, she heard Elspeth on the phone.

'She came to dinner last night here but then she started being unwell, and it's gone on all night. She slept in the end but she's not fit for work... Yes, Monday, she should be OK by then, I'll get her to ring you... OK.'

Elspeth returned to the kitchen. 'I expect you heard. Someone called Hattie? She said she'd tell the boss.'

'That should give them something to laugh about,' said

Judith. 'And Ed Cunningham probably thinks you're my secret lesbian lover.'

Elspeth laughed. 'Is that what he thinks?'

'Makes him feel better about me rejecting his advances,' said Judith, laughing despite herself. 'What am I going to do Elspeth? I can't tell my dad. He'll be knocking on the door before we can turn round, to whisk his little girl home to St Bees. I couldn't bear it.'

'Are you sure? It would be the most sensible thing to do.'

'I hate sensible,' said Judith.

'We just don't have room here,' said Elspeth, 'and I can't turn Sam out of the house after he's been so generous to us. It's his home.'

'I know that,' said Judith. 'It was very kind of you to put me up last night but I know I need somewhere else. Maybe Hattie would know somewhere. She seems to know everything about everybody. I'll have to tell them about the flat, but maybe later.' She reached for another piece of toast. 'How long do you think it'll take the police to do what they have to do?'

'From what Sam was saying, they'll have been there first thing this morning, to take photos, fingerprints, check with the neighbours. Probably won't take them more than a couple of hours. Tommy can go to play with his friend down the street and we'll go and clear up, find out what you'll need to claim on the insurance.'

'You'll help me with that?'

'Of course I will. What are friends for?'

Judith put down her toast. Tears pricked her eyes but she wiped them away.

❖ ❖ ❖

Later in the morning, the inevitable return to the flat couldn't be delayed any longer. Judith felt sick as she climbed the stairs. In the pale grey light of day the devastated rooms looked even more bleak than before. As they began to clear up the mess the owner of the house, alerted by the police, arrived, looked around in disgust and left, muttering about tenants being more trouble than they were worth, and suggesting to Judith that she find another place to live.

He rolled down the window of the van before he drove away. 'Should've sold the bloody place when the wife buggered off. Taken the money and gone to Spain. At least it's sunny down there, not like this dump.'

'Can he put me out?' Judith asked Elspeth.

'I don't think so, but you'd better check. What's the point in getting your place back to normal if he sells the house and you have to go?'

Judith felt as if her life was spiralling down into a hole. She had to sit down for a while in the wreckage of her flat and think about a future that seemed much less certain than before. She didn't know that the worst insults left by the flat wrecker had been removed by the police. As it was, they put on their Marigold gloves and Judith tried hard not to recognise the fragments of her life as they were shovelled, literally, into the rubbish bags. When the rubbish was cleared away, they mopped and scrubbed until their backs ached. Judith salvaged some clothes that were messy but not dirty and together they carried them in a suitcase back to Elspeth's. The washing machine was humming and Judith was making a list of items to be replaced, and wondering where she would sleep that night when the phone rang. Elspeth answered it, then turned to Judith. 'It's for you,' she said, passing the receiver in her cupped hand. 'Alan someone?'

'Judith?' said Alan Thornhill. 'It's taken me a while to track you down. Once a journo always a journo, eh? Hear you've had some trouble at the flat.'

'How did you know?'

'It was in the overnight incident book at the police station, the one you check every morning. Quite a shock when Andrew came back with his notes and there was your name. Then Hattie said someone phoned in for you, but we didn't know where you were. More phone calls, and eventually that new young CID chap gave us this number. We've been ringing all afternoon. Are you OK? Must've been a shock.'

'It was,' said Judith. 'I asked my friend to say I was sick, sorry.'

'Didn't want us asking a lot of questions?'

'Something like that,' said Judith. 'I've not been thinking very straight.'

'Not surprised,' said Thornhill. 'Nasty business. Did they make a mess?'

'Oh yes,' said Judith. 'We've been there since the police finished, clearing up, scrubbing.' She didn't want to tell Thornhill about the smell.

'Well there's someone here who wants to talk to you,' said Thornhill. There was a pause and then another voice came on the line.

'Judith, you poor girl.' They were the clear crisp tones of Irene Thornhill. 'What a thing to happen. It must have been dreadful for you. So where are you now?'

'In Roose, at a friend's house. She put me up last night.'

'Well that was very kind of her I'm sure, but we have a ridiculously huge house with just the two of us rattling around in it, and there's plenty of space. You can stay as long as you like.'

Judith took a minute to take in what Irene had said.

'Stay with you? Are you sure?'

'Of course. It would be such fun to have another woman in the house, and Alan is your employer, after all. He needs you at work. He thought you might want to leave Barrow and go back home – St Bees isn't it?'

'Yes,' said Judith. Irene obviously had a good memory.

'Well you can't come to work in Barrow every day from there, can you?'

'But –' Judith said. Things were happening too fast.

'But nothing, dear, it's all settled. Have you got some clothes, or will you need to go shopping?'

'They're in the washing machine,' she said.

'Splendid,' said Irene. 'We have a big dryer here so load them into a bag when they're done and we'll finish them off here. Might be some things of mine you could borrow if you need to. You know me and shopping.' Her laugh tinkled down the phone.

'There's my scooter. It's in the back yard of the house.'

'No problem. I'll arrange for someone with a van to come and pick it up.'

Two hours later the curtains in Elspeth's neighbours' houses twitched. Daimler cars weren't seen in Roose too often, and Irene's confident voice could be clearly heard once the TVs had been turned down. Judith had never been in such a large car. The suitcase and the bag of wet washing were on the back seat and Judith sat beside Irene, feeling like a film star going on holiday.

'This is so good of you,' she said, as the Daimler pulled away down Cannon Street. 'I don't know what to say.'

'Don't thank me, dear,' said her new landlady. 'It was the obvious answer right from the start. Alan knew that as soon I suggested it to him.'

'I don't even know where you live,' said Judith, as the car

turned off Abbey Road on a side road that Judith didn't recognise.

'We're just far enough out of town, if you know what I mean,' said Irene. 'On that little scooter of yours it'll take no time at all. Most people just keep going round by the coast don't they, but we live up on the hills in the middle of the peninsular, higher up. Lovely old village close by, and a view right round, out to the Irish Sea, and across to Blackpool Tower. In the winter on clear nights we can see the glow from the illuminations, but it takes hours to get there by car. There was a steamer across from Barrow in the old days, did you know?'

Judith did know, but Irene was talking so much that she wasn't sure how to interrupt. Irene looked across at her. 'I'm prattling aren't I?' she said. 'Really I'm so excited about having someone to stay. Life can get so dull these days. It'll be such fun.'

Judith began to wonder how long Irene expected her to stay. 'It's just until I can get the flat properly cleared and cleaned and get the insurance money,' she said.

'Oh yes, I know,' said Irene, 'You'll want to go back to your independent life, but it's bound to be a few weeks, isn't it.'

A few weeks? Judith hoped she was wrong about that. Irene was unlike anyone else Judith knew and she wasn't sure how to talk to her. She was the boss's wife, so she couldn't be a real friend, but there was something so lively and disarming about her. And so generous. Judith chided herself for being ungrateful, and she wondered what kind of house Irene was taking her to.

Bay View, as announced by the sign, was a massive house, bigger than Judith had anticipated, lying in its own grounds, at the end of a long drive up from the road. It stood on a low rise, flanked by what looked like an orchard on its south side, the small bare trees quite close together. Beyond that, a few houses straggled down the road towards the church and the rest of the village. Even in the fading light there was a wonderful view, now that a breeze from the northwest had cleared away the fog of the past few days. Irene parked the Daimler by the front door and helped Judith with the bag of wet washing and the suitcase.

'We'd better wash it all again, don't you think?' said Irene, dragging the heavy bag behind her across the tiled hallway. 'The utility room opens on to the back of the house, but now we're here I'll show you where it is and we can get this load started.'

Irene opened a door into what she called the utility room that looked to Judith about as big as her living room in the flat. A range of matching equipment faced them on the opposite wall. 'Ironing too,' said Irene. 'Look at this!' She pulled on what appeared to be a high cupboard and the door slid forward to reveal the ironing board and the iron perched above it on a shelf. 'Natty, isn't it!' she said. 'Edna says it's the best thing about this house. Edna's our housekeeper, by the way. She lives in the village and comes in every day, except Sunday of course. And she gets upset if there's nothing for her to do, so just drop your clothes in the basket in your room, dear, and they'll be back, washed and ironed when you get home from work. She's a treasure. She won't be in till Monday, so we'll put this lot on tonight just so you have something to wear tomorrow.' Irene looked Judith up and down. 'Or maybe you could borrow something of mine, just until Edna finishes everything off. What do you think? We'll have a look later. Leave your suitcase in the hall, dear. Alan will deal with that when he comes back from whatever meeting he has tonight. I lose track. He's out such a lot, meetings, heaven knows what.'

Judith had said almost nothing since she left Elspeth's and hoped that the flow of words would soon stop. It crossed her mind that Irene might be as nervous about Judith's arrival as Judith was to be here, in such exotic surroundings. She followed Irene through into a large living room that looked out to the west and the dark evening sky. Irene kicked off her shoes and plumped up the cushions on the sofa. 'You sit down there, Judith dear. You've had a pretty dreadful day or two, haven't you? Now, a drink … there's gin, vodka, wine, sherry, brandy, what would you like?'

Judith had to think for a moment. 'If you have some white wine,' she said finally, 'that would be lovely.'

'Of course,' said Irene, opening a cupboard in the sideboard, which was actually a fridge. 'Will Chardonnay do?'

Judith nodded, and a large amount of wine was poured and handed over. Irene mixed herself a gin and tonic in a tall glass, added ice from the fridge and sat down, raising her glass to Judith as she did so.

'Bottoms up, Judith, and welcome to Bay View,' she said.

'And thank you,' said Judith. I could get used to this, she thought. It felt like a dream, or something out of a glossy magazine that she'd strayed into by mistake. After a while, Irene pressed a button on the wall behind her chair and the curtains slid across the windows. Another button lit the side-lights around the room, and a third made music emerge from hidden speakers. By this time Judith had begun to adjust most heartily, helped by two more glasses of wine. They were talking merrily about clothes, or pop music, or something Judith couldn't later recall when they heard a taxi arrive, stop and drive away again. Minutes later Alan Thornhill put his head round the living room door.

'Here you are, Judith,' he said, smiling at her. 'Irene looking after you properly?'

Judith wanted to get up but felt a little unsteady. 'She certainly is. I'm so grateful to you both. It was horrible not to know where I was going to sleep. I felt like a refugee.'

'And she looked like one,' Irene giggled, 'dragging her stuff around in a big black bag.' The two women laughed out loud at this. Alan looked from one to the other, still smiling. 'Have you eaten?' he asked.

When Judith finally went upstairs, her bedroom felt like the hotel that she stayed in when Jessie and Lawrence had taken her to London for her eighteenth birthday. She had her own bathroom, an easy chair and even a desk. The bed was large and soft; sleep came quickly. When she woke in the morning with a fearful thirst and opened the curtains, the room was full of sky. Judith blinked, checked her watch and panicked, forgetting that it was Sunday and she didn't have to go to work. She looked down and saw that the long nightie she was wearing wasn't her own, nor was the dressing gown draped across the little chair in the corner of the room. They were both sleek and pale, gleaming in the morning light that bounced around the room as she opened the other set of curtains. She found the clothes she'd been wearing the day before in a basket in the bathroom and put them on before going downstairs.

'Hello, Judith,' said Irene. She was sitting at a table in the sunny window at the back of the house, in a long blue dressing down. 'Oh, you got dressed. Edna will do the rest of your things first thing tomorrow. I've told Alan you're not going in until after lunch tomorrow at the earliest, so some things should be ready by then if it's a good drying day. Or you're welcome to have a look through my wardrobe. And help yourself to orange juice and whatever you want in the kitchen, dear. We don't do a formal breakfast. If you open cupboards and the fridge and poke around you'll find most things. If you want anything cooking tomorrow, give Edna a shout.'

Judith found some juice and a banana, which was all she could face. She sat in the kitchen on her own for a while, trying to take in what had happened. In the light of morning it all seemed even more surreal than before. She couldn't believe that the Thornhills lived like this so close to the poorest streets of Barrow, or that they'd invited her to do the same. How much would everything cost, she wondered. He was the editor of a small provincial newspaper, and his wife went shopping. Alan couldn't possibly earn enough to live like this. They must have inherited money, or been very lucky with premium bonds.

The rest of Sunday passed in a blur. Alan and Irene went out in the car for a while in the afternoon and Judith ventured out between the showers. The wind had turned to the northwest and the skyline to the north and east was clear, as if someone had drawn it with a blue crayon. Barrow was just out of sight, but she could see Piel Castle and the south end of Walney Island with its white lighthouse. She walked to the end of the drive and sat on the wall for a while, her eyes drawn to the mouth of Morecambe Bay. Beyond it was the open ocean of the Irish Sea and she thought of the beach at St Bees and the house in Beach Road. Maggie would be complaining to John about another woman looking after her daughter, John would be calming her down, explaining that Judith was fine and needed to be close to work. Vince would listen to them both as he felt his way round the familiar house. Judith was glad to be away from it, however disorientating it was to have her little flat spoiled and inaccessible for a while. She would survive this. It was just stuff and could be replaced. Elspeth had called it 'desecration', but that was too strong. She wasn't hurt, and as her dad had said when she'd phoned him, 'That's what insurance is for.'

Judith went to bed early that night, suddenly overwhelmed by tiredness and unable to face any more of Irene's unrelenting chirpiness. She had a bath, read a crime novel she'd found downstairs, slept late and enjoyed the peace of the big room, the view and her own bathroom.

Before facing breakfast downstairs on the Monday morning, she called down to Irene, 'May I use the phone again, please?'

'Of course,' Irene called back. 'Use the one in your room if you want a bit of privacy. Breakfast's here when you're ready.'

Elspeth picked up on the second ring. 'Just about to go out,' she said. 'It's my late start today. How are things? Where do they live?'

'Not far really, on the fell behind where you live, quite high up.' Judith lowered her voice, 'Elspeth, you should see this house. It's like something out of a magazine or a film. I've got my own bathroom, and there's a housekeeper who does everything. I've only just got up.'

'Good for you,' said Elspeth. 'You needed a bit of comfort after all that nastiness and scrubbing. How long are you staying there?'

'Irene was talking about weeks, but it can't be as long as that, surely? As soon as I can get the money from the insurance I'll buy the things I need and move back in.'

'On your own? Aren't you worried about that?'

'What's Sam said? Have you spoken to him?'

'He rang about half an hour ago, and asked you to phone him back. Must be something about the flat. He's at the station. You've got the number? '

'Yes, thanks.' She put the phone down and dialled again. After a brief exchange with the duty sergeant, she heard Sam's voice.

'Judith,' he said. 'You got my message then. We couldn't find any of your paperwork in the flat. Where do you keep your notes, about the snooping around you've been doing?'

'You mean my legitimate enquiries,' said Judith. Sam had a knack for saying things that annoyed her. 'I keep them in my bag.'

'And you have your bag with you?'

'Yes, it's here. Hardly ever let it out of my sight. Why?'

'Well, we wondered whether that was what he was looking for.'

'Who?' said Judith. 'Do you know who did it?'

'Obvious, isn't it?' he said. 'Lennon has to be the main suspect, for this and the death of Desmond Harries. We've none of his fingerprints to match any prints we find here, so I'll need to talk to Donna. Did you say she works at the station in Morecambe?'

'You're not going there, are you?' said Judith. 'If the boyfriend finds out, he'll hurt her. You haven't met him. He's an awful man.'

'We can be discreet, you know,' he said. 'Didn't you say the bloke who runs the café likes Donna?'

'He lets her use the phone, and he worries about her.'

'Well then, he won't split to the boyfriend, will he?'

Judith thought for a moment. 'I'm coming with you,' she said. 'Donna won't talk to you, not without me there. She trusts me, you're just another copper.' She sensed his hesitation. 'It makes sense, Sam. I want to find Anthony as much as you do, especially if it was him who messed up my flat. I can go with you, or by myself. Your choice.'

There was silence for a few moments. 'When should I pick you up?'

'Not here' she said. 'And don't come to the newsroom, I'll meet you at Bruciani's at one. And don't tell anyone where we're going. If anything happened to Donna I'd never forgive myself.'

'OK', said Sam. 'See you then.'

CHAPTER 17

'Have you had enough to eat?' said Irene, as Judith was preparing to leave. 'Edna would love to make you something special, wouldn't you, Edna?' she shouted, so that Edna would hear from her usual place in the utility room. There was no response. Judith was embarrassed about Irene treating Edna like a pet or a servant, but she wasn't sure whether Edna enjoyed or hated it. How did it feel to serve someone else all the time? She couldn't imagine it being a pleasurable experience.

'I've had plenty, thanks,' said Judith quickly. She wanted to go into work before she had to meet Sam, but it was clear that Irene wanted her to stay longer. She seemed desperate for company and distraction.

'So, you're going in today, if you're sure you're up to it?'

Judith nodded. 'I'll be fine,' she said. 'Thanks.'

'What are you working on now?' said Irene. 'Alan doesn't tell me anything, even when he's here, which isn't often. I hope it's something important and useful, not all the boring stuff about men drinking too much on a Saturday night.'

Judith certainly wasn't going to mention that she was going to see Donna. 'Don't talk about the story before it's out' was advice she'd had on her journalism course and it was probably wise. She didn't want Irene and Alan talking about what she was doing, either between themselves or with anyone else.

'Just bits and pieces, but I really need to go to the newsroom today, Irene,' she said. 'Don't want Bill Skelly to think I'm wasting my time.'

'He's an old gasbag, isn't he?'

'What did you actually say to him, and to Ed, after I told you about how they were treating me?'

Irene laughed. 'I told Alan you weren't happy, and why – and Ed? Well I just fixed him with my best steely look and told him if he was rude to you again I'd have him sacked. Right there in his grubby alcove. He didn't know where to look. It was priceless!'

I bet it was, thought Judith. It was pretty clear that Irene enjoyed exercising whatever power she had. Aloud, she said, 'I have to go out later, so I may be late back.'

'Anywhere nice?' Irene ventured. 'You can tell me all about it later on. We'll have a drink and a good long chat.'

'Right-oh,' said Judith. 'And what are you up to today?'

'Oh, the usual, you know. Some business here, then into town. Nothing much.'

You're as vague as I am, thought Judith.

Going out of the back door of Bay View a little later, she was struck once again by the view. A skylark rose at a steep angle, singing its song. It was grey and cold, but the town and the arc of Walney Island were visible. It was like looking at a map. Smoke blurred the details, or it could have been dust kicked up by the continuous demolition and building work in Barrow. 'Too little, too late' was most people's view of what was happening to the town, unless they were still complaining about the old community that had been destroyed. No wonder Irene didn't want to be here.

Judith looked past the south end of Walney and then round into the bay. Even on this grey morning she could see where the tide was coming in, the mass of grey sea surging across the mudflats, shallow at first, then deeper, picking up sand and mud as it ran and churning against the clear water of the rivers that fed into the eastern reaches of the bay. She'd seen stories in the archives of people lost out there, trapped by the tide and swept off their feet, shouting for help that didn't come. Once, she'd read, the rescuers could hear the drowning man but couldn't see him in the fog, and by the time they reached him he was dead.

She left the Vespa behind the *Furness News* building as she often did and went upstairs to the newsroom. Time to sort out her notes, make sure Skelly knew she was working, and have a think about what she wanted to ask Donna. At least at Donna's work they might be safe from the ghastly boyfriend, but she wasn't sure that Donna would talk to Sam if she knew he was a policeman. Should they pretend Sam was another journalist? Was that ethical?

When she opened the door and walked in, every head looked up. Hattie came over and gave her a hug. 'You poor thing,' she said. 'It must have been awful for you.' Andrew smiled and gave an incongruous thumbs up, which was as close to fellow feeling as he could manage. Bill Skelly put a pencil behind his ear and looked across. 'Well, well,' he said. 'Look what the cat's dragged in. Thought you'd be still lying in luxury at your new digs, silk sheets and all. Lovely image that. But here you are. '

'Not for long,' she said. 'I'm doing a piece on the boys at Montgomery House, and it's going to be great.'

'Says who?' said Bill.

'You do, right now, when you tell me what a good idea it

is. Tugs at the heart strings, poor kids, snatched from home, far from families, one runs away and ends up dead, and so on. Good, eh?'

Bill walked across to her. 'Is that the line? Well I can tell you right now, girlie, that it won't get past me, so you can save your energy. If there is a line it's, "War hero who offers a lifeline to children from broken homes, devastated by tragic accident", and so on. Got that? No one has a bad word for the captain, and that Mrs Robinson's a saint.'

Judith looked for words but found none. The story she had in her mind lay in ruins, and she would have to find another one or there'd be nothing at all.

Bill was standing very close to her now. 'Dig up something on that bloke who hanged himself. Where, when, how, why, all the basic questions that you're supposed to ask, not some mealy-mouthed piece about a few delinquents. Now get on with it. Stories don't come to you, Miss Pharaoh, you have to go and find them.'

Hattie's typewriter resumed its regular thump. Andrew's head disappeared and on the other side of the room Ed Cunningham pushed back his chair and looked across at Judith, smiling and waving a nicotine-stained finger. Judith picked up her bag and left, without a word. At a table in the corner of Bruciani's, as far away as she could get from the hissing coffee machine, she sat and took stock. If she wanted to know if and why Anthony had wrecked her flat, Donna might help, story or no story. And she was sure that Sam and the police knew more about the whole Stevie business than they'd told her. She wanted to talk to Doc Hayward again, but he was still off sick. Maybe Bill's suggestion about Monty House and the saintly Mrs Robinson would work, and intrepid Captain Edwards might be flattered enough to tell her his story instead.

All was not lost. Surely Thornhill couldn't sack her while she was living in their house? And how long would that be? It was luxurious, Bill was right about that, but Judith didn't feel comfortable there. She would stay only until she could replace some of the stuff that had been damaged and make the flat fit to live in again.

If Irene offered her wine, or whatever else, tonight she would refuse. And she wouldn't drop everything after Skelly's outburst, even if she would have to do so eventually. She was taking Sam to meet Donna, and if that meant they could find Anthony, it would be worth risking Bill's temper. She wouldn't be intimidated by him, not today at least.

Talking to Sam in the car, with both of them facing ahead, felt easier than looking at him. She needed information to keep Skelly off her case, but Sam was so touchy that she would have to be careful.

'Are you still sure it was Anthony Lennon who broke into my flat?'

'Yes,' he said. 'Although, there was something odd what the fingerprint blokes found. And they'd like to take your fingerprints too, by the way, to help them see who else was there. Did you have many visitors?'

'No, nobody actually.'

'Judith no mates, eh,' said Sam, half turning towards her. 'Well they found clear fingerprints among things that they left at your place, underneath drawers and suchlike.'

'They? More than one person?' she asked, looking across at him. He nodded.

'Either Anthony had someone with him, or else it was someone else entirely, and more than one person.'

Judith faced ahead. For the first time she felt afraid. 'What were they looking for?' she asked.

'Could have been just a random burglary.'

'But they didn't take anything precious. The radio was still there, and the jewellery my gran left me.'

'Exactly. So they might have been looking for information about what you're working on.'

Judith's mind was racing. Who knew or cared about what she was doing?

'Or there's another possibility,' he said. 'They might have just wanted to frighten you. It could have been a warning.'

'Even if there were two people, and one of them might have been Anthony, why would he or they want to frighten me?'

'I don't know,' said Sam. 'But we still need to find Anthony to find out what he had to do with Harries's death. I told you there's some doubt about that.'

'You didn't tell me much,' said Judith.

'Everyone at the nick still reckons it was a straight suicide.'

'Do you?' asked Judith.

Sam shrugged. 'They're all telling me to let it go,' he said. 'If Anthony had found out about Harries's reputation, or thought he might have messed with Steven, it was enough motive for him to threaten Harries, and that could have tipped Harries over the edge. Messy business. Morrison and the bosses want it left alone, as far as I can see.'

'Is that OK with you?'

He shrugged again. 'Not much I can do about it, is there?'

After a long silence, they reached the outskirts of More-cambe. If Judith wanted any more out of him it would have to be now. 'Do you have enough to charge Anthony with anything?'

'At present, no,' he said. 'We need to find him. Donna needs to tell us more about where he might be. And she might even have something with his fingerprints on it. That would help a lot.'

'Are you going to tell her you're a policeman?'

They had stopped at a traffic light and he looked across at her. 'You've no idea, have you?' he said. 'Of course I have to tell her. Nothing would be admissible if I didn't.'

'Well don't tell her straight away,' said Judith. 'Let me talk first, or she'll just bolt. Her family don't talk to the police. When we get to the station, you wait in the car. If I can persuade her to talk to you, it might work.'

Sam thought for a moment. 'All right,' he said. 'But this is police work and it has to be me that does it. Don't make any promises, and don't lie to her, OK?'

He parked the car at the edge of the car park, out of sight of the main station entrance, and Judith walked across on her own. In the café, Donna was carrying a tray of tea. She saw Judith and smiled. Judith smiled back – that was a good start, she thought. She went through to the back to ask if she could see Donna alone for a few minutes and Fred, Donna's boss, came out to look after the customer standing by the counter.

'How are you, Donna?' she asked. 'No bruises today?'

'I think he's gone,' said Donna. 'One of 'is mates told me they'd heard Anthony was back and Ian just picked up his bag and left, two days ago.'

Judith sat back on the small wooden chair. 'Is that good?' she said. 'You were afraid of him, weren't you?'

'Still am,' said Donna. ''E wasn't bringing any money in, not that I saw any road, but I don't know where 'e is and 'e could be back, if 'e thinks Anthony's gone away again.'

'Where is Anthony, Donna, do you know?'

'Well you told me 'e'd been to see poor Stevie, so I guess 'e must be over Barrow way. Don't know where.'

Judith sipped the hot chocolate that the boss had brought over to them.

'There's been some trouble over there, Donna,' she said.

'What's 'e done?'

'Nothing's certain, but he may have found out something about what happened to Stevie, and we need to find him.'

'Stevie died in the mud, poor mite,' said Donna. 'What's that got to do with our Anthony?'

Judith was thinking quickly now. 'Anthony may have thought that someone at the home had been unkind to Stevie, may even have hurt him, which made him run away. We don't know exactly what happened, but we think Anthony may have threatened that person.'

'Well of course he did if someone hurt Stevie. Hit 'im, did 'e?'

'Well, the man killed himself.'

'Good,' said Donna.

Judith stared at her.

'If the man killed 'imself, that's not our Anthony's fault, is it? And good riddance. A nonce, was 'e? You know, a perv? If they'd caught 'im and locked 'im up 'e would've died anyway, in the nick.'

Judith was still lost for words. Eventually she said, 'The thing is, Donna, the police need to see Anthony because he was probably the last person to see this man before he killed himself. In fact,' Judith knew she had to say it, 'there's a policeman with me who would like to talk to you about it.'

Donna tried to stand up suddenly. 'Where?' she said.

Judith waved towards the door. 'He's out there. I told him not to come in. I knew it would bother you. But the police need to find out why Stevie ran away, Donna, why he died, and Anthony can help with that. He could be a witness, do you see?'

She knew it was only half the truth. Donna would probably hate her later, but she would face that when it happened.

'Will you talk to him, Donna, please? Help us find Anthony and we get justice for Stevie. You want that don't you?'

Donna sat down again. 'Stevie was a good lad,' she said. Judith nodded. 'Anthony was a wild one, miss, but 'e wouldn't hurt anyone, unless it were someone who hurt 'is family. I thought 'e might go for Ian. 'E might still.'

'Then he would be in trouble, Donna, even if he was only trying to protect you.' Judith waited again. 'Will you talk to the policeman? He's a nice man. I won't let him bully you.'

'You'll be there, with me?'

'We can talk in the car, and I'll be there.'

Donna thought for a while. Judith said, 'I'll ask Fred if we can borrow you for half an hour. That's all we'll need.'

Donna wouldn't sit in the front next to Sam. She crouched down in the back seat, hiding her head. She was afraid that someone might be watching.

'Donna's afraid her old boyfriend might try to hurt her,' Judith said carefully to Sam, hoping that he could see how nervous Donna was. 'I've explained to her that Anthony might be a witness and how you need to find him, about what happened to the man at the boys' home.'

'I'm Detective Constable Tognarelli,' said Sam quietly. 'I've been working on what happened to your brother Stevie, Donna, and we need to find Anthony as part of that enquiry. Judith thinks she's seen him in Barrow, but we can't be sure.

Do you have anything of his, with a picture of him, that we could look at?'

'I've got 'is passport,' said Donna. 'He left it with me, said it was safer.'

Sam's eyes widened. 'His passport?'

'Well 'e had to have one didn't 'e,' said Donna, as if Sam was a bit slow on the uptake, 'with coming all the way from Australia.'

'He was in Australia?' said Judith. She smiled. Vince had been right about that. 'When did he go there? '

Barnardo's sent 'im,' said Donna. 'They told him that his mum didn't want 'im no more and 'e might as well away and start again. So 'e went – 'e were about twelve.'

'So how did he get back here?' asked Sam.

'When 'e grew up, 'e got a job, saved some money. Said 'e always wanted to come 'ome.'

'But what about his passport?' Sam wondered about all the paperwork Anthony would have needed.

'Oh, 'e stole that,' said Donna, 'from some bloke over there. Had to change 'is name.'

'So what does he call himself now?' Sam asked, his little notebook in his hand.

'Can't remember,' said Donna. 'It's in 'is passport though. Do you want to see it?'

Donna insisted on walking home on her own, as she always did for a break between the lunchtime rush and the next shift that the boss had given her, that started at four o'clock. Sam and Judith sat in the car and waited.

'She won't come back,' Sam said. 'Do you know where she lives?'

'I do actually, but you're definitely not going there, and anyway, she will come back. She trusts me, and I told her that finding Anthony would help us know what really happened to Stevie. That's mostly true, isn't it?'

'Did you tell her about your flat?'

'No, but now you're telling me it might not have been him anyway. We could find out about that too, and the tape he sent to our office. I'm sure he made that tape. I told you he'd been in Australia.'

'So you did, and I told you it makes no difference where he'd been.'

'But now we'll see his passport.'

'Donna won't let us keep it, surely?'

Judith shrugged. 'God knows. People never fail to surprise me. Do some people surprise you?'

Sam thought about it. 'They do. When they don't, I'll know I've been in this job too long.'

The November afternoon was gloomy by the time Donna came back. She stood by the wall of the station, watching, before walking across towards them.

'Here,' she said, 'Anthony gave it to me in this envelope and told me to keep it safe, so I have.'

Sam's gloved hands intercepted the envelope as Donna handed it to Judith in the front seat. He held it carefully by the edges and slid the passport out onto his lap. Judith craned across to see. Sam opened the passport. 'Is this Anthony's picture?' he asked.

'He put it in 'imself. Clever, innit?' said Donna.

'And the name?'

'He kept the other man's,' said Donna. 'Had to learn the signature and that. I call him Anthony, like we always did, but to everyone else he's Roderick Arthur Petherbridge. What a laugh. Sounds real posh, doesn't it?'

'Can I keep the passport?' asked Sam.

'No, you bloody can't,' said Donna. 'If our Anthony said look after it, that's what I'll do. Can't just hand over his passport to some copper.' Sam looked down, making sure he remembered the face, the name, the signature, as many details as he could, before he handed the passport back to Donna. Judith noticed him slip the envelope down beside the seat.

Donna leaned forward to speak to Judith. 'Is that all you want, miss? I'm on now, till nine when we close. Extra shifts mean double the money.'

'What about your boyfriend.?' said Judith. 'What if he comes back?'

'Ex-boyfriend, you mean. He's scared shitless. Anyway, I'm going to stay with Mum for a bit. She invited me back pretty quick when she knew I was earning good money.'

'She's Mrs Bell now, isn't she?'

'That's her,' said Donna. 'Our Anthony will know where I've gone.'

'Address?' asked Sam.

'Get lost, copper,' said Donna. 'You keep away from us, and don't you dare say I've been talking to you, even it was for poor Stevie. Gotta go.' She got out of the car.

Sam leaned across and whispered to Judith. 'Go in with her. Get something with her prints on, anything.'

'How?' said Judith.

'Anything,' said Sam. 'Go on, quick.'

Judith went into the café. Five minutes later she was back. As she sat down in the front seat she pulled open her bag. Inside was a large spoon.

'I took hold of it with my sleeve, and then dropped it on the floor by Donna's feet,' she said. 'She picked it up and put it on the counter, and I pushed it into my bag when she went to get her overalls. Will that do?'

Sam reached into the glove compartment, found a brown evidence bag, dropped the spoon into it and put it on the back seat alongside another evidence bag containing the envelope. With any luck Forensics should be able to lift Anthony's prints.

They started the journey back to Barrow, round the foggy shore of the bay. Judith felt enclosed and oppressed by the gloom surrounding the car as Sam drove slowly out of the town.

'You pushed me into that,' she said to Sam.

'Nonsense,' he said. 'You loved it.'

It was true. Judith was ashamed of the excitement she'd felt, and now, more than ever, she wanted to talk to Anthony before the police did. It was still her story.

CHAPTER 18

'Is that you, dear?' cried Irene Thornhill. It was after six and quite dark; every light in Bay View seemed to be on as Judith steered the Vespa slowly down the drive, parked it and let herself in the back door with the key Irene had given her.

'It's Judith,' she called. 'Is it OK for me to let myself in?'

'Of course it is, dear,' said Irene, tapping into the kitchen in her high heels. She grasped Judith by the shoulders and feigned a kiss close to her ear. 'It's too cold to be riding that scooter. You could have rung from the office and I would have come down to pick you up.'

'I couldn't do that,' said Judith, taking off her thick jacket and leaving her boots by the door. 'I'm imposing on you enough as it is.'

'Not imposing at all. I've told you how much I enjoy having a guest, especially a guest like you, not those boring old army friends of Alan's. I told you he was in Malaya, didn't I? You'd think they would have had enough of it, but there's a group of them who can't seem to let go of it. They still get together and drink and talk about old times. Worse than watching paint dry. I try to avoid them whenever I can. They have this little club, you know, with a special tie and all that. A bit pathetic, actually, don't you think?'

231

A thought occurred to Judith. 'Is Captain Edwards from Montgomery House part of that group?'

'Who?' said Irene. 'I don't know anyone of that name, I'm sure.' She took Judith's hand and led her through into the warm lounge, where a fire was burning and the smell of logs mixed with the polish that Edna used so liberally around the house. Mum would love this room, Judith thought as she sank into the sofa.

Irene fussed with the food that Edna had left for them, and opened a bottle of wine. They sat with trays on their knees, with the television droning in the background. Judith felt the tension of the day draining away.

'Tell me all about it,' said Irene, filling Judith's glass for the second time. 'Where have you been today that made you so late back. Anywhere interesting?'

Judith knew she should keep quiet about what she was doing, but the wine and food and warmth were loosening her journalistic inhibitions.

'All the way to sunny Morecambe,' she said.

'What on earth took you there?' Irene enquired, looking at Judith over the rim of her glass. 'A fingerprint hunt,' said Judith, 'to track down whoever wrecked my flat.'

'Really,' said Irene. 'How enterprising of you. All on your own?'

'That pompous policeman came with me,' she said. 'He's all right actually. Certainly knows his business.'

'Does he work with Sergeant Morrison?' said Irene.

'That's the one,' said Judith. 'Not sure Morrison likes him though.' She giggled. 'Sam doesn't like him much either. Feels a bit like me and Skelly. He and Morrison both want to show us who's boss all the time.' She thought about this for a moment. 'Maybe they're threatened by youngsters like me and Sam.'

Irene smiled. 'But you young people are what we need. Energy, enthusiasm, it's so precious.' She waited. 'And have you found out who wrecked your flat?' Irene filled Judith's glass.

'Thanks, lovely,' said Judith. She hadn't drunk much good wine before and was beginning to understand why people enjoyed it. 'Haven't found the baddies yet,' she said, 'but we're close. And the insurance money should be here soon, and then I can move out and leave you alone.'

'And tell me about what's happening about that poor boy who died in the mud. Weren't you trying to find out what happened to him?'

'Looks as if everything's connected to the boy's older brother,' said Judith. 'We found out the name he's using today. It's a really funny name!' She giggled again. 'Would you believe, Roderick Arthur Petherbridge? What a handle. His sister thought it was a hoot.'

Irene got up to put another log on the fire, as Judith slipped down in her seat.

'Very warm in here,' she said, closing her eyes.

'You have a little rest,' said Irene, taking the glass and the tray before they slipped down too. 'Not too long though, or you'll not sleep properly later.' As Judith snoozed quietly, her head back on the cushion, Irene turned up the volume of the television and settled down to watch ITV Playhouse. She was still watching when Alan Thornhill came home an hour later.

'Everything all right?' he asked, looking at Judith who was still asleep on the sofa.'

'Fine,' said Irene. 'Talk to you later, dear.'

The following morning Judith woke with a start. She was wearing her underwear not her usual nightie and had no recollection of getting to bed. She was still wondering about it when Irene pushed open the door, carrying a cup of tea.

'I looked in earlier,' she said, 'but you were still spark out.'

Judith sat up on her elbows. 'I'm not used to the wine,' she said. 'Who helped me get to bed?'

'Irene laughed. 'Don't worry dear, it was only me. And I didn't tell Alan. Your secret's safe with me.'

Judith lay back on the pillow, relieved. 'Thank heaven for that. I had visions of my boss carrying me up the stairs, dead drunk.'

'Oh it wasn't as bad as that,' said Irene. 'I just helped you up and into bed. You'll remember it all perfectly once that tea hits the spot.'

Later, in the breakfast room, Judith repeated her belief that the insurance money would not be long.

'When it comes, we'll do some shopping, and make your home feel like yours again,' said Irene. 'No rush. You stay as long as you like.'

'You've been very kind,' said Judith, and she meant it, thinking about a present she could offer, and how grateful her parents would be when she told them about all the Thornhills had done for her.

'Delighted we could help,' said Irene. 'You'd better not be late. I promised Alan you'd be right as rain this morning.'

'He didn't see me asleep on the sofa, did he?' said Judith, embarrassed.

Irene patted her arm. 'Only in passing, don't worry. You're allowed to have a snooze after a busy day. He does it himself, many a time.'

By the time Judith arrived in the newsroom, she was already late for her regular walk across to the police station to check the overnight book. Andrew offered to go, but she insisted. Clearly, Skelly was keeping an eye on the feature she had claimed to be writing, and she wanted to make sure that her routine work was done, to give him no grounds for complaint. She picked up the usual list of burned out cars, broken windows and pub fights and turned to go, bumping into Sergeant Morrison coming out of the CID room. 'The girl with the hair,' he said. 'Still making a nuisance of yourself, are you?'

It took Judith a moment to recall the words on the tape that Morrison was referring to. 'We think we know who made the tape,' she said.

'Oh, we do, do we? Well I'm reassured, I must say. Good to know that people like you are out there doing our work for us.'

Behind her Sergeant Clark laughed at the obvious sarcasm, and she felt herself blush. Not worth rising to him, she said to herself, and pushed past him and out into the street. She wanted to tell Morrison what good police work Sam had been doing yesterday, but she knew Sam might not have told his boss what he was up to.

Sam meanwhile was with Officer Hobbs in Forensics, revelling in the possession of fingerprints that could help to answer all sorts of questions. He waited, watching anxiously, while Hobbs dusted and printed and compared.

'OK,' said Hobbs finally. 'The prints off the spoon belong to the sister, and are also on the envelope that had the passport in it. The only other prints on the envelope must be those of the man we know as Anthony Lennon, right?'

'Aka Roderick Arthur Petherbridge,' said Sam, reading from his notes. 'That was the name on the passport he nicked in Australia and doctored, to get him back here.'

'And you reckon he trashed that young woman's place as well?'

'I think so.'

'Well, think again, Nelly. No trace of those prints among the ones we lifted from the flat. Looks like there were two people involved there and neither of them was him.'

'Damn,' said Sam. 'I thought we had it all tied up. Anything on record for the prints we do have from the flat?'

Hobbs shook his head. 'Nothing,' he said. 'But we'll keep checking.'

'I'd really like to know who did it before it feels safe for her to go back there.'

'They wouldn't go back, would they? They must know it would be harder to get in now, and we'd be watching.'

'I suppose so,' said Sam. 'She's determined to go back anyway. Not sure why she's in such a rush. Moved in with the Thornhills, you know, the *Furness News* editor and his missus, and they live like royalty apparently.'

'Not easy living with the boss,' said Hobbs. 'I definitely wouldn't want to live with mine.'

'Nor me,' said Sam, and they both laughed.

'At least we've got the name this bloke's using,' said Sam. 'Looks as if he had something to do with that suicide, in the woods at Attercliff.'

'I heard that was some pervy bloke,' said Hobbs. 'Might have to give Roderick what's-'is-name a medal. He's not a nonce as well, is he?'

Sam shrugged. 'God knows. And that's not enough to kill yourself over these days. Can't go to jail any more for liking men.'

'But you can for liking boys,' said Hobbs, 'and whatever else those bastards get up to.'

❖ ❖ ❖

Sam took the forensic report back to the CID room and filed it with the other papers he was accumulating. It was time to pull some threads together. Stevie Stringer's death was off the list now, unless Doc Hayward suddenly had a brainstorm and changed his mind. Sam needed to check on how he was. Maybe illness and medication had affected him while he was working on the PM. Maybe there was some evidence somewhere, even if the boy's body was gone. Too many maybe's.

He turned his attention again to the two other pieces of the case, Harries's suicide and the trashing of Judith's flat. Fingerprint evidence seemed to rule out Anthony's direct involvement with the flat, but he needed to go back to the cigarettes found at Monty House and in the woods. He still wasn't convinced that Harries had tied the knots on the noose himself. He would have to go back to Monty House, no matter how much everyone wanted him to drop it. And still no word from the phone call he'd made to Gateshead CID. A trip there to follow up the trail to Harries's mother was another obvious move, but after the abortive visit to Lancaster he knew Morrison wouldn't allow it. Maybe there was another way.

He looked at the black phone resting on its cradle like a crouching cat. Only he and Hobbs knew that Lennon's fingerprints hadn't been found at Judith's flat. So if Hobbs kept quiet he could still pursue the Lennon connection for that reason and if he discovered anything compelling about Harries's death, he would have cause to ask Morrison to reconsider

Just before eleven, Sergeant Clark reminded him about the two minutes' silence for Remembrance Day and Sam heard the town hall clock strike as he stood to attention with others in Reception. Morrison arrived shortly afterwards and Sam had to convince him he was working diligently on the list that the sergeant had left for him. Then Harry Grayson hung around for a while and Sam continued the pretence of routine enquiries on other cases. He still wasn't sure he could trust Grayson to keep his mouth shut with Morrison, particularly with regard to his own enquiries. By the time the CID room was quiet again it was mid-afternoon and starting to get dark.

It took six phone calls to find the address and phone number of a Mrs Mollie Harries in Gateshead, a widow, with a son. Sam found the nearest police station to the address he had and dialled the number. When the duty sergeant answered Sam explained that they needed to find the next of kin of a man found dead the previous week.

'So what you want us to do,' said the sergeant finally, 'Is to visit this Mrs Harries and check that she has a son Desmond, who was a priest in Cumberland and then a padre. Last known address,' he paused, checking his notes, 'Montgomery House in Attercliff, Lancashire. That right?'

'Yes, and if all that's confirmed you can tell her that the son has died, and it's believed he took his own life. She might want to come down, if that's possible, or give us instructions about the body, all that.'

'OK,' said the sergeant.

'Oh, and get a sample of handwriting,' said Sam. 'Tell her he left a note and we need to verify.'

'If there is anything, what do want us to do with it?'

Sam thought of something. 'You don't have one of those telecopier machines do you, that takes a copy of something and sends it over a phone line?'

The sergeant laughed. 'You're joking right? We've got a copier, but that's it. If we get something from her, I'll put it in an envelope and send it. That's as advanced as we get here. Where do you want it sending to?'

Another decision. 'Send it to me,' said Sam. He gave Elspeth's address. 'Stuff goes missing here,' he explained. 'Could end up on someone else's desk, so home's easier. OK?'

'If you say so. Do you want me to let you know if and when we find Mrs Harries?'

'That'd be great thanks,' said Sam. 'Ask for DC Tognarelli, Barrow CID.'

'Anything to do with ice cream?' asked the sergeant, before he asked Sam to spell it.

It wasn't a great time to go to Montgomery House, but there were buses along the coast road at this time of night, and Sam didn't have to wait long. He reckoned he could claim to be calling in his own time if Morrison objected.

When he got to the house and the big door opened, he was very pleased to see Mrs Robinson there rather than Captain Edwards. And she seemed pleased to see him too, which was even better.

'The captain's not here,' she said. 'We're having to appoint another padre, of course, and he's at a meeting with some of the trustees in Broughton.'

'I'm sure you can pass on to him what I have to tell you both,' said Sam. 'It's not much, I'm afraid, but I know how anxious you must be to track down Mr Harries's next of kin.'

'Would you like some tea?' she asked. 'I was just about to have some myself. Have a seat in the office, I'm sure the captain wouldn't mind.'

'That would be very welcome, thank you,' he said, and she hurried away to arrange it.

Sam looked around the tidy office. The photos on the walls were all of groups of people. Some of them were of the boys, with the year written underneath. Another, on the far side of the hearth, was of a group of soldiers, by the look of it. They were all wearing hats with one side pinned up, and shorts. There was no caption on the photo. He looked more closely. One or two of the faces looked familiar. Mrs Robinson came back into the room carrying a tray of tea and a plate with slices of cake that gleamed with fruit and cherries. Sam's mouth watered.

'That's an interesting picture, isn't it?' she said, noticing where Sam was standing. 'Did you spot the captain?'

Sam looked again. There he was, in the middle of the front row.

'That was before his injury of course,' said Mrs Robinson, stirring the tea in the large teapot. 'Malaya somewhere, in the mid 'fifties I should think. This place has been going for ten years, and it took him a while to set it up after he was invalided out. We didn't hear much about that war, did we?'

'It was all about rubber plantations, wasn't it?' said Sam. 'Fighting off the Communists, as I remember.'

'The captain doesn't talk much about it, not to me at least,' said Mrs Robinson. 'Do you take sugar, detective?'

Sam was still surprised, and pleased too, when someone called him that. He took the tea from her hand, and accepted the proffered cake, too. It was as delicious as it looked. He watched Iris Robinson as they sat in silence for a few minutes. She must be in her fifties, he thought, and a good-looking woman in her time. The grey hair was full and swept up into a bun behind her head and the skin unlined and glowing in the light. She looked younger than she had that night when they found Harries hanging in the tree.

'I'm not sure we offered you condolences for your loss when my colleague and I were here that night,' he said. 'It must have been a terrible blow for all of you to lose Mr Harries so soon after Steven's accident.'

'It was,' she said. 'The captain was as distressed as I have ever seen him. The boys didn't say much, but they've learned to keep their feelings to themselves, in public at least.'

'And in private?' asked Sam.

'It was Stevie they were really upset about,' she said.

'That's understandable.'

'Of course. We had some nightmares. It was a terrible way to go, and some of the boys couldn't get it out of their minds.'

'Did any of them want to go to the funeral?' he asked.

She looked up. 'That was a hard decision for the captain,' she said. 'But he just felt that we couldn't rely on the boys to behave properly at the crematorium. Some of the older ones, at least. They seemed angry, as well as sad.'

'How so?' said Sam.

She hesitated. 'You'd have to ask the captain about that,' she said. After a moment she went on, 'Did you say you had some news about Mr Harries's mother?'

'We think we've found her, in Gateshead. Captain Edwards said it was Newcastle but they're very close, aren't they? I've asked my colleagues at the local station there to go and check and break the news to her. We were concerned that the family might not have found out about it. And we need contact with the next of kin before we know how to dispose of – er, what kind of funeral they would wish for.'

Iris nodded. 'Every mother's worst nightmare,' she said.

'Do you have children yourself?' he asked.

She shook her head. 'My late husband and I weren't blessed with children,' she said. 'Maybe that's why I love my work here, with the boys. They're like my family.'

Sam looked at her kind face. Surely, he thought, if anything untoward had happened to Steven here she would have known, and intervened. It was quiet in the office; he could hear the wall clock ticking.

'Mrs Robinson,' he began. 'We have heard that Mr Harries may have some trouble in the past, when he was a parish priest. It may have something to do with what he did.'

She looked up. 'What kind of trouble?' she asked.

'It was rumoured that he had been interfering with some young boys.'

'Oh, no!' she cried. The surprise and abhorrence were clear in her face. 'That can't be. Where do rumours like that come from? It's wicked.' She put down her tea and reached for a handkerchief. 'He had impeccable references when he came here. The captain would never employ anyone he had any doubt about, never.'

'I'm sorry to have to ask you this,' said Sam. 'But did any of the boys ever say anything, or complain about Mr Harries in that way?'

'Never,' she repeated fiercely. 'They're troubled children. They've seen more than you and I could ever understand, but about Mr Harries, never.'

Sam waited and wondered.

'What about anyone else?' he asked. She shook her head. 'The boys say things sometimes, things they make up in anger, or to wriggle out of trouble, like boys do,' she said. 'But nothing that worried me, really. No, nothing. I always checked with the captain in case there was anything we needed to follow up on. But there never was. He's always most particular.'

'What about visitors who come here?' Sam persisted.

'Friends of the captain, old army buddies, they visit from

time to time. And there are some quite famous people too, who organise fundraising for us, but they're not really strangers are they?' she said, recovering her composure. 'Dr Graham and the trustees come to see the boys, of course, and do their proper tour of inspection once a year as required, checking on safety, but they've never reported anything, nothing like that. Whoever spread stories about Mr Harries is wicked. Do you think that's maybe why he…?' Her words tailed away. Sam said nothing. She wiped her eyes and blew her nose.

'You'd better come back and see the captain about this,' she said. 'If it was something we missed, he needs to know.'

Sam stood up. 'I will, of course, Mrs Robinson. It's probably nothing, but we need to do things properly where children are concerned.' He stopped. 'Do you have any personal information about Mr Harries I wonder? Any record of illness, perhaps?'

'I might have,' she said. 'It would be in my office upstairs. I'll go and have a look.'

Sam heard her footsteps on the stairs, and her voice as she said. 'Never you mind who's down there. In your room, Mikey, please, and finish your homework.' Doors creaked, and then he heard her steps on the stairs again. She was empty-handed when she came back into the room. 'I can't lay my hands on the file I need,' she said.

'I could wait,' said Sam.

'No, not now,' she said. 'It gets busy again now with the younger children going to bed. It'll be tomorrow before I can look for it. And you said you wanted to see the captain?'

No point in arguing, he thought. Don't want anyone complaining to Morrison when I'm not supposed to be here. 'I'll come back in a day or two,' he said.

'Thank you for coming, Detective Tognarelli.' She smiled. 'I do appreciate it, and I'll tell the captain you called.'

Sam wanted to ask her not to mention it, but that was no good. He shook her hand. 'And thank you for the tea and cake. Most welcome after a long day.'

'Good night,' she said, opening the front door.

Sam stood at the bus stop, watching the moon over the bay. It was clear, but the weather forecast in the paper talked of fog. He pulled his coat collar up and thought about what she'd said.

CHAPTER 19

The Thornhills were both out, and Judith had the big house to herself. She had started making lists of things she would need to return to the flat, and was already looking forward to living alone again. Hospitality on this scale was impressive for a while, but it was beginning to feel like a gilded cage.

She pressed the button to close the curtains, although the cloud was down and so thick outside that no one could have seen in unless they were standing with their face pressed to the glass. Edna had gone home and wouldn't be back until the morning. Judith had spent most of her few days at Bay View in the main front room that Irene called the lounge, the kitchen on the other side, the breakfast room towards the back and her bedroom that was above the kitchen. Now she wanted to explore a little further. The Thornhills' bedroom and bathroom were on the right hand side of the landing, above the dining room and office downstairs, where Judith had never been. She pushed open the dining room door and peeped round. A long table dominated the room, with a matching sideboard and eight chairs. Must be quite a sight when it was all laid up for a special meal, she thought, with glasses and plates shining, and people in good clothes.

Further back beside the dining room on that side of the

house was what Irene called the office. Judith had glimpsed inside it only once. It was just after she'd moved in and she'd been coming down the stairs quietly very early one morning, still feeling like an intruder, as if she didn't belong there. When she heard Alan Thornhill's voice on the phone she froze where she was, embarrassed. 'Not now,' he'd said, 'No. I can't. We've got company. Tomorrow. Yes, I've got them.' She'd heard the telephone click onto the receiver and realised that she could see into the room. Thornhill was standing with his back to her, looking at some photos on the desk. Then he gathered them into a folder and put them into the desk drawer. He locked the drawer, took out the key and stretched his hand beyond her view. She heard a tinkle as if the key had been dropped into something. Then he'd begun to turn towards the door and Judith had carried on down the stairs. He'd said 'Hello' to her and gone out.

Now, with the house to herself, she wanted to see every room, but the office door was locked, so she went up the stairs to the really interesting place, the Thornhills' bedroom at the front of the house. There were two big beds and what looked like a walk-in wardrobe, and Judith felt particularly guilty looking through Irene's well-organised clothes – the colours, the fabrics, and shoes arranged in neat rows. It was like something out of *Vogue*. Alan's wardrobe took up half the space, but everything was just as well arranged – and the ties! She remembered what Irene had said about the club tie that Alan and his friends had. There were only a few ties that weren't plain or striped. One of them was dark blue, with a small image of an animal of some kind, a beaver maybe, with two curved daggers on either side. Maybe they all wore aprons and had funny handshakes as well, Judith thought, as she pulled the sliding wardrobe door back to where it had been before.

She crept back down the stairs, feeling as if she'd done something really bad and was afraid of being caught. It was only a house, she said to herself, and they'd told her over and again to treat it as her own, so she had. At the back of her mind, she still had doubts about their reasons for being so hospitable. They clearly wanted to look after her, but why? On the other hand, did it matter? She was free to leave any time she wanted, and there'd been no more talk about losing her job. Irene was probably supporting her, like she had before.

She was adding things to her list and wondering whether the insurance money would cover it all when she heard the car outside and the doors bang. The front door opened and Irene looked round the door of the living room. She looked flushed and happy.

'Alan's putting the car away,' she said, coming into the room. She kicked off her shoes and sat down heavily on one of the big pink armchairs. 'What an evening! Actually I'd much rather have stayed here with you and had a little drink and watched some TV.'

'Where have you been?' Judith asked.

'Oh, just a boring dinner with one of Alan's old chums and his wife. What a frump the woman was,' said Irene, lowering her voice. 'Let herself go terribly, and she can't be any older than me. Ghastly dress, haven't seen one like it since VE day!'

Alan Thornhill came in and smiled at his wife. 'Thanks for a lovely evening, darling,' she said to him. 'I was just telling Judith what fun we had. Mrs Fossey is a lovely woman, isn't she, and such a good cook.'

'I bet she didn't make that meal,' he said, 'any more than you make dinner when we have people coming. Thank God for Edna, I say.'

'There, Judith,' said Irene, 'the secret is out. Edna's a much better cook than me, but she's a well-kept secret, isn't she dear? My fondue is the talk of Barrow, thanks to her.'

Judith laughed along with them. Is this what being married is like, she wondered? Do people say things to each other that aren't true, and bother so much about appearances?

'Nightcap, Judith?' said Alan. 'Time for a proper whisky. Old Fossey's wasn't up to much.'

'And that wine,' said Irene. 'Life's too short to drink wine as bad as that. What can we get you, Judith?'

'Nothing, thanks. I've been drinking too much lately.'

'Suit yourself,' said Irene, pouring a wine for herself and a whisky for Alan from the glass decanter. 'So, what have you been up to with the house all to yourself?'

'Making lists, mainly,' said Judith, holding up the notepad.

'Stories that'll make us famous, eh Judith?' said Alan, raising his glass.

'No, sorry, just stuff I need for the flat, for when I go back.'

'Oh but you've only just got here,' said Irene. 'You can't leave just yet, can she Alan? It's so interesting having you here, seeing what you're working on. You never tell me anything about work, Alan, and Judith's been telling me all about it.'

'Not really,' said Judith, looking across at her boss and wishing Irene wouldn't talk so much.

'Bill tells me you're doing something about the boys at Montgomery House,' said Alan. 'How's that going?'

'It's not, I'm afraid. I wanted to take the line that the boys were victims of the system, if you know what I mean, but Bill didn't like that at all. I'll have to re-think.'

'Show me what you've got, if you like,' said Alan, 'and we'll see what we could make of it. Not tomorrow, in a day or two. I'm sure we'll work something out.'

'Thanks,' said Judith, surprised. Maybe he's being supportive because Irene's here, she thought. She seems to call the shots, despite the little wife act she puts on. Judith couldn't work out what they really saw in each other, but then most couples were a mystery to her.

Later, she lay in bed and wondered about another couple, Sam and his wife Christine, and the story Elspeth had told her. How could you do that, walk out without warning and strip the house too? No wonder Sam was so glum most of the time, and wary. He seemed a kind man, from what she remembered of seeing him talk to Tommy and Donna. Morrison probably thought he was a liberal softie, but that was a compliment coming from Morrison. And there was another mystery, why Sam put up with being bossed around by someone he obviously didn't respect. He could be a sergeant himself, she thought. That might make his life easier, and more money, too.

The cheque from the insurance people arrived the following day, and Judith rang home before she went to work, as she'd promised to do. 'That's good timing,' said her mother. 'I've just arranged for Gran to come down on Saturday and stay here with Vince. Dad's going walking, and I can come and help you. We'll need to shop, and then we can take everything to your place and make it feel like home again. Or do you want to find somewhere else, after that nasty mess they made?'

'Hang on,' said Judith. 'Are you sure you want to come all the way down here?' Already she had visions of Irene and her mother meeting each other, and the idea made her heart sink.

'Of course, it's not far, and your dad and I think we should say thank you to Mr and Mrs Thornhill for looking after you so well. He would come himself, but this walk's been arranged for a while.'

'Who's he going with?' asked Judith. John Pharaoh played golf almost every weekend, and didn't go walking in the hills nearly as often as he used to.

'With Lawrence,' said Maggie. 'Since Jessie died we haven't seen much of him at all, and your dad always liked him. He lives in Elterwater now. So he's going there and I'll get the train down to Barrow. We can get a taxi if we have lots of things to carry. It's not far, you said?'

'No,' said Judith. 'Just ten minutes or so into town. Are you sure?'

'Absolutely. Tell those nice people that they've done enough and now your family has to help. It's only right. I'll get the early train if I can, so we can make a good start. I'll let you know. See you Saturday, OK? It'll be fun. 'Bye, dear.'

Judith sensed that her weekend was going to be difficult. Maybe she could ask Elspeth to come over for a while, just to dilute the tension.

She explained their plan for Saturday to Irene, who seemed unable or unwilling to understand that Maggie Pharaoh wanted to have her daughter to herself. There was something overbearing and unstoppable about Irene that Judith noticed increasingly as she stayed in their house. However much Alan Thornhill was in charge at work, at home Irene was the boss. Maybe it's the same at our house, Judith wondered before she decided that it wasn't. Her mother was louder than John, but it was his calm presence that held the household together. John Pharaoh made the Thornhills seem shallow, and Judith missed him.

Judith's worst fears about Saturday were realised. From the moment Maggie stepped off the train and found Irene Thornhill waiting with Judith and the Daimler, the morning descended into farce, with the two women trying to outdo each other in their concern for the hapless Judith. They disagreed about practically everything.

'But you don't have enough money for those curtains, do you dear?' said Maggie as Irene picked out something glamorous and totally unsuitable for a small room in Cannon Street. 'They could be a gift from me,' said Irene gaily, at which point Judith thought her mother was about to implode.

'Certainly not, thank you Mrs Thornhill,' said Maggie. 'John and I will be helping Judith with some extra things, won't we, dear, after all the difficulties you've had. We do so much appreciate your kindness, Mrs Thornhill, and the loan of your lovely car, but I'm sure you must have things of your own to do this afternoon, and we can't impose on you any longer, can we Judith?'

'Oh,' said Irene. 'I see. Well I do have a bit of shopping to do myself. So if I meet you at the front of the shop in an hour or so and get you both back to Cannon Street with your bags…?'

'So kind,' said Maggie. 'Thank you so much. Now come along Judith, we still have more things to find.' And with that, Maggie tugged Judith away, leaving Irene standing with the curtains still in her hand.

Judith was annoyed and embarrassed. 'You didn't need to leave her standing like that,' she said when they were out of earshot.

'Well, she wasn't going to leave us alone, was she? Enough's enough, for heaven's sake. Does she have any children?'

'I don't think so, and there aren't any photos in the house.'

'She probably drove them away,' said Maggie, 'fussing too much.'

That's rich, thought Judith. 'They've both been very kind to me,' she said. 'And I didn't tell you how Irene helped me with a problem at work.' Damn, she thought, backtracking to avoid sharing anything about Ed Cunningham pestering her. 'Just the chief reporter being difficult,' she added quickly. 'Irene asked Mr Thornhill to have a word with him, not be so hard on me. Helped a lot.'

'Humph,' said Maggie. 'Too much interference if you ask me. Time you stood up for yourself. My dad wouldn't let anyone push him around.'

'That was down the pit, Mam,' said Judith, 'and a long time ago.'

'Anyway,' said Maggie, 'she can give us a lift to your place with all this stuff and then leave us alone.'

'Elspeth might come round this afternoon, to help. I told you about her, the friend who lives in Roose, with the baby.'

Maggie looked hard at her daughter. 'Is this another unsuitable friend?

She's a lovely woman,' Judith protested. 'You'll like her.'

'Come on up,' Judith shouted later, when the front door bell at Cannon Street jangled. The flat looked fresh and sunny after the previous foggy days, and Judith and her mother were busy making it look like home again. Footsteps sounded on the stairs and Judith was surprised to see not only Elspeth and Tommy, but Sam too.

'Brought someone for the heavy lifting,' said Elspeth, smiling, 'and something for the tins, too. Baked this morning, weren't they, Tommy?'

'I helped,' said Tommy. Elspeth rolled her eyes.

Judith turned to Maggie who was wiping her hands on her apron. 'This is my friend Elspeth, Mam,' she said, 'and her son, Tommy.'

'And her brother Sam,' said Sam, extending his hand to Maggie. 'Pleased to meet you Mrs Pharaoh.'

'And you,' said Maggie. 'Judith, you didn't say Elspeth had a brother.'

'Half-brother, actually,' said Elspeth, 'and my lodger too, at the moment.'

'Oh,' said Maggie, looking at Sam.

'Sam's a policeman, Mam,' said Judith. She and Elspeth winked at each other.

'Really,' said Maggie. 'How interesting.'

They worked till late afternoon, re-arranging furniture, putting up curtains, washing crockery and putting it back into newly cleaned cupboards. Elspeth made tea and they sat, the four of them, at the little table and ate Elspeth's cake, which Maggie said was delicious. Judith watched Sam talk to her mother with the same balance of politeness and interest that she had seen before, and with the same result. Maggie told him more about her family than Judith had heard her share before with a relative stranger. When she told Sam that she and her mother had both worked as screen lasses at a pit in Whitehaven, Judith almost choked on her cake.

After they'd done as much as they could, and the flat was looking habitable, they all walked to the station to see Maggie on to the last train back to St Bees, Sam carrying Maggie's bag and walking on the outside of the pavement, a gesture that Judith knew her mother would notice. As the train pulled away, Judith gave way finally to the laughter that had been building all day.

'Genius,' she said to Elspeth. 'Mam's had been on at me all day, and as soon as you all turned up I was off the hook. And Sam playing the gentleman, that was great.'

'He is a gentleman,' said Elspeth, 'aren't you, Sam?'

'Your mother reminds me of my own mother, and my aunts,' he said. 'I find older women easier.' He stopped, and shook his head. 'Come on, Elspeth, time we got Tommy home.' He turned to Judith. 'Are you going back to the Thornhills?'

'Just one more night there,' said Judith. 'Irene gave me the money for a taxi back to Bay View, and then Mam did, too. Didn't have the heart to refuse both of them.'

'What a charming woman your mother is, Judith,' said Irene, when Judith let herself in and joined the Thornhills in the lounge that looked even bigger after the small rooms of the flat. 'We must have them both here for dinner,' she said to Alan.

'I'm sure she's saying exactly the same to my dad,' said Judith. 'They're very grateful to you both for looking after me.'

'We'll run you down to the flat tomorrow, Judith,' said Alan. 'Are you sure you'll be all right there on your own?'

'Certain,' said Judith.

But in truth she wasn't so certain. Sam had told her that the fingerprints in the flat didn't match the ones they got from Anthony Lennon, but they still didn't know who'd wrecked the flat, or why. Sam seemed confident that they would pick up Anthony very soon, now that they knew the name he was using. The locks on the front door of the house and on Judith's flat had all been changed. All it needed was time for her confidence to return, and she hoped it would happen soon. Or she might wait forever and still feel no safer than she did now

The first night back in the flat was hard. She put the radio on very loud and stayed up as long as she could, to make sure that she would fall asleep without worrying about every sound in

the street. The new curtains were pulled tight shut, hiding the fog that had returned and encircled the orange street lights. Judith didn't look out. She didn't see the Landrover parked across the street and the two men who kept watch, their cigarettes glowing red in the night.

CHAPTER 20

'A letter came for you,' said Elspeth. Sam dropped his coat and a box of files on the stairs and picked up the envelope, holding it carefully by its edges through sheer force of habit. The writing was spidery, and the postmark Gateshead. He abandoned procedural caution and opened the envelope. Inside was a letter, and a postcard that swooped to the floor. Sam picked it up. On one side was a picture of the beach at Silloth and the coast of Scotland on the horizon. He turned it over and read the message:

Enjoying a day out here with the choir trip. Going well so far, apart from one lad who was sick on the coach before we'd hardly started! Hoping to come over at the end of the month to see you. Keep well, Desmond.

The letter was more difficult to read. It was from Desmond Harries's mother. Clearly the local police had tracked her down and told her the bad news about her son. He wondered how many letters to friends and family she would have written, and what she'd said in them. To Sam she had written:

Thank you for trying so hard to find me with this terrible news. Sergeant Noble who came to see me was very kind. He said you needed some of Desmond's handwriting so I have enclosed a postcard he wrote to me a couple of years ago which was the first thing that came to hand. I hope this is what you want. I have instructed an undertaker here who will make all the necessary arrangements to bring Desmond's remains back to us for burial.

Poor Desmond had been very sad for some years, and it was worse after his beloved father passed away three years ago. He rarely came to see me and I am not well enough to travel. He phoned me occasionally and I could tell he was unwell. Sergeant Noble did not tell me many details, and I don't really want them. At least poor Desmond is at peace now.

With kind regards,

Dorothea Harries (Mrs)

Poor woman, thought Sam. Hearing about her son's death from a policeman must have been hard to bear.

'I'll be down in a minute,' he called to Elspeth in the kitchen.

In his small, tidy bedroom he put down his coat and the letter and opened one of the files he'd brought home. Among the papers, exactly where he'd left it, was the note they'd found in Harries's pocket. Forensics had found nothing on it except Harries's own prints. Morrison said he'd checked the handwriting but Sam didn't trust him any more. Everyone just wanted the Harries business closed, but Sam wanted to prove that for himself. He smoothed out the creases in the note, laid it flat on the table he used as a desk, and put the postcard down next to it. He looked carefully from one to the other, checking the curve of the vowels, the height of the longer letters. They looked exactly the same. No sign of any duress, or abnormality of any kind. Someone more expert than him would have to check, but another of Sam's theories was crumbling. For whatever reason, and perhaps with an extra surge of guilt and fear from Anthony Lennon's anger, it looked as if Desmond Harries had written the note himself without external pressure, put it in his coat pocket, picked up an orange box and a rope from the yard outside Montgomery House, walked with them down to the wood, knotted the rope carefully around a branch and his own neck, kicked away the box, and died.

Sam sat on the bed. They'd all been right, and he wrong. No murder, no conspiracy, just a miserable, frightened man who'd finally cracked and done what he'd thought about for a long time. His own mother sounded sad, desperately sad, but not surprised. It was time to move on.

'You all right?' Elspeth asked as he came back downstairs. Sam looked tired and dispirited.

'I've just been proved wrong about something,' he said. 'It makes me wonder if I'm any good at this policing business.'

'Don't be daft,' she said. 'You can't be right all the time. At least you don't take the easiest way out like some do.'

Sam nodded. 'Grayson actually told me today to stop making work for myself. "Accident and suicide, open and shut," he kept saying. And something about me making the rest of them look bad.'

'He could be right,' said Elspeth. 'I bet he's not as tired as you are tonight.'

'I don't see the point of doing this job unless you're prepared to be thorough,' said Sam.

'Fine, but you'll get no thanks for it. Is Morrison still on your back?'

'He's worse than Grayson. Now he's dumped a rash of break-ins and car thefts on the Upgill estate on my desk and told me to do something useful for a change.'

'Those kinds of things matter to people,' she said, taking a casserole out of the oven. 'Do something useful for me and get some plates out. Are you hungry?'

Sam spent most of the next day checking and re-checking the several reports about the Upgill estate trouble, written up by the local bobby over the past few weeks. It looked as if only one person, or maybe two, might be responsible for all of them. The same M.O., same prints in those places where Forensics had managed to find any. They even had his blood type from a smear on the light switch inside a shed that had been burgled.

'You know this estate,' Sam said later to Constable Farrell in the tiny office that passed as the Upgill police station. 'You've worked here, how long?'

'Upgill born and bred,' said Farrell, proudly. 'Worked here all me life. They offered me a panda car, but they said I'd 'ave to wear a flat cap not me 'elmet, so I turned it down. Need to be on the street in a place like this, not sitting in a car. People need to see you.'

'So you must have some idea who did all these jobs?' said Sam.

'No evidence, not yet,' said Farrell, 'but look at this'. He pulled a fat file out of the top drawer of the rusty filing cabinet, and put it down carefully on the old plastic table. Sam opened it up and skimmed through.

'William Neil Noakes (aka Nocky) born 13.5.48, living in Winchester Crescent, when he wasn't inside one institution or another. 1957 Montgomery House Boys' Home, well, well, 1964 Boreham Green Borstal, 1967 HMP Lancaster.'

'What's the "well, well" about?' asked PC Farrell.

'Montgomery House,' said Sam. 'I was there the other day, on a case. That kid who we found in the mud, a week or two back.'

'Aye, I saw that,' said Farrell. 'Trying to run away, across the sands back to his mam, I heard. What did you make of the place?'

'Looks all right to me,' said Sam. 'Talked to the matron, Mrs Robinson. Probably too late by the time she gets them, but she cares about those lads.'

'Her man was killed in the war,' said Farrell. 'He were a good 'un too.'

'What do we need to do, to bring this idiot in?' asked Sam.

'He has a lock-up, down Stanley Street,' said Farrell. 'I reckon some of the stuff must be in there, but last time we had a look, it were empty, as if someone 'ad tipped him off. That were two months gone, so maybe we need to have another go.'

'What about the cars?'

'Some of them sold for parts, likely, but a couple turned up miles out of town, burned out. No prints, but I reckon he took 'em just to drive. The lad's nuts about cars.'

'Just him?'

'His mates come and go, but this last lot of jobs have been since he came out of Lancaster six months ago. God knows what he learned in there.'

'Right. Let's pay another visit to the lock-up then, as soon as possible.' said Sam. 'I'll sort it out back at the station, and let you know.'

When Sam arrived back in Barrow CID room, Morrison was there, looking at the papers on Sam's desk. 'Are you on with the Upgill estate stuff I left for you?' he asked.

'Well on with it, sarge. Farrell knows his patch all right.'

'Old school,' said Morrison. 'Straight as they come and going nowhere. He's worked up there as a PC for nearly twenty years. No ambition.'

'Nothing wrong with that, is there?' said Sam.

Morrison sneered. 'Mug's game,' he said. 'If you need a warrant, go ahead. Clear up as much as you can while you're at it. Good for the figures and I've got Chief Inspector God Almighty Cardine breathing down me neck. Proper police work this is, not trying to prove some loony theory about a nonce who topped himself.'

Sam said nothing, and Morrison was gone again, leaving another pile of unanswered messages on his desk.

Twenty-four hours later Sam was sitting across a table from Bill Noakes, aka Nocky, in an interview room in Barrow police station. An overflowing ashtray lay between them, and the table and chair were both screwed into the concrete floor.

'You might as well give it up, Mr Noakes,' said Sam patiently, after the suspect had sworn yet again that he knew nothing about the assorted electrical goods that had been found at his lock-up at seven o'clock that morning. 'We've got your prints all over the stuff, your blood type on the switch in the shed on Palatine Street, not to mention the prints in the car on the shore at Askam.'

Bill Noakes sat forward. 'There were no prints in that car,' he said.

The man in a suit sitting next to him lowered his head, and Sam turned to him.

'I think you need to talk to your client, Mr Althorpe,' he said. 'He hasn't got the sense he was born with, but you might persuade him that pleading guilty to the nine counts we have, and any more he'd like to tell us about, will save a lot of our time and make the court more well-disposed towards him. You may have to explain what that means. I'll be outside.'

The deal took longer than Sam expected. Either Mr Althorpe's powers of persuasion were fading with his advancing years, or Noakes was more confident than he should have been about his chances at trial.

'My client has agreed to plead guilty to the theft of goods found this morning, but he still denies knowing anything about the car in Askam.'

'Or the one in Ulverston,' said Noakes.

Sam sighed. 'Thank you Mr Althorpe. I have some more questions for Mr Noakes if you can stay a little longer.'

The solicitor looked disgruntled but he opened up his bag again and took the pen from his pocket.

'Now then, Mr Noakes. I'm going to give you another chance to tell some more of your story. I see you were in Montgomery House for quite a long time.'

'Six bleeding years,' said Noakes.

'And how was it?'

'What d'ye mean, how was it? Like a bloody 'oliday camp, compared to Borstal. Got your meals, went to school, did a lot of digging. Other lads were OK.'

'What about the staff?'

'Ma Robinson, she were good to us.'

'And the others?'

'What you after, copper?' said Noakes. 'What's he after, Mr Althorpe?'

'Just answer the questions, Bill.'

'Well, old peg leg, he started me on cars, gave me driving lessons and that.'

'You mean Captain Edwards. What did you do to deserve that?' asked Sam.

Bill Noakes coloured. He tried to push the chair away but it stuck fast. Sam stayed quiet, watching the young man's discomfort.

'Bill,' said Sam, leaning across the table. 'I'm trying to help you. You've obviously got a thing about cars.' Bill wriggled again, but Sam continued, his voice quiet.

'If we can say that this obsession of yours was caused by something that happened when you were very young, the court might be more sympathetic. You took the cars, Bill, we know that, and so do you. Do yourself a favour. Just answer the question.'

Bill Noakes looked desperately across at his brief, who stared fixedly at the cracked ceiling.

'I were just a lad,' he said. 'Edwards 'ad mates who came to the house. They said I 'ad to be nice to them.'

'How nice?' asked Sam. His heart was beating. He knew what was coming.

'You know, nothing much like, just a bit of, you know.'

'You mean sex?' said Sam.

Noakes stood up, gripping the table. 'Never,' he said. 'Not proper sex, just, you know, fooling around.'

'Do you want to tell me the details?' asked Sam. 'Mr Althorpe, perhaps you could help Mr Noakes explain what he means by "fooling around". If he could make a statement, it might help his case.'

Althorpe looked at Noakes, who had sat down again. 'Give me a few minutes, constable,' he said. 'And I think my client needs a drink.'

For twenty long minutes, Sam paced up and down the corridor outside. He heard raised voices. The interview room door opened and Mr Althorpe's tired face looked out. He beckoned to Sam. Inside the room, Noakes was sitting, staring at the small window high up on the wall.

'I'm afraid that my client has decided not to make a statement after all.'

Sam started to speak, but Althorpe raised his hand. 'Mr Noakes is not prepared to say anything about his stay at Montgomery House. He says it was a long time ago and it doesn't matter. He understands that this might not help his case, but he tells me he couldn't care less, or words to that effect.'

Sam was bitterly disappointed. For a moment he could see things that had been bothering him falling into place. They'd been just fragments, but a statement from Noakes would have given him something to work with. And now there was nothing except a lock-up full of TVs and a couple of burned out cars. He looked at Mr Althorpe. 'Are there any other offences Mr Noakes would like us to include in the charges we bring against him, just to clear the decks, so to speak?'

They both looked at Noakes, who shook his head.

'Not for you, copper,' he said. 'You're all the same, you bastards.' He spat at Sam, and missed. Spittle winked on the table between them.

Outside in the corridor, Althorpe said, 'What was all that about? Most people round here think Edwards should have a gong for what he does for those lads. What on earth made you start that line?'

Sam looked away. 'Nothing that was said in there will go any further,' he said, 'from me or you. I have good reason to ask those questions, and I'm not giving up yet.'

'Bad mistake,' said Althorpe. 'Leave it alone, constable, or you won't get very far in this town. Good afternoon to you.'

Morrison was delighted. Nine robberies and a guilty plea. Just the news he needed to take to his boss. Missed out on the two cars but they would probably be proven anyway, and the lad would go back to Lancaster or wherever, so long as it was miles away from their patch. 'Good man, Nelly,' he said. 'I owe you a pint.'

'Give it to Farrell,' said Sam. 'He did all the work.'

Morrison didn't like that idea one bit.

Before he went home, Sam sat in the quiet CID room and began to doodle on a piece of paper. Something was beginning to take shape in his mind. He wanted to look again at the beginnings of Montgomery House, who actually ran it, and who were these 'mates' who seemed to frequent the place? Who were the trustees, and what did their 'annual checks' consist of? Was Mrs Robinson really so confident that everything was fine? And what did any of this have to do with Steven Stringer, or even Anthony Lennon? Sam ran his hand down his face, noticing that he needed a shave. Bloody Anthony. Where the hell was he?

That evening Sam supervised Tommy in the bath and put him to bed. It was Elspeth's night off at the keep fit class she went to, which seemed to consist of half an hour's exercise followed by an hour in the pub. Tommy was nearly seven years old, thought Sam. Older than some of the boys at Montgomery House. Older than Bill Noakes was when he was taken from his home and family and placed in care, for his own good. And what good had it done him, or Anthony? Sam wanted to blame someone but didn't know who. He thought about what Bill had said about Edwards and the driving lessons. Could that really happen? Could a kid be persuaded to 'fool around' with strange men, just for a reward? What would have happened if Bill had refused, spat at Edwards' friends, whoever they were, like he'd spat at Sam? A beating?

One of the fragments circling slowly in Sam's head was

something Judith had told him, from her conversation with the lad at Monty House. He had told her about Stevie getting into trouble with a visitor and all the lads getting blamed. Sam wondered if there was more that Judith had kept to herself or had just forgotten. Eight o'clock, Elspeth would be back in half an hour. Judith might be home at the flat, or at the Feathers close to the *Furness News* offices where they often went after work. He searched for the number of the house in Cannon Street. The phone rang for a long time and he was just giving up when he heard her voice.

'Judith?'

'Who else, Sam?' she said. 'There's no one else here, thank heaven.'

'Not missing the delights of the Thornills' palace?'

'It was pretty good there, I can tell you. Big bed, all my washing done, far too much wine. but being around Irene and my boss all the time I could do without.'

'You all right, back in the flat?'

She hesitated. 'It's fine,' she said. 'Why? Have you found Anthony?'

'No. But I want to talk to you about something. Can I come over, or you come here?'

'I'll come to you,' she said. 'I'd got used to having a TV and it's a bit quiet without it.'

'You can watch it here if you like, but after I've asked you a few things. Can you bring your notebook?'

Judith and Elspeth saw each other approach the house from opposite directions.

'I thought it was you,' said Elspeth. 'Lucky you caught me, I've been out since six.'

'Sam rang me,' said Judith. 'Said he wanted to talk about something private.' Elspeth smiled. 'Is there something I should know?' she asked.

'No,' said Judith. 'Your brother's fingers got well and truly burned with wifey Christine, I reckon. And anyway, he's not my type.'

'And what type's that?' asked Elspeth. She had her key in her hand but wanted an answer before they went in.

'Taller,' said Judith, 'and more fun. Sam just thinks about work, all the time.'

The house was warm and smelled of food. Judith realised instantly that she was hungry. It must have showed in her face.

'Have you eaten?' asked Elspeth. 'We had supper early, but there's plenty left.'

When she'd loaded a plate for Judith, Elspeth discovered a sudden interest in something on the TV, leaving the other two sitting at the kitchen table, and Judith tucking into a sizeable portion of hotpot.

'Go on,' she said to Sam. 'I'm listening.'

'Just after Steven was found, you talked to the lad at Monty House, didn't you?'

'It was next door, by the field actually. I was hiding in a rhododendron bush and Mikey pretended to be cropping sprouts. It was ludicrous.'

'What did he tell you?'

'I told you before. Stevie was a nuisance, got them all into trouble.'

'Did he say why, or how?'

'Hang on,' said Judith. She fished her notebook out of her bag and leafed through it.

'What a mess,' he said. Even upside down, he could see bits of writing at different angles, arrows, crossings out. 'How do you make sense of it?'

'We all have our own ways of doing things,' she said. 'My ways happen to be organic, not like yours.'

'Organic? Who told you that?'

'See, I've found it. Conversation with Mikey, and the date. Didn't write it at the time, in the bushes, so I might have missed something. I might have forgotten it by the time I wrote it up. Here it is. Mikey said that Stevie spat at a visitor and didn't own up. They all lost their trips and comics and things.'

'Any more about the visitor, or any other visitors?'

Judith turned the page. 'Thought I remembered something,' she said. 'I asked whether they ever had any alcohol, and he said something about the captain having his old army mates over and they all got a bit noisy. I assume he meant they were drinking.' She looked up at Sam. 'Why are you asking about this?'

For a moment Sam wanted to tell her everything he was thinking, to share the burden. 'Just something I got from a suspect,' he said, 'who was at Attercliff when he was a lad. It started me wondering, but it's all guesswork. Just a theory, nothing I can prove.'

'Do you want to tell me?' she asked.

'Yes,' he said, 'but only some suspicions, nothing I can prove.'

CHAPTER 21

Elspeth looked at her watch. It was late and she wanted to stay out of their way until the steady sound of conversation had stopped. It was all work, she was sure of that. She wondered about Sam. Judith was a bit wild-looking, as unlike Sam's ex-wife Christine as could be, but he didn't seem to see her as anything but a work colleague. There was the occasional blush, but he could do that about anything. From what Judith had told her in their earlier conversations, she hadn't had a serious relationship with anyone since that bastard tutor. Both of them had been burned and scarred by other people – and herself too, she realised, but at least she had Tommy, not just a job, to absorb her love and her energy.

The kitchen door opened and Judith came out, putting on her coat, with Sam close behind. 'I'm going to walk back with Judith,' he said. 'Won't be long.'

'I've told him there's no need,' said Judith. 'Fog's so thick no one will see me anyway.'

'Well, take care, both of you. I'll leave the outside light on, Sam.' Elspeth hugged Judith, opened the front door and pushed them both out to close the door against the wisps of fog that threatened to invade the house.

Judith and Sam walked in silence. 'You can't be right about

what's going on at Montgomery House,' she said.

'I hope I'm not. I wasn't right about Harries's suicide.'

She looked across at him. 'What about it?'

'I thought the note in Harries's pocket might be a fake, but his mother sent some of his handwriting and it matches, as far as I can see. I've sent it to Forensics to check. God knows how long that'll take.' Sam kicked at a half brick lying in the middle of the pavement. Lorries passed along this road constantly taking the remnants of old demolished buildings to be dumped elsewhere. Fragments of Barrow's past fell off. The town was permanently covered in brick dust; it needed some real rain to sluice everything clean, and wind to blow away the fog.

Sam's dour mood was as thick as the air that swirled around them. 'Not sure I can stand working here much longer,' he said. 'Thought a fresh start somewhere would do me good, but it's not working.'

'Could you get promotion or something, get out from under people like Morrison?'

'Did the exams last year, but now I just have to wait. If your face doesn't fit, you could wait for ever, and my face doesn't fit.'

'How do you know? They must know how thorough you are.'

'That's the problem. They think I'm trying to show them up.'

Judith changed the subject. 'Any idea where Anthony is? I honestly don't think he's after me, but I know you want to find him.'

'We're checking all the places he might be staying, with both the names we know of, but he might not be using either of them. Wish I'd kept that passport. I gave as much as I could remember of his photo to the sketch artist, but those pictures never look like a real person. I'm sure he's still around. And if we do find him now, so what? All we've got is a suspicion that he had something to do with Harries's suicide.'

'You mean he pushed him into it?'

'Maybe, but no one at our nick or Ulverston seems to care about that. They're all sure Harries was a pervert.'

'Are you?'

Sam shrugged. 'Something's been going on at that place,' he said. 'I'm sure of it.' He stopped and held her arm. 'Promise me, you won't breathe a word of what we talked about tonight. Right or wrong, I'm in trouble either way if anyone knows what I'm thinking. People seem to think Edwards walks on water.'

'Do you think he'd know if anything was going on?'

'I'm sure he would, and Mrs Robinson would, too. But she thinks the sun shines out of him. It's the kids who come off worst, but I bet none of them will talk, especially the older ones. The suspect I talked to today, he had his chance to tell me something but he backed off it.'

'Afraid?'

'Not of me. The only thing that would bother him is what his mates would think, or other prisoners when he goes back to clink. Nothing worse than being a perv. It'll get you a beating in prison, or worse.'

They'd reached the corner of Cannon Street.

'I'll be fine now, Sam,' said Judith. 'Thanks for walking me back.'

'Sure? I'm dog tired,' he said. He pulled up his coat collar and looked down the road.

'Go home,' said Judith. She watched him walk away until he disappeared into the fog that closed around him. She turned back into her street and began to walk quickly into the gloom towards the house. The sound of her footsteps on the pavement bounced back from the foggy wall, exaggerating the silence.

A dark figure stepped in front of her wearing a long coat and hat pulled down over his face. She stopped, shocked, feeling her heart jump. She wanted to say something but no words came. She looked behind her. The street was empty and she turned to run. Too late. The steps behind her got closer and something pulled her back while a gloved hand closed over her mouth. She struggled but the arms were strong and the man pushed her back against a wall and then down an alley. 'If you scream I'll hurt you,' said the voice. 'Understand?'

She nodded.

He stood behind her, one arm round her shoulders, holding her. The hand eased away from her mouth. 'Not a sound,' he said. 'I could strangle you, I've done it before.'

She nodded again and breathed in the foggy air and the smell of his clothes.

'You know who I am, don't you?'

Judith nodded. 'Steven's brother,' she whispered.

'So you know what I want?'

'You want to know what happened to him.'

'He was just a kid. They killed him.'

'Who did?'

'Those bastards at the home.'

'How do you know?'

'I know,' he said.

'Stevie ran away,' said Judith.

'Of course he did. But they killed him.'

'What did you do to Mr Harries?'

'Who?'

'The man who hanged himself.'

'Our Stevie told me he was a nonce. I threatened 'im, but I didn't hang 'im. Wish I had. I found 'im hanging on that tree and I let him swing. Pervy bastard.'

'Did Harries tell you anything?'

'Nowt. Cried like a baby.'

'What about my flat. Did you wreck it?'

'Not me. Two men did it, I watched them go in.'

Judith stood quite still. Her neck was aching with the strain of his grip. She pulled away and he let her move, just a little.

She tried another question. 'Did you send that tape?'

'Had to do summat.'

'Why not a letter?'

'Can't write. Brothers at Bindoon didn't care. All we did there was work and get beaten.'

'What brothers?' Donna hadn't mentioned any more brothers.

'Bastards,' he said, and she heard him spit.

The car engine was close by before they heard it. He pulled her back into the shadow of the wall, and they both saw the square shape of a Landrover stop at the end of the alley before it slid past.

'It's them,' he said. She felt him twist to look up the alley. 'What's up there?'

'The back lane.'

He let go of her. 'Go home, quick,' he said. 'It's me they're after.'

He left her and ran down the alley, past Judith's back yard door and round the corner into the back lane. She waited, then followed and crouched to her knees at the end of the alley to look round the corner. To her left she saw one rear light on the Landrover, and beside it two men with a third slumped between them, his feet dragging on the road. As she watched, they let the man fall, opened the back door of the Landrover and picked up the lifeless figure, pushing it into the back. They jumped into the front and drove away, turning left at the end of the lane.

Judith ran to the back yard door and pulled her scooter off its stand. No point in calling the police, no time. She had to see where they were taking him. She waited in the alley. They could go either way, but she saw them pass down Cannon Street, back towards Abbey Road. At the end of the deserted street Judith looked both ways, peering into the gloom for the one brake light, not two. To the right, towards the town centre, a single red light glinted and she followed it until the blurred outline cleared. It was a motorbike. She swore and turned back towards the junction to take the other road, towards the outskirts of the town, urging the scooter as fast as it would go. The Landrover would hesitate to draw attention to itself by going too fast, but if she was stopped she could tell the police. There was no sign of a vehicle ahead of her. She wasn't thinking about why she was doing this, or what might happen. All she wanted was to do was to follow Anthony, to help him if she could.

At the next intersection the lights were on red, but she didn't stop, straining to see what lay ahead. She was almost across the junction when she saw the single red light to her left and the back wheel of the scooter slid on the greasy road as she turned too quickly. She had left her helmet behind and her hair streamed behind her, some of it across her face. As she pulled strands away from her eyes the Vespa wobbled, but stayed upright.

She knew now where they were going, to the coast road and away from the town. She had no idea who they were but they had wrecked her flat and now they had taken Anthony and she was angry. She slowed to keep the red light just at the edge of her vision and switched off the scooter's headlight. They might not see her, and if they did, she might not matter enough to them. Who were they? She hated them.

Where the road swung east along the shore of the bay she followed it round but the fog was less thick and she realised quite quickly that the Landrover was not ahead of her. There was only one way they could have gone and she doubled back, taking the lane that led down towards the sea. There was the red light again, to her left, heading out across the sands towards the flowing channels that carried the rivers across the bay. She stopped the scooter where fresh tyre tracks led off the road, through the gap in the sea wall and down towards the shore. She couldn't follow them on the scooter. She looked around, desperate, unsure what to do. The pub was another quarter of a mile away, but it was late and they might be closed already or drinking after hours behind a locked door. Fog drifted in patches. She saw the red light, then lost it, then saw it again. For a while it disappeared, but then she heard the sound of an engine and hid behind the wall as the Landrover emerged from the gloom, bumping and splashing across the nearer channels, heading east. Judith pushed the scooter against the wall and stood for a moment. Then she pulled her coat round her, tied the belt as tight as it would go, and ran down the beach.

The first of the channels was shallow and she waded through it, but the second flooded her boots with icy water, weighing her feet down. She had thought of discarding the boots all together but decided to keep them on, to protect her feet from stones. The soles were soon clogged with mud and she fell sideways. In righting herself she lost her bearings and had to wait until a gap in the fog revealed where she had started from. She turned back and formed an imaginary straight line to guide her. He was out there. She was certain that they had dumped him and driven away. She had no idea of the time. Was the tide coming in, to find him and finish him off? She would have to be quick.

She dragged herself, sodden and heavy, across the mudbank, and into another channel. In the middle of it she stopped and looked down. The water was flowing from her right. She knew what that meant. The tide was coming in. On the far bank she looked around. She was lost, and for the first time she was afraid. Then she heard it. A low moan, then louder, ahead and to her left. The bank was steep and she slipped again. As she got to her feet, brushing mud from her hands, she saw a dark pile of something on the sand, lapped by the water. The moan came again and the pile moved, then stopped.

She reached him and knelt down. Anthony's hat was gone, his face streaked with mud and sand. He lay on his side, one knee underneath, the other leg bent at an unnatural angle. Blood seeped from his nose and the side of his mouth. His mouth moved and she moved closer.

'Done,' he said. On the side of his chest was the handle of a knife with a dark stain around it. She put her hand towards it.

'No,' he groaned. 'Leave it.'

She was panting now, and the tears came, tears of disgust and anger, but not sadness, not yet.

She looked around. There was nothing, no light, no sound except the lap of the tide as it began to cover his legs. She stood up. The water was still rising and flowing past them more urgently, pulled into the vast bay by forces that she could not stop or control. Anthony spat out the salty mud that had reached his mouth and turned his face towards the sky.

'Go,' he mouthed. Red bubbles broke on his lips. 'Go.'

She knelt again, cradling his head. She could not leave him

there to drown or bleed to death. If she could hold on to him the water might take his weight and she could drag him towards the shore and leave him safe and go for help. She put her arms round him from behind and held him. Relentless water pushed and rolled them over, but as it deepened around them they did not float. Anthony's body rolled over her leg, pinning her down. She pushed with all her strength against him, her boots sliding in the mud, straining for purchase. After a few moments, exhausted, she lay back, salt water slipping over her chin. She wiped a muddy hand down her face. As she looked up towards the sky, blackness replaced the grey, just for a moment. A single star gleamed. She turned her head. Above her the night sky was clear, but all around was a wall of grey.

A surge of the tide took Anthony's solid body and pushed it off her aching leg. She cried with pain and fear and rolled over onto her front, raised her head and then pulled one knee underneath her, pushing up, then the other knee. Her heavy coat streamed as she lifted herself, watching Anthony rolling away. He made no sound. Kneeling now, the water up to her shoulders, she sat back, then stood, fell, stood again. The stars had disappeared. The rising water in the channels twisted and snaked, deceptive, taunting. She rose from her knees and tried to walk with the flow, following the body that was slipping away into the gloom, but after a few stumbling steps she stopped. He was gone. The water lapped and pushed. Following intuition, nothing more, and knowing that she had crossed a channel before finding Anthony's body, she reached for deeper water and pushed through it, feeling for the incline of the far bank. Finding it at last, she struggled up and pulled breath into her lungs, trying to keep the same direction and pushing forward again. Another channel. This time she drifted, feeling the flow pushing her to the side. Only with the final stretch did her foot touch the sand and she pushed against her toes. She dropped to her knees, her head below the water to push herself up the bank of the channel, find her feet and stand. Wet hair and sand caked her face and she pushed them back, looking to left and right. She was too tired now to go much further and the water tugged at her, pulling her off her feet.

As she slipped again, the air lightened, just for a second and she saw a gleam of something orange to her left before the curtain closed again. It had to be the single streetlight on the shore near the gap in the wall. A burst of energy pushed her upright again and she held the now invisible light in her memory, pushing against the water that flowed against her, pushing, straining, breathing and pushing again. Once more the orange glow appeared, again to her left, and again she bent toward it before it faded and was gone. The water was shallower now, but her boots were sticking in the mud, sinking and cloying. She bent down and pushed the top of one of the boots, heaving at her foot until it slid out. The surging tide pivotted her round, twisting her knee, making her cry out as she fell. She lay for a moment, weighed down by her sodden coat, and then knelt, stood and stumbled forward, up onto shingle. When the shingle softened into turf and the orange light enveloped her, she knelt again, panting, before rolling over to rest.

CHAPTER 22

Something was licking her face. Judith turned her head and smelled the dog's breath as it stood over her. She was cold. Pain thumped in her head. She opened her eyes. There was a shout, the dog backed away and another face appeared, reeking of tobacco. A calloused hand stroked strands of hair from her face. The man took off his jacket and covered her with it. 'Awreet, lass,' he said. 'Going for help, Meg'll stay with ye.'

He spoke to the dog, who lay down beside Judith, shielding her from the wind that had blown away the fog into a grey dawn.

She began to shiver and the dog came closer, its paws across her legs. Oyster catchers mewed at the tide's edge, rooks cawed in ancient trees, and Judith lay, memories of the night flickering into her mind. The man came back with a heavy blanket and a cushion that he eased under her head.

'Hold on, lass,' he said to her. 'Help's coming. Here, drink.'

He held up her head and put a cup to her mouth. The tea was hot and sweet, but most of it dribbled down her neck.

'Try again,' he said. 'Need to get warm.'

A bell sounded, far away, and came closer.

'Ambulance,' said the man. 'They'll see you reet. Hold on.'

Suddenly there were voices, the sound of boots on gravel,

and strong hands straightened out her body and lifted her onto a stretcher. Judith felt herself slide into the darkness, heard the bang of doors and the rumble of the engine. Beside her a young man said to her, 'What's your name, love?'

'Judith,' she heard her voice croak. 'Judith Pharaoh.'

'You're very cold, Judith,' said the young man, 'so we're taking you to hospital to check you over and warm you up. You'll be all right. Someone will ask you about all this, but not yet.' He wiped streaks of mud from her face, then reached down to massage her numb feet. 'You're in a right mess, eh,' he said. 'Dinna fret. We'll have you sitting up soon enough.'

They wheeled her into the hospital. Voices murmured. She could feel the movement of the trolley and saw the ceiling of the corridor slide past over her head. More hands lifted her up and down, and then a woman's voice said. 'Hello, Judith. Need to warm you up, so we're going to get you into a bath. Only me here, all the men have gone. You help me get these wet clothes off and we'll be right as rain, OK?'

The water was warm and silky against Judith's cold skin and she lay back as the nurse soaped and washed her. Her knees began to smart and blood seeped into the water.

'Good sign,' said the nurse. 'Blood starts again when you warm up. Just a few cuts and bruises. You were lucky, pet.'

Warm and dry again, Judith sat up in the tight bed and looked around her. Blue curtains were pulled around and she could hear the sounds of talking beyond them.

'Just a few minutes,' the nurse's voice said. 'She's in shock still. Needs to rest.'

The curtains opened and Sam stood beside her, looking down. His pale face didn't smile.

'Sergeant Clark called me,' he said. 'I shouldn't have left you. I let that bastard do this.'

She shook her head. 'They took him,' she whispered. 'Two men, they took him and I followed them.' She remembered. 'My scooter…'

'We've got it. What were you doing out there?'

'They stabbed Anthony. Have you found him?'

He stared at her. 'Who stabbed him?'

'The two men, in the Landrover.'

He leaned over her. 'Judith,' he said. 'We found you, just you. Where is Anthony?'

Judith raised her head in desperation. 'He's out there. The tide came and took him. I had to leave him.' She started to cry. He pulled a tissue from the box on the locker and handed it to her. Judith felt the hot tears on her face. Sam turned away and opened the curtains. 'Nurse!' he called.

'All right, that's enough,' said Nurse Froggatt, stroking Judith's damp hair. 'Whatever you want to know, it'll have to wait. The doctor will decide when she's fit to talk any more.'

'But –' he began.

She held up her hand. 'No buts, constable. That's enough for now. She's in no fit state. Now off you go and we'll tell you when she's ready. Shoo.'

'It's Nurse Froggatt,' she said, turning back to Judith. 'I'm going to bring you some tea, and something to eat. The doctor will be round soon. Just rest. No one's going to bother you.'

Judith lay back and turned her head to one side. Behind her eyes she could see Anthony's body rolling, twisting, disappearing into the fog.

'No serious damage, Miss Pharaoh,' said the doctor a while later. 'You were very cold, good thing someone found you when they did. Bruises, and you've twisted your knee, but that's about all. Have they asked you who we should call, family, and so forth?'

Judith shook her head. 'My dad,' she said. 'John Pharaoh, at Sellafield. What time is it?'

He looked at his watch. 'Just gone eleven,' he said.

'In the morning?'

'Yes,' he smiled. 'In the morning. Looks as if you'd been out there all night.'

'Have they found Anthony?' she asked.

He frowned. 'Just you, as far as I know. Was someone with you?'

'Anthony, but he was hurt. I couldn't hold on to him.'

'We'll let the police deal with that, shall we?' he said. 'My job is to get you back to yourself again, and we're halfway there. A few more hours and you'll be much better. Need to sleep, though. I'll ask Nurse Froggatt to give you something. See you later.'

A few minutes later the nurse returned with a pill and a cup of water. Judith did as she was told, and drifted away into dreamless darkness.

The next thing she saw was her father's face.

'She's awake,' he said. 'Judith, it's me, Dad. They called me at work and I came straight down.' She felt his warm hand on her cheek and looked into his face and his brimming eyes.

'I'm all right Dad,' she said. 'I'm still here.'

He sobbed. 'They say you could have died, pet. From the cold. Out there all night. What happened to you?'

Judith didn't know what to say. 'I saw a man I know get taken away. They hurt him and dumped him out on the sand, so I went to find him.'

John shook his head. 'Have you told the police?'

'Not yet. Is Sam still here?'

'There's a young man outside. Is that him? He looked very upset.'

'Can you ask him to come in, Dad? I need to talk to him.'

John didn't move. 'Not yet,' he said. 'You're not fit to answer questions.'

'How long will I be here?' she asked. 'I'm not badly hurt, the doctor said.'

'You need to rest,' said her father. 'As soon as you can leave here, I'm taking you home. I'll get you some clothes.'

Judith said nothing, holding her father's hand as he blinked back his tears.

Three hours later, Judith was sitting by the side of her bed, wearing clothes that her father had brought from the flat. The curtains had been pulled back and she watched the nurses come and go. Women in other beds looked across and smiled at her. The door at the far end of the ward opened and Sam walked towards her. He was smiling, too.

'Good to see you looking more yourself,' he said, as he pulled up a chair and sat down next to the bed. 'Doc says I can ask you the questions we need to have some answers to, before your dad takes you away to St Bees. Elspeth wanted you to stay with us, but he wouldn't hear of it. Has anyone from your work been?'

'Don't know,' said Judith. 'They made me sleep for a while. Then Dad came, and now you. Nurse Froggatt's pretty fierce, she might have sent them away.'

'Quite right, too,' he said. 'This is a police investigation, and the press will have to wait.'

'Have you found Anthony?' she asked again, although she knew that he was dead.

He shook his head. 'Tide's come and gone, and there was no sign of anyone where you were found. It was a high tide last night, could have taken him anywhere.'

She rested her head on the high chair and turned away.

He lowered his voice. 'Tell me what happened, Judith, right from the time I left you at the corner last night.'

She told him, every detail she could remember, and the tears came again. He looked around, fearful that Nurse Froggatt would intervene, but the ward was quiet and she was nowhere to be seen.

'He told you that the two men who went to your flat were in a Landrover?'

'He said "they're here" when the Landrover went past the end of the alley.'

'And when you found him, there was a knife in his chest? What kind of a knife, can you remember that?'

She shook her head. 'I wanted to pull it out, but he stopped me.'

Sam nodded. 'Why did you stay with him so long? You could have drowned.'

'I thought I might be able to save him, if the water took his weight and I could get us both towards the shore. I didn't want him to die like Stevie.' She felt the tears in her eyes again.

'What else did he tell you?'

She dredged her memory. 'He said he'd threatened Harries, and found his body, but he didn't kill him.' She hesitated, thinking. 'He sent the tape to the paper 'cos he couldn't write, and something about the brothers at Bindoon not caring about them. I didn't understand that.'

'Maybe something to do with Australia. That was all?'

She nodded. 'He told me to go, said he was done. I don't remember much after that.'

'So we're left with these two men,' said Sam. 'Can you remember anything about them, anything at all?'

'It was dark, and it was all over so quickly. When I saw them, they were holding Anthony between them, then they pushed him in the back of the Landrover.'

'Tall, short?'

'Hard to tell. They looked taller than Anthony, but he was hanging down, feet dragging on the floor.'

'And the Landrover?'

'I think it was red,' she said. 'Dark red, but the lights were orange and it was foggy.'

'Number plate?'

'Not all of it.' She closed her eyes, trying to see it. 'I think the first letter was A, and the numbers, I don't know. Maybe 26 or 28? It was so dark. It had only one light at the back. They drove away in it. It must be somewhere.'

'Did they know you were following them?'

Judith shrugged. 'I tried to hide, but they could have spotted me. If they know where I live, they probably know about the scooter.'

Sam looked at her. 'You can't stay in Barrow,' he said. 'Go back to St Bees with your dad and we'll tell the police up there to keep an eye on you.'

'Where is my dad?'

'The nurse said he's gone to get some more things for you, and he'll be back. Stay home a while, let things cool down. Give me the telephone number and I'll let you know what's going on.'

As she spoke, he wrote the number down and put his notebook away. He looked at her again. 'Thank God you're still here. We could have lost you.'

'But you didn't,' she said. 'So cheer up.'

❖ ❖ ❖

It was dark when John's car pulled away from the hospital. Judith sat beside him with a rug over her knees.

'I look like the Queen Mum with this on,' she said.

He laughed. 'Can't imagine anyone less like the Queen Mum than you.'

'What's that suitcase on the back seat?' she asked.

'I took your keys, but when I went to the flat, I couldn't find clothes that looked clean, so I just went out and bought a few things. Hope I got the sizes right. Mum will take you shopping when you're ready. She'll love that.'

'Thanks,' she said, dreading the prospect of a shopping trip to Whitehaven with Maggie, and probably Granny Violet in tow as well. 'Has anyone told work where I am?'

'That young detective said he was going to see them,' said John. 'Apparently Mrs Thornhill offered to have you to stay again, but he told them you were coming back with me.' He hesitated. 'Your mother wasn't too happy about you staying with them last time.'

'That was different,' said Judith. 'I had to work, but now I can take some time off.' She glanced at her father. 'Not long though, Dad. You'll tell Mum that, won't you? Don't let her think I'm coming back for good.'

'We'll see,' he said.

The homecoming was much as Judith had expected, and she did her best to sound pleased to be there. 'Bit drastic wasn't it?' said Vince. 'I knew you really wanted to come home, Jude, but you didn't have to get half drowned before we'd let you in.'

She smiled, and punched his arm. 'Right,' she said.

'Granny Violet wanted to come over, but I told her to wait until you were better,' said Maggie when she brought Judith tea and sandwiches on a tray. 'We'll have a proper dinner later, this is just to put you on. Your room is aired and ready, whenever you want to go and rest. Do you want to put your feet up?'

'I'm all right Mum, really. My knee hurts a bit, but that's all, honestly.'

The next day Judith woke with a start. It was light and for a moment she couldn't remember where she was. In the flat the window was to her right, but now everything was the wrong way round. She heard the phone, but where was it? She lay back, trying to remember. The bedroom door was pushed open and Vince put his head round.

'Jude? Are you awake? Do you want to speak to your boss?'

'Vince,' Maggie called up to him. 'Leave Judith alone. Who's on the phone?'

'As you were,' said Vince. 'She who must be obeyed is calling.'

Judith heard him tread slowly down the stairs. He'd left the door open and she could hear her mother's raised voice.

Several minutes later Maggie came into Judith's room carrying a cup of tea. 'That's told him,' she said, putting down the tea and perching on the bed. 'Mr Thornhill. Can he help at all, indeed? Thanks, but no thanks. And what kind of job puts a young woman in such danger, I'd like to know.'

Judith groaned. 'He didn't send me out there, Mum.'

'Well who did?' said Maggie. 'What on earth possessed you?'

'Not now, Mum, please,' said Judith. 'Don't ask me any more questions.'

Sam had questions. They'd been piling up in his mind, and one of them he'd asked before leaving the hospital. 'Doctor

Hayward was discharged three days ago,' was the answer. 'He's quite unwell, but it was felt he would be more comfortable at home.' Sam had checked his watch, found Hayward's home number, and called it from the hospital payphone.

'This is the second call we've had about my husband in the past twenty-four hours,' said Mrs Hayward. 'I shall tell you what I told the other one. My husband is ill and tired and does not wish to speak to anyone, least of all the police. I'd be grateful if you could respect that and leave us alone.'

'Who was the other person who called?' asked Sam.

'Inspector Morrison, of course,' said Mrs Hayward. 'He's pestered my husband for far too long, and you can tell him from me that he's not welcome here. Goodbye, constable.'

Back at the CID room the following morning, Sam called to the WPC who was in the outer office doing some filing. She came through, notepad in hand.

'Can you get on to Records for me, Kath? I've got a possible number plate. Not much, but's it's a red Landrover and there can't be too many of those.' He handed over a piece of paper. 'And can you ask them for anything they've got on two villains using a Landrover. Probably have some previous, assault, GBH and local enough to know about the sands, tides, that kind of stuff. Doesn't ring any bells with me, but I'm new here.'

'What about Sergeant Morrison?' said Kath Tunnycliffe. 'He's been around forever, knows all the locals. He came in a while back. Told me to get his desk cleared up. That's a joke.'

'You get going with Records, I'll plough through the stuff on his desk again,' said Sam. 'Maybe he has a system that works like carbon dating, with the really old valuable stuff at the bottom.'

'Good luck with that,' said WPC Tunnycliffe. 'I suppose you'll want some tea.'

'I'll get it,' said Sam. Tunnycliffe must be about the same age as Judith, he thought, and people treat her like a skivvy. If that happens at Judith's office, no wonder she gets so grumpy.

He looked down at Morrison's desk, put one hand under the pile of papers, lifted them up and turned the whole lot over, so that the deepest layer was on top. He turned over some of the items. Most of it was inconsequential and outdated, but his eye was caught by a name at the bottom of a note. *Need to talk to you. Call me at home. Hayward.*

Sam checked the date. It was three days after Stevie's body was found on the sands. He replaced the pile of material as he had found it and went to fill the kettle.

'Where's Grayson?' he asked WPC Tunnycliffe. 'I need to check something with him.'

'He's off today. You might get him at home.'

Sam went back in the office and picked up the phone.

'Harry?' he said, when Grayson eventually answered the phone. 'Got some more information about the suicide at Attercliff. Took a statement today from someone who heard Anthony Lennon admit that he'd threatened Harries, and found his body in the woods, but says he didn't kill him.'

'Well, that deals with the question of the cigarettes. Lennon must have smoked a couple there while he watched Harries's body swinging in the wind. Nice. Who's the witness?'

'Judith Pharaoh,' said Sam. He knew what reaction there'd be.

'That nosey bitch,' said Harry. 'How did she find Lennon before we did? And where is she now?'

Sam told him as little of the story as he needed to know.

'Is she all right?' asked Harry, more gently.

'Shocked, mild hypothermia apparently, but she's recovered from that now. Seems all right to me. She's gone back home with her dad, but I'll go up there and take a statement. She was so done in she couldn't think straight at the hospital.'

'We assume Lennon's dead, do we?'

'Looks like it,' said Sam. 'No report of a body, but in the bay it could take a while to turn up.'

'And what about the pair in the Landrover?'

'No sign of them either,' said Sam. 'We're still looking.'

'Let me know if you need me,' said Harry and rang off.

WPC Tunnycliffe put her head round the door. 'I've been on to Records,' she said. 'No joy with the number plate so far, but there's new information. Lancashire police in Hest Bank have been on. A red Landrover was found out there a couple of hours ago. Looks like someone tried to torch it.'

'Good,' said Sam. 'Something happening, at last. Have you got a contact, and the location?'

She waved a piece of paper at him. 'All here,' she said. 'And I've got you a car for tomorrow.'

'Is there a registration plate on the Landrover?'

'I asked but they said it was missing. Do you want me to carry on with what we've got?'

Sam agreed, but he feared it would be like a needle in a haystack.

It was just after eight on Friday morning when Sam walked into the car pool yard to pick up the keys.

'What time d'you call this, constable?' said Sergeant Morrison. 'I've been waiting here ten minutes. You driving?'

They were well on the way to Ulverston before Sam said, 'Thought this was my case, sarge.'

Morrison drew on his cigarette. 'It was lad, for too long. Not enough happening and I've been asked the question.

Now some nosey bitch has got herself involved and we're waiting for the big front pager from the *News* asking what the police are doing, blah, blah. So the DI leans on me and I lean on you. That's the way it works.'

Sam didn't respond.

'What the fuck was she doing out there anyway?' Morrison went on. 'From what I gather Lennon was over from Australia on false papers and got himself in bother with some of the locals. Dumping him in the bay was a bit stupid. Could have bumped him off quietly anywhere if they'd wanted to. That's assuming it's the same Landrover.'

'Didn't know you were taking such an interest, sarge.'

'No thanks to you, lad. Good job I keep my ear close to the ground.'

'Where did you hear about the Landrover?'

'From the press, God help us. Thornhill told me, last night.'

And who told him, Sam wondered.

'So here I am, Nelly, and we'll have a proper look at this Landrover, or what's left of it. They're taking it to the compound at Lancaster nick. Know where that is?

'I was in the Lancashire force for three years, sarge,' said Sam. 'I think I know where I'm going.'

'Touchy, constable. You still look about nineteen to me.'

They found the Landrover standing forlorn in the corner of the police compound covered with a tarpaulin.

'Bit late for worrying about the rain, isn't it?' said Morrison. 'Looks as if the water's probably washed away most of what we're looking for. Any prints?'

'Some,' said the Forensics man. 'Not too good, but worth checking. Everything was pretty sodden by the time we got it out. And they'd tried to torch it but the tide must have caught them out. Registration plates gone.'

'Any sign of where they went?'

'Nothing. Too wet, and the tide washed out any bootprints too. It's not far to the road from where it was dumped. They could have walked, or got a lift.'

'What about blood?' asked Sam, remembering what Judith had said about the knife.

'Some stains in the back, we're checking those now. Do we know the blood type of the bloke they snatched?'

Morrison looked at Sam. 'Well? Do we?'

'No,' said Sam. 'He was completely under our radar, false papers, no address.'

'A mystery man,' said Morrison. 'Kidnapped by persons unknown for reasons unknown. Great.'

'He had a sister,' said Sam, 'in Morecambe. Donna. Works at the station café.'

Morrison looked at him. 'Did he? So she's Steven Stringer's sister, too, is she?'

'Half sister probably,' said Sam. 'Mother gets around a bit.'

'Family couldn't even be bothered organising the lad's funeral,' said Morrison, 'so why should we care?'

'It's our job, isn't it?' said Sam.

Morrison pulled him by the arm, out of earshot of the others. 'Don't get pompous with me, lad,' he whispered. 'I've been in this job more years than you've had hot dinners, and don't you forget it. So we'll get the wrapping off this vehicle, go over it with a fine toothcomb, find whatever there is to find, and get back to Barrow before day's end. And no more smart remarks from you. Right?'

Sam knew there was no point in saying anything, so he didn't. Now that prints and blood samples had been taken, they took the Landrover apart. Morrison had already given up and was standing talking to someone he knew when Sam saw in his torch beam a glint of something down beside the handbrake. It could have been part of the underside of the car, visible through a gap in the chassis, but it looked too bright. He poked at it with the blade of his penknife, and it took a few minutes before he prised something small and circular into his hand. It looked like a badge, something off a lapel. The pin had broken off. Sam turned the badge and wiped the dirt off with his gloved hand. Two tiny curved daggers, and above them an animal of some kind.

Sam walked across to Morrison. 'What do you make of this?' he asked, showing the sergeant what he had found. Morrison had already taken off his gloves, so looked at the badge carefully without touching it. 'Where d'you find this?' he asked. 'How come they missed it first time?'

'I could just see the edge of it shining in the torchlight. Took me a while to get it out,' said Sam.

'Let's hope it was worth the effort,' said Morrison. 'Could be anything, or been there for years.'

Sam dropped the small object into an evidence bag. 'I'll take that,' said Morrison, taking the bag from Sam and putting it in his pocket. 'By the way, have you taken a full statement from the Pharaoh girl yet?'

'I asked her a few things while she was in hospital,' said Sam, 'but she was pretty shaken up and exhausted. Wasn't the right time to get all the details.'

'Well, it needs doing,' said Morrison, 'and don't leave it too long. Where is she now?'

'At her parents' in St Bees.'

Morrison snorted. 'Could have done it myself while I'm on duty this weekend, but I'm not dragging all the way up there. It'll have to wait till Monday.'

'Do you want me to do it?' asked Sam. Morrison was probably the last person Judith would want to talk to. 'I could take the statement,' he said. 'Nothing planned this weekend, and it's an easy trip on the train.'

Morrison looked at him curiously. 'What's this, constable?' he said. 'Interested in her, are you?'

Sam felt his face redden. 'Just want to get the job done, sir,' he said. 'We don't seem to be getting very far.'

Morrison sniffed, looking up as it began to rain. 'Good police work takes time, lad. No point in rushing and having to go back over things. We've done what we can here, leave the rest to the forensic boys. Friday afternoon. Might as well get started back before the roads get too busy.'

'What about the statement?' asked Sam. '

'If you want to give up your own time, constable, that's up to you, so long as you don't put it down as overtime.' Morrison smiled and nudged him with his elbow. 'Could be worth your while, eh? I fancy getting my hands in that hair. You'll have to tell me all about it.'

Sam couldn't speak. The man was disgusting. He turned away and set off towards the car.

For a while they drove in silence. Sam waited until his desire to punch Morrison had subsided. Why was he interfering all of a sudden?

'I've got WPC Tunnycliffe checking with Records for me today,' Sam said. 'Maybe she can chase that badge thing down too.'

Morrison rolled his eyes. 'Tunnycliffe? Bad enough having women in the force, Nelly,' he said. 'For God's sake don't give them anything important to do. Tunnycliffe's not the sharpest knife in the drawer, is she? All right for making a brew, and a few other things beside, I've heard, but keep her well away from anything that matters, right? Right?' He felt in his pocket for the bag and the badge, pulled on a glove and slid the badge out of the bag onto his palm. 'Leave this with me,' he said.

Nothing more was said as Sam drove back to Barrow through the Friday afternoon traffic and Morrison lolled in the seat next to him, dozing with his mouth wide open. Sam looked across at him, then back at the road. He wasn't sure how much more of Morrison he could take.

Chapter 23

Sam dropped off Sergeant Morrison in town outside the Crown where he had people to see, apparently. People to drink with more like, Sam thought, but he said nothing except 'Goodnight, sir.' The 'sir' stuck in his throat, but he knew Morrison would comment if he didn't say it. He took the car back to the yard and went in the main entrance of the police station. Sergeant Clark looked up. 'How's young Judith?' he asked. 'She were bloody lucky by the sound of it, but what the 'ell was she doing there at all?'

'I'm still working on that,' said Sam. Clark was the force's most enthusiastic gossip, which made him a source of good information, but you had to careful what you told him.

'She'll still be off work, likely?' said the sergeant, fishing for titbits.

'Aye, likely,' said Sam. 'Is Tunnycliffe still around?'

'She were asking if I'd seen you,' he said. 'She'll be through there somewhere.'

'Thanks, George,' said Sam.

WPC Tunnycliffe looked up when he pushed open the door. She smiled and picked up a piece of paper. 'Records came up with something about two blokes who use a Landrover,' she said. 'One's got a sheet as long as your arm, wounding, B & E, sounds like a nasty piece of work. He was in Strangeways on a seven-year stretch, got out last year. Colin Peter Blakey, born 1928. No fixed abode. Known to frequent the Lancaster area. Apparently he was pulled over last year for various motoring things, no insurance. He was driving an old grey Landrover, registration number's here if you want to check it.'

'Grey? Could have changed it, I suppose,' said Sam, looking through the paper that she handed to him. The registration number bore no resemblance to what Judith had given him. Another dead end. 'What about the other bloke?'

'No known associates,' she said, 'but he was in the army in the '50s. Military service I suppose. In Malaya apparently.' She frowned. 'What was going on there?'

Sam laughed. 'How old are you?' he said. 'Communist guerillas were trying to get rid of the old colonial rubber planters. We didn't hear much about it, and they called it an emergency, not a war. Don't know why. Apparently the guerillas got supplies and such from the local population so they tried to move people out of villages into camps, to stop that happening. Probably what the Yanks are doing in Vietnam now.'

Kath Tunnycliffe looked at Sam. 'How come you know so much about all that?' she said. He shrugged. 'Read the papers, that's all. The proper papers, not the rubbish ones.'

'Well, anyway,' said Kath. 'That's where he was, and Records reckon he hangs out with other ex-army people.'

'Anyone in particular?'

'No names on here,' she said. 'Could be family.'

'That's really helpful, thanks, Kath.' said Sam. 'I owe you a drink.'

'It made a change from the usual stuff,' she said. 'And don't bother about the drink, sir. Chapel and teetotal, that's me.'

'Really? You must be the only one round here that doesn't drink like a fish.'

'You don't, do you? Are you Chapel, too?'

Sam laughed. 'I'm not anything. It's all myth and superstition, whichever church or chapel it is.'

'That's a shame. Should I pray for you?' she added. 'Well, I'm off. Friday evening at Gran's, like always. You going anywhere?'

Sam hesitated. 'No,' he said. 'Weekend off, just for a change. Have a good one, Kath.'

He sat at his desk for a while after she'd gone. There was no one else around. Morrison was probably on his third pint of the evening. Sam flicked through his notebook looking for the St Bees number Judith had given him. A young man's voice answered the phone.

'Could I speak to Judith Pharaoh, please,' said Sam. 'It's DC Tognarelli, Barrow CID.'

'Hang on,' said the young man. Sam heard him call out. 'Mum, the police are on the phone for our Judith.'

There was a pause and some whispering. 'Hello,' said a woman this time. 'This is Mrs Pharaoh. I'm afraid Judith can't come to the phone at present.'

'Sorry to bother you, Mrs Pharaoh,' said Sam in his best telephone voice. 'I'm investigating what happened to Judith, both the incidents, as we think they may be connected.'

'You mean the people who killed that man were the ones who wrecked her flat? Is she in danger?'

'It's early days yet to know anything very clearly, so please don't worry too much. The more Judith can tell us, the better. I saw her in the hospital but that wasn't a good time to take a full statement from her.'

'Indeed it wasn't,' said Maggie. 'She's had a very difficult time.'

'I appreciate that, Mrs Pharaoh. Is she feeling any better now?'

'She's more rested, thank you, constable, but she's not herself, if you know what I mean.'

'Of course,' he said, although he wasn't certain what it meant for Judith to 'be herself'. 'I wonder if I could come and talk to her while she's with you, and take the full statement we need? It's important that we track down the men concerned as quickly as possible. It is a murder enquiry after all, and Judith is central to the investigation.'

'I'm not sure,' said Maggie. She hesitated. 'You're the young man who helped at Judith's flat, aren't you? Elspeth's brother?'

'Yes, that's me,' said Sam, 'on official business this time. If I come to St Bees tomorrow, would Judith be able to talk to me? I'm sure it wouldn't take very long.'

'Well,' said Maggie. 'She's asleep at the moment. Let me ask my husband. Hold on.'

There was a long delay before Maggie's voice spoke again. 'We're not very happy about this, actually. Judith's very tired still, and quiet. She hasn't wanted to talk to us about what happened. But if you need her statement so urgently, then we feel you should be able to talk to her. Not for long mind, is that clear?'

'Quite clear, Mrs Pharaoh,' said Sam. 'Tomorrow afternoon?'

The train was the best way to get up to St Bees on Saturday morning. Much of the route was new to him and he sat looking out at the narrow strip of green farmland that lay between the railway and the coast for much of the way, except where the line ran right along the top of the beach. The day was fine and calmer than of late. The edge of the outgoing tide created another horizontal band, different in colour and light from the sand and rock pools in front, the flat grey sea beyond and the pale blue and white of the sky. Sam was struck by the difference in the seascape between this coast on the open sea and the mud and sand of Morecambe Bay only a few miles to the south across the Furness peninsular.

St Bees was different, too. Instead of the broad streets and industry of Barrow here was a picturesque station, the sandstone of the old school and priory and fields with sheep and horses. The narrow hill that ran down through the village gave way to a flat green valley floor where the rail line ran from the south. To the north dark red cliffs rose steep from the beach, blocking the train's route, and the railway turned sharply east along the valley. Sam looked around, wondering what had made Judith so keen to be in Barrow when she could live in this idyllic spot. Perhaps she really was as perverse as she appeared to be.

The house on Beach Road wasn't hard to find, and spoke of comfort and an easy life. He felt for his warrant card as he pressed the doorbell outside the porch and heard the chime inside the house. When the door was opened, a young man stood, looking in Sam's direction but not looking at him. Sam held out his warrant card but the young man didn't look at it, turning instead to call over his shoulder, 'Mum, the policeman's here.' Maggie Pharaoh appeared, pushed the young man to one side, glanced at Sam's proffered warrant card, and stood back to invite him into the hallway.

'Do come in, constable. We seem to meet when Judith's in trouble, don't we?' Maggie said. She turned to the young man who was still hovering in the hall. 'This is my younger son Vince. His eyesight isn't good, but he will insist on answering the doorbell.' Vince was tall and smiling and Sam shook the proffered hand. 'My husband will be back shortly. It's his golf day, you know.'

'Of course,' said Sam. He hoped Judith's father would arrive before he left. He'd seen him at the hospital, but only for a few minutes.

Judith came slowly down the stairs wearing a long blue dressing gown, her feet bare. Sam was shocked by what he saw. The energy he remembered about her seemed to have drained away. Her face was pale, dark under the eyes, and even her hair was dull, drawn back more severely than usual. She tried to smile.

'I wasn't expecting you today,' she said.

Maggie turned to Sam. 'We did tell her it was today, but she's been a bit confused about dates.'

'I didn't want to wait till Monday,' Sam said to Judith. 'Do you want me to come back later?' He wondered whether she was fit enough to give him the details he needed.

'But you've come all this way,' said Maggie. She seemed embarrassed by Judith's confusion. 'It'll be fine, won't it, Judith, now that the constable has come all this way? Why don't you pop back upstairs and put something on while I make us a cup of tea?' She gestured to her daughter and Judith turned reluctantly and went back up the stairs, while Maggie ushered Sam into the front room. Vince followed him in and sat down. 'Judith's been really upset by all this, you know,' he said. 'I don't think she knew the man she was trying to save, but it must have been awful to watch him just float away like that, and then nearly drown herself.'

'Is that what she told you?' asked Sam.

'Just yesterday,' Vince went on. 'I took her some tea and I'm sure she was crying. I could hear it in her voice. Did she know the man?'

'She'd spoken to him,' Sam said. 'That was all, as far as I know. But it's a bad business all round. I'm not surprised she's upset.'

Maggie came back into the sunny room, carrying a tray. 'I'm sure she won't be long,' she said. 'At least your visit will get her out of bed for a while. I've never seen her so exhausted.'

'It's probably shock,' said Sam. 'The impact can last for days, longer even. Is she having nightmares about what happened?'

'She is, she told me,' said Vince. 'Flashbacks, that wake her up. At least I can't remember anything about falling off the wall.'

Maggie looked at Sam. 'Vince had an accident,' she said. 'That's when his eyesight faded.'

'I'm sorry to hear that,' said Sam, wondering whether he should have waited until Judith was back in Barrow.

They were almost finished with the first cup of tea and talking about the joys of living in St Bees when the door opened slowly and Judith came in.

'There you are, dear,' said her mother briskly. Judith's dressing gown had been replaced by jeans and a big brown jumper, but she still looked frail.

'Cup of tea?' Maggie asked. Judith shook her head, but Maggie poured one anyway. 'You need it,' she said. 'Too much sleep can make it worse, don't you think, constable?'

Sam said nothing. Judith's mother seemed very tense, he thought, as if the daughter's distress somehow reflected on her.

'Are you sure you're able to talk to me for a while, Judith?' he asked. 'It won't take long I'm sure. We talked before at the hospital didn't we, so I just need a few more details, then I can write the statement and all you have to do is confirm and sign it. Will that be OK?'

Judith nodded. 'There,' said Maggie. 'That'll be fine, I'm

sure,' she said. 'Would you like us to leave you to it? Come on, Vince.' She took Vince's arm and pulled him out of the room, shutting the door behind them.

Judith sat back in her chair and closed her eyes. 'She fusses,' she said quietly.

'That's what mothers do, isn't it?' said Sam.

Judith shook her head. 'She wants me to live here, work at Sellafield like my dad. It would drive me mad.'

Sam smiled. 'You'll be better soon,' he said. 'Back in your little flat, pleasing yourself.'

'Hurray,' said Judith, and this time the smile reached her eyes. 'Come on, then,' she said. 'What do you want to know?'

He wrote carefully as Judith repeated the story she'd told him a few days before. When she paused, he looked back over his notes. 'You said you thought the men in the Landrover had probably seen you following them.'

'Did I? Not sure. It was dark and very foggy. There's only one headlight on the scooter and they might not have noticed it like two headlights on a car. When I saw them going out onto the sand I kept well down behind the wall.' She hesitated. 'If they'd seen me, wouldn't they have done something?'

Sam didn't want to think what they might have done. 'Perhaps,' he said. 'The knife, what did you notice about that?'

She shook her head. 'Anthony wouldn't let me touch it. It wasn't a very big knife. I couldn't see the blade. The handle seemed bent, not straight, but I couldn't be sure about that. It might still … when you find his body?'

He knew what she meant, but it could be days before the body surfaced. Harry had told him that bodies sometimes disappeared for years out on the sands, and all that finally came to light were bones. The knife would have gone, unless it was stuck very deep.

'While you were holding Anthony and trying to get him out of the water, did he saying anything to you, any names maybe?

Judith closed her eyes, remembering. 'Nothing. He said he was done for and that I should go.'

'And what did he say before that,' said Sam, 'before the Landrover passed you in Cannon Street?'

'I've told you all that,' she said, her voice raised. Sam realised he might be pushing her too hard, but after a moment's pause she carried on. 'I asked him about Harries and the flat, and he said he'd sent the tape. The only name he mentioned was "Bindoon", or maybe it was "Ben Doon". I don't know who that is.' Judith looked at him. 'Sorry. I'm trying to forget it, but something's…' She looked away, towards the sunny window where the gauzy curtains moved a little in the draught.

'No, I'm sorry,' said Sam, 'for putting you through all this again. You've done really well, and we're almost finished. I'll write up these notes properly now. You can read it over before you sign it, and then I'll leave you alone.'

Sam moved his chair over to the small table to write on the larger paper he'd brought with him. He felt that Judith was watching him but he didn't look up.

There was a tap on the door, and Maggie put her head round before bustling in. 'Is it all done?' she asked. 'I'll take the tray out of your way, constable. Why don't you walk him back to the station, Judith? You need some fresh air, get some colour on those cheeks.' She leaned towards Judith, who flinched away. 'Come on now,' Maggie persisted, turning to Sam. 'She does need a walk, get out of that stuffy bedroom.'

When Maggie picked up the tray and left the room, Sam smiled at Judith who rolled her eyes. 'See what I mean?' she said, and he nodded.

'Come on,' he said. 'It's not far. And there's something else I want to ask you about.'

Maggie came back carrying Judith's coat and helped her into it. 'It's quite windy,' she said, as if to a child, 'so keep it buttoned up.'

It was only when they had closed the garden gate and turned along the road towards the station that Judith undid the top buttons and put her head up towards the racing sky, shaking her head from side to side until wisps of hair escaped their moorings and danced around her face.

'Some of the time I feel almost normal,' she said, 'but then it starts again. I can hear the water rushing, and everything feels blurred, as if I'm going to faint. All I want to do is go back to bed.' She turned to Sam. 'How long's it going to last?'

'It depends,' he said. 'Delayed shock can go on for a while. You need to look after yourself. Or let your mother look after you.'

Judith groaned. 'Should I go to the doctor? Would that help?'

'They'd probably put you on sleeping pills or tranquillisers or something,' said Sam. 'Is that what you want?'

She shook her head. 'I just want to be able to think straight, and stop seeing things. Just blot them out.' She paused. 'I keep seeing his white face, floating away.'

She stopped and Sam stopped beside her, looking at her. She shook her head.

'What was it you wanted to ask me?'

'Are you sure?'

'Yes, the cold air's helping. I might remember something.'

'There was something we found in the Landrover. I

wondered if it would make any sense to you.' He took out his notebook and flicked back through the pages until he found the page he wanted. 'There was something under the seats, like a badge without the pin. It must have fallen off and slipped down. It had a design on it, like this.' He showed her the page where he had drawn the image on the badge that Morrison had taken from him.

Judith stared at it. 'I've seen that before,' she said. 'I'm sure I have. But where?' She put her hands to her face, straining to remember. Something to do with Alan Thornhill,' she said.

'Thornhill? Your editor?'

She looked up. 'It was on a tie, in his wardrobe,' she said, triumphantly. 'I saw it.'

'What were you doing, looking in his wardrobe?' Sam asked.

'They were out, and I was poking around,' she said.

Sam frowned. 'It could mean anything,' he said. 'It's the kind of badge that regiments have. Was he in the army?'

'He was in Malaya, in the 'fifties. Irene told me that.'

'Everyone in the regiment might have a tie like that, if it was a regimental symbol. Or a badge.'

'So the men in the Landrover might have been in Malaya, too?'

'Not necessarily,' said Sam. 'Someone else who'd been in the Landrover might have been. It's a pretty thin link.'

Judith's face suddenly brightened and she turned to Sam. 'I'm sure there's something funny about Thornhill,' she said. 'I've been thinking about it. He doesn't earn that much and they have this huge house, big car, pots of money.'

'Could have inherited it,' said Sam, glancing at his watch. 'Come on, the train'll be here soon.'

Judith caught hold of his sleeve. 'But what if he's up to something?'

'I doubt it,' said Sam. 'Look how helpful he's been to you, with the story, and taking you into his own home.' He changed the subject. 'Doc Hayward's not well, by the way. He's at home.'

'You do believe me, don't you, about what he said to me about Steven's death?'

Sam hesitated. Judith was angry now. 'He told me, in the pub, that Steven didn't drown. I've not made that up.'

'But there was nothing about that in the PM report. The coroner said it was an accident. That's all we have.'

They'd reached the station and Judith turned away, her loose hair blowing across her face. There were tears in her eyes. 'Just the wind,' she said, brushing them away. The signal clattered, heralding the train's arrival 'You don't believe me,' she said.

'I do believe you,' he said. 'But there's no proof of anything.'

Judith snorted. 'Another kid turning up dead. Would that help?'

Sam was angry now. 'I have to go,' he said. 'Go home, Judith. Get well again, and we'll talk. It's too complicated. Just give it some time.'

Judith turned and walked away. Frustrated and annoyed, Sam watched her retreating back before he climbed on the train and let it take him back to Barrow and reality.

The view of sea and sky beyond the salt-smeared window didn't lift Sam's spirits. He longed to lift the weight of isolation from his mind, but he couldn't discuss the case with anyone. Morrison, Harry, the people at Montgomery House, no one wanted to know that there were problems about how Steven died, or what had really happened to Harries. Grayson kept repeating, 'Accident, suicide, accident, suicide', but Sam's doubts still refused to go away. And now his mind was seething with other possibilities, even more worrying than before. He wanted to share more of what he was thinking with Judith, but would that be fair? She was clearly exhausted and increasingly irrational. He needed to trust her, but he couldn't do so, not now, not yet.

CHAPTER 24

On Monday morning, finding Dr Graham's number was easy but deciding on the approach to take with him was harder. It felt as if everyone Sam wanted to talk to was connected to someone else, in patterns that he didn't understand. He had to make it sound like a routine enquiry; maybe he would start by asking about the overall health of the boys, then about Steven Stringer and whether there might have been any reason why he chose to run away. But when Dr Graham came to the phone and Sam explained what he wanted, the immediate response sounded surprised and annoyed.

'It's some time since the poor boy died, constable, and I understand there was nothing in the PM report that delayed his funeral, so what's all this about? Has some new information come to light?'

'No, sir, just a few loose ends. I'd be grateful if you could give me half an hour of your time.'

Graham sighed audibly. 'I suppose you have to do these things. I'm very busy today so it will need to be quick.'

Dr Graham's housekeeper showed Sam into a darkly furnished library in a large house outside Broughton. Curtains were half drawn against low winter sun. Dr Graham was short and suited, grey hair carefully combed over his head. His small eyes looked Sam quickly up and down. He didn't seem as bad-tempered as Sam had expected.

'Detective Constable Tognarelli,' he said, reading Sam's warrant card with exaggerated care. 'That's quite an unusual name for these parts. A Scottish connection by any chance?'

'My father, sir,' said Sam. 'Raised in Glasgow.'

'And you?'

'Raised in Bolton,' said Sam. 'People tell me my voice is a bit of a mixture.'

Graham smiled with his mouth, but not his eyes. 'So many local accents and dialects in this part of the world, I'd have thought you came from further up the coast, or Carlisle way. Now what can I do for you? I can only give you a few minutes, I'm afraid.'

Sam was all affability. 'Purely routine, sir. My sergeant just asked me to tie up a few loose ends of two cases that happen to involve Montgomery House.'

'Would that be Sergeant Morrison?' said Dr Graham. 'Captain Edwards mentioned that he had taken a personal interest. It's been a difficult few weeks for Edwards.' He looked at Sam. 'We all go back a long way together,' he said. 'That's how the idea for Montgomery House started, you know, when we served together in Malaya, in the early 'fifties.'

'Sergeant Morrison too?' asked Sam, trying to work out how old that would make him. 'No, not Morrison, but his boss, and your boss too.'

'Chief Inspector Cardine? He was in Malaya?'

'Indeed he was. Small world, isn't it?'

Getting smaller by the minute, thought Sam. He wondered how many others were in this select band.

Dr Graham was more pleasant now that he'd clarified Sam's lowly position on the local totem pole. 'So, constable, what can I help you with?'

'First of all, sir, about the boy who was found drowned,' said Sam, looking at his notebook. 'Was there anything about him that you know of that might have caused him to run away?'

'Do you mean his health, or being bullied perhaps?'

'Exactly,' said Sam. 'Mrs Robinson says how well cared for the boys are at Montgomery House, but there might be something that would explain his behaviour.'

'As I recall the lad, he'd had a rough start and it showed. Mrs Robinson was looking after him, better than at any time earlier in his life, but he was still underweight for his age.'

'Could he have been picked on, perhaps?'

'Oh, quite possibly. Boys will be boys, as they say. But any serious bullying would have been spotted and stopped I'm sure. Only twenty boys, constable. Not hard to know what's going on. I can assure you that nothing untoward had been brought to our attention as trustees.'

'Thank you, sir,' said Sam, turning his page and still not looking up.

'The experience in Malaya touched us all, constable,' said Dr Graham. He poured himself a coffee from the pot that the housekeeper had left, but he didn't offer any to Sam. 'We had to move the villagers into camps, to keep them away from the rebels, cut their supply lines, you know.'

Sam said nothing, wondering what had set off this train of thought.

'Things were pretty bad,' Graham went on. 'Food was short. We were outside the cage, they were inside it. We had enough food, they didn't. Some of the children were prepared to do anything for food. Maybe their parents put them up to it. Either way, it was pretty bad. I came back wanting to do something for children like that, who had nothing, abandoned by their families. Do you understand? That's where Montgomery House came from, from that ideal. We give our time for nothing, you know. All of us.'

Sam listened politely, wondering what lay underneath what the doctor was saying.

'That's very interesting, thank you,' said Sam. 'Just one other matter, before I go, regarding Mr Harries.'

Graham sipped his coffee. 'Ah,' he said. 'That was a very unfortunate business,'

'Can you tell me how Mr Harries came to be appointed as padre to the school?'

The older man hestitated. 'Is this relevant to anything, constable?'

'If you wouldn't mind, sir,' said Sam.

'Well, as I recall,' said Graham, 'we were about to advertise for a teacher who would also serve as chaplain – "padre" the captain called it – and Edwards said he'd found someone who seemed ideal for the position, so we could save ourselves the trouble of interviews and all that. Of course the board's appointments committee had a look at all the relevant information before we confirmed the decision.'

'Of course,' said Sam. 'And was there any indication of previous difficulties, from when Mr Harries had been a parish priest in Cumberland?'

'What sort of difficulties?'

Sam looked up. He wanted to see the expression on Graham's face. 'There had been rumours of some sexual misconduct, with boys in the parish.'

Dr Graham's face paled and he put down his cup. Sam heard the china rattle. 'Rumours?'

'No evidence was brought, and no official enquiry, but Mr Harries moved on to another parish, and then into the army as a padre.'

The doctor blinked and sat up a little straighter. 'Did Captain Edwards know about this? He certainly never mentioned any such thing to us.'

Sam did not respond and Dr Graham continued. 'I can assure you, constable, that any such information, even if unproven, would have been considered seriously by the Board. These boys are so vulnerable, you know...'

'Indeed so, sir,' said Sam. 'So we can conclude that this information was not known to you at the time of Mr Harries's appointment?'

'Certainly not to me, or to the Board to my knowledge. Have you asked Captain Edwards the same question?'

'Not yet, sir. I needed to know how the appointment was made, and you've been clear about that.'

Dr Graham sat back in his chair. 'You are not suggesting, are you, constable, that there is any connection between these two "loose ends", as you call them?'

'Not at all, sir.' Sam adopted his most neutral expression. 'It would be very useful to have a full list of the Board members for Montgomery House, if you have one?'

Graham looked irritated. 'I'm sorry, constable. I don't have time to dig all that out now, and I'm not sure it's my job to do so. You can find out anything you need from the usual channels. The place is a charity, after all. There are records of these things.'

'Right,' said Sam. No point in pushing that question any further. 'Thank you for your time, sir.'

'Give my regards to Sergeant Morrison,' said Dr Graham, as he showed Sam to the door. He's making sure I know he's connected, thought Sam. It was like a club where all the members knew each other, all of them confident and comfortable. Maybe they think I'll want to join them, he said to himself. Actually, what he wanted to do was knock their complacent heads together. But they could ruin him, and he would need to tread very carefully indeed.

It wasn't far down the Furness peninsular to Attercliff. He'd already ascertained that Monday was Iris Robinson's day off, which was very convenient as he really wanted to talk to her away from Montgomery House. At her suggestion they were meeting at a small house in the village, where she lived with her ageing father when she wasn't on duty.

Out of uniform, she looked quite different, more vulnerable. 'Come in, constable,' she said, smiling. 'My father's having his after lunch nap. Have you eaten, by the way? I made a few sandwiches, just in case.'

Sam could smell tomatoes and saw them peeping from between fresh bread, making his mouth water. For a few minutes all thought of Montgomery House gave way to the pleasure of eating, first the sandwich and then a piece of chocolate cake that Iris produced from a large tin.

'Don't get the chance to bake very often,' she said, 'but father still loves cake.'

'Me too,' said Sam. He reached for his notebook. 'Now I don't want to push you on this issue, Mrs Robinson, but we do need to check for any possible impropriety that the boys at Montgomery House might have been exposed to.'

Iris rose a little out of her chair. 'Oh, really!' she said. 'This is too much. I told you last time we spoke that it was cruel gossip, and it still is.' She sat down and pulled a handkerchief from her pocket. 'I didn't tell Captain Edwards last time about what you'd said, but this time...'

Sam waited until she'd calmed down a little. 'I know how difficult this must be for you, Mrs Robinson,' he said quietly. 'You give those boys all your attention and care and it must be very painful to imagine that others might not do so. But there will be times, when you're here with your father for example, that things at Montgomery House might not be quite as they should be. And you couldn't be expected to know, could you? No one could blame you in any way.'

'But that's not the point, is it?' she said, turning towards him, her eyes still filled with tears. 'You're accusing people I know of terrible things, a betrayal of all the trust those boys have in us, all of us.'

'Not accusing,' Sam began, but she waved a hand to cut him off.

'As good as,' she said. 'I'm not worried about blame, not for me. But it's Montgomery House, and the captain. That's what upsets me most, that you or anyone could think that anything ... anything like that might happen. That place is his life, constable. I've seen how much it means to him, and how hard he works for those boys. He provides for some of them out of his own pocket, did you know that? Trips away, walking on the fells, driving lessons, all out of the goodness of his heart. And what does he get in return? Slurs and accusations from dirty-minded people who can't bear to see goodness at work.' She blew her nose. Sam said nothing.

'I'm sorry, constable,' she said after a pause. 'I know you're only doing your job.'

'Have other people made accusations like this?' he asked. 'When I last saw you,' he looked at his notes, 'it was on Remembrance Day, you said "the boys say things sometimes, things they make up in anger, like boys do." Do you remember that, Mrs Robinson? What kind of things have the boys said to you?'

She screwed up the handkerchief in her lap, and looked away. The room was silent for a few moments. A clock on the mantelpiece ticked. Finally, she spoke.

'Once or twice,' she said, 'over the years, a boy might say that someone had, you know, got too close. Not anyone who worked here, someone who came to the house.'

'You said various people visit, are these all friends of the captain?'

'Maybe not friends, but people he knows. Some of them he was overseas with.' She paused. 'My father was in the war. I could never get him to talk about it but when he met his old mates, they would chatter away. The rest of us can't really understand, can we?'

'Anyone else?' asked Sam.

'We do get some important people,' she said. 'There's a chap from the TV, he's been a few times. The boys love to see famous people. Well, we all do, don't we, and he does such a lot for us, raising money and so on. Oh, and I think the captain introduced me to one of our local councillors, but that was a while ago now. I don't meet all the visitors, sometimes I'm off duty or here with my father. Captain Edwards likes to invite people who can raise money for us. It all helps, he says. And Mr Thornhill from the *Furness News*, he makes sure the pictures get in the paper, so everybody's happy.'

'What did you mean about visitors getting too close? Is that what the boys said?'

She looked away. 'No, not exactly.'

Sam waited. The clock ticked.

'There was one boy,' she said quietly. 'It was quite a long

316

time ago. He showed me, and he said that someone had hurt him. He was quite upset, begged me not to tell anyone. But I was worried and I asked the captain about it. He told me that the boy was lying, playing people off against each other like he had done all his life.' She looked up at Sam. 'I trust the captain. If he tells me that there's nothing to worry about, I believe him. I have to believe him.'

'Can you remember the boy's name?' said Sam.

She looked down at her hands and the twisted handkerchief.

He was called Bill,' she said. 'But the boys called him Nocky.'

'Do you know where he is now?' Sam asked.

She looked up. 'No. Do you?'

'He's back in Lancaster prison where he's been on and off for most of his adult life.'

She put her hand to her mouth. 'He was so angry,' she said.

'He still is,' said Sam. He hesitated. 'Iris, please, I want you to do something for me. I want you to keep this conversation to yourself. You have done nothing wrong, and nothing you have said to me can harm the captain, not as it stands. But I may need to take a more formal statement from you, at some point, and to talk to the boys again. Do you understand?'

She nodded.

'Have you heard if visitors are due to come to Montgomery House?'

She shook her head. 'The last few weeks have been so difficult. The captain has been very low. There was something planned for next weekend I think, but he may have cancelled it.' She looked at Sam. 'Whatever may have happened in the past, constable, I swear to you that I didn't know, and nor did Captain Edwards. Those boys are his life. He's an honourable man. You must believe me.'

'I want to believe you, Mrs Robinson, truly I do,' said Sam. 'But if any of your boys have been harmed, it's my duty to investigate.'

She nodded again.

'Thank you for your time and the delicious lunch.'

'And you'll let me know what you find out?'

'You'll be informed about the official enquiry, if and when it happens. At present all I'm doing is following up a complaint. Please remember what I asked, that you keep this to yourself.'

She shook his hand at the door, still visibly upset. Sam wondered how long it would be before Captain Edwards heard all about his visit.

When he got back to the police station, WPC Tunnycliffe motioned to him. 'Morrison's looking for you,' she whispered. 'He looks really mad. What have you done?'

The door to the CID room opened and Sergeant Morrison pointed at Sam.

'You!' he said. 'In here, now!'

Sam followed him into the room.

'Get out, Grayson,' said Morrison and Grayson was out of the door in seconds, closing it behind him.

Sam stood straight, not looking at his superior officer. He could see what was about to happen.

'How many times, constable?' Morrison said, leaning into Sam's face. 'How many times do I need to tell you to back off anything to do with Montgomery House and get on with your job? You are clear who's in charge here, aren't you?'

'Sir, yes, sir,' said Sam, still looking straight ahead, past Morrison's looming head.

'So tell me, constable, why one of the trustees of Montgomery House, a highly respected local man, has been visited by my constable, and interrogated about who does what, when it's none of that constable's damn business?'

Sam said nothing.

'Let's get this really clear, shall we?' Morrison went on. 'That business with Harries is closed. Coroner said suicide, we say suicide, his poor grieving mother says suicide, and the man is in the ground. There is no evidence, none, that he ever laid a finger on any of the boys. If he had, the captain and the Robinson woman would have dealt with it. Right?'

'Right, sir,' said Sam. He was breathing as slowly as he could.

'And Harries isn't the only one with a death wish,' Morrison went on, turning away to walk up the room and back again. 'If you don't get back to doing what I tell you, you're killing your job here as quick as that sad nonce broke his own neck. Am I making myself clear?'

'Sir,' said Sam.

'I never want that pompous git Cardine to speak to me again like he spoke to me this morning. "Keep your men under control, sergeant," he says. If you'd been in that room, constable, I'd have whipped you like a dog. And I still could, once you've got kicked out, and no one would care.'

Morrison picked up his jacket. 'I've given you a long list of matters that demand your attention. It's on your ridiculously tidy desk. You will address yourself to that list, and nothing other than that list, and report to me tomorrow morning. Is that clear?'

'Yes, sir,' said Sam.

Morrison stamped out of the room, and Sam sank onto his chair. His hands were shaking as he picked up the list and saw the familiar litany of petty crime. Kath Tunnycliffe pushed open the door. 'He's gone. Are you OK?'

Sam nodded.

'Cup of tea?' she asked.

'Please, Kath. Plenty of sugar.'

It was the end of the road. All he had were fragments, insubstantial bits of a picture that could only be guessed at. He was guessing that the Monty House boys had been abused, but others might see a picture of benevolent concern undermined by malicious children who were well-versed in playing off adults against each other. And now the invisible web of connections had succeeded in tying him up, a hapless fly that had stumbled into it.

The phone rang.

'Constable Tognarelli?' said a woman's voice. 'It's Ann Hayward. My husband is asking for you. He's very agitated. Can you come?'

Sam didn't hesitate, not for a moment. On his way out he said, 'Kath, if Clark or Morrison ask, I'm off to the probation office, right? Back in an hour.'

Kath raised her eyebrows, but he was gone.

CHAPTER 25

Dr Hayward tried unsuccessfully to push himself up on his pillows. He looked grey: cheeks hollowed below tight bone while folds of skin sagged around his neck, as if his face had dropped from its bearings. The air in the darkened bedroom was stale and smelled of age and sickness. Sam tried not to react and focussed on the old man's eyes, watery and bright. Behind him, Ann Hayward said, 'He wants to talk to you, constable, but be patient when he gets breathless. There's an oxygen mask just by the pillow. And you,' she continued, pointing at her husband, 'don't be stubborn about the oxygen. If you need it, use it. The young man's in no hurry. I'll be downstairs if you want anything.'

Sam looked around for a chair and pulled one up as close to the head of the bed as he could manage. Hayward was already straining for breath.

'Talk as quietly as you like,' said Sam. 'I'll hear you. Take your time.'

Hayward's voice was low and hoarse. He started to cough, and put a tissue to his mouth to catch whatever had come up. 'That PM, on the wee boy.'

'Steven Stringer,' said Sam.

'Aye. He didn't drown.'

'No water in his lungs,' said Sam.

Hayward nodded. 'Couldn't say it....', he pulled at the air, 'in the report.'

'Why not?'

'Morrison made me change it. Ask Ann. She knows.'

Sam started to make notes.

The old man reached out to him. 'Wait. Not finished,' he gasped. 'I took samples. From the lad. As insurance. At the mortuary. Labelled "unknown". Morrison doesn't know.'

Sam took a moment to understand what he was hearing. 'You took samples from Steven's body during the post-mortem, and they're in the mortuary labelled as "unknown". They were insurance if you needed to defy Morrison?'

Hayward nodded, then stretched for the oxygen mask and put it over his mouth and nose, breathing hungrily.

'Don't speak,' said Sam. 'Have you checked the samples?'

Hayward shook his head. Above the mask his bright eyes followed Sam's face.

'But what do you think?'

Hayward frowned. He pulled the mask away from his mouth. 'Drugs, maybe booze.'

Sam was writing in his notebook. 'And it was definitely Sergeant Morrison who made you change the PM report?'

'Yes, Morrison.'

'Any other marks on the body?'

Hayward looked away. 'Bruise. Neck.' He pushed the mask back onto his face and breathed.

Sam thought for a moment then pointed with his little pencil to the back of his own neck. Hayward watched and nodded, just once. Sam closed his eyes, then he spoke again. 'If I need to get those samples checked, who can I go to?'

The old man took off the mask. 'Ask Ann,' he said. He

moved his hands to mimic writing something down.

'You've given your wife the name of someone I could go to?'

Hayward nodded and replaced the mask, pulling air into his ravaged lungs.

'Not long,' he said. He waved Sam away. 'Go.'

Sam reached for the papery hand and shook it. 'Thank you,' he said.

Doctor Hayward let his head fall back onto the pillow, drew on the oxygen and closed his eyes.

Sam crept out of the room and down the stairs. Ann Hayward called out to him 'In here,' and he walked into the kitchen. She was standing at the sink with her back to him.

'What did he tell you?'

'That there are some samples at the mortuary from a boy who died a few weeks ago. He said you know where I should take them. He told me about Morrison. That was all he could manage.'

Ann turned towards him, and Sam could see that she'd been crying. 'He hasn't got long,' she said. 'They sent him home when they knew there was nothing more they could do. His lungs are finished and his heart won't take the strain. It all happened so suddenly. We've been together for forty years. I can't imagine life without him.'

She wiped her face on the edge of her apron and sat down at the small kitchen table. 'I suppose you want to know the rest of it?'

'Tell me,' said Sam.

She told Sam the story from the beginning, from the time her husband started drinking. Morrison had found out, knew there'd been mistakes and threatened to report him.

'We should have told him where to go there and then,' said

Ann. 'But he wanted a favour with a report, to leave something out that would have affected a friend, he said. It was nothing very serious, but he threatened to report the drinking and David did what he wanted. Foolish. I knew as soon as he told me that it would go on, and it did. He had enough to get David struck off. I pleaded with him to face Morrison down, but he just kept drinking. He got sicker and sicker and wouldn't get help. Forgetting things, blacking out.' She wiped her eyes. 'And that bastard, he just kept on, and anything he wanted he got. Cases swept under the rug, blood samples ignored, nothing too drastic, but it was all wrong.'

'How long?' Sam asked.

'When did it start you mean? Two years or so. I begged David to stop. Then when they told him at the hospital how long he had left, he just broke down. This morning he told me to find you, and he gave me this.' She took an envelope from her apron pocket and handed it to Sam. The writing was only just legible. '*Prof. Adrian Phillips, Lancaster Med School.*'

'There's a note inside,' she said. 'He and Adrian were students together, and they still see each other, but not for a while, since this business started. I think David was too ashamed to face him. He wants you to get those samples from the mortuary and take them to Adrian personally. Show him the note and do what he tells you. And don't let anyone else know.'

'When did you see Morrison last?' Sam asked.

'Just after David got out of hospital, he rang. I told him David was too ill to talk, but he kept ringing. I don't pick up the phone now.'

'What does he want, do you think?'

'I'm not sure. Maybe something about the boy who died. Then we heard about Judith Pharaoh and that business out on the sands. David was very upset by that, he likes Judith. He told me to record what Morrison said if he rang again.'

Sam stared. 'Record? How? With a machine?'

'No, just write down what he said, verbatim, and date it. He said it might have to stand up in court.'

'What did Morrison say, exactly, that you have a record of?'

She frowned. 'He said that he had enough on David to ruin him and if he ever wanted another favour, he'd better get it.'

'Where are those notes now?'

'At the bottom of the sugar jar. It was David's idea. I told him it felt like MI5.'

'Leave them there for now,' said Sam. 'Have you told anyone else about this?'

She shook her head. 'No one.'

'Why me?' he asked.

'He told me you play it by the book.' She smiled. 'He said you were a prig, but he had to trust someone. He wanted to tell Judith but he was frightened what might happen to her. You can stand up for yourself. That's what he said.'

Sam sat back, his pencil poised over his notebook. His mind was racing. 'Leave it with me,' he said. 'I know what I have to do.'

'What about Morrison?' she said.

'Leave that with me, too,' said Sam. 'I'll think of something. First thing is to pick up those samples and get them checked. Who do I need to see at the mortuary?'

'Oh, yes,' she remembered, 'he told me that. He can't be sure of the other doctor, but the technician knows what you're looking for and he's expecting someone to pick them up. His name's Kumar. He's from Pakistan.'

'Does Kumar know anything else?'

'No, and David says he wouldn't ask. He says because he's brown everyone just ignores him.'

'Including Morrison?'

'Especially Morrison.'

'How long will it take to get those samples checked?'

'He said if Adrian does what it says it could be quick.'

'How quick?'

She shrugged. 'I don't know. How are you going to get to Lancaster?'

Sam was thinking. 'That'll be tricky,' he said. 'Morrison's got me on a short lead, but I'll think of something. I may need to call you. Can you pick up the phone if it rings? If it's Morrison just put it down again.'

Elspeth and Tommy weren't in the house when Sam let himself in later. He made tea and found a biscuit in the tin. Apart from the sandwich and cake at Mrs Robinson's he'd eaten nothing all day and he felt shaky. 'Running on empty' Elspeth called it, and said how bad it was for him. He couldn't wait for supper at home, and when the two of them returned he was halfway through fish, chips and mushy peas. He looked so guilty that they all laughed.

Sam found that reading to Tommy at night was the best way to relax. 'Better than any amount of beer or pills for calming me down,' he said to Elspeth when he came downstairs.

'Anything special that's winding you up?' she asked. Sam longed to tell her, but he knew he couldn't. He shrugged. 'Just the normal stuff, and Morrison on my back again.'

'The man's a menace,' said Elspeth.

'That he is,' said Sam.

The next day started quietly enough and his Tuesday morning meeting with Morrison went better than expected. Sam was deferential, and the work he'd done the previous evening in updating all the various case files was impressive, even to someone who was determined to find fault.

'What about that Upgill case?' the sergeant asked. 'Haven't we got some more stuff we could hang on him? Won't make much difference to him, he's going down anyway, and it would make our clear-up figures look better. Can't you threaten him with something? What did PC Plod Farrell tell you about him?'

Sam looked at the file. 'Farrell mentioned a girlfriend with a kid.'

'That'll do,' said Morrison. 'Tell him you'll get the kid taken into care unless he coughs to more jobs. That might shift him.'

Sam didn't react. He could see an opening.

'Noakes is in Lancaster, sir,' he said, 'on remand.'

'Well get over there and get it sorted,' said Morrison. 'I don't need to hold your hand on this one, do I?'

'No, sir,' said Sam. His heart was thumping. A trip to Lancaster under Morrison's instructions was better than he could have hoped for. Before he picked up a car he went over to the mortuary to find Kumar, the technician. When he mentioned the samples that Dr Hayward had left, Kumar knew immediately what he was looking for. They were parcelled up and Sam slipped them into the bag he carried for his files. The size of the parcel stopped the bag from closing properly, but when he held it under his arm it wouldn't have been noticed as he walked across to get the car.

Professor Adrian Phillips read the note that Sam gave him and took off his glasses. 'I told you when you arrived out of the blue that I'm not happy about unannounced visits like this, constable. This is a busy place. We already have more work than we can handle.' He pinched the bridge of his nose, as if to demonstrate the inconvenience that reading the note had presented to him.

'David Hayward's a good friend,' he said, 'but all this sounds highly irregular. I assume those are the samples he's referring to, in your bag? Have they been properly preserved and packed?'

'The technician at the mortuary knows what he's doing,' said Sam. 'I can't tell you why Dr Hayward asked me to bring them to you, but I can assure you we both feel it's necessary to have your objective opinion about whatever these samples might show. It's a complicated case, that's all I can say.'

Phillips looked steadily at him. 'I can do what Hayward wants me to do. That's not the issue. But you must appreciate that there's a professional risk involved. I have a good relationship with the police here in Lancaster, and they wouldn't look kindly on anything unofficial going on. Hayward doesn't say why there's been no official request from your force. Who's in charge of this case?'

'Sergeant Morrison, sir.'

'And can you tell me why Sergeant Morrison is not mentioned, and why a detective constable has been given this task, apparently without authority? No offence, but it's not the normal way to do these things.'

Sam looked away. He'd guessed this would happen.

'All I can say, sir, is that Dr Hayward didn't want my sergeant involved at this time. If you'd like to call them, Mrs Hayward might be able to explain.'

'You have their number?'

Damn, thought Sam. This could take forever. It was too late to speculate about that now, and he handed over the Haywards' telephone number, praying that Mrs Hayward would be at home and willing to talk to him.

Ten minutes later Professor Phillips returned.

'Give me the samples,' he said. 'I'm satisfied that the information is needed and that this is the only way to proceed, in the circumstances.'

Sam handed over the parcel, wondering whether David Hayward had been able to speak to Phillips himself.

'How long will it take?' Sam asked.

'Come back tomorrow,' said Phillips. 'We should be able to complete everything by then, and I'll need to write my report. You'll have enough trouble with the chain of evidence if anything comes of this, and my report will have to pass court scrutiny.'

'Tomorrow?' Sam was horrified. 'I thought, maybe later this afternoon?'

Phillips scowled at him. 'Don't push your luck, constable. I'm agreeing to this only out of respect for a colleague, and against my better judgment. If I say tomorrow, it'll be tomorrow. I can give you the bare bones over the telephone and send my full report on by post. I presume that will be sent to you, or to Dr Hayward?'

'Dr Hayward, I think, sir,' said Sam, happy to keep the official channels working among the medics if nowhere else. 'I'm acting on his behalf, so it makes sense for the results to go to him.'

'Very well. Leave the necessary details with my secretary, and tell her that you'll be calling for the results by four o'clock tomorrow. Understood?'

'Yes, sir,' said Sam. It was the best he could do.

Adrian Phillips hesitated. 'Have you seen Dr Hayward yourself recently?'

'Yes, sir, when he asked me to bring the samples to you. I saw him at home. Talking was difficult for him. Was he able to speak to you himself?'

'No, he tried, but his wife had to take over. The poor man

could hardly speak.' Phillips shook his head. 'He was a fine doctor, one of the best in this business. What a waste.'

Phillips turned away and left the room, his white coat flapping, holding the parcel with both hands raised, like an offering to the gods of medicine.

Possibilities were still buzzing in Sam's head when he parked the car in the visitors' car park at Lancaster jail. Before he began the tedious process of gaining entry, he sat for a while, thinking about the man he was about to talk to. Sam wanted Noakes to open up about what might have happened at Montgomery House several years before. He needed dates and names, and something more specific than Iris Robinson's flustered assurances that nothing untoward ever happened, or ever could happen while her blessed captain was in charge. Her loyalty to him was unbreakable, so far at least. What might induce a hardened criminal like Noakes to tell the truth and deal with the consequences, which might be worse for him than for the people who'd hurt him? The only bargaining possibilities were some leniency with the latest misdemeanours, and the man's concern for his girlfriend and her child. Sam wondered whether Noakes was the child's father, and whether that would make any threats to the child and its mother more potent? He hung his head. Had it come to this? He was planning to threaten a child's future to get information about children being damaged in the past. It was absurd and he was disgusted with the whole business. He felt like a fish caught in a net: the more he struggled the tighter the mesh wrapped around him. 'Just do the job,' he told himself. 'First essential is to keep Morrison off my back, and that's what I've come for. Get Noakes to cop to more offences, by whatever means I have, and move on. I've no choice, not yet, so stop fretting and get on with it.'

❖ ❖ ❖

Lounging in the small chair, Bill Noakes looked anything but cooperative, taking without comment the cigarette that Sam offered to soften him up. Sam noticed that his left cheek was bruised and the eye swollen.

'What happened?' he asked.

'Walked into a door didn't I?' said Noakes.

'Look,' said Sam, 'my sergeant wants to clear up as many of the Upgill jobs as we can. You give us some help with that and we'll see about getting you transferred out.'

Noakes said nothing for a while, and the tip of his cigarette glowed in the gloom of the dingy interview room. Finally he said, 'What jobs do you want to know about?'

Sam got the files out of his case, and slapped them down on the table one at a time, describing the bare details of each one as he did so. 'They've got your signature all over them,' he said. 'All of them. Another seven counts on top of what we got you for. What difference will that make?'

'So why bother?'

'Cos it makes my sergeant look good, that's why,' said Sam, 'and that means he's nice to me and everybody's happy.'

One by one, Noakes admitted his involvement in the extra jobs, and wrote his unwieldy signature to that effect. Job done. Noakes stubbed out the cigarette in the tiny ashtray and held out his hand for another one. Sam put the packet down on the table between them but kept his hand over it. He hadn't finished yet.

'What about the other thing we discussed? I told you it could help if you gave me some more details about Monty House.'

Noakes leaned back in the fragile chair, folding his arms.

'Told you before,' he said. 'No sale. How long d'you think I'd last in any nick if anything like that came out?' He pointed to his damaged face. 'This is nothing,' he said. 'Find some other idiot to cough to what goes on in that fucking place. You'll get nowt out of me.'

He stared at Sam and snatched the cigarette packet off the table. 'Guard!' he shouted, getting up and standing by the door.

'Wait,' said Sam. He waved the guard away. 'I've been to see Sharon,' he lied. 'And the bairn.'

Bill looked hard at him. 'What about them?'

'They want you back, Bill. You'll do five years, more, unless we can say you cooperated. You know what that means. Clearing up piddling little theft jobs is one thing, nailing some rich bastards for touching up kids, that's something else. You could name some names, Bill, give us some details. We do the rest. Wouldn't necessarily have to come out if we can find some more leads and use them. Then Sharon wouldn't have to be on her own for so long.'

'What? She got someone else already?'

Sam shook his head. He hated lying but it was getting easier. 'Not yet, but you know how it is. Kids need a father.'

Noakes pushed back the chair that clattered backwards onto the floor. He lunged across the table and grabbed at Sam's tie, pulling him forward. The guard blew a whistle and in a moment three men were pulling Bill away. They pushed him hard against the wall. As they handcuffed him, Noakes turned his head and spat at Sam.

'You're all bastards, all of you. Leave my kid alone, or I'll wait till I get out and I'll do you, I swear. Fuck that place, and fuck you.'

They led Noakes away, still struggling and swearing, and Sam sank into the chair, pulling his tie straight and feeling his neck for the imprint of the strong fingers. He was breathing hard. At least he'd tried. Even a lost man like Bill Noakes had stood up for himself, and part of Sam was glad of that. What a mess, to respect a criminal more than his own sergeant.

CHAPTER 26

Cool water was underneath her, seeping through her clothes. Something was making Anthony's body roll backwards and forwards. She could hear him groaning, and the handle of the knife sticking out of his chest hit his coat buttons, gently, tap, tap, tap. Someone said her name, far away, at the edge of hearing. She opened her eyes and the fading light of a winter afternoon slipped past the edge of the curtains onto her face. The tapping stopped. More light as the bedroom door opened slowly. She sat up.

'Jude?' said Vince. 'You OK? I could hear a funny noise, like someone groaning.'

'It was Anthony,' she said.

Vince looked around, sightless and confused. 'What? Have you got someone with you?'

'No, of course not,' she said. She lay back. The back of her nightie was sodden and sitting up had let cold air into the bed. She shivered. Vince felt his way over to the foot of the bed and sat down.

'What day is it?'

'Tuesday.'

'And what's the time?' she asked. She had no idea how long she'd been lying there.

'Past lunchtime. Mum went out a while ago. Frank said Granny Violet wasn't feeling good and she went out, to see her, I suppose. She had an argument with Frank about it. I could hear her shouting at him.'

Judith turned over, away from the light. The noises in her head had stopped and a dull cloud had descended again. Her mouth tasted sour.

'Do you want a drink?' he said. 'I can manage a cup of tea without making too much of a mess. And Mum's left some sandwiches for you. '

Judith didn't answer. She was thinking about Donna, Anthony's sister. She'd lost two brothers, and no one could tell her why. She might not even know about Anthony. As far as Judith knew there'd been no sighting of his body, and only her word that he was dead. But then again, perhaps she wanted to believe he was already gone when she released her hold and watched him float away, pale face turned towards the sky. He could have died later, alone, drowned in the scum of the incoming tide, and that thought was even harder to bear.

'Jude,' said Vince. 'I'm still here. Do you want a drink? It's a one-time offer and unlikely to be repeated.'

Judith reached out and took his hand. 'I'm thinking about the man on the sands. He has a sister in Morecambe and she may not know about him. They haven't found him, and maybe they don't want to tell anyone until they're sure.' She shifted in the bed. 'Don't make me a drink, Vince. I think I need to go out.'

'Out where?'

'I need to speak to Donna, the sister. She deserves to know what I know. Imagine if it was you and no one told me where you were or what happened. I don't think the police care about things like that, unless you're someone important.'

'You're not going to Morecambe, are you?'

'Wish I could but I don't think I'm well enough. All I want to do is sleep, but I keep dreaming about him. Maybe talking to Donna would help. I like her. She has a hard life. I've got her number at the café where she works. I'll go to the phone box.'

'Don't be daft,' said Vince. 'There's a perfectly good phone downstairs. If you don't want Mum to know what you're doing, I won't tell, you know that.' He reached for her hand and she gave it to him. He squeezed it hard. 'I think you're amazing, you know that, don't you? Or else you're crazy, not sure which. You could have such an easy life, letting Mum and Dad fuss, working down the road, nine to five, safe as houses, but you're out there, digging up stories, taking on the world. I envy you that. I'd love to get away, but I can't, not like this.' He sniffed and looked towards the light that seeped past Judith's drawn curtains. 'I'll bring you that tea.'

It took Judith longer than she expected to find the phone number of the station café in Morecambe where Donna worked. Her mind seemed sluggish, and she couldn't work out when it was that she'd first gone to Morecambe to track down the boy they'd found on the shore. In the end she just scanned the pages of her notebook, looking for numbers rather than words, and there it was, written sideways down the page. She thought of Sam's meticulous notes and regretted her carelessness.

'Station café,' said Fred's voice. Judith was glad that she'd made a note of his name.

'Is that you, Fred?' she said. 'This is Judith Pharaoh, do you remember me, from the *Furness News*?'

'The lass with all the hair,' said Fred. 'You brought that copper to see Donna.'

'Is she still with you?' Judith asked. 'Is she all right?'

'Aye, as right as she'll ever be now that useless man is back and bossing her around. I've begged her to get away from him. She could have more hours here and have enough to get by, but she won't leave him.'

'Is she there now, Fred? I need to talk to her.'

'Not more bad news, is it? She's on her break. Hang on, I'll see if she's back.'

There was a long pause, then Donna's quiet voice. 'Judith? What is it — 'ave they found Anthony?'

Judith wished she hadn't made this call. She'd been right in guessing that no one had said anything to Donna about what had happened, and Judith didn't want to tell her.

'It's about Anthony, Donna. I met him, in Barrow, last week —' she paused, searching for the words.

'Is 'e all right?' Donna interrupted her.

Judith forced herself to say it. 'Donna, someone drove him out to the sands near Barrow and dumped him there. I followed them and tried to drag him to shore, but the tide came in and I couldn't….'

'Where is 'e, then?' Donna cried.

'We don't know…'

'He'll be OK — 'e's tough our Anthony, 'e's had to be.'

Judith hesitated. 'He could have got out, further down the shore.' She knew it wasn't true, but that was what came out of her mouth. Why did she think she could tell her this way, over the phone?

'Who did that to 'im?' Donna went on, as if it was a prank that Judith was talking about, not a murder.

Tell her the truth, the voice screamed in Judith's head, but she didn't.

'We don't know,' said Judith. At least that was true.

'Maybe 'is mates would know,' said Donna.

'What mates?'

'The ones who came looking for him,' Donna said. 'Must've been a week or so after you and that copper came, these two blokes turned up. They asked if I was Anthony's sister, said they were old mates and wanted to know if I knew where 'e was. One of them looked a bit older, but the young one said 'e'd been in care with Anthony. Seemed nice enough blokes. Paid for my lunch.'

'Did you see if they had a car?'

'Not a car, a jeep thing.'

'Was it red?' Judith asked.

'That's it,' said Donna. 'I said I thought 'e was in Barrow, from what you'd said. One of 'em said they might put a piece in the *Furness News* looking for him and they both laughed. They said they knew the boss and 'e owed them a favour. I didn't know what they were on about. Isn't that where you work?'

'Yes,' said Judith.' She felt weak suddenly, sat down on the stairs and put her head down, keeping the phone to her ear. 'Did you get their names?'

'Tom and Gerry, they said. I thought they were taking the piss, but they said they was really called Tom and Gerry. Mebbe they were. Anyways, they were friendly enough. Our Anthony could be with them, couldn't 'e? E's not been 'ere, if that's what you're asking.'

Judith couldn't say any more. She felt dizzy and it was too hard.

'If I hear anything, I'll let you know, Donna,' she said finally. 'Write this number down. You call me if you hear any more, or if those mates of his come back, OK?'

Judith gave Donna the St Bees number, put down the phone

338

and sat on the stairs until Vince found her and pushed her back up the stairs to bed, where a tide of exhaustion carried her away once again.

Hours passed. Judith slept and the family left her alone.

The following morning Vince shook her shoulder and sat down on the bed.

'You need to wake up,' he said. 'It's Wednesday. That policeman came on Saturday and then you made that call to Morecambe yesterday and that's all you've done for days.'

He sat still for a while. Judith waited for him to speak again. 'It's awful downstairs,' he said. 'We tiptoe around, and Mum's taking it out on me. And she says you're being selfish.'

Judith rolled over again and looked at Vince. He was staring at the window and looked miserable.

'Sorry,' she said. 'I'm not sleeping much, dreaming a lot. Awful dreams. I think I'm drowning, and people are watching, but not doing anything. I thought making that phone call would help, but it didn't.'

'Dad says it's a reaction to what happened and it will wear off. Don't you want some food?'

She shook her head. 'But I think I'll try to get up.'

'Thank God for that,' said Vince. 'I'll get you some tea.'

Judith picked up the pillows from the floor and put them behind her head. She could see the play of sunlight on the curtains but didn't open them. The chair in the corner where she had left her clothes was empty.

'What's happened to my clothes?' she asked Vince when he re-appeared with a mug of tea and a biscuit.

'Mum took them all for the wash,' he said. 'She said they smelled horrible and needed proper washing. She's been fussing even more than normal. It's pretty bad. Dad must be glad to get out to work every morning. This morning she made him agree to take some time off.'

'What for?'

'To take you and Mum away for a week somewhere.'

The mug slipped in Judith's hand and tea stains dripped onto the sheet. 'Away where?'

'Don't know. Granny Violet will come here to look after me and they're going to take you away, for a proper rest, they said, and a "change of scene". That's what Mum kept going on about. She wore Dad down in the end.'

Judith felt trapped. She could feel her heart beating faster. 'I don't want to go away,' she said. 'They can't make me.'

'Doctor Albright might insist, Mum said. It's either that or they start pumping pills into you.'

'There's nothing wrong with me,' said Judith. 'I'm just fed up and tired. And no one believes me.'

'About what?'

'Anything.'

'You had a row with that policeman, didn't you?' said Vince. 'I liked the sound of him. Great voice, a mixture of Lancashire and Scottish I think. Has a sort of lilt to it.'

Judith snorted. 'Lilt, my arse,' she said. 'He's a boring, fussy, pompous prick. Can't make a move without checking every stupid little thing he's supposed to do.'

'That's a bit harsh, isn't it? What are you arguing about?'

'Doesn't matter,' said Judith, lying down again. 'I've been working it all out, lying here. It's a clear as day what's been going on but Mr Plod has to play it safe.'

Vince shook his head. 'I've no idea what you're on about. Maybe you do need a holiday. Get this rubbish out of your head.'

Judith pushed back the covers and put both feet on the floor. The sudden movement reeled in her brain and she put both hands to her head. Vince stood up. 'Now what are you going to do?' he said. 'I didn't really mean it, about you needing a holiday. Can't be on my own with Granny Violet. You have to help me, Judith. Don't let them take you away, please.'

'Where are my clothes?' she said.

'Most of them are on the line still. It rained a bit earlier on. They won't be dry yet.'

Judith was out of the bed now, opening drawers and the wardrobe. 'There's nothing here,' she said. 'Mum said she wanted to burn most of it,' said Vince, standing uncomfortably by the door. 'That's the other thing she's going to do, take you shopping.'

Judith groaned. 'There must be something.' She opened the door of the wardrobe wide and peered inside. 'Old pair of jeans,' she said, picking something up off the floor of the wardrobe. 'That's a start. Let me have something of yours, Vince. A shirt and a jumper, that's all I need.'

'Need for what?' said Vince.

'To get out of here, before they kidnap me,' said Judith.

They both heard the door open downstairs and their mother's voice. 'I'm home, Vince. Everything all right? Where are you?'

'Go, go,' whispered Judith. 'Tell her I've had some tea and gone back to sleep. And get me a shirt.'

Judith got back into bed and pulled the tea-stained sheet over her head, while Vince pulled the door closed behind him.

She lay quite still, trying to hear what was being said downstairs but she couldn't. She hoped Vince wouldn't give her away. The tea and the activity had cleared her head a little. Pieces of the puzzle that had been floating around for days were beginning to slow down and form into larger chunks, but there were still yawning gaps. She was sure now that Steven Stringer had been hurt or killed before he was dumped in the quicksand, but why and where and by whom and how? Anthony had come back from Australia and found his brother, and someone had wanted him dead, but who and why? Then there was Harries. Pat O'Toole kept saying they were only rumours about him, but rumours have to start for some reason. Maybe Anthony threatened him. Maybe that was why they were after Anthony, but why take the risk of killing him?

The memory of what Donna had said hit her again. The men in the Landrover knew Thornhill, said he owed them a favour. He was in this up to his neck, she was sure now. Everything added up, and she was amazed she hadn't seen it right from the start. All that concern for her welfare? A sham. He'd given her the Monty House story because he could control her more than he could control Bill Skelly. And having her staying at their house made it even easier to keep an eye on her. He sent the Landrover men to find Anthony. Did he know what they would do to him? Did he tell them to do it? Was that the favour he owed them?

Her mind pushed the pieces of the picture around. Why was Anthony such a danger to them? And where did all Thornhill's money come from? Maybe they were fiddling the books at Monty House, or getting money from all the visitors. Judith gasped as the last piece fell into place, what Anthony had found out about, what got him killed. Monty House was a brothel, with young boys' bodies for sale to anyone who would pay. It was obvious, but who would believe her? Her heart was racing, adrenalin pushing her into action.

Judith got out of bed, found a dressing gown that had escaped the laundry purge and crept along the landing to the bathroom. Cold water splashed her face. Footsteps were coming up the stairs and she sat on the toilet seat behind the locked door, trying to control the panic rattling in her head. 'You in there, Judith?' said Maggie's voice close to the door. 'Come downstairs when you're finished, dear. You need some food, you've not had anything to eat.' The steps retreated. Judith tried to think about what to do. She couldn't let them take her away, not now. She had to escape, to prove what only she knew.

She had to pretend to be the dutiful daughter. They thought she was ill, so she could fool them until it was too late and she had gone. She would lie to Vince about where she was going so they would go looking for her in the wrong place. The prospect of deceiving them all excited her. The fever in her head had turned into a plan. She stood up carefully, washed and brushed her hair into some kind of submission and went downstairs, breathing slowly, calming herself.

'That's better,' said her mother when she saw her. 'You've lain up there in that stuffy room for too long, our Judith, but look at you now. Washed and brushed, almost back to normal.'

'Thanks for washing my clothes,' said the dutiful daughter. 'I've let things slip a bit lately.'

'Well it's nearly done. Just the ironing tonight and you'll be ready for a little holiday with me and your father. We're going on Friday, up to Galloway, where we went on our honeymoon. Last time we left you with Granny and Grandad in West Row and this time you're coming with us. Granny's coming here to look after Vince, so she gets a little holiday too. It's all settled.' Vince shook his head.

Judith desperately wanted to protest at decisions being made without her agreement, but she held her tongue, to give herself more chance of getting away. Vince looked imploringly at her. 'That sounds good,' she said, as cheerfully as she could muster. 'I've never been to the other side of the Solway.'

'Beautiful country,' said Maggie. 'Quiet, no crowds, just what you need. Your dad took a bit of persuading but it'll be good for him, too. He's been worried sick about you.'

'Sorry,' said Judith.

'Oh, none of it was your fault, pet, was it? That poor man died and you nearly did too, but it's all over now, isn't it? I expect you'll leave that Barrow job now, won't you, so this is a good chance to decide about coming home for good.'

With the certainty of mothers who like to dictate their children's lives, Maggie bustled around while Judith sat watching her, planning the details of her escape. She would wait till she had some clothes, take her biggest shoulder bag with the things she might need and say she wanted to go for a walk. Her mother would think this would be another sign of her recovery, and would go and see Violet before their holiday started. With the right timing, it could be late afternoon before she realised that Judith was gone. She would get the train to Barrow, pick up the Vespa and make sure Thornhill wasn't at home. If Irene was there, all the better. Judith was sure that Irene had no idea what her husband and his cronies were up to, and she wanted to break it to her gently.

Now that her head was clear, Judith ate a good supper, chatted amicably to her parents and exuded calm common sense. It was only Vince who heard the false cheerfulness in her voice, pitched slightly higher than normal. He wasn't sure what she was up to, but she was definitely up to something. He was in his room when he heard Judith coming upstairs later and he called to her.

'What's going on?' he asked. 'You're very excited about something, I can hear it, and I don't think it's about going to

Galloway on Friday with the parents.'

Judith giggled. 'Can I trust you, Vince?' she said.

He nodded.

'I'm going to run away, tomorrow, when Mum goes to see Granny. I've worked it all out. I know what's been going on, and all I need now is the proof and I know where to find it.'

'Proof of what?' Vince asked, puzzled. Judith couldn't resist sharing what she now knew. 'If I tell you, you have to promise not to tell anyone. OK?'

She told him the story, in a continuous whisper, about Steven's death, and Anthony and Harries and Thornhill's duplicity and the conspiracy, and the tie and the badge and the men in the Landrover. Vince listened with increasing alarm. This was not the sister he knew, this was an obsessed person, wild-eyed, convinced beyond reason that she and she alone knew the truth that would soon be revealed. It reminded him of someone he'd heard on the TV talking about the existence of flying saucers.

When Judith finally stopped talking, he had to respond. 'Does anyone else know all this?' he asked.

She shook her head. 'Just me. I worked it all out. Don't know why it took me so long to see it.'

'And what are you going to do?'

'Find the proof of course, and help Irene Thornhill get away from that awful man. She has no idea what's he's been doing, how could she?'

'What's the big rush?' said Vince. 'Do you have go down there straight away?'

'I was going to wait, but I can't now, can I, or they'll take me away. And it's too important, don't you think? One kid's died, they killed Anthony, where will they strike next?'

'It could be you next, Judith, have you thought of that?'

'That's why I have to act,' she said, triumphantly. 'And you have to help me, Vince. When Mum gets home tomorrow, tell her I've gone to see Elspeth and Tommy in Barrow, and I'll be back later.'

'Is that true?'

'No, of course not,' said Judith. 'But that will put them off the scent. I just need an hour or two to do what needs doing.'

'And what's that?' he asked, hoping that his face didn't betray his belief that his sister had lost her reason.

Judith giggled again. 'Never you mind,' she said. 'I've told you too much already. You have to keep it all to yourself, whatever happens. Promise?'

'OK,' said Vince. There seemed little point in trying to dissuade her. It was a fantasy, and she was going to embarrass herself and make others angry, but maybe that would draw a line under the whole stupid business.

'Hope I can sleep,' said Judith. 'Tomorrow will be busy.'

'Good night,' he said.

'We'll stop in Whitehaven on the way through tomorrow,' said Maggie to her daughter at the breakfast table. Judith had got up and dressed as normally as necessary, to feed her mother's conviction that it was only a matter of time before she had her prodigal daughter back home for good.

'I'm going to take Granny to the Ladies' Tea and Chat as normal this afternoon, so you make a list of the clothes you need tomorrow. Some of the old stuff is only fit for the ragman.'

Judith spent the rest of the morning upstairs, on the pretext of cleaning and tidying her room. She gathered the things she thought she would need, including the keys to Bay View that were still in her bag. If she got the train around two o'clock, she could be at the her flat in Cannon Street to pick up the Vespa well before four, and out to Bay View after Edna had left for the day and before Thornhill would get home from the office. Pick up the tie, talk to Irene, find whatever there was to find in the office, and away. She could see the story already in the national papers as well as the locals, and the by-line, maybe even a picture.

As soon as Maggie left the house Judith put her plan into operation. First she rang the newsroom to check on Thornhill's plans for the day. Hattie was pleased to hear her sounding so cheerful. 'We heard you'd taken it all rather hard,' she said.

'Oh, I was fine,' said Judith. 'Tired of course, but no problem. Should be back next week, all being well, if I can persuade my mother to stop fussing.' Hattie laughed. 'And can you tell me where the boss is today, Hattie?' she added nonchalantly. 'He's away at a meeting all afternoon,' said Hattie. 'Irene was in earlier, moaning about him being late back again.'

'So she'll be at home, will she?' Judith asked. Better and better.

'That's what she said,' Hattie replied. 'One of these days while she's complaining about her life, I'm going to slap her, I swear I will. That woman has everything and she's never satisfied.'

'That's always the way, isn't it?' said Judith. 'I'll see you next week and we can moan about her together.'

'Shall I tell Bill and Ed about you coming back?'

'No, please don't, Hattie. Just in case, you know, something happens. It'll be a surprise.'

Vince listened to Judith's excited chatter on the phone with increasing admiration. She's fooling all of them, he said to himself. Whatever she's planning, she's thought it all out.

Judith went back upstairs and returned carrying a large shoulder bag. 'I've got some spare clothes,' she told Vince. 'If things work out the way they should, I'll be away for a few days. The police will need to take statements, get search warrants, that kind of thing. By the weekend it might be all wrapped up. Could be on the TV news. That'll make Mum take my job seriously, at last.' She checked her watch. 'Train just after two, and away we go. Wish me luck.'

'I do,' said Vince. 'Oh, and you'd better leave me the number of that friend of yours in Barrow, the one I have to say you've gone to see. Elspeth, isn't it?'

Judith fished in her bag for her little book, found the number and gave it to him.

'Elspeth doesn't know anything about all this,' she said, 'so she'll be suitably mystified and unhelpful. That'll give me enough time to do what I have to do.'

'Good luck, then,' said Vince.

It'll be fine, he told himself, as Judith kissed him goodbye and pulled the front door closed behind her. Later he regretted not picking up the phone straight away, but he went back to his music and turned it up as loud as he could before his mother came home.

CHAPTER 27

For most of Thursday Sam busied himself with the files that Morrison had piled onto his desk.

'You're very quiet,' said Harry Grayson. 'Tunnycliffe says you've been in all day, not swanning around like normal.'

Sam pointed at the pile of folders. 'See how Morrison loves me,' he said. 'Hardly speaks to me for weeks, takes no interest in anything I'm doing and all of a sudden he's all over me like a rash and finds dozens of vitally important things for me to do.'

Grayson smirked. 'Keeps you off the street, and out of everyone else's hair. They're all grumbling about you.'

'What have I done now?'

'Just the usual,' said Grayson. 'Too busy, too serious, finding fault with the way we do things. That kind of stuff.'

Sam sat back, scratching his short hair with his pencil. 'It's a shambles round here. You know it is. We learned all that stuff in college, then you get on the job and the old hands tell you to forget all of it and just do what they do. That's the easy way, but it stinks.'

'Works for me,' said Grayson. 'Took me about three weeks to pick it up, and they've left me alone ever since. You should try it. Do what they tell you, don't think for yourself, cut corners all you like and never, ever, grass on your mates. Then just keep your head down, wait your turn and get to be sergeant when your face fits. That's where you're going wrong, Nelly. Listen and learn, my son.'

Sam shook his head. He knew he would have to do something about Morrison, and soon, but for that he needed Hayward's story in a proper statement, not just some scribbled notes about a phone call.

It was three o'clock. Professor Phillips had told him to call back at four, but Sam couldn't wait any longer, and it might be better to phone from home before Elspeth and Tommy came home from school.

'Have to go out for a bit,' he said to Grayson. 'You going to be here a while?'

'No choice,' said Grayson. 'Got enough here to keep me busy for hours.'

Sam walked the mile or so to the house. It was clear and cold but black clouds lay heavily to the west and he pulled his coat collar up against the wind. The first attempt to find Phillips on the phone didn't work. He was bounced around from place to place, ending up with the secretary who told him that Professor Phillips was very busy and couldn't be disturbed for at least half an hour. Sam sat on the stairs by the phone and waited, thinking about Judith. It was five days since he'd seen her in St Bees and he'd heard nothing from her. Nor had Elspeth, which was more surprising. He knew that Elspeth had sent a get well card, but there'd been no response. He'd noticed Judith's up and down moods – depressed, angry, unreasonable – and being with her mother probably wasn't going to help. She was a difficult person; he wondered what had happened in her life to make her so. Maybe Elspeth knew, but she probably wouldn't tell him even if he asked.

He made himself a drink to pass the time and the minutes ticked by. Half an hour on the dot since his first attempt, he dialled the Lancaster number again, and this time he heard Phillips' educated drawl.

'Ah, constable,' he said. 'You want the test results on the samples you brought in yesterday. What was the boy's full name again? Steven Clifford Stringer, that's fine, and you don't have the date of birth, do you?'

Sam did, and gave it to him.

'Right. Well, Dr Hayward was right to be curious. We know the boy didn't drown and it looks as if he might have died from an overdose of alcohol and drugs. It wouldn't take much in such a young, slight body to slow the heart down irretrievably.'

Sam stopped scribbling. 'An overdose? Of what?'

'Well, alcohol of some kind, probably spirits to hit him so hard, and sedatives. They could have been prescribed for him, I suppose, but unlikely.'

Sam was silent, thinking.

'Where did the boy live?' Phillips asked.

'In a children's home, Montgomery House, just a few miles from here,' Sam said.

'Ah,' said Phillips. 'In a home. All boys, is it?'

'Yes, why?'

'I'm afraid I've come across cases like this before. Boys, various ages, usually in care. If we had the body still we could double check, but it's likely he's been abused.'

'In what way?'

'Sexually abused, constable. Raped.'

Sam didn't respond. The doctor continued. 'If you're going to deal with cases like this you need to know the details. Children are given alcohol to soften them up, so to speak, but for

351

boys there needs to be something to relax the muscles, so that someone can… Do I need to spell this out, constable?'

'No,' said Sam. 'I understand.'

'They often use Diazepam. It's an effective sedative and has this very useful side-effect, useful if you want to assault small boys, that is.'

Sam heard the casual remark but for a moment he couldn't speak.

'You still there, constable?'

'I'm here,' said Sam. 'You're saying that someone gave these drugs to Steven, for sex, and killed him?'

'That's what could have happened. It probably wasn't deliberate, but there's always a risk. If the boy wasn't actually dead he would be deeply unconscious and they must have panicked, whoever did this to him.'

Sam made himself think about what had happened. 'So they could take him out onto the sands where he was found, and the quicksand would have sucked the body down.'

'Oh dear, what a mess,' said Phillips. 'Makes no difference to me, obviously. But I assume you're investigating the place where all this happened? It probably isn't an isolated case. They just slipped up this time, and little Steven paid the price. Sad.'

Sam couldn't bear to listen to this man for much longer.

'Is there anything else, constable?' Phillips went on. 'I'll put all the details in my report for Dr Hayward.' He hesitated. 'Oh, and considering the seriousness of the implications, I've already alerted the police. Other boys are at risk, and it needs to be followed up immediately. I called your superior just before you rang.'

Sam's heart thumped in his chest.

'Who did you speak to?'

'Right to the top with this one,' said Phillips. 'Your Chief

Inspector Cardine, isn't it? Had to leave a message, the bare facts as I knew them and asked him to call me back urgently.'

Sam mumbled something and put down the phone. His head was reeling. For a while he sat on the stairs without moving, rousing himself finally when he couldn't bear the thought of seeing Elspeth and Tommy. How could someone do that, to a child? Was that why Harries killed himself? Disgust, guilt, self-loathing? Sam would have helped string the bastard up if he'd known then what he knew now. Why did Phillips have to tell Cardine? From what Dr Graham had said, Cardine was already part of the group of men who all knew each other: him, Edwards, Thornhill, Morrison, they all scratched each others' backs. How many more were there? Sam pulled on his coat, put his precious notebook in his inside pocket and left the house, knowing what he needed to do next and hoping he wasn't too late.

'What do you want now?' said Ann Hayward. 'He's been easier in himself since you were here last, and I don't want him getting wound up again.' She was standing at the door and showed no sign of inviting Sam into the house.

'I promise I won't stay long, Mrs Hayward, but things are happening and I need to talk to him.' She hesitated. 'Please,' said Sam. 'More boys could be at risk.'

She stood aside and he went into the dark hall. The smell of sickness hit him immediately, and she noticed his reaction.

'I know,' she said. 'You get used to it after a while. The district nurse and I keep him as clean as we can, but … he's in the back room now. We had to move him downstairs.'

The room was dark. Mrs Hayward went to the window and pulled the curtain back just a little. Sam could hear the patter of rain and the intermittent rattle in the old man's chest.

'Are you awake, David?' said his wife. 'That constable's come to see you again. The one who works for Morrison.'

Hayward turned his head and raised a mottled hand off the sheet. 'Back again?' he said.

'How are you, doc?' Sam asked. Ann pulled up a chair for him and he sat down, tasting the sour breath close to his face.

'Finished,' said Hayward.

'I took those samples to Lancaster,' said Sam. Hayward's eyes reacted. 'Phillips?'

Sam nodded. 'He did the tests, gave me the results today.'

Hayward said nothing. Sam continued. 'He thinks Steven died of alcohol and sedatives that slowed his heart.'

Hayward's eyes filled with tears.

Sam went on. 'We know Steven could be difficult, and the sedatives might have been prescribed for him, but Dr Graham said nothing about it when I saw him, and if it was accidental they would have reported it surely, not just dumped the boy's body on the sands.'

Still Hayward said nothing, looking steadily at Sam. He pulled for breath before he spoke, groping for the oxygen mask beside the pillow. 'Happened before,' he said, after a long pause. 'Older kid. Car accident. I did the PM. First time.' He put the mask over his mouth and drew in.

Sam tried to fill the gaps. 'You mean that was the first time Morrison made you alter a PM, when he threatened you?'

Hayward nodded slowly, and lowered the mask.

'Car accident where?' Sam asked, reaching for his notebook.

'Coast Road. Older man driving.' Deep breath. 'He was OK.'

'What drugs did you find?'

The old man spelled out the syllables. 'Diazepam.'

They looked at each other. Sam nodded. 'Same again,' he said. 'I can find the record of the accident. Can you remember a name?'

Hayward strained his memory, his eyes watering.

'Feversham,' said Ann's voice from behind Sam. 'The driver was called Maurice Feversham. He was a friend of Edwards. The lad's name was Edward, Eddie Stretch. He was fifteen. No one asked any questions.'

Sam leaned forward, oblivious to the smell. 'You must have thought about this, doc. Who was Morrison trying to protect?'

Hayward breathed. 'All of them, the old soldiers.' Breath. 'And their mates.'

'Cardine?' Nod. 'Edwards?' Nod. 'Thornhill?' Nod.

'Anyone else?' asked Sam.

Hayward turned his head away.

'He's had enough,' said his wife. 'He wants all this to stop. To forget.'

'He can let it go soon,' said Sam. 'Can he still sign his name?'

'Yes, if we help him. And we could witness it. Is that what you want?'

'I need to have a proper statement,' said Sam. 'It may be the last chance.'

'I know,' she said. 'I've got an old typewriter. We can check what he wants to say, line by line, and we can all sign it. Will that do?'

'Thank you, Mrs Hayward,' said Sam. 'I know how painful this must be for you.'

She smiled. 'If it helps him to die at ease with himself, that's all I want, constable.'

And so they wrote the dying man's statement, and when it was done Dr Hayward lay back in his bed and went to sleep.

Back in the office, Grayson was still at his desk, working in a pool of light from a lamp. He looked up when Sam came in.

'You've been a while,' said Grayson. 'I've had to cover for you.'

'Why?'

'Morrison. He phoned, looking for you. I said you were out chasing something up from the Upgill cases. Where have you been?'

'Doesn't matter,' said Sam. 'I need the phone.'

'Help yourself,' said Grayson.

Sam found Judith's number and called. It was gone five o'clock and someone should be home. A young man answered. 'It's the policeman, isn't it?' he said, when Sam asked for Judith. 'Recognise the voice.'

'Is she there, Vince?' asked Sam. 'I need to speak to her.'

'Actually she's not, and when Mum comes in there's going to be a fuss. Judith went to Barrow after lunch. She said she was escaping, before Mum and Dad dragged her off on holiday.'

'Escaping?'

'That's what she called it.'

'Did she say where she was going?'

Vince hesitated. 'She asked me to say she was going to see Elspeth. That's your sister, isn't it?'

'She's not there,' said Sam. 'Where has she really gone?'

'Honestly, I'm not sure, constable.'

'Call me Sam, please,'

'OK. Actually, Sam, Judith's gone a bit weird. She lay in her room for days after you came to see her at the weekend, and then all of a sudden she got up and dressed and told me this long, complicated story and said she had to find the proof. If you ask me, I think she's gone off her head.'

'What story?'

'About that boy at Montgomery House who died, and then someone called Harries and the other bloke who died on the sands and a Landrover. And there was something about a badge. On and on. Made no sense to me.'

Sam's mind raced. 'So where do you think she's gone?'

'She was ranting on about Thornhill, her boss. "Have to warn Irene", she said. Is that his wife? They're the people she stayed with, aren't they?'

Shit, shit, shit, Sam said to himself. Out loud he said, 'When did she leave?'

'Just after lunch, when Mum went out. She took a bag and said she might be away a few days, until it was all wrapped up, something like that.'

'Is that all?'

'Yes,' said Vince. 'Is she all right?'

'I'm sure she'll be fine,' Sam lied.

'Wait,' Vince shouted into the phone. 'What do I do now? She told me to cover for her.'

'You've done what you needed to. Leave it with me now.'

'What do I say to Mum? She'll be back soon.'

'Tell her Constable Tognarelli will find Judith and bring her home.'

'Is Judith in trouble? Should we call the police ourselves?'

'No,' said Sam, as firmly as he could. 'Leave it with me Vince, OK? I have to go.'

One more call. It was late, and a long time passed before someone picked up the phone.

'Newsroom, Andrew.'

'This is the police,' said Sam. 'We're looking for Judith Pharaoh.'

'She rang in earlier,' said Andrew. 'Hattie spoke to her.' He paused. 'I was listening.'

'Did she say where she was going this afternoon?'

'She asked about Mr Thornhill, but he was out. Hattie told her Mrs Thornhill would probably be home. She said Judith sounded really cheerful. We thought she was ill.'

'She's not well,' said Sam. 'That's why we want to find her.'

'That's all I know,' said Andrew. 'Sorry.'

The phone rang again as soon as Sam put down the receiver. 'Nelly?' said Morrison. 'Where the fuck have you been? Bloody Cardine's been on to me again. Some long tale about a forensics bloke in Lancaster. What's Lancaster got to do with it? What's going on?'

'Nothing sir,' said Sam. 'Must be mixing it up with the Noakes business in Lancaster, when I went there.'

'Rubbish! Don't lie to me, you arrogant prick,' Morrison shouted, making Grayson wince on the other side of the room. 'I want you to stay right there, d'you hear me? Don't move till I get there. You'll tell me what's going on or I'll have your badge.' The line buzzed as he rang off.

'What's going on, Nelly?' Grayson repeated with a feeble attempt at Morrison's accent.

Sam looked at him. 'Harry, I want you to come with me, now, before Morrison gets here.'

'Where?'

'We'll need a car. Too far to walk.'

'Where?' shouted Grayson.

'I'll tell you later. Hurry, man. God knows where Morrison was calling from, but we need to get out of here. Come on.'

Grayson picked up his coat. 'I must be bloody mad,' he said.

Sam pushed him towards the door. 'I'll tell him it was my idea, acting on information received, I needed backup, no time to wait, anything you like. It'll be fine, but we can't hang around.'

At the carpool they had to wait for someone to respond to the bell.

'Need a car, right away,' said Sam. 'Just for an hour or two.'

'No can do, son' said the man. 'One's out, one's on the blink. Starter motor gone.'

'When's it due back?'

'Any minute, actually, but they're often late. You'll have to wait. Warmer inside. Cuppa?'

Grayson was heading into the office but Sam pulled him back. 'We can't wait,' he said. In the carpool office the phone rang and the man turned to answer it. Grayson said, 'You've not even told me where we have to go in such a hurry, or why. I like a bit of excitement, but this is crackers.'

'Have you got a car?' asked Sam.

'Me, no chance. Got a bike.'

'A push bike?'

'Please! Look at me. No, a motorbike.'

'Where is it?'

'Back at the station, in the back yard.'

'Come on,' said Sam, pulling Grayson after him.

They headed out of town on the motorbike, Sam hanging on to Grayson's coat. The rain was holding off but it was cold, and without gloves Sam's hands were going numb.

'Take a left after Roose,' Sam shouted into Grayson's ear. 'House is called Bay View, on its own, on the hill somewhere.'

'Could be anywhere,' Grayson shouted back.

'Just keep going,' said Sam. 'Find a pub, and we'll ask.'

All they got in the first pub were shaking heads, until Sam mentioned Thornhill's name and someone pointed. 'Further on, bloody great big place, you can't miss it.'

'Try the Black Cock,' said another, 'they'll tell you.'

'Hold the front page,' someone shouted to general amusement.

The landlord at the Black Cock looked askance at Sam's warrant card.

'It's only a scooter,' he said. 'We just picked it up and put it out of the way. No need to send the flying squad.'

'What scooter?' said Sam, puzzled.

'Red Vespa,' said the landlord. 'That girl who stayed with Thornhills a while back, she left it in our yard, right in front of the cellar door.'

'When?' Sam asked.

The landlord thought about it. 'Six'ish now isn't it? About an hour ago. I called them about it when I saw their lights on.'

'Who answered?'

'Thornhill, of course. His house, isn't it?'

CHAPTER 28

The Black Cock was closed and looked deserted when Judith drove the Vespa slowly into the yard at the back. It was nearly half past four, the light was fading, and she pushed the scooter into the dark shadow of the wall where it couldn't be seen from the road. Bay View was a hundred yards up the hill, sitting on the ridge. No one else had ever built up there. 'Too draughty,' Edna had told her. 'Most folk build houses in more sheltered spots. Have to be rich to live up high like this.'

At least I don't have the heavy bag, Judith thought as she began to walk up the hill. It'll be at the flat when I need it later. And I might even have Irene with me. She won't stay here when she knows what he's been doing.

Coming round the last bend in the road, she noticed that the house on the skyline was in darkness. No lights down the long drive, or in the house itself. The windows were black. Maybe Irene wasn't home after all. Or not yet? It was dark but not late. She was probably still in town, or shopping. A car passed her going down the hill and Judith decided not to let herself be seen walking down the long drive. She would get over the wall and go round to the back through the little orchard, out of sight of the road. No one would see her. She gripped the key in her pocket.

When she reached the back door, she knocked on it hard just in case there was someone at home. She had a story prepared about having left something in a drawer upstairs, but there was no response, and she opened the door noiselessly and slipped inside. Out of the wind it was very quiet in the house and smelled of the familiar lilac scented polish. She thought for a moment about the layout of the rooms and wondered how long it would be before Irene arrived.

First things first. Judith felt her way through to the hall and up the stairs while her eyes adjusted to the gloom. In the main bedroom she padded across the dense carpet to the wardrobe on the other side and slid back the door. If the tie was where she'd seen it before, it would be in one of the small drawers to the side of the main hanging space. She needed more light and cursed herself for not bringing a torch. It was a plain tie, and there were several quite visible among the striped and patterned ones that were arranged neatly in two of the drawers. She drew out the first plain one, but it was black and had no design. Must be the one he wore for funerals. Another turned out to be dark red when she turned towards the uncurtained window for a little more light. She put the wrong ones back carefully and pulled out the third. Bingo. Here it was, dark blue with the small round design. She took it over to the window and peered at it. The handles of the two knives reminded her of Anthony and the movement of his dying body in the encroaching tide. She folded the tie and put it carefully into her jacket pocket.

One goal achieved. When they compared the tie with the badge Sam had found in the Landrover, everyone would know that Thornhill had something to do with Anthony's death. Now for the next step, to get into the office and see what Thornhill had hidden away in the desk drawer. If he was running some kind of business, making money out of Montgomery House as she had discovered, then the desk contents would have to be revealed. Irene wasn't here to help, so she would have to do it on her own. Her heart was beating strongly but she felt more alive and alert than she'd felt in days.

Downstairs Judith tried the door of the office but wasn't surprised to find it locked. She knew where all the room keys were kept, on the back of a cabinet door in the kitchen, and there they all were, more than she had envisaged. This could slow things down. She glanced at her watch. Nearly five. She'd expected Irene to be back by now, but it was OK. Judith knew what was meant by Alan Thornhill being 'back late'. That meant very late, hours away.

Taking a few keys at a time, Judith tested each one in the office door. She was crouching down by the kitchen cabinet, replacing the first batch and picking out some more, when a light flickered through the window onto the wall of the kitchen above her head. A car was coming down the long drive. It might be Irene coming home, but there was no way to be certain. Judith threw the keys into the cabinet, closed the door and crawled across the hall into the living room on the far side. She looked around, excited but not frightened. She'd stay out of sight until she was sure who it was. The largest of the two sofas sat with its back to the wall, and she pulled it out slightly to get behind it, while the tyres of the car crunched on the gravel outside and she heard the car door bang. It must be Irene, Judith thought. Who else could it be? A second door banged. Was that the boot, or did Irene have someone with her? She sat quite still, waiting.

A key clicked in the front door and light flared in the living room doorway. Judith smelled Irene's familiar perfume, and heard the anticipated shopping bags drop onto the floor. Irene, still unseen, went into the kitchen and Judith heard the sound of water running. Another set of footsteps crunched the final few yards from the car to the door. The front door was closed and the feet were hushed by the carpet down the hall.

'Cup of tea?' Irene's voice called.

'Love one,' said Alan Thornhill. Why was he here, Judith asked herself as his footsteps passed by the living room. The kitchen door stayed open and she could hear running water, the clink of china, drawers opening and closing. She thought about the keys she'd not had time to put back on their pegs. Would someone look in there? What else was in that cabinet? It was down low, next to the sink and it smelled of bleach. That was OK. There'd be no reason to open the door. Judith settled herself into a more comfortable position and wondered what to do. It was silly hiding there, but she didn't move. The Thornhills had started to talk in the kitchen and the excitement of eavesdropping overcame any remaining shreds of caution in her exalted mood. She felt invisible, untouchable. Even her hearing felt sharper than before.

'Do you think we've got enough?' Irene was saying.

'It's enough,' said Alan. 'Photos, plenty of them and good ones too. Even got some video the last time. Not much but it would kill him in court.'

'It'd never get to court,' said Irene. 'The family would never dare let it go that far. They've probably been covering up for him for years. We've got him. And there's plenty of money. Start small like we usually do and then turn it on.'

Judith was puzzled. She couldn't think what this had to do with Montgomery House.

Chairs scraped over the kitchen floor. There was a short silence before Alan Thornhill's voice began again. 'I still think it's time we packed it in. I know I've said so before but this time I'm sure. Morrison's getting twitchy. That nosey bastard copper went to see Graham, in his home. He was furious. Complained to Cardine, Cardine shouted at Morrison. I've told Brian to shut him down but he doesn't listen to me.'

Irene snorted. 'Who does listen to you? I don't any more. You're at it again, bleating about giving up, just because things aren't working out as smoothly as you like.'

'It's going wrong, I can feel it.'

Judith listened, puzzled. She couldn't recognise the two people she was hearing, although she knew their voices well.

'First the damn kid,' Alan's voice continued. 'All Harries had to do was get him further out where the tide would take him, but we end up with the body just down the road. Then the bloody man tops himself practically on our doorstep. He must have known the police would have to ask questions. The man was an idiot.'

Silence. Judith tried to concentrate, to make sense of it.

'So you think it's all over,' said Irene.

'Time to take the money and run.'

She laughed. 'That's your advice, is it?'

'We could go to Spain. They'd never find us there.'

'And never come back?'

'Depends what happens.'

'So I might have to stay in Spain with you for the rest of my life?' Judith heard the chair scrape again. 'I can't think of anything worse. A bloody life sentence in the sun with the snivelling wreck of a man called my husband. No thanks.'

'Don't start all that again,' Alan's voice rose. 'I had no choice about moving up here. They were my parents. Edwards was here already, and I knew what he'd be up to.'

'There are always choices. And don't give me the dutiful son speech either. I've heard it all before.'

'I need a drink,' came the reply and Judith froze. The drinks cabinet was just next to the sofa where she was hiding. The switch on the wall snapped and light flooded the room. She didn't breathe, feeling the vibration in the floor as Thornhill walked across it. She heard the cabinet door squeak as it always did, the rattle of bottles, clink of a glass, the sound of liquid pouring, being drunk, pouring again. Thornhill slumped into the sofa, which slid back towards the wall, crushing Judith into a smaller space. Her knee throbbed and she could hardly breathe.

Irene had followed him into the room and helped herself to a drink.

'This time I mean it,' she said. 'I've had enough.'

'What do you mean?'

'You put the money in my name, remember?'

'I had to.'

'Well I've left you a hundred pounds in the account, the rest is in my suitcase.'

Alan moved on the sofa and Judith felt the pressure on her legs.

'You've done what?' he shouted. 'We earned that money, together. You can't just take it.'

'Watch me,' she said. 'What will you do, tell the police?' She laughed. More fluid poured into a glass. 'You started all this,' Irene said. She was close by. Judith smelled her perfume strongly. 'You and your pervy friends. All they wanted to do after Malaya was carry on molesting little boys like they'd done in those bloody camps, and you were happy to drool and take pictures. Then Edwards got greedy and invited more boy fanciers to the party, used them to raise money, and everybody's having a jolly time. But not enough money in that for us, is there? Whose idea was it to make them pay us to keep quiet? That's where all the real money upstairs comes from, and who's idea was it? Not yours, you pathetic waste of space. Mine. That money's mine, all of it. And now you've all cocked it up, giving that kid too much stuff, not even getting rid of him properly.'

'You can't blame me for that.' Thornhill was whining, wilting under his wife's scorn.

Judith felt him lurch further back in the sofa. The meaning of what she was hearing burst into her mind and she felt sick. None of this should be happening. Irene was her friend, not this snarling monster. She had to get away from them, but how? What would they do if they found her? Her sore knee was twisted and hurting but she couldn't move, not until Alan got up, or they both left the room. She was stuck, and no one knew where she was.

Suddenly Thornhill stood up, and the pressure on Judith's legs eased. Thank God, she thought. Now go, out of the room, turn out the light, leave the house. Let me get out.

'Are you going to leave me?' Alan whimpered.

'Yes, at last,' Irene said. 'Should have done it months ago. If I wait any longer, you could fold up completely, blow us all away'

'Is there someone else?'

She laughed, that same short harsh laugh. 'Why do I need another pathetic man?' she said. 'Look at you all, poncing around, having sex with young boys, not a real man amongst you. All these years I've been the good wife, dressed up, made meals, gone to those god-awful dinners. Bored, bored, bored out of my skull. No, there's no one else. I'm getting the hell out, and you won't find me, so don't even try.'

Irene walked away and her husband followed her. Judith could hear them. Footsteps up the stairs. Thornhill was pleading with his wife, 'Don't leave me, Irene, please,' his voice fading as they went into the bedroom. Judith thought about how long it would take her to push back the sofa, get out into the hall, out of the door and away. Then the telephone rang, very loud, right above her head, on the table next to the sofa. She shrank back as footsteps came down the stairs, but it was the phone in the kitchen that Alan picked up. She couldn't hear him very clearly and moved her head slightly towards the end of the sofa. If he stayed there for a few minutes, and Irene stayed upstairs, she might manage to get out. Her knee was very painful now, but it wasn't far to the door. She began to move her legs.

Too late. 'OK, thanks, that's fine,' Alan said, and the phone clicked into silence.

'Irene,' Alan called up the stairs. 'That was George at the Black Cock. They found Judith's scooter in the yard, parked by the beer cellar door. He was telling me they had to move it. They know it's hers.'

Irene came to the top of the stairs. 'Judith? What's the little bitch up to now? I thought she was having a breakdown in St Bees.'

'She was,' said Alan.

Irene ran down the stairs. 'Christ, she's been here. Did you get her doorkey off her?'

'I didn't know she had a key. Why would she come here?'

'God knows. She's in with that copper, the one Morrison can't control. And you can't control her, can you?' They were both standing in the hall.

'Where is she?' said Irene. 'The scooter's still there. Where is she?'

She ran to the office. Judith heard the door rattle. 'Thank God she's not got in here.' More footsteps, into the kitchen.

'Christ,' said Irene. 'Look at this. She's been looking through the keys. She might have got in the office and then locked up again. Open it up Alan, don't just stand there. See if anything's missing.'

Judith heard the office door open, drawers being pulled. 'All the files are here,' he said. 'Looks like nothing's been touched.'

'Where is she?' Irene screamed. 'Come out, you little bitch. You can't hide. You look down here,' she said to Alan. 'I'll do upstairs. Look everywhere. Don't screw this up, too.'

Judith couldn't breathe. She pushed herself down towards the floor, as far as the pain in her knee would allow, and waited. Could she reach the phone before he came back?

The sofa was hauled away and Judith shrank down. Above her head Thornhill's voice said, 'Oh, God!'

'I didn't hear anything,' said Judith, her voice rising in panic. 'Just voices, but I don't know what you were saying.' She looked up. Alan didn't move, he just kept staring down at her over the back of the sofa. Irene's face appeared, distorted with anger.

'You stupid bitch,' she said. 'You couldn't leave it alone, could you? Poking around in other people's business. And look at you now, lying behind the damned sofa like a dead cat.' She pushed the sofa back hard towards the wall and pain blazed in Judith's knee, making her cry out.

'Stay there,' said Irene. 'So now what do we do?' she asked her husband. There was no response. 'Do you realise what she's heard?' she went on. 'Everything, every damn thing. We can't let her go.'

Judith wanted to beg them to let her leave, but the words dried in her mouth.

Footsteps retreated and returned.

'Where did you find that?' asked Alan.

'In the desk. It's been there for years, since you came back from the war. Had you forgotten?'

'What are you going to do with it?'

'Not me,' said his wife. 'You. I'm taking the money and getting out of here before that copper boyfriend of hers turns up. You have to deal with her, and make it good. Say you found her in the house and it was an accident. Tell them anything you like, but just do it, or she'll tell them everything.'

'No,' he said.

The sofa was pulled back. Irene was holding a revolver. 'See this?' she said to Judith. 'This is where the talking stops. Get up.'

Judith struggled to her feet, holding on to the back of the sofa. She looked into Irene's eyes and saw the hatred coming back at her. Irene pointed the revolver at her and gestured with it. 'Sit down there where we can see you, away from the phone,' she said. 'Get something to tie her with,' she said to Alan. 'Anything. You were a Boy Scout, weren't you? Hurry up.'

Thornhill came back carrying some parcel string. Irene sighed. 'All right, use plenty. Put her wrists behind her.'

Thornhill stood still and Irene thrust the gun into his hands. 'For God's sake, man. Hold this.'

She took the string, pulled Judith's hands behind her back and started to bind her wrists together, tight, very tight. Judith cried out.

'Shut up,' said Irene. 'It won't matter when he puts a neat little bullet into you, will it? Now put your legs out.' Judith winced as Irene tied the ankles too, and pushed her back on to the sofa, trussed like a chicken and unable to stop herself from falling over sideways.

'I can't do it here,' said Alan. 'And now she can't move.'

'Not my problem. The carpet cost a fortune but it doesn't matter how much mess you make. I won't be here. I'm taking the car.'

'Where can I take her?' he said.

'Anywhere, but don't leave it too long. That young policeman's no fool.'

Judith could see Alan out of one eye. He was looking around him in desperation.

'Don't leave me,' he said again.

Irene was out of Judith's vision, but she heard drawers opening in the office, then her quick footsteps going upstairs. A couple of minutes later Irene came down again, with something heavy bumping down the stairs behind her.

'Put the gun down and help with this bag,' she ordered.

He won't help, surely, thought Judith, but he did, holding the gun in one hand and helping his wife drag the bag to the front door and out towards the car parked outside. Judith struggled but she couldn't move. The car engine started and the wheels crackled on the gravel as it turned and disappeared down the drive. Judith rolled against the back of the sofa so she could see out of both eyes. Alan Thornhill stood in the living room doorway looking at her.

'You can't do this,' Judith said.

'I have to.'

'Just leave me here. I won't tell.'

'You know you will.'

'I can wait, until you're away. Take my scooter and the money from my purse. You could be on a train and away before they find me.'

'Are they coming?'

'Of course, but you still have time.'

He shook his head. He walked carefully round her and went

to the drinks cabinet, picked up a bottle of brandy. Then he switched off the lights in the hall and the living room and sat down in an armchair on the other side of the room, pulled the stopper out with his teeth, spat it away and took a long drink from the bottle. In the faint light from the kitchen Judith saw a trickle of brandy glisten as it ran down his chin.

'You can't kill me,' she said.

'I've killed before,' said Thornhill, taking another swig from the bottle.

'But this is different,' she said. She watched him. 'What happened to you?'

He stared at her.

'It was the war,' he said after a long pause. 'When we came home, everything was so dull. I wanted more. Edwards offered something, and I wanted it. I couldn't do it, with the boys. I just watched, took the pictures. Blackmail was Irene's idea, to get more money. It worked. So many of them on the hook. I wanted to stop, but she wouldn't.'

'What happened to Steven Stringer?'

'We gave him the stuff, to keep him quiet, and he just faded away. We couldn't wake him. Harries was crying. We told him to take the boy away and lose him.'

'And Anthony?'

Thornhill drank more brandy. He was slumped back in the chair, the hand holding the gun resting on the arm. Judith could see his eyes trying to focus before he spoke.

'No one knew where he came from. He just turned up, pushed Harries into suicide and then it all started to go wrong. So we got two of our lads to deal with it.'

'He was Steven's brother,' said Judith.

Thornhill nodded and took another drink. 'The lads tracked him down.'

'The men in the Landrover?'

'Stupid,' he said. 'Why did you try to help him? What's it to you?'

'I didn't want him to die,' said Judith.

Thornhill grunted, pushed himself up and lifted the gun off the arm of the chair, gripping it with both hands. He pointed the gun unsteadily at Judith. She closed her eyes.

Sam and Grayson left the motorbike by the road to make less noise as they approached the house. They'd seen Thornhill's Daimler speeding away down the hill, and they were running along the drive towards Bay View when they heard the shot and stopped. Sam shouted. 'Go back, call it in. We need backup, and an ambulance. Go, go!'

Sam ran on, using the grass at the side of the drive to avoid making a noise on the gravel. Lights were on in the room to the left of the front door, but on the right the window was dark and curtains closed. Close to the front door he dropped to a crouch, crawled the last few feet and put his ear to the door. There was a sound, someone moaning. He strained to hear more but the moaning stopped.

The front door was impenetrable. He ducked under the lighted window and peeped in. Kitchen. Empty. Shopping bags lay by the door. Round the side of the house he could see a small window on the upper floor of the house, but no way to reach it and too small. At the back was another door, also locked, but the top third of the door was frosted glass. A quick check on windows on the other side but all were shut and dark. Wind swirled round the hillside and an owl hooted in the trees. There was no moon yet and Sam peered in to the darkness of the back garden, searching for a spade or something to break the glass. He picked up a rock from what looked like a rockery in the corner of the garden. It was heavy and he needed both hands to carry it to the back door. He leaned against the door listening, but there was nothing except the sound of the wind. He raised the rock and launched it at the glass pane. It cracked but held, and the rock dislodged from his grip, falling onto his foot. The pain gave him strength as he smashed his elbow into the glass pane, which broke and clattered inwards, leaving shards around the frame.

Pushing his arm through the hole, he found the lock inside, opened it and stepped over the broken glass into the kitchen, ducking down to lower his profile against the light. He heard a voice calling and crawled forward, stopping to take a splinter of glass from his knee. The pain in his foot hammered. Light from the kitchen door flooded into the hall and he stopped. Standing now, he inched along the wall, listening for any movement. 'In here,' said the voice. Sam froze.

'Police!' he called. 'The house is surrounded. Put down the gun.'

Nothing. Sam peered through the hall doorway and saw a body, lying on a sofa on the far side of the large living room, under the window. It moved and he shrank back. The air smelled of blood.

'Sam?' Judith coughed. 'Is that you? I think he's dead.'

In the gloom of the living room, Sam saw Thornhill lying back in the chair, a dark stain around his head, his dead hand still holding the gun.

'Sam,' said Judith. 'Help me.'

'Thank God,' he said, reaching the sofa where Judith lay and took her bound body in his arms.

CHAPTER 29

Sam's best shoes were tight around the throbbing foot. The church was almost empty. At the far end of the nave, near the altar steps, wooden trestles stood waiting for the coffin. He chose a pew near the back and sat for a while, thinking. He wanted to close his eyes, but couldn't risk the dizziness that had plagued him for several days. Keeping his head down helped, and people would think he was praying and leave him undisturbed.

In his mind, the same memories: the smell of furniture polish overlaid with blood, black stains in the half light, a body sprawled in death. Sam's head told him he had done the right thing, but regret hammered on his rational mind and stole his sleep. He should have believed her, tried harder, moved more quickly, not let Morrison get in his way. Someone began playing the organ, very softly, and a figure in clerical robes flitted around the choir stalls. People were coming past him down the aisle but he didn't look up. He wondered who might be there from the station. Morrison hadn't turned up at the crime scene, and had not been seen since. Called away suddenly, family crisis, Sergeant Clark had said, but Sam couldn't believe Morrison would dare show his face, not after all that had happened.

Someone slipped into the pew beside him. 'Can you move up a bit,' said a familiar woman's voice, 'or are you waiting for someone?'

He turned and smiled. 'How are you?' he asked.

'Better. Still having trouble sleeping.'

'Me too,' he said.

'Mum says I should talk to a priest,' said Judith. 'How's your foot?'

'These shoes don't help. Will you?'

'What? Talk to a priest? Not a chance,' she said. 'Faith like hers must be a comfort, but not for me.'

'How was Scotland?'

Judith lowered her head to whisper, aware of other people pushing into the pew in front of them. 'Not as ghastly as I thought it might be. Mum was too shocked to fuss much, and Dad was fine. He's just parking the car down the road. Lots of cars and people outside. I thought you might be in here already.'

'We need to talk,' he said.

'I know, but not here. Are you going to the do afterwards at the hotel?'

'I wasn't, but I will if we can find somewhere quiet there.'

'OK,' she said.

John Pharaoh sat down beside his daughter and leaned across to shake Sam's hand.

'Good to meet you again, Mr Pharaoh,' said Sam. 'I wasn't sure Judith would be able to come.'

'Her mother wasn't either,' John whispered. 'But she wanted to pay her respects, didn't you, Judith, so I brought her down in the car. What about you, Sam? How are you doing?'

Sam shrugged. 'It's complicated,' he said. 'We can't really talk here.'

'You talk to Judith later, maybe, and she'll tell us the bits she can. I know it must be tricky.'

'It is,' said Sam.

The big doors at the back of the church opened with a creak that echoed in the vaulted space, and the mourners stood as the coffin progressed down the aisle, carried by six bearers of various ages. Sam guessed they must be relatives. Behind the coffin was Ann Hayward, supported by a younger woman who looked like her. They were both pale, but their heads were high and they were past tears. Judith wiped her eyes and Sam put an arm round her shoulders for a few moments until she moved slightly and he took it away.

They sang the old hymns and listened to people talking about the father, brother, friend and colleague that Hayward had been to all of them. Sam could see that Chief Inspector Cardine was among the crowd, but he took no part in the service. The church was full, and some stood at the back, adding to the volume of men's voices that made Sam's heart swell and caught the hymn in his throat. They followed the coffin out into the cold morning and round to the churchyard where the grave yawned beside a mound of red Furness earth. Standing at the back of the group, they missed most of the vicar's words as they were snatched away by the wind. When the coffin was lowered Sam and Judith queued with others to pay their respects to the family. Mrs Hayward gripped Sam's hand. 'Thank you,' she whispered, and pulled Sam towards her to speak quietly to him. 'He waited for someone he could trust.'

The hotel was just round the corner on Abbey Road. On the way in among the file of people in dark clothes, John Pharoah met an old work colleague. 'You and Sam want to talk,' he said to Judith. 'I'll be fine here. Come and look for me when you want to leave.'

Judith and Sam juggled cups of tea and a plate of sandwiches between them and sneaked out of the crowded room, down the hall to a small room at the back. There were no chairs but they stood by the mantelpiece, leaning awkwardly to catch the crumbs.

'Are you all right standing up like this?' Sam asked.

'I'm fine for a while, really,' she said. 'Tell me what's been happening?'

He thought back over the previous two weeks, sifting out the things that mattered from the mass of conversations and discoveries of the previous days.

'You remembered so much about what happened that night,' he said. 'Even as shocked as you were, all that detail was really useful. Irene's car was found at Manchester airport. We think she took a flight to Madrid, although the description from the airport staff didn't sound like her, and she might have moved on from there. Basically, we have no idea where she is. And we found some things in the desk in Thornhill's office that confirmed what you told us, about the blackmail scheme, but only fragments. We think she must have taken most of the files with her, to destroy or to use later. You said she had a heavy bag with her and the files would have weighed a lot. She may need them. Whatever money she had won't last forever.'

'What about Monty House? Is it still going?

'It's strange. No, more than strange, it's awful,' said Sam, 'as if nothing had really happened. Captain Edwards has been interviewed, obviously, after what we heard from you, but apparently he's claiming that everyone who visits the house is OK, and he knew nothing about what the Thornhills or others were up to. They haven't let me anywhere near him.'

'But how can he say that?'

Sam shrugged. 'Everyone thinks Harries was the one bad apple, and no one else in the barrel can be blamed, including Edwards who says he was duped by Harries himself when he was appointed. False references, all that. It was Harries who abused Steven, an isolated incident, and then he killed himself and that removed the problem.'

Judith shook her head. 'I don't get it,' she said. 'Irene's blackmail scheme couldn't work if that was true.'

'But the only real evidence of blackmail that we have is your statement about conversations heard while you were trespassing and hiding behind a sofa. Both the others are gone.'

'My evidence isn't enough, and the ones who are left are still regarded as good people whose only fault is their trust in the goodness of others? Is that how it goes?'

'Pretty much,' said Sam. 'One of the good people is Iris Robinson, I'm pretty certain about that, and she still won't hear a word against the captain.'

'Didn't you say you had some evidence from the man who's in jail, who was in Monty House himself?'

'He won't make a formal statement, not yet at least. And anyway, if it's his word against Edwards I know which way a jury would jump.'

'I think I need to sit down,' said Judith, feeling energy and courage and faith in justice draining out of her.

The woman in the hotel reception protested for a moment when Sam appeared and picked up a chair from beside her, but he smiled and explained, and carried the chair back to Judith. 'Do you want me to find your dad?' he asked. She shook her head. 'I'll be all right. Don't leave me. Tell me more.'

Sam felt suddenly tired too and sat on the floor beside her, his legs stretched out. His foot hurt, and he wondered what anyone who saw them there would think.

'Not sure what else there is to tell you. Sorry it's so dismal.'

'What about Anthony?'

Sam looked at his shiny shoes. 'Ah,' he said. 'Of course, you don't know about that.'

'Tell me,' she said.

'A body washed up, not far from where we found Harries actually. It was a mess, but we knew who it was. He'd been stabbed, but the knife had gone. I went to fetch Donna, and she identified him. Poor girl. Two brothers, both dead in the tide. She wasn't close to Anthony, not with all the years he'd spent away, but it was still a shock. I think she realised that the blokes who asked her about him probably killed him. She was terribly upset that she might have led them to him.'

'Is she still with that awful boyfriend?'

Sam smiled. 'No, that's one good thing that came out of it. Do you remember Fred, her boss at the café?'

Judith smiled too. 'He was always fond of her.'

'He took her in, and saw off the boyfriend.'

Judith clapped her hands. 'Thank God for Fred.'

'I think I need some air,' said Sam. 'There's a garden round the back where we could sit. Or do you want to find your dad? He's probably anxious to get you home.'

'He'll be yacking away to his old mate,' said Judith. 'I'm in no rush to get back home. Show me the garden. With any luck there'll be a proper seat.'

The rain had stopped and sun shone brightly onto the little patch of green saved from the encroachment of the car park. A wooden bench stood beside a bare flowerbed dotted with heavily pruned roses that pointed at the sky.

'Must be lovely out here in summer,' said Judith. 'Just enough space for two of us on the bench.' They sat in silence for a moment, feeling the sun on their faces.

'Why do men do that with children?' she asked, opening her eyes but not looking at him. 'I can understand that some men might love other men rather than women, but why these boys?'

'It's not love,' said Sam. 'I think it's about power. They do it because they can. The children have no power and they can use them, make them do things they don't want to do. It's cruelty, like beating a dog.'

They sat quietly for a while before Judith asked 'What will happen to those boys, the ones who've been abused?'

'They must be pretty messed up by it all, but some of them were pretty messed up to start with. And no one believes them, so after a while they just don't bother complaining. If they can't make Iris believe them, what chance do they have?'

'You believe it all happened, don't you?' Judith asked.

'I believe what you heard, and I wish I'd believed you earlier when you began to think Thornhill was involved, but I was just thinking about the practicalities, getting a search warrant or grounds for an arrest, and there wasn't enough evidence.'

'What made you know where to find me?' she asked.

'When Vince told me you wanted to help Irene, I knew where you'd gone. He thought you'd gone a bit loopy, you know.'

'I did,' she said. 'Probably delayed shock or something, I don't know. I was convinced that Thornhill was evil and that I had to rescue Irene. It took me a while to believe what I was hearing when they started talking about it. And then she was so vicious. She told Alan to shoot me, just to shut me up. And I thought he was going to do it.'

She put both hands to her face. Sam sat awkwardly beside her, wanting to comfort her, but afraid to do so.

'Come on,' he said. 'We can't torture ourselves any more with this.'

'Wait,' said Judith. 'What are you going to do?'

'Just what I've done since it happened. Finish the paperwork, gather the evidence, do what we can to find Irene and get her back. Without Morrison around, it's actually easier to get on with the job.'

'Where is he?'

'No one's saying. All sorts of rumours. Clarky says he's on a training course somewhere, but then he winks and you know that's what we're supposed to think. I don't care where he is actually as long as he's not here.' He looked across at her. 'And what about you? Are you going back to the *News*?'

'I doubt it,' she said. 'Skelly's stepped up into the editor's office and they got George Falcon back straight away. According to Hattie, he was desperate to get back to work and away from his wife. I can understand that. Work can be such a relief sometimes. Cunningham's still there, and Andrew. They're probably glad to see the back of me.'

'Do you think you've recovered properly?'

'Not sure how I would know, or how long it should take. The doctor said it could be a long time before the nightmares fade, and I still get some ringing in my ears from that gunshot. It was terribly loud.'

'A Webley revolver,' said Sam, 'brought back from Malaya probably.'

'I was lucky,' she said. 'I know that.'

'Irene might have done you a favour, from what you said. Thornhill was so devastated by her leaving him to carry the can that he took the easy way out, on an impulse.'

'And he was very drunk by then,' said Judith. 'Nearly a whole bottle of brandy.' She put her hand over her eyes. 'I can still see it,' she said. 'The gun barrel shaking in his hand, pointing at me. I was sure he was going to kill me.'

This time Sam did put his arm round her, pulled her up and led her back inside.

It was after Judith and John had gone and Sam was looking for his coat that Chief Inspector Cardine found him, propelled him back into the cloakroom, closed the door and leaned his back against it. He was a big man, with white hair oiled into shape and a thin white moustache.

'Leaving, detective, before we've had the chance to talk?'

'Yes, sir,' said Sam. 'I only came down here to catch up with a friend.'

'Ah, the dashing Miss Pharaoh,' said Cardine. 'She's recovered from her ordeal, I assume? She'll need to be in good form for the inquest when it comes around.'

Sam frowned. 'There's no doubt about Thornhill's cause of death, is there? Judith heard and saw everything a coroner would want to know about.'

'As I said, she'll be centre stage for all that. No doubt she'll enjoy it.'

'What do you want to talk about, sir?' asked Sam. He would not be drawn into an argument about Judith.

'You have some decisions to make, don't you?' said Cardine, 'About your future in the force?'

'Do I?' said Sam.

'I think you do, constable,' Cardine went on, 'and you should think about them very seriously. You've had some problems since you came to us, lack of discipline, disrespect for your seniors. Things can't go on as they were, can they?'

Someone knocked on the cloakroom door. Cardine called, 'Just a minute,' but he didn't move. 'You will report to me tomorrow, constable, for a discussion about your future. Nine o'clock tomorrow, at my office. Is that clear?'

Sam nodded.

'Is that clear?' Cardine repeated.

'Yes, sir,' said Sam.

Sam said nothing to Elspeth that evening. He was fairly certain what was coming, but there was no point in worrying Elspeth until it did. Cardine did not keep him waiting the following morning. At nine o'clock Sam was standing at attention in front of the chief inspector's desk, looking at the wall.

'You may be interested to know, constable,' said Cardine without looking up, 'that Detective Sergeant Morrison won't be returning to us. He's been offered a senior job in the Hong Kong force, accepted it and resigned as of last Friday. We're all very pleased for him. So that leaves a vacancy as detective sergeant, doesn't it?'

Sam nodded. With any luck he would never see Morrison again.

'I wonder if you would consider going for that job, constable? You've done the sergeant's exams I understand?'

'Yes, sir,' said Sam.

'Well, just in case that was in your mind, I think I should tell you not to waste your time. I've seen your report and your allegations about Sergeant Morrison's dealings with Dr Hayward. It's all nonsense, of course. Everyone knows about Hayward's drinking, and his failing faculties. Nothing he might have said to you will count for anything, and he can't be questioned about it now that he's dead.'

Sam stared ahead as he took in Cardine's words..

'So your report will backfire, constable, not on Sergeant Morrison but on you. No one wants a sergeant who would make such unfounded allegations about a fellow officer. I certainly don't, and my word counts for something in these parts, and a few others.' Sam lowered his eyes. Cardine was still looking down at the file on his desk. 'Am I making myself clear, constable?'

'Yes, sir,' said Sam.

'I've also read the statement you took from that hysterical girl, and all the allegations she's making based on what she heard from behind a sofa. Do you honestly expect that to be taken seriously?'

'Yes, sir, I do,' said Sam. He was looking directly at Cardine now. 'We found some evidence at the house to support what she said, and what she heard. It's all in the file.'

'Yes, I have it,' said Cardine. 'And it'll be my decision what to do with it. These are very serious allegations, against men personally known to me, with unimpeachable reputations in this town, one of whom took his own life when his wife left him. If there was criminal wrongdoing, the evidence points to the guilt of Mrs Thornhill first and foremost, and so far we don't know where she is.'

'But, sir —' said Sam. Cardine raised his hand.

'Save your breath,' he said. 'What you think or say cuts no ice with me or anyone else. Maybe in uniform you might have had a chance of a career, but as a detective, you're finished. As I said, you've got some decisions to make.'

Chief Inspector Cardine put the file to one side and sat behind his polished empty desk, his hands resting calmly in front of him. 'I want a letter from you on my desk by the end of the day. I think you understand what's needed. That's all, constable. Close the door on your way out.'

Sam turned on his heel and left the office. Back in the CID room he sat for a while, until his hands had stopped shaking.

Chapter 30

Judith lay in her quiet bedroom at the back of the house on Beach Road. Now that the wind had dropped she had opened the top window just enough to hear the sea and savour the smell of it as she breathed in slowly. She was pleased that she'd been at Doc Hayward's funeral, but the conversation with Sam had left her low. John must have said something to his wife, and Maggie had treated her daughter more softly than usual when they arrived home.

Later she ventured downstairs. Maggie and Vince were in the front room with the radio on and John was sitting in the kitchen with the newspaper. He put it down, and pulled out a chair for Judith to sit with him.

'How are you feeling now?' he asked.

'OK,' she said, 'just sad, really. Sam thinks nothing will happen about Monty House. Edwards is still there. They can't deny what happened to Stevie Stringer but they're treating it as an isolated case and blaming Harries.'

'Who's conveniently dead,' said John.

'Exactly,' said Judith. 'Sam wasn't sure what would happen next, if anything.'

'I like that young man,' said John.

Judith knew he was fishing for a reaction, and she thought

about what to say. 'He's getting better. To start with I thought he was a pompous prick.'

'Judith! What a thing to say, after all that expensive education.'

'Well he was, and he probably still is,' said Judith. 'But it's a strength as well. He plays by the rules. I think he's really upset about how the police are reacting to what happened. No one seems prepared to do anything. They just want to keep the lid tight and carry on. Irene Thornhill is the villain now, and she can't be questioned either because she's disappeared. Spain, apparently.'

'Plenty of crooks there these days,' said John. 'It's really hard to get them out.' He looked at his daughter's pale face and wild hair. 'Do you want a drink?'

Judith shook her head. 'I'm trying to decide what to do about work. I've been off for nearly two weeks already.'

'Doctor Albright will write you another sick note if you need it.'

'I know. I still don't know whether I really want to go back. But I don't want to work at Sellafield either. Sorry, Dad, but I don't.'

'I didn't really expect you to do that,' he said. 'It's a big place, but you can't thrive in my shadow. You need to strike out on your own.'

She nodded. 'Does Mum understand that?'

'I doubt it, but let me deal with that.'

Judith leaned across and kissed her father on the cheek. 'So what do you think I should do, Dad?'

'Honestly?' he said. 'I always thought you would make a great journalist, but you were wasted and exploited in that job. They never really trusted you, did they, quite apart from all that nastiness you told me about.'

Judith thought about the newsroom and what happened there. He was right.

'Now that Bill's the editor, they'll need a chief reporter,' she said, without conviction.

'But Falcon is back, isn't he, at least for a while, and can you see Bill Skelly picking you for that job, Judith, and all the aggravation of working with a stroppy woman like you?'

'Stroppy? Is that what you think?'

'Not me, them,' said John. 'I saw what happened to my mother. It was twenty years ago, and you're not quite as stroppy as she was, but things haven't changed all that much.'

'You sound like a feminist,' said Judith.

'Am I allowed to be a feminist?' he said, smiling. 'I'm not saying you should have that job because you're a woman, but you shouldn't have to fight like you've had to do. It's a waste of your energy and your talent and they don't deserve you.'

Judith watched him, surprised by his vehemence.

'There's no rush,' he went on. 'Something will turn up, and you'll know if it's what you want. I can help, if you need me to. We're not short of money, and I'm very happy to support you in a new venture, if you find something you want to do.'

She squeezed his arm.

The tides were unusually high over the next few days, and on Saturday, as Vince wasn't at college, Judith walked with him down to the shore at high tide, to listen and feel the spray on his face. Clusters of foamy bubbles blew up the beach and over their boots, and Judith felt like a child again, running up the stony slope away from encroaching waves.

'We're lucky living here,' Vince said as they walked back to the house, blown along by the westerly.

'A honey trap,' said Judith. 'I have to escape before it sucks me in and I'm stuck for good.'

'College is good for getting me out of the house,' he said. 'And Dad says they can use me at Sellafield when I've done my exams. So at least I'll be earning, even if I can't have my own place.'

'I want out, too,' said Judith. 'But I don't know where or what. Dad keeps on about letting things just happen but I'm not very good at being patient.'

Judith was alone in the house the next day when the phone rang just after ten. It was Sam. He enquired after her health, as he always did, but she could hear that something else was on his mind.

'Will you be coming back to Barrow at all?' he asked. 'I could do with a chat.'

'No plans,' said Judith. 'I'm still off sick officially, but I couldn't face it even now I'm feeling better.'

'Have you decided about work?'

'The one thing I know is that I'm not going back to the *News*. Not sure about anything else.'

'We need to talk,' he repeated, 'so I'll come to you.'

'No,' she said. 'I need a break and you always come here. We could meet halfway…' She thought about the possibilities. 'How about Silecroft? We could walk to the beach if the weather's OK, or go to the Miners if it's not. It's right next to the station.'

It was cold but clear the following afternoon. Sam waited in the Miners for Judith's southbound train to arrive. The wind had dropped and the sky was clearing from the west, so they decided to risk the walk to the shore.

'It'll take us ten minutes,' he said. 'Can you manage that?'

'Come on, Sam.' She grabbed his arm. 'I'm not in my dotage

yet. Walking's good for us. And you keep saying we need to chat, so chat away.'

Sam told her what Cardine had said to him at the funeral.

'That's awful,' she said. 'Can't you complain to someone, take it further?'

'Maybe, but I've taken the hint and decided to leave the force.'

Judith stopped, shocked. 'But Sam, you can't do that. That means they've won. You love being a policeman. Why not just move to another job, away from Barrow? What about the Met?'

'I thought about that,' he said. 'But do I want to live in London? Not really. And I'm not sure things will be straight-forward there, either. What if I saw other things going on I didn't approve of?' He laughed. 'Makes me sound a real tight arse, doesn't it?'

'Well you are, I suppose,' said Judith. 'Hayward said you play it by the book. That's probably why he told you about Morrison.'

'And look where that got me,' said Sam. He walked on, and she followed, past a pair of incongruously large houses and up the final rise that led to the sea. Spread before them the long beach was wet and gleaming from the receding tide, the horizon a pale grey line dividing sea from sky. Sam spoke again, his eyes blinking against the salty breeze. 'Cardine wanted my resignation, and that's what I gave him. I need to work but there are other things I could do. Always fancied being a postman.'

'A postman? Well, you'd be back in uniform again.'

He smiled. 'But at least I wouldn't feel ashamed of it.'

'Is that how you feel, about the force?'

Judith had turned to face him, her hair blowing free across her face. Sam looked out at the frothy lines of surf rolling in one after another.

'I know it's not the whole force,' he said. 'One day soon we'll have the guts to clear out people like Cardine and Morrison, but there's no place for me until that happens. Everyone hates a grass, and that's what I am.' He hesitated. 'Look,' he said, 'Rain, you can see it out to sea. If we start back we might avoid it.'

But the rain caught up with them. By the time they got back to the shelter of the Miners they were both wet and cold enough to justify something stronger than beer. Judith's brandy burned her throat.

'I understand why you have to leave,' she said, 'but it's such a waste. I've seen how clever you are with people. And you're fussy about details. You're good at what you do, Sam.' She smiled as a thought came to her. 'You could be Sam Spade, like in the films. 'Sam Tognarelli, Private Eye'. Sounds good.'

Sam smiled too. 'Good idea, thanks. I'll brush up my American accent and buy a big hat.'

'And I could answer your phone and keep the beautiful women at bay,' said Judith.

'That would be a waste, too,' he said. 'What will you do, really? You need time, don't you, to get over all this nastiness? Policemen know they have to deal with villains and violence, but you didn't sign up for that. It's bound to affect you for a while. Are you sleeping OK?'

Judith took another sip of brandy. 'Yes, I sleep. It was bad to start with, but getting better now. I can talk to Dad about it, and Vince. That helps. Mum doesn't want to know. She thinks it's just too sordid. And she's more worried about Granny Violet than she is about me.'

'Give it time,' said Sam. 'You can afford to look around, can't you?'

'Only if I live at home. It feels like my life's going backwards.'

They sat quietly, watching the fire and thinking about the future.

Sam said, 'Perhaps we'd better not see each other for a while. Put the whole business behind us.'

Judith looked up. 'Is that what you want?'

'No, not really, but I think it's what we need.'

'How long?'

He shrugged. 'I need to find another job, and then a place to live if I have to move out of Barrow. Could be anywhere, miles away.'

'I've still got my scooter,' said Judith, and they both laughed.

If you've enjoyed this story, you may want to…

- Order another copy of *Cruel Tide* to pass to a friend.

- Read one of the books in Ruth Sutton's trilogy, entitled *Between the Mountains and the Sea* shown on the next page:

    A Good Liar tells the story of Jessie who risks career and independence with a love affair, whilst her secret past draws ever closer.

    Forgiven is set among the coal mines and fells of the Cumberland coast. Jessie's struggle for happiness continues.

    Fallout features the nuclear disaster at Windscale, which brings a compelling stranger into Jessie's world.

- Follow Ruth Sutton's blog on *ruthwords. wordpress.com* and check her website *www.ruthsutton.co.uk* for latest news of her writing.

- Follow Ruth Sutton on *Twitter@ruthsutton* and on Facebook.

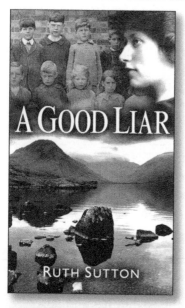

A GOOD LIAR

RUTH SUTTON

FORGIVEN

RUTH SUTTON

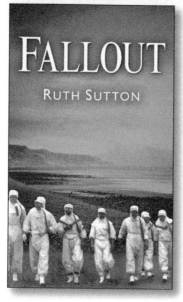

FALLOUT

RUTH SUTTON

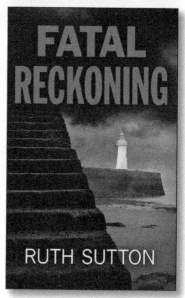

FATAL RECKONING

RUTH SUTTON